THE
PAGAN STONE

Nora Roberts

HOT ICE
SACRED SINS
BRAZEN VIRTUE
SWEET REVENGE
PUBLIC SECRETS
GENUINE LIES
CARNAL INNOCENCE
HONEST ILLUSIONS
DIVINE EVIL
PRIVATE SCANDALS
HIDDEN RICHES
TRUE BETRAYALS
MONTANA SKY
SANCTUARY
HOMEPORT
THE REEF
RIVER'S END
CAROLINA MOON
THE VILLA
MIDNIGHT BAYOU
THREE FATES
BIRTHRIGHT
NORTHERN LIGHTS
BLUE SMOKE
ANGELS FALL
HIGH NOON
TRIBUTE
BLACK HILLS
THE SEARCH
CHASING FIRE
THE WITNESS
WHISKEY BEACH
THE COLLECTOR
TONIGHT AND ALWAYS
THE LIAR
THE OBSESSION

Series

Irish Born Trilogy
BORN IN FIRE
BORN IN ICE
BORN IN SHAME

Dream Trilogy
DARING TO DREAM
HOLDING THE DREAM
FINDING THE DREAM

Chesapeake Bay Saga
SEA SWEPT
RISING TIDES
INNER HARBOR
CHESAPEAKE BLUE

Gallaghers of Ardmore Trilogy
JEWELS OF THE SUN
TEARS OF THE MOON
HEART OF THE SEA

Three Sisters Island Trilogy
DANCE UPON THE AIR
HEAVEN AND EARTH
FACE THE FIRE

Key Trilogy
KEY OF LIGHT
KEY OF KNOWLEDGE
KEY OF VALOR

In the Garden Trilogy
BLUE DAHLIA
BLACK ROSE
RED LILY

Circle Trilogy
MORRIGAN'S CROSS
DANCE OF THE GODS
VALLEY OF SILENCE

Sign of Seven Trilogy
BLOOD BROTHERS
THE HOLLOW
THE PAGAN STONE

Bride Quartet
VISION IN WHITE
BED OF ROSES
SAVOR THE MOMENT
HAPPY EVER AFTER

The Inn BoonsBoro Trilogy
THE NEXT ALWAYS
THE LAST BOYFRIEND
THE PERFECT HOPE

The Cousins O'Dwyer Trilogy
DARK WITCH
SHADOW SPELL
BLOOD MAGICK

The Guardians Trilogy
STARS OF FORTUNE
BAY OF SIGHS
ISLAND OF GLASS

Ebooks by Nora Roberts

Cordina's Royal Family
AFFAIRE ROYALE
COMMAND PERFORMANCE
THE PLAYBOY PRINCE
CORDINA'S CROWN JEWEL

The Donovan Legacy
CAPTIVATED
ENTRANCED
CHARMED
ENCHANTED

The O'Hurleys
THE LAST HONEST WOMAN
DANCE TO THE PIPER
SKIN DEEP
WITHOUT A TRACE

Night Tales
NIGHT SHIFT
NIGHT SHADOW
NIGHTSHADE
NIGHT SMOKE
NIGHT SHIELD

The MacGregors
PLAYING THE ODDS
TEMPTING FATE
ALL THE POSSIBILITIES
ONE MAN'S ART
FOR NOW, FOREVER
REBELLION/IN FROM THE COLD
THE MACGREGOR BRIDES
THE WINNING HAND
THE MACGREGOR GROOMS
THE PERFECT NEIGHBOR

The Calhouns
COURTING CATHERINE
A MAN FOR AMANDA
FOR THE LOVE OF LILAH
SUZANNA'S SURRENDER
MEGAN'S MATE

Irish Legacy
IRISH THOROUGHBRED
IRISH ROSE
IRISH REBEL

LOVING JACK
BEST LAID PLANS
LAWLESS

BLITHE IMAGES
SONG OF THE WEST
SEARCH FOR LOVE
ISLAND OF FLOWERS
THE HEART'S VICTORY
FROM THIS DAY
HER MOTHER'S KEEPER
ONCE MORE WITH FEELING
REFLECTIONS
DANCE OF DREAMS
UNTAMED
THIS MAGIC MOMENT
ENDINGS AND BEGINNINGS
STORM WARNING
SULLIVAN'S WOMAN
FIRST IMPRESSIONS
A MATTER OF CHOICE

LESS OF A STRANGER
THE LAW IS A LADY
RULES OF THE GAME
OPPOSITES ATTRACT
THE RIGHT PATH
PARTNERS
BOUNDARY LINES
DUAL IMAGE
TEMPTATION
LOCAL HERO
THE NAME OF THE GAME
GABRIEL'S ANGEL
THE WELCOMING
TIME WAS
TIMES CHANGE
SUMMER LOVE
HOLIDAY WISHES

Nora Roberts & J. D. Robb

REMEMBER WHEN

J. D. Robb

NAKED IN DEATH
GLORY IN DEATH
IMMORTAL IN DEATH
RAPTURE IN DEATH
CEREMONY IN DEATH
VENGEANCE IN DEATH
HOLIDAY IN DEATH
CONSPIRACY IN DEATH
LOYALTY IN DEATH
WITNESS IN DEATH
JUDGMENT IN DEATH
BETRAYAL IN DEATH
SEDUCTION IN DEATH
REUNION IN DEATH
PURITY IN DEATH
PORTRAIT IN DEATH
IMITATION IN DEATH
DIVIDED IN DEATH
VISIONS IN DEATH
SURVIVOR IN DEATH
ORIGIN IN DEATH
MEMORY IN DEATH
BORN IN DEATH
INNOCENT IN DEATH
CREATION IN DEATH
STRANGERS IN DEATH
SALVATION IN DEATH
PROMISES IN DEATH
KINDRED IN DEATH
FANTASY IN DEATH
INDULGENCE IN DEATH
TREACHERY IN DEATH
NEW YORK TO DALLAS
CELEBRITY IN DEATH
DELUSION IN DEATH
CALCULATED IN DEATH
THANKLESS IN DEATH
CONCEALED IN DEATH
FESTIVE IN DEATH
OBSESSION IN DEATH
DEVOTED IN DEATH
BROTHERHOOD IN DEATH
APPRENTICE IN DEATH

Anthologies

FROM THE HEART
A LITTLE MAGIC
A LITTLE FATE

MOON SHADOWS
(with Jill Gregory, Ruth Ryan Langan, and Marianne Willman)

The Once Upon Series
(with Jill Gregory, Ruth Ryan Langan, and Marianne Willman)

ONCE UPON A CASTLE   ONCE UPON A ROSE
ONCE UPON A STAR   ONCE UPON A KISS
ONCE UPON A DREAM   ONCE UPON A MIDNIGHT

SILENT NIGHT
(with Susan Plunkett, Dee Holmes, and Claire Cross)

OUT OF THIS WORLD
(with Laurell K. Hamilton, Susan Krinard, and Maggie Shayne)

BUMP IN THE NIGHT
(with Mary Blayney, Ruth Ryan Langan, and Mary Kay McComas)

DEAD OF NIGHT
(with Mary Blayney, Ruth Ryan Langan, and Mary Kay McComas)

THREE IN DEATH

SUITE 606
(with Mary Blayney, Ruth Ryan Langan, and Mary Kay McComas)

IN DEATH

THE LOST
(with Patricia Gaffney, Mary Blayney, and Ruth Ryan Langan)

THE OTHER SIDE
(with Mary Blayney, Patricia Gaffney, Ruth Ryan Langan, and Mary Kay McComas)

TIME OF DEATH

THE UNQUIET
(with Mary Blayney, Patricia Gaffney, Ruth Ryan Langan, and Mary Kay McComas)

MIRROR, MIRROR
(with Mary Blayney, Elaine Fox, Mary Kay McComas, and R. C. Ryan)

DOWN THE RABBIT HOLE
(with Mary Blayney, Elaine Fox, Mary Kay McComas, and R. C. Ryan)

Also available . . .

THE OFFICIAL NORA ROBERTS COMPANION
(edited by Denise Little and Laura Hayden)

THE
PAGAN STONE

NORA ROBERTS

BERKLEY

NEW YORK

BERKLEY
An imprint of Penguin Random House LLC
1745 Broadway, New York, NY 10019

ISBN: 9781984804921

Jove mass-market edition / December 2008
Berkley trade edition / August 2019

Printed in the United States of America
1   3   5   7   9   10   8   6   4   2

Cover images by Shutterstock
Cover design by Rita Frangie
Book design by Laura K. Corless

For old friends

Where there is no vision, the people perish.

—Proverbs 29:18

I have nothing to offer but blood, toil, tears, and sweat.

—Winston Churchill

PROLOGUE

———◦◦◦———

Mazatlán, Mexico
April 2001

Sun streaked pearly pink across the sky, splashed onto blue, blue water that rolled against white sand as Gage Turner walked the beach. He carried his shoes—the tattered laces of the ancient Nikes tied to hang on his shoulder. The hems of his jeans were frayed, and the jeans themselves had long since faded to white at the stress points. The tropical breeze tugged at hair that hadn't seen a barber in more than three months.

At the moment, he supposed he looked no more kempt than the scattering of beach bums still snoring away on the sand. He'd bunked on beaches a time or two when his luck was down, and knew someone would come along soon to shoo them off before the paying tourists woke for their room-service coffee.

At the moment, despite the need for a shower and a shave, his luck was up. Nicely up. With his night's winnings hot in his pocket, he considered upgrading his ocean-view room for a suite.

Grab it while you can, he thought, because tomorrow could suck you dry.

Time was already running out: it spilled like that white, sun-kissed sand held in a closed fist. His twenty-fourth birthday was less than three months away, and the dreams crawled back into his head. Blood and death, fire and madness. All of that and Hawkins Hollow seemed a world away from this soft tropical dawn.

But it lived in him.

He unlocked the wide glass door of his room, stepped in, tossed aside his shoes. After flipping on the lights, closing the drapes, he took his winnings from his pocket, gave the bills a careless flip. With the current rate of exchange, he was up about six thousand USD. Not a bad night, not bad at all. In the bathroom, he popped off the bottom of a can of shaving cream, tucked the bills inside the hollow tube.

He protected what was his. He'd learned to do so from child-hood, secreting away small treasures so his father couldn't find and destroy them on a drunken whim. He might've flipped off any no-tion of a college education, but Gage figured he'd learned quite a bit in his not-quite-twenty-four years.

He'd left Hawkins Hollow the summer he'd graduated from high school. Just packed up what was his, stuck out his thumb and booked.

Escaped, Gage thought as he stripped for a shower. There'd been plenty of work—he'd been young, strong, healthy, and not par-ticular. But he'd learned a vital lesson while digging ditches, hauling lumber, and most especially during the months he'd sweated on an offshore rig. He could make more money at cards than he could with his back.

And a gambler didn't need a home. All he needed was a game.

He stepped into the shower, turned the water hot. It sluiced over tanned skin, lean muscles, through thick black hair in need of a trim. He thought idly about ordering some coffee, some food, then decided he'd catch a few hours' sleep first. Another advantage of his profession, in Gage's mind. He came and went as he pleased, ate when he was hungry, slept when he was tired. He set his own rules, broke them whenever it suited him.

Nobody had any hold over him.

Not true, Gage admitted as he studied the white scar across his wrist. Not altogether true. A man's friends, his true friends, always had a hold over him. There were no truer friends than Caleb Hawkins and Fox O'Dell.

Blood brothers.

They'd been born the same day, the same year, even—as far as anyone could tell—at the same moment. He couldn't remember a time when the three of them hadn't been . . . a unit, he supposed. The middle-class boy, the hippie kid, and the son of an abusive drunk. Probably shouldn't have had a thing in common, Gage mused as a smile curved his mouth, warmed the green of his eyes. But they'd been family, they'd been brothers long before Cal had cut their wrists with his Boy Scout knife to ritualize the pact.

And that had changed everything. Or had it? Gage wondered. Had it just opened what was always there, waiting?

He could remember it all vividly, every step, every detail. It had started as an adventure—three boys on the eve of their tenth birthday hiking through the woods. Loaded down with skin mags, beer, smokes—his contribution—with junk food and Cokes from Fox, and the picnic basket of sandwiches and lemonade Cal's mother had packed. Not that Frannie Hawkins would've packed a picnic if she'd known her son planned to camp that night at the Pagan Stone in Hawkins Wood.

All that wet heat, Gage remembered, and the music on the boom box, and the complete innocence they'd carried along with the Little Debbies and Nutter Butters they would lose before they hiked out in the morning.

Gage stepped out of the shower, rubbed his dripping hair with a towel. His back had ached from the beating his father had given him the night before. As they'd sat around the campfire in the clearing those welts had throbbed. He remembered that, as he remembered how the light had flickered and floated over the gray table of the Pagan Stone.

He remembered the words they'd written down, the words they'd spoken as Cal made them blood brothers. He remembered the quick pain of the knife across his flesh, the feel of Cal's wrist, of Fox's as they'd mixed their blood.

And the explosion, the heat and cold, the force and fear when that mixed blood hit the scarred ground of the clearing.

He remembered what came out of the ground, the black mass of it, and the blinding light that followed. The pure evil of the black, the stunning brilliance of the white.

When it was over, there'd been no welts on his back, no pain, and in his hand lay one-third of a bloodstone. He carried it still, as he knew Cal and Fox carried theirs. Three pieces of one whole. He supposed they were the same.

Madness came to the Hollow that week, and raged through it like a plague, infecting, driving good and ordinary people to do the horrible. And for seven days every seven years, it came back.

So did he, Gage thought. What choice did he have?

Naked, still damp from the shower, he stretched out on the bed. There was time yet, still some time for a few more games, for hot beaches and swaying palms. The green woods and blue mountains of Hawkins Hollow were thousands of miles away, until July.

He closed his eyes, and as he'd trained himself, dropped almost instantly into sleep.

In sleep came the screams, and the weeping, and the fire that ate so joyfully at wood and cloth and flesh. Blood ran warm over his hands as he dragged the wounded to safety. For how long? he wondered. Where was safe? And who could say when and if the victim would turn and become attacker?

Madness ruled the streets of the Hollow.

In the dream he stood with his friends on the south end of Main

Street, across from the Qwik Mart and its four gas pumps. Coach Moser, who'd guided the Hawkins Hollow Bucks to a championship football season Gage's senior year, gibbered with laughter as he soaked himself, the ground, the buildings with the flood of gas from the pumps.

They ran toward him, the three of them, even as Moser held up his lighter like a trophy, as he splashed in the pools of gas like a boy in rain puddles. They ran even as he flicked the lighter.

It was flash and boom, searing the eyes, bursting in the ears. The force of heat and air flung him back so he landed in a bone-shattering heap. Fire, blinding clouds of it, spewed skyward as hunks of wood and concrete, shards of glass, burning twists of metal flew.

Gage felt his broken arm try to knit, his shattered knee struggle to heal with pain worse than the wound itself. Gritting his teeth, he rolled, and what he saw stopped his heart in his chest.

Cal lay in the street, burning like a torch.

No, no, no, no! He crawled, shouting, gasping for oxygen in the tainted air. There was Fox, facedown in a widening pool of blood.

It came, a black smear on that burning air that formed into a man. The demon smiled. "You don't heal from death, do you, boy?"

Gage woke, sheathed in sweat and shaking. He woke with the stench of burning gas scoring his throat.

Time's up, he thought.

He got up, got dressed. Dressed, he began to pack for the trip back to Hawkins Hollow.

ONE

—◦◦❋◦◦—

Hawkins Hollow, Maryland
May 2008

The dream woke him at dawn, and that was a pisser. From experience, Gage knew it would be useless to try to find sleep again with images of burning blood in his brain. The closer it got to July, the closer it got to the Seven, the more vivid and vicious the dreams. He'd rather be awake and doing than struggling with nightmares.

Or visions.

He'd come out of the woods that long-ago July with a body that healed itself, and with the gift of sight. Gage didn't consider the precognition wholly reliable. Different choices, different actions, different outcomes.

Seven years before, come July, he'd turned off the pumps at the Qwik Mart, and had taken the added precaution of locking Coach Moser in a cell. He'd never known, not for certain, if he'd saved his friends' lives by those actions, or if the dream had been just a dream.

But he'd played the odds.

He continued to play the odds, Gage supposed as he grabbed a pair of boxers in case he wasn't alone in the house. He was back, as he was every seventh year. And this time he'd thrown his lot in with the three women who'd turned his, Fox's, and Cal's trio into a team of six.

With Cal engaged to Quinn Black—blond bombshell and paranormal writer—she often spent the night at Cal's. Hence the inadvisability of wandering downstairs naked to make coffee. But Cal's attractive house in the woods felt empty to Gage, of people, of ghosts, of Cal's big, lazy dog, Lump. And that was all to the good, as Gage preferred solitude, at least until after coffee.

He assumed Cal had spent the night at the house the three women rented in town. As Fox had done the headfirst into love with the sexy brunette Layla Darnell, they might've bunked at the house, or Fox's apartment over his law offices. Either way, they'd stay close, and with Fox's talent for pushing into thoughts, they had ways of communicating that didn't require phones.

Gage put coffee on, then went out to stand on the deck while it brewed.

Leave it to Cal, he thought, to build his home on the edge of the woods where their lives had turned inside out. But that was Cal for you—he was the type who took a stand, kept right on standing. And the fact was, if country charm rang your bell, this was the spot for it. The green woods with the last of the spring's wild dogwoods and mountain laurel gleaming in slants of sunlight offered a picture of tranquility—if you didn't know any better. The terraced slope in front of the house exploded with color from shrubs and ornamental trees, while at the base the winding creek bubbled along.

It fit Cal to the ground, just as his lady did. For himself, Gage figured the country quiet would drive him crazy within a month.

He went back for the coffee, drank it strong and black. He took a second mug up with him. By the time he'd showered and dressed, restlessness nipped at him. He tried to quell it with a few hands of solitaire, but the house was too . . . settled. Grabbing his keys, he headed out. He'd hunt up his friends, and if nothing was going on, maybe he'd zip up to Atlantic City for the day and find some action.

It was a quiet drive, but then the Hollow was a quiet place, a splat on the map in the rolling western Maryland countryside that got itself juiced up for the annual Memorial Day parade, the Fourth of July fireworks in the park, the occasional Civil War reenactment. And, of course, the madness that flowed into it every seven years.

Overhead, the trees arched over the road; beside it, the creek wound. Then the view opened to rolling, rock-pocked hills, distant mountains, and a sky of delicate spring blue. It wasn't his place, not the rural countryside nor the town tucked into it. Odds were he'd die here, but even that wouldn't make it his. And still, he'd play the long shot that he, his friends, and the women with them would not only survive, but beat down the thing that plagued the Hollow. That they would end it this time.

He passed the Qwik Mart where foresight or luck had won the day, then the first of the tidy houses and shops along Main. He spotted Fox's truck outside the townhouse that held Fox's home and law office. The coffee shop and Ma's Pantry were both open for business, serving the breakfast crowd. A hugely pregnant woman towing a toddler stepped out of the bakery with a large white bag. The kid talked a mile a minute while Mom waddled down Main.

There was the empty gift shop Fox's Layla had rented with plans to open a fashion boutique. The idea made Gage shake his head as he turned at the Square. Hope sprang, he supposed, and love gave it a hell of a boost.

He gave a quick glance at the Bowl-a-Rama, town institution and Cal's legacy. And looked away again. Once upon a time he'd lived above the bowling center with his father, lived with the stench of stale beer and cigarettes, with the constant threat of fists or belt.

Bill Turner still lived there, still worked at the center, reputedly five years sober. Gage didn't give a flying fuck, as long as the old man kept his distance. Because the thought burned in his gut, he shut it down, tossed it aside.

At the curb, he pulled up behind a Karmann Ghia—property of one Cybil Kinski, the sixth member of the team. The sultry gypsy shared his precog trait—just as Quinn shared Cal's ability to look back, and Layla shared Fox's reading of what was hidden in the now. He supposed that made them partners of sorts, and the supposing made him wary.

She was a number, all right, he thought as he started up the walk to the house. Smart, savvy, and sizzling. Another time, another place, it might've been entertaining to deal a few hands with her, see who walked away the winner. But the idea that some outside force, ancient powers, and magic plots played a part in bringing them together had Gage opting to fold his hand early.

It was one thing for both Cal and Fox to get twisted up with their women. He just wasn't wired for the long-term deal. Instinct told him that even the short-term with a woman like Cybil would be too complicated for his taste and style.

He didn't knock. They used the rental house and Cal's as bases of sorts, so he didn't see the need. Music drifted—something New Agey—all flutes and gongs. He turned toward the source, and there was Cybil. She wore loose black pants and a top that revealed a smooth, tight midriff and sleekly muscled arms. Her wild black curls spilled out of their restraining band.

The toes of her bare feet sported bright pink polish.

As he watched, she braced her head on the floor while her body lifted up. Her legs spread, held perpendicular to the floor, then somehow twisted, as if her torso were a hinge. Fluidly, she lowered one leg until her foot was flat on the floor, forming her into some erotic bridge. With movements that seemed effortless, she shifted herself, tucking one leg against her hip while the other cocked up behind her. And reaching back, she gripped her foot to bring it to the back of her head.

He considered the fact that he didn't drool a testament to his massive power of will.

She bent, twisted, flowed, *arranged* herself into what should have been impossible positions. His willpower wasn't so massive he didn't imagine that any woman that flexible would be amazing in bed.

She'd arched back, foot hooked behind her head, when a flicker in those deep, dark eyes told him she'd become aware of him.

"Don't let me interrupt."

"I won't. I'm nearly done. Go away."

Though he regretted missing how she ended such a session, he wandered back to the kitchen, poured himself a cup of coffee. Leaning back on the counter, he noted the morning paper was folded on the little table, the dog bowl Cal left there for Lump was empty, and the water bowl beside it half full. The dog might've already had breakfast, but if anyone else had, the dishes had already been stowed away. Since the news didn't interest him at the moment, he sat and dealt out a hand of solitaire. He was on his fourth game when Cybil strolled in.

"Aren't you a rise-and-shiner this morning?"

He laid a red eight on a black nine. "Cal still in bed?"

"It seems everyone's up and about. Quinn hauled him off to the gym." She poured coffee for herself, then reached in the bread bin. "Bagel?"

"Sure."

After cutting one neatly in half, she dropped it in the toaster. "Bad dream?" She angled her head when he glanced up at her. "I had one, woke me at first light. So did Cal and Quinn. I haven't heard, but I imagine Fox and Layla—they're at his place—got the same wake-up call. Quinn's remedy, weights and machines. Mine, yoga. Yours . . ." She gestured to the cards.

"Everybody's got something."

"We kicked our Big Evil Bastard in the balls a few days ago. We have to expect him to kick back."

"Nearly got ourselves incinerated for the trouble," Gage reminded her.

"*Nearly* works for me. We put the three pieces of the bloodstone back together, magickally. We performed a blood ritual." She studied the healing cut across her palm. "And we lived to tell the tale. We have a weapon."

"Which we don't know how to use."

"Does it know?" She busied herself getting out plates, cream cheese for the bagels. "Does our demon know any more about it than we do? Giles Dent infused that stone with power more than three hundred years ago in the clearing, and—theoretically—used it as part of the spell that pulled the demon, in its form as Lazarus Twisse, into some sort of limbo where Dent could hold it for centuries."

Handily, she sliced an apple, arranged the pieces on a plate while she spoke. "Twisse didn't know or recognize the power of the bloodstone then, or apparently hundreds of years later when your boyhood ritual released it, and the stone was split into three equal parts. If we follow that logic, it doesn't know any more about it now, which gives us an advantage. We may not know, yet, how it works, but we know it does."

Turning, she offered him his plated bagel. "We put the three pieces into one again. The Big Evil Bastard isn't the only one with power here."

Just a bit fascinated, Gage watched Cybil cut her half bagel in half before spreading what he could only describe as a film of cream cheese over the two quarters. While he loaded his own half, she sat and took a bite he estimated consisted of about half a dozen crumbs.

"Maybe you should just look at a picture of food instead of going to all the trouble to fix it." When she only smiled, took another minuscule bite, he said, "I've seen Twisse kill my friends. I've seen that countless times, in countless ways."

Her eyes met his, dark with understanding. "That's the bitch of our precog, seeing the potentials, the possibilities, in brutal Technicolor. I was afraid when we went into the clearing to perform the ritual. Not just of dying, though I don't want to die. In fact, I'm firmly against it. I was afraid of living and watching the people closest to me die, and worse, somehow being responsible for it."

"But you went in."

"We went in." She chose an apple slice, took a stingy bite. "And we didn't die. Not all dreams, not all visions are . . . set in stone. You come back, every Seven, you come back."

"We swore an oath."

"Yes, when you were ten. I'm not discounting the validity or the power of childhood oaths," she continued, "but you'd come back regardless. You come back for them, for Cal and Fox. I came for Quinn, so I understand the strength of friendship. We're not like them, you and I."

"No?"

"No." Lifting her coffee, she sipped slowly. "The town, the people in it, they're not ours. For Cal and Fox—and now in a very real sense for Quinn and Layla—this is home. People go to great lengths to protect home. For me, Hawkins Hollow is just a place I happen to be. Quinn's my home, and now so is Layla. And by extension, by connection, so are Cal and Fox. And so, it seems, are you. I won't leave my home until I know it's safe. Otherwise, while I'd find all this fascinating and intriguing, I wouldn't shed blood for it."

The sun beamed in the kitchen window, haloed over her hair, set the little silver hoops at her ears glinting. "I think you might."

"Really?"

"Yeah, because the whole thing pisses you off. Wanting to kick its ass weighs on the side of you staying, seeing it through."

She took another tiny bite of bagel and smiled at him. "Got me. So here we are, Turner, two pairs of itchy feet planted for love and general pissiness. Well. I want my shower," she decided. "Would you mind staying at least until Quinn and Cal get back? Ever since Layla had her 'snakes in the bathroom' event, I've been leery about showering when I'm alone in the house."

"No problem. You going to eat the rest of that?"

Cybil pushed the untouched quarter bagel toward him. As she rose to go to the sink to rinse out her coffee mug, he studied the black-and-blue cloud on the back of her shoulder. It reminded him they'd taken a beating on the night of the full moon at the Pagan Stone, and that she—unlike Cal, Fox, and himself—didn't heal within moments of an injury.

"That's a bad bruise on your shoulder there."

She shrugged it. "You should see my ass."

"Okay."

With a laugh, she glanced over her shoulder. "Rhetorically speaking. I had a nanny who believed that a good paddling built character. Every time I sit down I'm reminded of her."

"You had a nanny?"

"I did. But paddling aside, I like to think I built my own character. Cal and Quinn should be back soon. You might want to make another pot of coffee."

As she walked out he gave the ass in question a contemplative study. Top of the line, he decided. She was an interesting, and to his mind, complicated mix in a very tidy package. While he had a fondness for tidy packages, he preferred simple contents when it came to fun and games. But for life and death, he thought Cybil Kinski was just what the doctor ordered.

She'd brought a gun along on their hike to the Pagan Stone. A little pearl-handled .22, which she'd used with the cold, calculated skill of a veteran mercenary. She'd been the one to do the research on the blood rituals—and she'd done the genealogies that had proven she, Quinn, and Layla were descendants of the demon known as Lazarus Twisse and Hester Deale, the girl it had raped over three centuries before.

And the woman could cook. Bitched about it, Gage mused as he rose to put on another pot of coffee, but she knew her way around the kitchen. He respected the fact that she generally said what was on her mind, and kept a cool head in a crisis. This was no weak-kneed female needing to be rescued.

She smelled like secrets and tasted like warm honey.

He'd kissed her that night in the clearing. Of course, he'd thought they were all about to die in a supernatural blaze and it had been a what-the-hell kind of gesture. But he remembered exactly how she'd tasted.

Probably not smart to think about it—or to think about the fact that she was upstairs right now, wet and naked. But a guy had to have some entertainment during a break from fighting ancient evil. And strangely, he was no longer in the mood for Atlantic City.

He heard the front door open, and the quick burst of Quinn's bawdy laughter. As far as Gage could see, Cal had hit the jackpot in Quinn for the laugh alone. Then you added in the curvy body, the big baby blues, the brain, the humor, the guts, and his friend rang all the bells, blew all the whistles.

Gage topped off his coffee, and hearing only Cal's footsteps approach, got down another mug.

Cal took the mug Gage held out, said, "Hey," then opened the refrigerator for milk.

For a man who'd likely been up since dawn, Cal looked pretty damn chipper, Gage noted. Exercise might release endorphins, but if Gage was a betting man—and he was—he'd put money on the woman putting the spring in his friend's step.

Cal's gray eyes were clear, his face and body relaxed. His dark blond hair was damp and he smelled of soap, indicating he'd show-ered at the gym. He doctored his coffee, then took a box of Mini-Wheats out of a cupboard.

"Want?"

"No."

With a grunt, Cal shook cereal into a bowl, dumped in milk. "Team dream?"

"Seems like."

"Talked to Fox." Cal ate his cereal as he leaned back against the counter. "He and Layla had one, too. Yours?"

"The town was bleeding," Gage began. "The buildings, the streets, anyone unlucky enough to be outside. Blood bubbling up from the sidewalks, raining down the buildings. And burning while it bled."

"Yeah, that's the one. It's the first time the six of us shared the same nightmare, that I know of. That has to mean something."

"The bloodstone's back in one piece. The six of us put it back together. Cybil puts a lot of store in the stone as a power source."

"And you?"

"I guess I'd have to agree, for what it's worth. What I do know is we've got less than two months to figure it out. If that."

Cal nodded. "It's coming faster, it's coming stronger. But we've hurt it, Gage, twice now we've hurt it bad."

"Third time better be the charm."

He didn't hang around. If routine held, the women would spend a good chunk of the day looking for answers in books and on the Internet. They'd review their charts, maps, and graphs, trying to find some new angle. And talking it all to death. Cal would head over to the Bowl-a-Rama, and Fox would open his office for the day. And he, Gage thought, was a gambler without a game.

So he had the day free.

He could head back to Cal's, make some calls, write some

e-mails. He had his own research lines to tug. He'd been studying and poking into demonology and folklore for years, and in odd corners of the world. When they combined his data with what Cybil, Quinn, and Layla had dug up, it meshed fairly well.

Gods and demons warring with each other long before man came to be. Whittling the numbers down so that when man crawled onto the scene, he soon outnumbered them. The time of man, Giles Dent had called it, according to the journals written by his lover, Ann Hawkins. And in the time of man only one demon and one guardian remained—not that he was buying that one, Gage thought. But there was only one who held his personal interest. Mortally wounded, the guardian passed his power and his mission to a young human boy, and so the line continued through the centuries until there was Giles Dent.

Gage considered it as he drove. He accepted Dent, accepted that he and his friends were Dent's descendants through Ann Hawkins. He believed, as did the others, that Dent found a way, twisting the rules to include a little human sacrifice, to imprison the demon, and himself. Until hundreds of years later, three boys released it.

He could even accept that the act had been their destiny. He didn't have to like it, but he could swallow it. It was their fate to face it, fight it, to destroy it or die trying. Since the ghost of Ann Hawkins had made a few appearances this time out, her cryptic remarks indicated this Seven was the money shot.

All or nothing. Life or death.

Since most of his visions featured death, in various unpleasant forms, Gage wasn't putting money on the group victory dance.

He supposed he'd driven to the cemetery because death was on his mind. When he got out of the car, he thrust his hands into his pockets. It was stupid to come here, he thought. It was pointless. But he began to walk across the grass, around the stones and monuments.

He should've brought flowers, he thought, then immediately

shook his head. Flowers were pointless, too. What good did flowers do the dead?

His mother and the child she'd tried to bring into the world were both long dead.

May had greened the grass and the trees, and the breeze stirred the green. The ground rolled, gentle slopes and dips where somber gray markers or faithful white monuments rose, and the sun cast their shadows. His mother and his sister who'd died inside her had a white marker. Though it had been years, many years, since he'd walked this way, he knew where to find them.

The single stone was very simple, small, rounded, with only names and dates carved.

CATHERINE MARY TURNER

1954–1982

ROSE ELIZABETH TURNER

1982

He barely remembered her, he thought. Time simply rubbed the images, the sounds, the *feel* of her to a faded blur. He had only the vaguest memory of her laying his hand against her swollen belly so he could feel the baby kick. He had a picture, so he knew he favored his mother in coloring, in the shape of his eyes, his mouth. He'd never seen the baby, and no one had ever told him what she looked like. But he remembered being happy, remembered playing with trucks in the sunsplash through a window. And yes, even of running to the door when his father came home from work, and screaming with fun as those hands lifted him up high.

There'd been a time, a brief time, when his father's hands had lifted him instead of knocking him down. The sun-splashed time, he supposed. Then she'd died, and the baby with her, and everything had gone dark and cold.

Had she ever shouted at him, punished him, been impatient?

Surely, she must have. But he couldn't remember any of that, or chose not to. Maybe he'd idealized her, but what was the harm? When a boy had a mother for such a brief time, the man was entitled to think of her as perfect.

"I didn't bring flowers," he murmured. "I should have."

"But you came."

He spun around, and looked into eyes the same color, the same shape as his own. As his heart squeezed, his mother smiled at him.

TWO

She's so young. That was his first thought. Younger, he realized, than he as they stood studying each other over her grave. She had a calm and quiet beauty, a kind of simplicity he thought would have kept her beautiful into old age. But she hadn't lived to see thirty.

And even now, a grown man, he felt something inside him ache with that loss.

"Why are you here?" he asked her, and her smile bloomed again.

"Don't you want me to be?"

"You never came before."

"Maybe you never looked before." She shook her dark hair back, breathed deep. "It's such a pretty day, all this May sunshine. And here you are, looking so lost, so angry. So sad. Don't you believe there's a better place, Gage? That death is the beginning of the next?"

"It was the end of before, for me." That, he supposed, was the black and white of it. "When you died, so did the better."

"Poor little boy. Do you hate me for leaving you?"

"You didn't leave me. You died."

"It amounts to the same." There was sorrow in her eyes, or perhaps it was pity. "I wasn't there for you, and did worse than leave you alone. I left you with him. I let him plant death inside me. So you were alone, and helpless, with a man who beat you and cursed you."

"Why did you marry him?"

"Women are weak, you must have learned that by now. If I hadn't been weak I would have left him, taken you and left him and this place." She turned, just a bit, so she looked back toward the Hollow. There was something else in her eyes now—he caught a glint of it—something brighter than pity. "I should have protected you and myself. We would have had a life together, away from here. But I can protect you now."

He watched the way she moved, the way her hair fell, the way the grass stirred at her feet. "How do the dead protect the living?"

"We see more. We know more." She turned back to him, held out her hands. "You asked why I was here. I'm here for that. To protect you, as I didn't during life. To save you. To tell you to go, go away from here. Leave this place. There's nothing but death and misery here, pain and loss. Go and live. Stay and you'll die, you'll rot in the ground as I do."

"Now see, you were doing pretty well up till then." The rage inside him was cold, and it was fierce, but his voice was casual as a shrug. "I might've bought it if you'd played more Mommy and Me cards. But you rushed it."

"I only want you safe."

"You want me dead. If not dead, at least gone. I'm not going anywhere, and you're not my mother. So take off the dress, asshole."

"Mommy's going to have to spank you for that." With a wave of its hand the demon blasted the air. The force knocked Gage off his feet. Even as he gained them, it was changing.

Its eyes went red, and shed bloody tears as it howled with

laughter. "Bad boy! I'm going to punish you the most of all the bad boys. Flay your skin, drink your blood, gnaw your bones."

"Yeah, yeah, yeah." In a show of indifference, Gage hooked his thumbs in his front pockets.

The face of his mother melted away into something hideous, something inhuman. The body bunched, the back humping, the hands and feet curling into claws, then sharpening into hooves. Then the mass of it twisted into a writhing, formless black that choked the air with the stink of death.

The wind blew the stench into Gage's face, but he planted his feet and stood. He had no weapon, and after a quick calculation, decided to play the odds. He bunched his hand into a fist and punched it into the fetid black.

The burn was amazing. He wrenched his hand free, jabbed again. Pain stole his breath, so he sucked more of it and struck out a third time. It screamed. Fury, Gage thought. He recognized pure fury even when he was flying over his mother's gravestone and slamming hard to the ground.

It stood over him now, stood atop the gravestone in the form of the young boy it so often selected. "You'll beg for death," it told him. "Long after I've torn the others to bits, you'll beg. I will dine on you for years."

Gage swiped blood from his mouth, smiled, though a wave of nausea rolled over him. "Wanna bet?"

The thing that looked like a boy dug its hands into its own chest, ripped it open. On a mad roll of laughter, it vanished.

"Fucking crazy. The son of a bitch is fucking crazy." He sat a moment, catching his breath, studying his hand. It was raw and red with blisters, pus seeping from them and the shallow punctures he thought came from fangs. He could feel it healing as the pain was awesome. Cradling his arm, he got to his feet and swayed as dizziness rocked the ground under him.

He had to sit again, his back braced on the gravestone of his mother and sister, until the sickness passed, until the world steadied. In the pretty May sunshine, with only the dead for company, he breathed his way through the pain, focused his mind on the healing. As the burning eased, his system settled again.

Rising, he took one last look at the grave, then turned and walked away.

He stopped by the Flower Pot and bought a splashy spring arrangement that had Amy, who worked the counter, speculating on who the lucky lady might be. He left her speculating. It was too hard to explain—and none of Amy's damn business—that he had flowers and mothers on the brain.

That was one of the problems—and in his mind they were legion—with small towns. Everybody wanted to know everything about everyone else, or pretend they did. When they didn't know enough, they were just as likely to make it up and call it God's truth.

There were plenty in the Hollow who'd whispered and muttered about him. Poor kid, bad boy, troublemaker, bad news, good riddance. Maybe it had stung off and on, and maybe that sting had gone deep when he'd been younger. But he'd had what he supposed he could call a balm. He'd had Cal and Fox. He'd had family.

His mother was gone, and had been for a very long time. That, he thought as he drove out of town, had certainly come home to him today. So he'd make a gesture long overdue.

Of course, she might not be home. Frannie Hawkins didn't hold a job outside the home—exactly. Her work *was* her home, and the various committees she chaired or participated in. If there was a committee, society, or organization in the Hollow, it was likely Cal's mother had a hand in it.

He pulled up behind the clean and tidy car he recognized as hers in the drive of the tidy house where the Hawkinses had lived as long as Gage remembered. And the tidy woman who ran the house knelt on a square of bright pink foam as she planted—maybe they were petunias—at the edges of her already impressive front-yard garden.

Her hair was a glossy blond under a wide-brimmed straw hat, and her hands were covered with sturdy brown gloves. He imagined she thought of her navy pants and pink T-shirt as work clothes. She turned her head at the sound of the car, then her pretty face lit with a smile when she saw Gage.

That was, always had been, a small wonder to him. That she smiled, and meant it, when she saw him. She tugged off her gloves as she rose. "What a nice surprise. And look at those flowers! They're almost as gorgeous as you are."

"Coals to Newcastle."

She touched his cheek, then took the offered flowers. "I can never have too many flowers. Let's go in so I can put them in water."

"I interrupted you."

"Gardening is a constant work in progress. I can't stop fiddling."

The house was the same for her, he knew. She upholstered, sewed, painted, made crafty little arrangements. And still the house was always warm, always welcoming, never set and stiff.

She led him back through the kitchen and into the laundry room, where, being Frannie Hawkins, she had a sink for the specific purpose of flower arranging. "I'm just going to put these in a holding vase, then get us something cold to drink."

"I don't want to hold you up."

"Gage." She waved off his protest as she got down a holding vase, filled it. "Go, sit out back on the patio. It's too pretty to be inside. I'll bring us out some iced tea."

He did as she asked, mostly because he needed to figure out exactly what he'd come here to say to her, and how he wanted to say it. She'd been busy in the back garden as well, and with her container pots. All the color, the shapes, the textures seemed somehow magically perfect and completely natural. He knew, because he'd seen her, that she routinely sketched out her plans for her beds, her pots every year.

Unlike Fox's mother, Frannie Hawkins absolutely never allowed other hands to weed. She trusted no one to tug out bindweed instead of petunias, or whatever. But he'd hauled his share of mulch for her over the years, his share of rocks. He supposed, in some way, that made her magazine-cover gardens his, in a very limited sense.

She stepped out. There was iced tea with sprigs of mint in a fat green glass pitcher, the tall coordinating glasses, and a plate of cookies. They sat at her shaded table, looking out over trim grass and flowing flowers.

"I always remember this backyard," he told her. "Fox's farm was like Adventure World, and this was . . ."

She laughed. "What? Cal's mom's obsession?"

"No. Somewhere between fairyland and sanctuary."

Her smile faded into quiet warmth. "What a lovely thing to say."

He knew what he wanted to say, Gage realized. "You always let me in. I was thinking about things today. You and Fox's mother, you always let me in. You never once turned me away."

"Why in the world would I?"

He looked at her then, into her pretty blue eyes. "My father was a drunk, and I was a troublemaker."

"Gage."

"If Cal or Fox had trouble, I probably started it."

"I think they started plenty of their own and dragged you into that."

"You and Jim, you made sure I had a roof over my head—and you made it clear I could have this one, I could have yours whenever I needed it. You kept my father on at the center, even when you should've let him go, and you did that for me. But you never made me feel like it was charity. You and Fox's parents, you made sure I had clothes, shoes, work so I had spending money. And you never made me feel it was because you felt sorry for that poor Turner kid."

"I never thought of you, and I don't imagine Jo Barry ever thought of you, as 'that poor Turner kid.' You were, and are, the son of my friend. Your mother was my friend, Gage."

"I know. Still, you could've discouraged Cal from hanging out with me. A lot of people would have. I'm the one who had the idea of going into the woods that night."

The look she gave him was pure *mother.* "And neither one of them had anything to do with it?"

"Sure, but it was my idea, and you probably figured that out twenty years ago. You still kept the door open for me."

"None of that was your fault. I don't know a lot of what you're doing now, the six of you, what you've discovered, what you plan to do. Cal keeps a lot of it from me. I guess I let him. But I know enough to be certain what happened at the Pagan Stone when the three of you were boys wasn't your fault. And I know without the three of you, and all you've done, all you've risked, I wouldn't be sitting here on my patio on this pretty day in May. There'd be no Hawkins Hollow without you, Gage. Without you, Cal, and Fox, this town would be dead."

She laid a hand over his, squeezed. "I'm so proud of you."

With her, maybe particularly with her, he couldn't be less than honest. "I'm not here for the town."

"I know. For some odd reason, it only makes me prouder that you're here. You're a good man, Gage. You are," she said, with some heat when she saw the denial on his face. "You'll never convince me otherwise. You've been the best of friends to my son. You've been the best of brothers. My door isn't just open to you. This is your home, whenever you need it."

He needed a moment to settle himself. "I love you." He looked back into her eyes. "I guess that's what I came here to say. I can't remember my mother very well, but I remember you and Jo Barry. I guess that's made the difference."

"Oh. That's done it." So she cried a little as she got up to wrap her arms around him.

To make it two for two, Gage hit the nursery just outside of town. Figuring Joanne Barry would appreciate a plant even more than flowers, he found a flowering orchid that fit his bill. He drove out to the farm, and when he found no one at home, left the orchid on the big front porch with a note under the pot.

The gestures, the talk with Frannie had smoothed out the rough edges from his visit to the cemetery. He considered heading home and doing some solo research, but reminded himself—for better or worse—he was part of a team. His first choice was Fox, but when he drove by the office, Fox's truck was no longer parked out front. In court, Gage assumed, or off meeting a client. With Cal at the bowling center, and the old man working there, that avenue simply wasn't an option.

Gage swung around and made the turn toward the rental house. It appeared it would be ladies' day for him.

Both Cybil's and Quinn's cars were out front. He walked into the house as he had that morning, without knocking. With coffee on his mind, he started back to the kitchen as Cybil appeared at the top of the steps.

"Twice in one day," she said. "Don't tell me you're becoming sociable."

"I want coffee. Are you and Quinn in the office up there?"

"We are, just a couple of busy demon-researching worker bees."

"I'll be up in a minute."

He caught the sexy arch of her eyebrow before he continued back. Armed with a mug of coffee, he backtracked and headed up the stairs. Quinn sat at the keyboard, her quick fingers tapping. They continued to tap even as she glanced up and sent him her big, bright smile. "Hi. Have a seat."

"That's okay." Instead he wandered over to the town map tacked to the wall, studied all the colored pins ranged over it that repre-sented incidents involving paranormal activity.

The graveyard wasn't a favorite, he noted, but it got some play. He moved on to the charts and graphs Layla had generated. There, too, he noted the graveyard wasn't a usual *haunt*, for lack of a better term. Maybe it was too clichéd to meet the Big Evil Bastard's stan-dards.

Behind him, Cybil sat studying her own laptop screen. "I've found a source that claims the bloodstone was originally part of the great Alpha—or Life Stone. It's interesting."

"Does it tell us how to use it to kill the fucker?"

Cybil glanced up briefly, spoke to Gage's back. "No. It does, however, speak of wars between the dark and the light—the Alpha and the Omega, the gods and the demons—depending on which version of the mythology I've found. And during these wars, the great stone exploded into many fragments, infused with the blood and the power of the gods. And these fragments were given to the guardians."

"Hey now." Quinn stopped typing, swiveled to face Cybil. "That's hitting close to home. If so, the bloodstone was passed down to Dent as a guardian. And he, in turn, passed it to our guys here in three equal fragments."

"I've got other sources that cite the bloodstone's use in magickal rituals, its ability to stimulate physical strength and healing."

"Another bingo," Quinn said.

"It's also reputed to aid in regulating the female menstrual cycle."

Gage turned at that. "Do you mind?"

"Not a bit," Cybil said easily. "But more to our purposes, the bloodstone is, by all accounts, a healing stone."

"We already knew that. Cal and Fox and I did our homework on the stone years ago."

"All of this comes to blood," Cybil went on. "We know that, too. Blood sacrifice, blood ties, bloodstone. And also fire. Fire's played a role in many of the incidents, and was a major factor the night Dent and Twisse tangled, and the night you and Cal and Fox first camped at the Pagan Stone. Certainly on the night the six of us fused the stone back into one whole. So think about this—what do you get when you strike stones together? A spark, and sparks lead to fire. The creation of fire was, arguably, the first magickal act of man. Bloodstone—fire and blood. Fire not only burns, it purifies. Maybe it's fire that will kill it."

"What, you want to stand around banging stones together and hope a magic spark lands on Twisse?"

"Aren't you in a cheery mood?"

"If fire could kill it, it would already be dead. I've seen it ride on flames like they were a damn surfboard."

"*Its* fire, not ours," Cybil pointed out. "Fire created from the Alpha Stone, from the fragment of that stone passed to you, through Dent, by the gods. Fusing it that night made one hell of a blaze."

"How do you propose to light a magic fire with a single stone?"

"I'm working on it. How about you?" Cybil countered. "Any better ideas?"

This wasn't why he was here, Gage reminded himself. He hadn't come to debate magic stones and conjuring the fire of gods. He wasn't even sure why he was baiting her. She'd come through, he reminded himself, all the way through in fusing the three parts of the stone into one.

"I had a visit today, from our resident demon."

"Why didn't you say so?" All business, Quinn reached for her tape recorder. "Where, when, how?"

"In the cemetery, shortly after I left here this morning."

"What time was that?" Quinn looked at Cybil. "Around ten, right? So between ten and ten thirty?" she asked Gage.

"Close enough. I didn't check my watch."

"What form did it take?"

"My mother's."

Immediately, Quinn went from brisk to sympathetic. "Oh, Gage, I'm sorry."

"Has it ever done that before?" Cybil asked. "Appeared in a form of someone you know?"

"New trick. That's why it had me conned for a minute. Anyway, it looked like her, like I remember her. Or, actually, I don't remember her that well. It looked like pictures I've seen of her."

The picture, he thought, his father had kept on the table beside his bed.

"She—it—was young," he continued. "Younger than me, and wearing one of those summer dresses."

He sat now, drinking his cooling coffee as he related the event, and the conversation nearly word for word.

"You *punched* it?" Quinn demanded.

"Seemed like a good idea at the time."

Saying nothing, Cybil rose, crossed to him, held out her hand for his. She examined his, back, palm, fingers. "Healed. I'd wondered about that. If you'd heal completely if it was able to wound you directly."

"I didn't say it wounded me."

"Of course it did. You punched your fist into the belly of the beast, literally. What kinds of wounds were there?"

"Burns, punctures. Fucker bit me. Fights like a girl."

She cocked her head, appreciating his grin. "I'm a girl, and I don't bite . . . in a fight. How long did it take to heal?"

"A while. Maybe an hour altogether."

"Longer, considerably, than if you'd sustained burns from a natural source. Any side effects?"

He started to shrug that off, then reminded himself every detail mattered. "A little nausea, a little dizziness. But it hurt like a mother, so you'll have that."

She cocked her head, sent him a speculative look. "What did you do afterward? There's a couple of hours between then and now."

"I had some things I needed to do. We punching time clocks now?"

"Just curious. We'll write it up, log it in. I'm going to make some tea. Do you want any, Quinn?"

"I want a root beer float, but . . ." Quinn held up her bottle of water. "I'll stick with this."

When Cybil walked out, Gage drummed his fingers on his thigh a moment, then pushed to his feet. "I'm going to top off my coffee."

"You do that." Quinn held her own speculative look until he'd left. Rocks weren't the only things that shot off sparks when they slapped together, she mused.

Cybil put the kettle on, set out the pot, measured her tea. When Gage stepped in, she plucked an apple from the bowl, cut it neatly in quarters, then offered him one.

"So here we are again." After getting a plate, she quartered a second apple, added a few sprigs of grapes. "When Quinn starts talking root beer floats, she needs a snack. If you're looking for something more substantial, there're sandwich makings or cold pasta salad."

"I'm good." He watched her as she added a few crackers, a handful of cubed cheese to the snack plate. "There's no need to get pissy."

She cocked that brow at him. "Why would I be pissy?"

"Exactly."

Taking one of the apple slices, she leaned back against the counter, and took a tiny bite. "You're misreading me. I came down because I wanted tea, not because I was annoyed with you. Annoyance wasn't what I felt. You probably won't like what I was feeling, what I do feel."

"What's that?"

"Sorry that it used your personal grief against you."

"I don't have any personal grief."

"Oh, shut up." She took another, and this time angry, bite out of the apple. "That *is* annoying. You were in the cemetery. As I sincerely doubt you go there for nature walks, I have to conclude you went to visit your mother's grave. And Twisse defiled—or tried to—your memory of her. Don't tell me you don't have grief for the loss of your mother. I lost my father years ago, too. And he chose to leave me, chose to put a bullet in his brain, and still I have grief. You didn't want to talk about it, so I gave you your privacy, then you follow me down here and tell me I'm pissy."

"Which is obviously off," he said dryly, "as you're not in the least pissy."

"I wasn't," she muttered. She let out a breath, then nibbled on the apple again as the kettle began to sputter. "You said she looked very young. How young?"

"Early twenties, I guess. Most of my impressions of her, physically, are from photographs. I . . . Shit. Shit." He dug out his wallet, pulled a small picture from under his driver's license. "This, this is the way she looked, down to the goddamn dress."

After turning off the burner, Cybil moved to him, stood side-by-side to study the photo in his hand. Her hair was dark and loose, her body slim in the yellow sundress. The little boy was about a year, a year and a half, Cybil judged, and propped on her hip as both of them laughed into the camera.

"She was lovely. You favor her."

"He took this out of my head. You were right about that. I haven't looked at this in . . . I don't know, a few years maybe. But it's my clearest memory of her because . . ."

"Because it's the one you carry with you." Now Cybil laid her hand on his arm. "Be annoyed if that's how you have to handle it, but I'm so sorry."

"I knew it wasn't her. It only took a minute for me to know it wasn't her."

And in that minute, she thought, he must have felt unbearable grief and joy. She turned back to pour the water into the pot. "I hope you hit a couple of vital organs, if organs it has, when you punched it."

"That's what I like about you, that healthy taste for violence." He slipped the picture of his mother back into his wallet.

"I'm a fan of the physical, in a lot of areas. It's interesting, isn't it, that in this guise, its first push was to try to convince you to leave. Not to attack, not even to taunt as it has before, but to use a trusted form to tell you to go, to save yourself. I think we have it worried."

"Yeah, it looked really concerned when it knocked me on my ass."

"Got up again, didn't you?" She arranged the plate, the pot, a cup on a tray. "Cal should be here in another hour, and Fox and Layla shortly after. Unless you've got a better offer, why don't you stay for dinner?"

"Are you cooking?"

"That is, apparently, my lot in this strange life we're leading at the moment."

"I'll take that offer."

"Fine. Carry this up for me, and we'll put you to work in the meantime."

"I don't make charts."

She shot him that smug look over her shoulder as she started out ahead of him. "You do today if you want to eat."

Later, Gage sat on the front steps, enjoying the first beer of the evening with Fox and Cal. Fox had changed out of his lawyer suit into jeans and a short-sleeved sweatshirt. He looked, as Fox habitually did, comfortable in his own skin.

How many times had they done just this? Gage wondered. Sat, sharing a beer? Countless times. And often when he was in another part of the world, he might sit, sip a beer, and think of them in the Hollow.

And there were times he came back, between the Seven, because he missed them as he'd miss his own legs. Then they could sit like

this, in the long evening sunlight without the weight of the world—
or at least this corner of it—on their shoulders.

But the weight was there now with less than two months left
before what they all accepted was do or die.

"We could go back to the cemetery, the three of us," Fox suggested. "See if it wants another round."

"I don't think so. It had its fun."

"Next time you go wandering around, don't go unarmed. I don't
mean that damn gun," Cal added. "You can pick up a decent and
legal folding knife down at Mullendore's. No point letting it try to
take a chunk out of your hand."

Idly, Gage flexed the hand in question. "Felt good to punch the
bastard, but you're right. I didn't even have a damn penknife on me.
I won't make that mistake again."

"Can it just come back as the dead—? Sorry," Fox added, laying
a hand on Gage's shoulder.

"It's okay. Quinn brought that up earlier. If it can take the form
of the living, it's a big skill. The dead's hard enough. Cybil thinks
not. She had some convoluted, intellectual theory, which I stopped
listening to after she and Quinn started the debate. But I'm leaning
toward Cybil's end of it. It had substance. But the image, the form—
that was like a shell, and the shell was . . . borrowed, was the gist
of Cybil's long, involved lecture on corporeal changes and shape-
shifting. It can't borrow from the living because they're still wearing
the shell, so to speak."

"Whatever," Fox said after a moment. "We know Twisse has a
new twist. If he wants to play that game again, we'll be ready."

Maybe, Gage thought, but the odds were long. And getting longer every day.

THREE

—◦◦◦◦◦◦—

n loose cotton pants and a tank she considered suitable only for sleeping, Cybil followed the life-affirming scent of coffee toward the kitchen. It was lovely to know someone in the household woke before she did and had a pot going. The chore, all too often, fell to her as she was up and about before any of the others.

Of course, none of the others slept alone, she thought, so they got coffee *and* sex. Didn't seem quite fair, she decided, but that's the way the cookie crumbled. Still, the cookie meant she wasn't required to make precaffeine conversation, and had a quiet interlude with the morning paper until the frisky puppies rolled out of bed for the day.

Halfway between the stairs and the kitchen, she stopped, sniffed the air. That, she realized, was more than coffee. Bacon scented the air, which made it a red-letter day. Someone besides Cybil was cooking.

At the doorway, she saw Layla busy at the stove, humming away as she fried and flipped, her dark hair pulled back in a little stub at the nape of her neck. She looked so happy, Cybil thought, and wondered why she felt this big-sister affection for Layla.

They were of an age, after all, and while Layla might not be as well-traveled as she was, her housemate had lived in New York for several years, and even in cropped pants and a T-shirt wore urban polish. With Quinn, there'd been an instant connection for Cybil—a click the moment they'd met in college. And now, there was Layla.

She'd never had that same affinity, that *click* with her own sister, Cybil thought. But then she and Rissa never fully understood each other, and her younger sister tended to get in touch primarily when she needed something or was embroiled in yet another mess.

Cybil decided she should count herself lucky. There was Quinn, who'd been like a missing piece of herself, and now Layla sliding smoothly into the slot, to make the three of them a unit.

With the bacon set aside to drain, Layla turned for a carton of eggs and jolted when she saw Cybil. "God!" On a laugh, she clutched at her heart. "You scared me."

"Sorry. You're up early."

"And with a yen for bacon and eggs." Before Cybil could do it herself, Layla got down a cup and poured coffee. "I made plenty of bacon. I figured you'd be down before I finished, and Fox is always up for a meal."

"Hmm," Cybil said, and dumped milk into the coffee.

"Anyway, I hope you're hungry, because I seem to have fried up half a pig. And the eggs are fresh from the O'Dell farm. I got the paper." Layla gestured toward the table. "Why don't you sit down and have your coffee while I finish this up?"

Cybil took that first mind-clearing sip. "I'm forced to ask. What are you after, Darnell?"

"Transparent as Saran Wrap." With a wince, Layla broke the first egg in the bowl. "There is this little favor, and I'd be bribing Quinn with breakfast if she were here instead of at Cal's. I have the morning off, and a fistful of paint samples. I was hoping I could talk you and Quinn into going over to the shop with me this morning, help-ing me decide on my color scheme."

Cybil pushed her hair back, drank more coffee. "Here's a ques-tion. Why would you think either of us would let you get away with deciding on the color scheme for your own boutique without us bad-gering you with our opinion?"

"Really?"

"Nobody escapes my opinion, but I'll be eating bacon and eggs."

"Good. Good. It just seems crazy, worrying about paint chips when we've got life-and-death issues to worry about."

"Color schemes are life-and-death issues."

Layla laughed, but shook her head. "We've got a demon who wants us dead, coming into full power in about six weeks, and I'm pursuing the wild hare of opening my own business in the town it wants for its personal playground. Meanwhile Fox has to interview and train—or I have to train—my replacement as his office manager while we figure out how to stay alive and destroy ancient evil. And I'm going to ask Fox to marry me."

"We can't stop living because . . . Whoa." Cybil held up a hand, and waited for her morning-fuzzy brain to clear. "In my journalism classes, that's what we called burying the lede. Big time."

"Is it crazy?"

"Of course, you never bury the lede." Since it was there, Cybil reached over and took a slice of bacon. "And yes, of course, marriage is insane—that's why it's human."

"I don't mean marriage, I mean asking him. It's so unlike me."

"I would hope so. I'd hate to think you go around proposing to men all willy-nilly."

"I always thought when everything was in place, when the time was right, that I'd wait for the man I loved to set the scene, buy the ring, and ask." Sighing, Layla went back to breaking eggs in the bowl. "*That's* like me—or was. But I don't care about everything be-ing in place, and how the hell can anybody know, especially us, if the time's right? And I don't want to wait."

"Go get him, sister."

"Would you—I mean under the circumstances?"

"You're damn right I would."

"I feel . . . Here he comes," Layla whispered. "Don't say any-thing."

"Damn, I was planning to blurt it all out, then toss a few hand-fuls of confetti."

"Morning." Fox sent Cybil a sleepy smile, then turned a dazzling one on Layla. "You're cooking."

"My boss gave me the morning off, so I've got time to spare."

"Your boss should always give you whatever you need." He reached in the fridge for his usual Coke. And, popping the top, looked from one woman to the other. "What? What's going on?"

"Nothing." And thinking of his ability to read thoughts and feel-ings, Layla pointed her whisk at him. "And no peeking. We were just talking about the boutique, paint chips, that sort of thing. How many eggs do you want?"

"A couple. Three."

Layla sent Cybil a satisfied smile when Fox leaned in to nuzzle her and cop some bacon behind her back.

The building that would house Layla's boutique had an airy feel to it, good light, good location. Important pluses, to Cybil's mind. Layla had years of experience in fashion retail, as well as an excellent eye for style—other major advantages. Added to them was her shared ability with Fox to sense thoughts, and that sense of what a customer really wanted would be an enormous advantage.

She wandered the space. She liked the old wood floors, the warm tones of it and the wide trim. "Charming or slick?" Cybil asked.

"Charming, with slick around the edges." Standing at the front window with Quinn, Layla held one of the paint chips up in the natural light. "I want to respect the space, and jazz it up with little touches. Female, comfortable, but not cozy. Accessible, but not altogether expected."

"No pinks, roses, mauves."

"None," Layla said decisively.

"A couple of good chairs for customers to sit in," Quinn suggested, "to try on shoes, or wait for a friend in the changing area, but no floral fabrics, no chintz."

"If this were a gallery, we'd say your stock would be your art."

"Exactly." Layla beamed over at Cybil. "That's why I'm thinking neutral tones for the walls. Warm neutrals, because of the wood. And I'm thinking instead of a counter"—she waved the flat of her hand waist-high—"I might find a nice antique desk or pretty table for the checkout area. And over here—" She pushed the chips into Quinn's hand, crossed the bare floor. "I'd have clear floating shelves in a random pattern, to display shoes, smaller bags. And then here . . ."

Cybil followed as Layla moved from section to section, outlining her plans for the layout. The image formed clearly—open racks, shelves, pretty glass-fronted curios for accessories.

"I need Fox's father to build in a couple of dressing rooms back here."

"Three," Cybil said. "Three's more practical, is more interesting to the eye, and it's a magickal number."

"Three then, with good, flattering lighting, and the torturous triple mirror."

"I hate those bastards," Quinn muttered.

"We all do, but they're a necessary evil. And see, the little kitchen back here." With a come-ahead gesture, Layla led the way. "They kept that, through its various retail incarnations. I thought I could do quirky little vignettes every month or so. Like, ah, candles and wine on the table, some flowers—and a negligee or a cocktail dress tossed over the back of the chair. Or a box of cereal on the counter, some breakfast dishes in the sink—and a messenger- or briefcase-style handbag on the table, a pair of pumps under it. You know what I mean?"

"Fun. Clever. Yes, I know what you mean. Let me see those chips." Cybil snatched them from Quinn, then headed back to the front window.

"I've got more," Layla told them. "I've sort of whittled it down to those."

"And have your favorite," Quinn finished.

"Yeah, I do, but I want opinions. Serious opinions, because I'm as scared as I am excited about this, and I don't want to screw it up by—"

"This. Champagne Bubbles. Just the palest gold, really just the impression of color. Subtle, neutral, but with that punch, that fun factor. And any color you put against this will pop."

Lips pursed, Quinn studied the chip over Cybil's shoulder. "She's right. It's great. Female, sophisticated, warm."

"That was my pick." Layla closed her eyes. "I swear, that was my pick."

"Proving the three of us have excellent taste," Cybil concluded. "You're going in to apply for the business loan this week?"

"Yeah." Layla blew out a breath that fluttered her bangs. "Fox says it's a slam dunk. I have references from him, Jim Hawkins, my former boss from the boutique in New York. My finances are—hah—modest, but in good order. And the town wants and needs businesses. Keep revenue local instead of sending it out to the mall and so on."

"It's a good investment. You've got prime location here—Main Street only steps from the Square. You were raised in the business, as your parents owned a dress shop. Work experience, a canny sense of style. A very good investment. I'd like a piece of it."

Layla blinked at Cybil. "Sorry?"

"My finances are healthy—not bank-loan healthy, but healthy enough to invest in a smart enterprise. What have you projected as your start-up costs?"

"Well . . ." Layla named a figure, and Cybil nodded and wandered. "I could manage a third of that. Quinn?"

"Yeah, I could swing a third."

"Are you kidding?" was all Layla could say. "Are you *kidding*?"

"Which would leave you to come up with the final third out of your modest finances or the bank loan. I'd go with the loan, not only to give yourself breathing room, but for tax purposes." Cybil brushed back her hair. "Unless you don't want investors."

"I want investors if they're you. Oh God, this is—wait. You should think about it awhile. Seriously. You need to take some time, think about it. I don't want you to—"

"We have been thinking about it."

"And talking about it," Quinn added. "Since you decided to go for it. Christ, Layla, look what we've already invested in each other, and in this town. This is only money—and as Gage would probably say, we want to ante up."

"I'll make it work. I will." Layla brushed away a tear. "I will. I know what we are to each other, but if you do this, I want it all legal and right. Fox will . . . He'll fix it, he'll take care of that part. I know I can make it work. Now, especially, I know I can."

She threw her arms around Quinn, then opened up to pull Cybil into the hug. "Thank you, thank you, thank you."

"Not necessary. Remember what else Gage might say," Cybil reminded her.

"What?"

"We could all be dead before August." With a laugh, Cybil gave Layla a pat on the butt, then stepped back. "Have you thought of any possible names for the place yet?"

"Again, are you kidding? This is me, here. I have a list. In fact I have three lists, and a folder. But I'm tossing them because I just thought of the perfect name." Layla held her hands out to the sides, palms up. "Welcome to Sisters."

They separated, Layla to the office, Quinn to have lunch with Cal's mother to discuss wedding plans, Cybil back home. She wanted to pursue the bloodstone-as-weapon angle, and push deeper into the idea of it being a fragment of a larger mystical power source.

She liked the quiet and the solitude. It was good for thinking, reshuffling thoughts, for moving them around like puzzle pieces until she found a better fit. Because she wanted a change of venue, she brought her laptop and the file of notes she'd printed out that dealt specifically with the bloodstone down to the kitchen. With the back door and windows open to the spring air, she made iced tea, fixed a small bowl of salad. Over lunch, she reviewed her notes.

July 7, 1652. Giles Dent (the Guardian) wore the bloodstone amulet on the night Lazarus Twisse (the Demon) led the mob it had infected to the Pagan Stone in Hawkins Wood, where Giles had a small cabin. Prior to that night, Dent had spoken of the stone, and shown it to Ann Hawkins, his lover and the mother of his triplet sons (who would be born on 7/7/1652). Ann wrote of it, briefly and cryptically, in the journals she kept after Dent sent her away (to what would become the O'Dell farm) in order to birth their sons in safety.

When next documented, the stone had been divided into three equal parts, and was clutched in Cal Hawkins's, Fox O'Dell's, and Gage Turner's fists, after they had performed their blood brother ritual, at the Pagan Stone at midnight on their shared tenth birthday (7/7/1987). The ritual—blood ritual—freed the demon for a period of seven days, every seven years, during which time it infected certain people in Hawkins Hollow, said infection causing them to perform acts of violence, even murder.

However, as the demon was freed, the three boys gained specific powers of self-healing and psychic gifts. *Weapons.*

Cybil nodded at the word she'd underscored. "Yeah, these are weapons, these are tools that kept them alive, kept them in the fight. And those weapons sprang from, or are certainly connected to, the bloodstone."

She reviewed her notes on Ann Hawkins's journal entry about bringing three back to one, and her conversations—such as they'd been—with Cal, with Layla. One into three, three into one, Cybil mused, and found herself mildly annoyed Ann hadn't elected to appear to her.

She thought she'd like to interview a ghost.

She began to type her thoughts, using the stream-of-consciousness method that served her best, and could and would be refined later. From time to time she paused to make a quick handwritten note to herself on her pad, on some point she wanted to dig into later, or a reference area that needed a closer look.

When she heard the front door open, she kept working—thought fleetingly: Quinn's back early. Even when the door slammed, sharp as a shot moments later, she didn't stop the work. Wedding tension, she supposed.

But when the door behind her slammed, and the thumb bolt on the lock snicked, it got her attention. She saved the work—it was second nature to save the work, and her mind barely registered the automatic gesture. Over the sink, the window slid down, the slow movement somehow more threatening than the slammed door.

She could hurt it, she reminded herself as she rose to sidestep to the knife block on the counter. They'd hurt it before. It felt pain. Drawing the chef's knife out of the block, she promised herself if it was in the house with her, she would damn well cause it some pain. Still, her instincts told her she'd do better outside than locked in. She reached for the thumb bolt.

The shock ripped up her arm, had her loosing a breathless scream as she stumbled back. On a sudden, thunderous burst, the kitchen faucet gushed blood. She stepped toward the phone—help, should she need it, was only two minutes away. But when she reached for the phone, a second, more violent shock jolted her.

Scare tactics, she told herself as she began to edge out of the kitchen. Trap the lone woman in the house. Make a lot of noise, she added when the booming shook the walls, the floor, the ceiling.

She saw the boy through the living room window. Its face was pressed against it. It grinned.

I can't get out, but it can't get in, she thought. Isn't that interesting? But as she watched, it crawled up the glass, across it, down, like some hideous bug.

And the glass bled until it was covered with red, and with the buzzing black flies that came to drink.

They smothered the light until the room, the house, was dark as pitch. Like being blind, she thought as her heart began to buck and kick. That's what it wanted her to feel. It wanted to claw through her to that old, deep-seated fear. Through the booming, the buzzing, she braced a hand on the wall to guide her. She felt the warm wet run over her hand, and knew the walls bled.

She would get out, she told herself. Into the light. She'd take the shock, she'd handle it, and she *would* get out. Wall gave way to stair banister, and she shuddered with relief. Nearly there.

Something flew out of the dark, knocking her off her feet. The knife clattered uselessly across the floor. So she crawled, hands and knees. When the door flew open, the light all but blinded her. She came up like a runner off the mark.

She plowed straight into Gage. Later, he'd think she would have gone straight through him if she could've managed it. He caught her, fully expecting to have a clawing, kicking, hysterical female in his hands. Instead, she looked into his eyes with her own fierce and cold.

"Do you see it?" she demanded.

"Yeah. Your neighbor out sweeping her front walk doesn't. She's waving."

Cybil kept a viselike grip on Gage's arm with one hand, turned, and waved with the other. On the front window, the boy scrabbled like a spider. "Keep it up." Cybil spaced her words evenly. "Waste all the energy you like on today's matinee." Deliberately she released Gage and sat on the front steps. "So," she said to Gage, "out for a drive?"

He stared at her for a moment, then shaking his head, sat down beside her. The boy leaped down to race around the lawn. Where it ran, blood flowed like a river. "Actually, I'd stopped in to see Fox. While I was there, he got this little buzz in the brain. A lot of static, he said, like a signal just off channel. Since Layla said you were the only one on your own, I came up to check."

"I'm very glad to see you." Fire sprang up from the bloody river. "I wasn't sure I was getting through, with our psychic Bat Signal." To help keep herself steady, she reached out, took Gage's hand.

On the lawn, the thing screamed in fury. It leaped, and it dived into the stream of flaming blood.

"Impressive exit."

"You've got balls of fucking steel," Gage murmured.

"A professional gambler should be able to read a bluff better than that."

As every inch of her began to shake, Gage took her chin in his hand, turned her face to his. "It takes balls of fucking steel to bluff like that."

"It feeds on fear. I was damned if I was going to give it lunch. But I'm double damned if I'm going back in the house alone, right at the moment."

"Do you want to go back in, or do you want to go somewhere else?"

His tone was casual, almost careless, without a trace of *there, there, honey*. The last hard knot in her belly loosened, and she realized that last little one had been pride, not fear. "I want to be in Bimini, sipping a Bellini on the beach."

"Let's go."

When she laughed, he went with instinct rather than judgment, and took her mouth with his.

Stupid, he knew it was stupid, but smart couldn't be half as satisfying. She tasted like she looked—exotic and mysterious. She didn't feign surprise or resistance, and instead took as he did. When he released her, she kept her eyes on his as she leaned back.

"Well, that was no Bellini in Bimini, but it was very nice."

"I can do better than nice."

"Oh, I have no doubt. But . . ." She gave his shoulder a companionable pat as she rose. "I think we'd better go inside, make sure everything's all right in there." She looked out over the lush green lawn, toward the front window sparkling now in the afternoon sunlight. "It probably is, but we should check."

"Right." He got up to go inside with her. "You should call Fox's office, let them know you're okay."

"Yeah. In the kitchen. That's where I was when it started." She gestured to the living room chair lying on its side. "That must've been what flew across the room and knocked me down. The little bastard threw a chair at me."

Gage righted it, then picked up the knife. "Yours?"

"Yeah, too bad I didn't get to use it." She stepped into the kitchen with him, let out a slow breath. "The back door's closed and locked, and so's the window. It did that. That was real. It's best to know what's real and what isn't." After rinsing the knife and sliding it back into the block, she picked up the phone to call Layla.

Assuming she'd want it the way it was, Gage unlocked and opened both door and window.

"I'm going to cook," Cybil announced when she hung up the phone.

"Fine."

"It'll keep me calm and centered. I'll need a few things, so you can drive me to the market."

"I can?"

"Yes, you can. I'll get my purse. And since I now have Bellinis on the brain, we'll stop by the liquor store and pick up some champagne."

"You want champagne," he said after a beat.

"Who doesn't?"

"Anything else on our list of errands?"

She only smiled. "You can bet I'm getting a pair of rubber gloves. I'll explain on the way," she said.

She browsed, studied, examined the offerings in produce. She selected tomatoes with the care and deliberation he imagined a woman might use when selecting an important piece of jewelry. In the brightly lit market with its mind-melting Muzak and red dot specials, she looked like some fairy queen. Titania, maybe, he decided. Titania had been no pushover either.

He'd expected to be irritated, or at least impatient with the household task of food shopping, but she was fascinating to watch. She had a fluid way of moving, and a look in her eyes that said she noticed everything. He wondered how many people could be terrorized by a demon, then coolly stroll behind a grocery store shopping cart.

He had to admire that.

She spent a full fifteen minutes over poultry, examining, rejecting chickens until she found one that somehow met her standards.

"We're having chicken? All this for chicken?"

"Not just chicken." She tossed back her hair, gave him that sidelong smile of hers. "It's a roasted chicken made with wine, sage, garlic, balsamic—and so on. You'll weep with joy at every bite."

"I don't think so."

"Your tastebuds will. Your travels have probably taken you to New York a time or two over the years."

"Sure."

"Ever dined at Piquant?"

"Fancy French place, Upper West."

"Yes, and a New York institution. The chef there was my first serious lover. He was older, French, absolutely perfect for the first serious lover of a woman of twenty." That smile turned knowing, and just a little sultry. "He taught me quite a bit—about cooking."

"How much older?"

"Considerably. He had a daughter my age. Naturally, she despised me." She poked at a baguette. "No, I'm not settling for the bread here, not this late in the day. We'll stop by the bakery in town. If nothing there works, I'll just bake some."

"You'll just bake some bread."

"If necessary. If I'm in the mood to, it can be therapeutic and satisfying."

"Like sex."

Her smile was quick and easy. "Exactly." She rolled the cart into line. Leaned on the handle. "So, who was your first serious lover?"

She didn't notice, or didn't appear to care, that the woman ahead of them in line looked back over her shoulder with wide eyes. "I haven't had one yet."

"Well, that's a shame. You've missed all the wild passion, the bitter arguments, the mad yearnings. Sex is fun without it, but all the rest adds intensity." Cybil smiled at the woman ahead of them. "Don't you agree?"

The woman flushed, moved her shoulders. "Ah, yeah, I guess. Sure." And developed a sudden—and to Gage's eyes, bogus—interest in the tabloids on the rack before the belt.

"Still, women are more prone to look for all that emotion. It's genetic—hormonal," Cybil continued conversationally. "We're more sexually satisfied, as a gender, when we let our emotions engage, and believe—even if the belief is false—our lover's emotions are as well."

When the belt cleared enough, she began to load her purchases on. "I cook," she told Gage, "you pay."

"That wasn't mentioned."

She gave the bird a pat as she set it on the belt. "If you don't like the chicken, I'll give you a refund."

He watched her load. Long fingers, palely painted nails, a couple of sparkling rings. "I could lie."

"You won't. You like to win, but like women and emotion and sex, the win isn't as satisfying for you unless you play it straight."

He watched the items ring up, and total. "It better be damn good chicken," he said as he pulled out his wallet.

FOUR

⸺◦◖◗◦⸺

She'd been right about the chicken; he'd never had better. And he thought she'd been right to decree no discussion of her experience, or any demon-related topic during the group meal.

It was fascinating how much *other* the six of them had to talk about, even though they'd been in one another's pockets for months. Wedding plans, new business plans, books, movies, celebrity scandals, and small-town gossip bounced around the table like tennis balls. At any other time, in any other place, the gathering would have been exactly as it appeared—a group of friends and lovers enjoying each other and a perfectly prepared meal.

And how did he fit into the mix? His relationship with Cal and Fox had changed and evolved over the years as they'd gone from boys to men, certainly when he'd yanked out his roots in the Hollow to move on. But at its base it was what it had always been—the friendship of a lifetime. They simply were.

He liked the women they'd chosen, for their own sakes, and for the way they'd meshed with his friends into couples. It took unique women to face what they were all facing and stick it out. It told him that if any of them survived, the four of them would buck the odds and make the strange entity of marriage work.

In fact, he believed they'd thrive.

And if they survived, he'd move on again. He was the one who left—and who came back. That's how he made his life work, in any case. There was always the next game, and another chance to play. That's where he fit in, he supposed. The wild card that turned up after the cut and shuffle.

That left Cybil, with her encyclopedic brain, her genius in the kitchen, and her nerves of steel. Only once since they'd come together had he seen her break down. Twisse had triggered the deepest personal fear in all of them, Gage remembered, and for Cybil that was blindness. She'd wept in his arms when that was over. But she hadn't run.

No, she hadn't run. She'd stick it out, all of them would. Then if they lived through it, she'd move on. There wasn't a single cell of small-town girl in that interesting body of hers. Adaptable she was, he thought. She'd settled smoothly enough into the Hollow, the little house, but it was . . . like Frannie Hawkins's holding vase, he realized. This was just a temporary stop before she moved on to something more suited to her style.

But where, and to what would she move? He wondered that, wondered about her more than was wise.

She caught his glance, arched a brow. "Looking for a refund?"

"No."

"Well then. I'm going for a walk."

"Oh, but, Cyb—" Quinn began.

"Gage can come with me, while the four of you deal with the dishes."

"How come he gets out of kitchen duty?" Fox wanted to know.

"He shopped, he paid. I want a little air before we bring the Big Evil Bastard to the table. How about it, big guy? Be my escort?"

"Take your phone." Quinn caught Cybil's hand. "Just in case."

"I'll take my phone, and I'll put on a jacket. And I won't take candy from strangers. Relax, Mommy."

When she breezed out, Quinn turned to Gage. "Just don't go far, okay? Keep her close."

"This is Hawkins Hollow, everything in it's close."

She put on a light sweater and slipped black skids onto feet that were so often bare. The minute she stepped outside, she breathed deep. "I like spring nights. Summer's even better. I like the heat, but under the circumstances, I'm hoarding spring."

"Where do you want to go?"

"Main Street, of course. Where else? I like knowing my ground," she continued as they walked. "So I walk around town, drive around the area."

"And could probably draw a detailed map of both by now."

"Not only could, have. I do have an eye for detail." She took another breath, this one loaded with the scent of peonies rioting pink in someone's front garden. "Quinn's going to be happy here. It's so absolutely right for her."

"Why?"

He saw the question surprised her—or, he thought more accurately, the fact he'd asked surprised her.

"Neighborhood. That's Quinn. Developments, suburbia, no, not so much. Too . . . formed. But neighborhood, where she knows the tellers at the bank, the clerks at the market by name? That's all Q. She's a social creature who needs her alone time. So, the town—that gives her the neighborhood. And the house outside town—that gives her the alone. She gets it all," Cybil decided. "And the guy, too."

"Handy Cal falls in there."

"Very. I admit, when she first talked about Cal, I thought Bowling Alley Guy? Q's gone deep end." Laughing, she shook back her hair. "Shame on me for assuming a cliché. Of course, the minute I met him, I thought, oh, Really Cute Bowling Alley Guy! Then seeing them together clinched it. From my standpoint, they're both getting it all. I'll enjoy coming back here to visit them, and Fox and Layla."

They turned at the Square, and onto Main Street. One of the cars stopped at the light had its windows open and Green Day blasting. While Ma's Pantry and Gino's remained open—and a few teenagers loitered outside the pizza joint—the shops were closed for the night. By nine, Ma's would be dark, and just after eleven, Gino's would lock it up. The Hollow's version, Gage thought, of rolling up the sidewalks.

"So, no yen to build yourself a cabin in Hawkins Wood?" he asked her.

"A cabin in the woods might be nice for the occasional weekend. And the small-town charm," she added, "is just that—charming for visits. I love visiting. It's one of my favorite things. But I'm an urbanite at heart, and I like to travel. I need a base so I have somewhere to leave from, to come back to. I have a very nice one in New York, left to me by my grandmother. How about you? Is there a base, a headquarters, for you?"

He shook his head. "I like hotel rooms."

"Me, too—or to qualify, a room in a well-run hotel. I love the service, the convenience of my well-appointed chamber in a hive where I can order up Do Not Disturb and room service at my whim."

"Twenty-four hours a day," he added. "And somebody comes in and cleans it all up while you're out doing something a lot more interesting."

"That can't be overstated. And I like looking out the window at a view that doesn't belong to me. Still, there are other types in the world, like many of the people in this town Twisse is so hell-bent to destroy. And they like looking out at the familiar. They need and want the comfort of that, and they're entitled to it."

That brought it back to square one, Gage thought. "And you'd bleed for that?"

"Oh, I hope not—at least not copiously. But it's Quinn's town now, and Layla's. I'd bleed for them. And for Cal and Fox." She turned her head, met his eyes. "And for you."

There was a jolt inside him at that, at the absolute truth he felt from her. Before he could respond, her phone rang.

"Saved by the ringtone," Cybil murmured, then drew out her phone, glanced at the display. "Hell. Damn. Fuck. Sorry, I'd better deal with this." She flipped the phone open. "Hello, Rissa."

She took a few steps away, but Gage had no trouble with the logistics or the ethics of eavesdropping on her end of the conversation. He heard a lot of "no"s between long, listening pauses. And several chilly, "I've already told you"s and "not this time"s followed by an "I'm sorry, Marissa" that spoke of impatience rather than apology. When she closed the phone, that impatience was clear on her face.

"Sorry. My sister, who's never quite grasped the concept that the world doesn't actually revolve around her. Hopefully she's pissed enough at me now to lay off for a few weeks."

"This would be flat-tire sister?"

"Sorry? Oh." And when she laughed, he could see her click back to the night they'd met when they'd nearly run into each other on a deserted county road as each of them traveled toward Hawkins Hollow. "Yes, the same sister who'd borrowed my car and left a flat spare in my trunk. The same who routinely 'borrows' what she likes, and if she remembers to return it, generally returns it damaged or useless."

"Then why did you lend her your car?"

"Excellent question. A weak moment. I don't have many, at least not anymore." Annoyance darkened her eyes now, the steely kind.

"I bet."

"She's in New York, flitting back from wherever she flitted off to this time and doesn't see why she and whatever leeches currently sucking on her can't stay at my place for a couple weeks. But golly, the locks and the security code have been changed—which was necessary because the last time she stayed there with a few friends, they trashed the place, broke an antique vase that had been my great-grandmother's, borrowed several items of my wardrobe—including my cashmere coat, which I'll never see again—and had the cops drop by at the request of the neighbors."

"Sounds like a fun gal," he commented when Cybil ran out of breath.

"Oh, she's nothing but. All right, I'm venting. You have the option of listening or tuning out. She was the baby, and she was pampered and spoiled as babies often are, especially when they're beautiful and charming. And she is, quite beautiful, quite charming. We were children of privilege for the first part of our lives. There was a lot of family money. There was an enormous and gorgeous home in Connecticut, a number of pied-à-terres in interesting places. We had the best schools, traveled to Europe regularly, socialized with the children of wealthy and important people, and so on. Then came my father's accident, his blindness."

She said nothing for a moment, only continued to walk, her hands in her pockets, her eyes straight ahead. "He couldn't cope. He couldn't see, so he wouldn't see. Then one day, in our big gorgeous home in Connecticut, he locked himself in the library. They tried to break down the door when we heard the shot—we still had servants then, and they tried to break it down. I ran out, and around. I saw through the window, saw what he'd done. I broke the glass, got inside. I don't remember that very well. It was too late, of course. Nothing to be done. My mother was hysterical, Marissa was wild, but there was nothing to be done."

Gage said nothing, but then she knew him to be a man who often said nothing. So she plowed on.

"It was afterward we learned there'd been what they like to call 'considerable financial reversals' since my father's accident. As his untimely death gave him no time to reverse the reversals, we would have to condense, so to speak. My mother dealt with the shock and the grief, which were very real for her, by fleeing with us to Europe and squandering great quantities of money. In a year, she'd married an operator who squandered more, conned her into funnelling most of what was left to him, then left her for greener pastures."

The bitterness in her tone was so ripe, he imagined she could taste it.

"It could've been worse, much worse. We could've been destitute and instead we simply had to learn how to live on more limited resources and earn our way. My mother's since married again, to a very good man. Solid and kind. Should I stop?"

"No."

"Good. Marissa, as I did, came into a—by our former standards—modest inheritance at twenty-one. She'd already been married lavishly, and divorced bitterly, by this time. She blew through the money like a force-five hurricane. She toys with modeling, does very decently with magazine shoots and billboards when she bothers. But what she wants most is to be a celebrity, of any sort, and she continues to pursue the lifestyle of one—or what she perceives to be the lifestyle of one. As a result, she's very often broke and can only use her charm and beauty as currency. Since neither has worked on me for a long time, we're usually at odds."

"Does she know where you are?"

"No, thank God. I didn't tell her, and won't, first because as big a pain in my ass as she is, she remains my sister and I don't want her hurt. Second, more selfishly, I don't want her in my hair. She's very like my mother, or as my mother was before this third marriage settled and contented her. People always said I took after my father."

"So he was smart and sexy?"

She smiled a little. "That's a nice thing to say after I've unloaded on you. I've wondered if being like my father meant I wouldn't be able to face the worst life threw at me."

"You already did. You broke the window."

She let out a breath that trembled in a way that warned him there were tears behind it. But she held them back—major points for her—and turning, looked up at him with those deep, dark eyes. "All right, you've earned this for listening, and I've earned it for being smart enough to dump it on a man who would."

She gripped his shirtfront, rose on her toes. Then she slid her hands over his shoulders, linked her arms around his neck.

Her mouth was silk and heat and promise. It moved over his, a slow glide that invited him in, to sample or to taste fully. The flavors of her wound through him, strong and sweet, beckoning like a crooked finger.

Come on, have a little more.

When she started to ease away, he gripped her hips, brought her back up to her toes. And had a little more.

She didn't regret it. How could she? She'd offered, he'd answered. How could she regret being kissed on a quiet spring night by a man who knew exactly how she wanted to be kissed?

Hard and deep, with just a hint of bite.

If her pulse tripped, if her belly fluttered, if this sample caused her system to yearn, to burn, she chose to ride the excitement, not step away with regret. So when she stepped back, it wasn't with regret, it wasn't with caution, but with the clear understanding that a man like Gage Turner respected a challenge. And giving him one would undoubtedly prove more satisfying to both of them.

"That might've been a slight overpayment," she decided. "But you can keep the change."

He grinned back at her. "That *was* your change."

She laughed, and on impulse held out a hand for his. "I'd say our after-dinner walk did both of us good. We'd better get back."

In the living room, Cybil sat with her feet tucked up, a mug of tea in her hand as she relayed the incident from that afternoon for the group, and Quinn's recorder.

She didn't skimp on the details, Gage noted, and she didn't flinch from them.

"There was blood in the house," Quinn prompted.

"The illusion of blood."

"And the flies, the noise. The dark. You saw and heard all that, too?" Quinn asked Gage.

"Yeah."

"The doors and windows were locked from the inside."

"The front door opened when I tried it, from the outside," Gage qualified. "But when we went back in, the kitchen door was still locked, so was the window over the sink."

"But it—the boy," Layla said slowly, "was outside, on the window. It never came in."

"I think it couldn't." Cybil took a thoughtful sip of tea. "How much more threatened would I have felt if it was locked in here with me? If it could have gotten in, I think it would have. It could cause me to see and hear—even feel things that weren't real inside the house. It could lock the door, the window in the room where I was when it started. Not the front," she said. "Maybe it used up that area of its power on the back of the house. It could only make me *think* the front door was locked. Stupid. I never thought of it when it was happening."

"Yeah." Cal shook his head at her. "It's pretty stupid of you not to cop to that when the house was bleeding and shaking and you were stuck in the dark with demon boy crawling on the window."

"Now that we've established Cybil completely loses her head in a crisis, we should ask ourselves why it couldn't come in." Fox sat on the floor, scratching Lump on his big head. "Maybe it's like the vampire deal. Has to be invited."

"Or, keeping Dracula inside of fiction where he belongs, it just wasn't up to full power. And won't be," Gage reminded them, "for a few more weeks."

"Actually . . ." Cybil frowned. "If we consider vampyric lore, it's not impossible the undead, drinker of blood, and so forth, doesn't have its legitimate roots in this demon. Some of that lore speaks of the vampire's ability to hypnotize its victims or foes—mind control. It feeds off human blood. This is more your area, Quinn, than mine."

"You're doing fine."

"All right, to stick with this channel, vampires are often said to have the ability to turn into a bat, a wolf. This demon certainly shape-shifts—which adds the possibility of the shape-shifter, of which the lycanthrope is a subset, found in various lore. To some extent, these might be bastardizations of this demon."

She picked up her own notebook, scribbled in it as she continued. "Undead. We know now that it can take the form of someone who's died. What if this isn't, as we thought, a new trick, but an ability it had before Dent imprisoned it, and is only now, as what we're told is the final Seven approaches, able to pull that out of its hat again?"

"So it kills Uncle Harry," Fox proposed, "then for fun, it comes back as Uncle Harry to terrorize and kill the rest of the family."

"It does have a sick sense of fun." Quinn nodded. "Should we start sharpening stakes?"

"No. But we'd better figure out how the weapon we do have works. Still, this is interesting." Thoughtfully, Cybil tapped her pencil on the notepad. "If it couldn't come in, that might give us a little more security, and peace of mind. Have any of you ever seen it inside a home?" Cybil asked.

"It just gets the people in it to kill themselves, or each other, or burn the place down." Gage shrugged. "Often all of the above."

"Maybe there's a way to block it, or at least weaken it." Layla slid off her chair to sit on the floor beside Fox. "It's energy, right? And energy that feeds on, or at least seems to prefer, negative emotions. Anger, fear, hate. At every Seven, or the approach of one, it targets birds and animals first—smaller brains, less intellect than humans. And it recharges on that, then moves, usually, to people who're under some influence. Alcohol, drugs, or those emotions again. Until it's stronger."

"It's coming out stronger this time," Cal pointed out. "It's already moved past animals, and was able to infect Block Kholer to the point he nearly beat Fox to death."

As Layla took Fox's hand, Cybil considered. "That was target specific, and it wasn't able to infect the chief of police when he got there and dragged Block off. Target specific might be another advantage."

"Unless you're the target," Fox pointed out. "Then it seriously sucks."

Cybil smiled at him. "True enough. It doesn't just feed off hate, it hates. Us especially. As far as we know, everything it's done or been able to do since February targets one of us, or the group as a whole."

She set her notebook on the arm of the sofa. "It's expending a lot of energy to scare us, hurt us. That's a thought I had today when it had me trapped in here. Well, before it went dark and I wasn't so cocky. That it was using up energy. Maybe we can taunt it into using more. It's stronger, yes, and it's getter stronger yet, but anytime it puts on a big show, there's a lull afterward. It's still recharging. And while there might not be a way to block or weaken it, there might be a way to divert it. If it's aiming at us, its ability to infect the Hollow may be diminished."

"I'm pretty sure I can state categorically it's been aimed at us plenty, and still managed to wreak havoc in the Hollow."

Cybil nodded at Fox. "Because you've always been in the Hollow trying to save lives, fight it off."

"What choice do we have?" Cal demanded. "We can't leave people unprotected."

"I'm suggesting they might not need as much protection if we were able to draw it away."

"How? And where?"

"How might be a challenge," Cybil began.

"But where would be the Pagan Stone. Tried that," Gage continued. "Fourteen years ago."

"Yes, I've read that in Quinn's notes, but—"

"Do you remember our last trip there?" Gage asked her. "That was a walk on the beach compared to getting through Hawkins Wood anywhere close to the Seven."

"We made it that time, two Sevens ago. Barely," Fox added. "We thought maybe we could stop it by repeating the ritual at the same time, the same place. Midnight, our birthday—the dawn of the Seven, so to speak. Didn't work, obviously. By the time we got back to town, it was bad. One of the worst nights of this ever."

"Because we weren't here to help anyone," Cal finished. "We'd left the town unprotected. How can we risk that again?"

Cybil started to speak, then decided to let it go for now. "Well, back to the bloodstone then. That's one of the new elements on our side of the scoreboard. I've got some avenues I'm exploring. And was about to push a little deeper earlier today when I was so rudely interrupted. I'll get back on that tomorrow. I was also going to suggest, if you're up for it, Gage, that you and I try what Cal and Quinn have, and Fox and Layla."

"You want to have sex? Always up for it."

"That's so sweet, but I was staying on topic and speaking of combining abilities. We have past." She gestured to Cal and Quinn. "We have now, with Fox and Layla. You and I see forward. Maybe it's time to find out if we see further, or clearer, together."

"I'm game if you are."

"How about tomorrow then? I'll drive out to Cal's, maybe about one."

"Ah, about that." Cal cleared his throat. "After today, I think we have to limit solo time as much as possible. Nobody should be staying here or at my place alone at night, for one thing. We can split that up, so there's at least two—better three—in one place. And

during the day, we should use the buddy system whenever possible.
You shouldn't drive out to my place alone, Cybil."

"I'm not going to disagree about safety and strength in numbers.
So, who's going to buddy up with Fox whenever he has to drive up
to Hagerstown, to the courthouse? Or with Gage when he's zipping
from here to there?"

Fox shook his head sadly at Cal. "Warned you, didn't I?"

"For the record, I'm not the least bit insulted that you'd want to
protect me and my fellow females." Cybil smiled at Cal. "And I agree
we should stick together as much as possible. But it's not practical or
feasible that we can avoid basic alone time or tasks for the duration.
We're six weeks out. I think we can all promise to be sensible and
cautious. I, for one, won't be lighting the candle and creeping down
to the basement at midnight to investigate strange noises."

"I'll come here," Gage told her.

"No, because now it's a matter of principle. And I think we'd
have more luck with this at Cal's. This house still feels . . ."

"Smudged," Quinn finished. She reached over to rub Cybil's
knee. "It'll fade."

"Yes, it will. Well, while you all work out who's sleeping where
tonight, I'm going to bed." Rising, she glanced at Gage. "I'll see you
tomorrow."

She wanted a long hot soak in the tub, but that struck her as
too close to going down into a dark basement. Both were horror-
movie clichés for a reason, after all. She settled on the nightly routine of cleanser, toner, moisturizer. As she started to turn down the
bed, Quinn came in.

"Cal and I are staying here tonight."

"All right, but wouldn't it make more sense for you two to go
home, with Gage?"

"Fox and Layla are bunking at Cal's. I wanted to be here tonight."

Because she understood, Cybil's eyes stung. She sat on the side of the bed, took Quinn's hand, laid it against her cheek as Quinn sat beside her.

"I was all right until the lights went out. More interested, even intrigued than scared. Then they went out, and I couldn't see. Nothing was as horrible as that."

"I know. I can sleep in here with you tonight."

Cybil shook her head, tipped it to Quinn's shoulder. "It's enough to know you're across the hall. We all felt it, didn't we? That smudge like you said, that smear it left on the house. I was afraid it was just me, just being paranoid."

"We all felt it. It'll fade, Cyb. We won't give ground."

"It'll never understand how we are together, or what we are together. It would never understand that you knew I'd sleep better tonight with you in the house, or that I'd be better talking to you for a few minutes alone."

"It's one of the ways we'll beat it."

"I believe that." She sighed. "Marissa called."

"Crap."

"Yeah, and it was—the usual crap. 'Can't you do this, can't I have that? Why are you so mean?' It just added to an upsetting day. I dumped a good chunk of my unfortunate family history on Gage's head."

"Really?"

"Yes, I know, not my usual style. It was a weak moment, but he handled it well. He didn't say much, but he said exactly the right thing. Then I kissed his brains out."

"Well." Quinn gave her a friendly shoulder bump. "It's about damn time."

"Maybe it is, I don't know. I don't know if it would complicate things, simplify them, or make no damn difference at all. But while I'm sure the sex would be good—in fact superior—I'm equally sure it would be as risky as going down in the basement to see what the banging's about."

"It could be, but since there'd be two of you involved, you wouldn't be going down to the basement alone."

"True." Pursing her lips, Cybil studied her own toes. "And there would be some comfort when we were both hacked to death by the ax murderer."

"At least you'd've had sex first."

"Superior sex. I'll sleep on it." She gave Quinn a squeeze. "Go on, go snuggle up with your adorable guy. I'm going to do a little yoga to help me relax before I go to bed."

"Just call if you need me."

Cybil nodded. That was the thing, she thought when Quinn left her. That was a constant in her life. If she needed Quinn, all she had to do was call.

FIVE

She'd been in his dreams, and in his dreams, she came to his bed. In his dreams her lips, soft and seeking, yielded to his. Her body, sleek and smooth, arched up, long arms, long legs wrapping him in warmth, in fragrance. In female.

The wild glory of her hair, dark against white sheets, spilled away from her face while those deep, seductive eyes watched him.

She rose. She opened. She took him in.

In his dreams, his blood beat like a heart, and his heart pounded its fist in his chest. Inside him, joy and desperation rolled into one mad tangle of need. Locked, lost, he took her lips again. The taste, the taste that burned through him like a fever while their bodies raced together. Faster. Faster.

While around them the room began to bleed, and to burn.

She cried out, her nails biting like teeth into his back while the sea of bloody flames rolled over them. And the word she cried as they were consumed was *bestia*.

He woke, once again at first light. And that, Gage thought, had to stop. He had no particular affinity for mornings, and now it seemed he was doomed to deal with them. There'd be no going back to sleep after the little movie clip his subconscious had drummed up. It was too damn bad such a promising dream had taken a turn so far south at the—ha—climax.

He could pick apart the symbolism, he thought, staring at the ceiling of Cal's guest room. But then, it was easy to identify the springboard for the lion's share of tonight's entertainment.

He was a guy. He was horny.

Moreover, it suited his fantasy to have her come to him rather than him pursuing her. They'd made a pact not that long ago on this very topic. How had she put it? *You won't try to seduce me, and I won't pretend to be seduced.*

Remembering made him smile into the dim, dawn light. But if she made the moves, all bets were off as far as he was concerned. The challenge would be to con her into making those moves so she believed it was her idea in the first place.

Then again, the interlude in the dream had ended badly. He could ascribe that to his own cynical, pessimistic nature, or he could consider it a portent. Or, third option, a warning. If he let himself become involved with her—because it hadn't just been sex in the dream, he'd been *involved*—they could both pay the ultimate price. Blood and fire, he thought—as usual. And it hadn't been her lover's name she'd cried out when she'd been consumed by passion and flame, but *bestia.*

Latin for beast. A dead language used by dead gods and guardians.

Simply put, the distraction of sex would blur their focus, and the Big Evil Bastard would strike when they were defenseless. Meaning, any of the three options indicated the smart money was on keeping it in his pants, at least as far as Cybil Kinski was concerned.

He rolled out of bed. He'd shower off the dream, and the urges it stirred. He was damn good at controlling his urges. If he was restless and horny, it meant he needed a game and sex. So he'd make it a point to find both. A quick trip to AC would meet both needs, eliminate any possible complications or consequences.

And he and Cybil would use the sexual tension between them as an energy source for the greater good. Of course, if they won, if they lived, he'd make damn sure he found a way to get her naked. Then he'd find out if her skin was as soft as it looked, her body as limber, her . . .

That line of thinking wasn't going to help him control his urges.

He toweled off, opted out of shaving (what the hell for?), then pulled on jeans and a black T-shirt because they were the handiest. As he started downstairs he heard the murmur of voices, and a quick, sexy giggle behind the closed bedroom door. So the lovebirds were up early and already cooing, he mused. Odds were they'd be at it long enough for him to have a quiet, solitary cup of coffee.

In the kitchen, he started the first pot of the day, and while he brooded, he walked out of the house to hike down to the road and the paper box. Cal's front slope was a riot of blooms. The azaleas— one of the few ornamentals Gage actually recognized—were in full, showy bloom. Some sort of delicate weeper arched over, dripping pink. All that color and shape tumbled down toward the gravel lane, cheerful as children, while the woods stood along the edges with its thickening green hiding its secrets. Its joy and its terrors.

Birds trilled, the winding creek murmured, and his footsteps crunched. Some of Cal's blooms were fragrant, so their perfume fluttered in the air while dappled sunlight played over the ribbon of the creek.

Soothing, he thought, the sounds, the scents, the scene. And for a man like Cal, unquestionably satisfying. He enjoyed it himself for short stretches, Gage admitted, as he reached into the blue box and pulled out the morning paper. And he needed, again unquestionably, infusions of Cal and Fox. But if those stretches played out too long, he'd start jonesing for neon, for green baize, for horns and crowds. For the action, the energy, the anonymity of a casino or a city.

If they killed the bastard and lived through it, he thought he'd buzz off somewhere for a few weeks. Cal's wedding in September would bring him back, but in the meantime, there was a big world out there, and a lot of cards to be dealt. Maybe Amsterdam or Lux-embourg for a change of pace.

Or, if he was in the get-Cybil-naked mode, he might suggest Paris. Romance, sex, gambling, and fashion all in one shot. He thought she'd like the idea. After all, she shared his affection for travel and a good hotel. Finding out how they traveled together might be a nice way to celebrate living beyond his thirty-first birthday.

She was bound to bring him luck—good or bad was yet to be seen—but a woman like that tipped scales. He was willing to gamble they'd tip his way.

A couple of weeks, pure fun, no strings, then they'd come back, watch their friends get hooked up, and part ways. It was a good blueprint, he decided, one that could easily be adjusted to whim and circumstance.

With the paper tucked under his arm, he started back the way he came.

The woman stood just over the other side of the little wooden bridge that spanned the creek. Her hair fell loose and free around her shoulders, and glowed pale gold in the delicate sunlight. Her long dress was a quiet blue, high at the neck. His heart gave one hard thump as he knew her to be Ann Hawkins, dead for centuries.

But just for an instant, for one quick beat when she smiled, he saw his mother in her.

"You are the last of the sons of the sons of my sons. You are what came from me and my love, what came from passion, cold blood, and bitter sacrifice. Faith and hope came before you, and must remain steadfast. You are the vision. You and she who came from the dark. Your blood, its blood, our blood. With this, the stone is whole once more. With this, you are blessed."

"Blah, blah, blah," he said, and wondered if the gods struck you dead for mouthing off to a ghost. "Why don't you tell me how to use it, and we'll finish this thing and get on with our lives?"

Ann Hawkins tilted her head, and damned if he didn't see the *mother* look on her face. "Anger is a weapon as well, if used judiciously. He did all that he could, gave you all you would need. You have only to see, to trust what you know, to take what is given. I wept for you, little boy."

"Appreciate it, but tears didn't do me a lot of good."

"Hers will, when they come. You are not alone. You never were. From blood and fire came the light and the dark. With blood and fire, one will prevail. The key to your vision, to the answers, is in your hand. Turn it, and see."

When she faded, he stood where he was. Typical, he thought, typical female. They just couldn't make things simple. Irritated now, he crossed the bridge and climbed the slope of the lane to the house.

The lovebirds were in the kitchen, so he'd lost his chance for that quiet and solitary cup of coffee. They were wrapped around each other, naturally, lip-locked in front of the damn coffeepot.

"Break it up." Gage bumped Fox with his shoulder to nudge him clear of the pot.

"Hasn't had his first cup yet." Fox gave Layla a last squeeze before picking up the Coke he'd already opened. "He's bitchy until."

"Do you want me to fix you some breakfast?" Layla offered. "We've got time before we have to leave for the office."

"Aren't you Mary Sunshine?" On this grouchy pronouncement, Gage pulled a box of cereal out of the cupboard, then dug in for a handful. "I'm good." Then he narrowed his eyes as Fox opened the paper. "I walked down for that, I get it first."

"I'm just checking the box scores, Mr. Happy. Any Pop-Tarts around here?"

"God, you're pathetic."

"Man, you're eating Froot Loops out of the box. Pot, kettle."

With a frown, Gage glanced down. So he was. And since the coffee kicked the worst of his crabbiness down, he looked back at Layla with an easy smile. "Hey, good morning, Layla. Did you say something about fixing breakfast?"

She laughed. "Good morning, Gage. I believe I did mention that, in a weak moment. But since I am feeling pretty sunny, I'll follow through."

"Great. Thanks. While you are, I'll tell you guys about the visitor I had on my morning stroll."

Layla froze with her hand on the handle of the refrigerator. "It came back?"

"Not it. She. Though technically maybe a ghost is an it. I haven't given it much thought."

"Ann Hawkins." Fox tossed the paper aside. "What's the word?"

Topping off his coffee, Gage told them.

"Everyone's seen her now, one way or the other, but Cybil." Layla set a platter of French toast on the breakfast bar.

"Yeah, I bet that'll tick her off. Cybil, that is," Gage added as he forked up two slices.

"Blood and fire. There's sure been a lot of that, in reality and in dreams. And that's what put the bloodstone back together. That was Cybil's brainstorm," Fox remembered. "Maybe she'll have one about this."

"I'll fill her in when she gets here later today."

"Sooner's better." With a generous hand, Fox poured syrup on his stack of French toast. "Layla and I will swing by the house before we go to the office."

"She's just going to want me to go through it all again when she gets here."

"Still." Fox sampled a bite, grinned at Layla. "This is great."

"Well, it's not Pop-Tarts."

"Better. Are you sure you don't want me to go into the bank with you this afternoon? Being you, your paperwork's in order, but—"

"I'm fine. You've got a busy schedule today. Plus, with my two investors, I'm not applying for a big, fat loan. More of a slim, efficient one."

So they segued, Gage thought, from ghosts to interest rates. He tuned them out, started to scan the headlines in the paper he'd stolen back from Fox. Then caught a stray comment.

"Cybil and Quinn are investing in your shop?"

"Yeah." Layla's smile radiated like sunlight. "It's great. I hope it's great for them—I'm going to make it great for them. It's just wonderful, and staggering, that they'd have that kind of faith in me. You know what that's like. You and Fox and Cal have always had that."

He supposed he did, just as he supposed this was one more tangible aspect of how the six of them were entwined. Ann had said he wasn't alone. None of them were, he realized. Maybe it was that, just that, that would weigh the odds in their favor.

When he had the house to himself, he spent an hour answering and composing e-mails. He had a contact in Europe, a Professor Linz, whose expertise was demonology and lore. He was full of theories and a lot of verbose rhetoric, but he had come through with what Gage considered salient information.

And the more data you tossed into the hat, the better the chance the winning ticket was in there. It wouldn't hurt to get Linz's take on Cybil's newest hypothesis. Was the bloodstone—*their* bloodstone— a fragment of some larger whole, some mythical, magickal power source?

Even as he wrote the post, he shook his head. If anyone outside of his tight circle of friends knew he spent a great deal of his time searching out information on demons, they'd laugh their asses off. Then again, those outside that circle who knew him only saw what he let them see. Not one of them reached the level he'd call friend.

Acquaintances, players, bedmates. Sometimes they won his money, sometimes he won theirs. Maybe he'd buy them a drink, or they'd stand him a round or two. And the women—away from the tables—they'd give each other a few hours, maybe a few days if it suited both of them.

Easy come, easy go.

And why did that suddenly seem more pathetic than a grown man wanting a Pop-Tart for breakfast?

Annoyed with himself, he combed his hands through his hair, tipped back in the chair. He did as he pleased, and lived as he wanted. Even coming here, facing this, was a choice he'd made. If he didn't make it past the first week of July, that would be too damn bad. But he couldn't complain. He'd had thirty-one years, and he'd seen the world on his own terms. From time to time, he'd lived pretty damn high. He'd rather live, and work his way back up to that high a few more times. A few more rolls of the dice, a few more hands dealt. But if not, he'd take his losses.

He'd already accomplished the most important goal of his life. He'd gotten out of the Hollow. And for fifteen years and counting, when someone raised a fist to him, he hit back, harder.

The old man had been drunk that night, Gage remembered. Filthy drunk after falling face-first off the shaky wagon he'd managed to ride for a handful of months. The old man was always worse when he fell off than when he waved that wagon on and kept stumbling down the road.

Summer, Gage thought. The kind of August night where even the air sweated. The place was clean, because the old man had been since April. But being up on the third floor of the bowling center meant that sweaty air just rose and rose until it squatted there, laughing at the constant whirl of the window AC. Even after midnight, the whole place felt wet, so the minute he stepped in, he wished he'd crashed at Cal's or Fox's.

But he'd had a sort of a date, the sort where a guy had to peel off from his pals if he wanted any kind of a chance to score.

He figured his father was in bed, sleeping or trying to, so he toed off his shoes before heading into the kitchen. There was a pitcher half full of iced tea, the instant crap that always tasted too sweet or too bitter no matter how you doctored it up. But he drank down two glasses before looking for something to kill the aftertaste.

He wished he had pizza. The alley and the grill were closed, so no chance there. He found a half a meatball sub, surely several days old. But small matters such as these didn't concern teenage boys.

He ate it cold, standing over the sink.

He cleaned up after himself. He remembered too clearly what the apartment smelled like when his father was drinking heavily. Bad food, old garbage, sweat, stale whiskey, and smoke. It was nice that, despite the heat, the place smelled normal. Not as good as Cal's house or Fox's. There were always candles or flowers or those girly dishes of petals and scent there. And the female aroma he guessed was just skin touched with lotions and sprayed with perfume.

This place was a dump compared, not the kind of place he'd want to bring a date, he thought with a glance around. But it was good enough, for now. The furniture was old and tired, and the walls could use some new paint. Maybe when it cooled off in the fall, he and the old man could slap some on.

Maybe they could swing a new TV, one that had been manufactured in the last decade. Things were pretty solid right now with them both working full-time for the summer. He was squirreling away some of his take for a new headset, but he could kick in half. He had a couple more weeks before school started up, a couple more paychecks. A new TV would be good.

He put his glass away, closed the cupboard. He heard his father's step on the stairs. And he knew.

The optimism drained out of him like water. What was left in him hardened like stone. Stupid, he thought, stupid of him to let himself believe the old man would stay sober. Stupid to believe there'd ever be anything decent in this rat trap of an apartment.

He started to cross to his room, go inside, shut the door. Then he thought the hell with it. He'd see what the drunken son of a bitch had to say for himself.

So he stood, hip-shot, thumbs in the front pockets of his jeans, a defiant red flag eager to wave at the bull. His father pushed open the door.

Weaving, Bill Turner gripped the jamb. His face was red from the climb, from the heat, from the liquor. Even across the room, Gage could smell the whiskey sweat seeping out of his pores. His T-shirt was stained with it under the arms, down the front in a sodden vee. The look in his eyes when they met Gage's was blurry and mean.

"'Fuck you looking at?"

"A drunk."

"Had a couple beers with some friends, don't make me a drunk."

"I guess I was wrong. I'm looking at a drunken liar."

The meanness intensified. It was like watching a snake coil. "You watch your fucking mouth, boy."

"I should've known you couldn't do it." But he *had* done it, for nearly five months. He'd stayed sober through Gage's birthday, and that, Gage knew, had been when he'd started to believe. For the first time since his father had stumbled down the drunken path, he'd stayed on that wagon over Gage's birthday.

This disappointment, this betrayal was a sharper slash than any lash of the belt had ever been. This killed every small drop of his hope.

"None of your goddamn business," Bill shot back. "This is *my* house. You don't tell me what's what under my own roof."

"This is Jim Hawkins's roof, and I pay rent on it just like you. You drink your paycheck again?"

"I don't answer to you. Shut your mouth, or—"

"What?" Gage challenged. "You're so drunk you can barely stand. What the hell are you going to do? And what the hell do I care," he finished in disgust. Turning, he started toward his room. "I wish you'd drink yourself dead and finish the job."

He was drunk, but he was fast. Bill lunged across the room, slammed Gage back against the wall. "You're no good, never been any damn good. Never should've been born."

"That makes two of us. Now take your hands off me."

Two quick slaps, front and back, set Gage's ears ringing, split his bottom lip. "Time you learned some goddamn *respect*."

Gage remembered the first punch, remembered plowing his fist into his father's face, and the shock that fired in his father's eyes. Something crashed—the old pole lamp—and someone cursed viciously over and over. Had that been him?

The next clear memory was standing over his father as the old man sprawled on the floor, his face bruised and bleeding. His own fists had screamed from the pounding, and the healing of his swollen, bloody knuckles. His breath wheezed in and out of his lungs, and sweat soaked him like water.

How long had he beaten on the old man with his fists? It was a hot red haze. But it cleared now, and behind it was ice cold.

"If you ever touch me again, if you ever lay a fucking hand on me again in your life, I'll kill you." He crouched down to make sure the old man heard him. "I swear an oath on it. In three years, I'm gone. I don't care if you drink yourself to death in the meantime. I'm past caring. I've got to live here at least most of the time the next three years. I'll give my share of the rent straight to Mr. Hawkins. You don't get a dime. I'll buy my own food, my own clothes. I don't want anything from you. But however drunk you are, you'd better be able to think this one thought. Hit me again, you motherfucker, you're a dead man."

He rose, walked into his room, shut the door. He'd buy a lock for it the next day, he thought. Keep the bastard out.

He could go. Exhausted, he sat on the side of the bed and dropped his head in his hands. He could pack up what was his and if he showed up on Cal's doorstep or at Fox's farm, they'd take him in.

That's the kind of people they were.

But he needed to stick this out, needed to show the old man and, more, show himself, that he could stick it out. Three years till his eighteenth birthday, he thought, then he'd be free.

Not quite accurate, Gage thought now. He'd stuck it out, and the old man had never raised a hand to him again. And he'd taken off when his three years were up. But freedom? That was another story.

You carried the past with you, he thought, dragging it behind you on a thick, unbreakable chain no matter how far you looked ahead. You could ignore it for good long stretches of time, but you couldn't escape it. He could drag that chain ten thousand miles, but the Hollow, the people he loved in it, and his goddamn destiny just kept pulling him back.

He pushed away from the computer, went down to get himself more coffee. Sitting at the counter, he dealt out a hand of solitaire. It calmed him, the feel of the cards, the sound of them, their colors and shapes. When he heard the knock on the door, he glanced at his watch. It appeared Cybil was early. He left the cards where they were, grateful the simple game had kept his mind off the past, and off the woman as well.

When he pulled open the door, it was Joanne Barry on the front deck. "Well, hey."

She only looked at him for a moment. Her dark hair was braided back, as she often wore it. Her eyes were clear in her pretty face, her body slim in jeans and a cotton shirt. Then she touched his face, laid her lips on his forehead, his cheeks, his lips in her traditional greeting when there was love.

"Thank you for the orchid."

"You're welcome. Sorry I missed you when I dropped it off. Do you want to come in? Do you have time?"

"Yes, I'd like to come in, for a few minutes."

"Probably something to drink back here." He led the way back toward the kitchen.

"Cal's got a nice place here. It's always a surprise."

"Really?"

"That he—all of you—are grown men. That Cal's a grown man with this very nice home of his own, with its beautiful gardens. Sometimes still, just every so often, I wake up in the morning and think: I've got to get those kids up and off to school. Then I remember, the kids are grown and gone. It's both a relief and a punch in the heart. I miss my little guys."

"You'll never be rid of us." Knowing Jo, he skipped right over all the sodas, whittled her choices down to juice or bottled water. "I can offer you water or what I think might be grapefruit juice."

"I'm fine, Gage. Don't bother."

"Could make some tea—or you could. I'd probably—" He broke off when he turned and saw a tear sliding down her cheek. "What is it? What's wrong?"

"The note you left me, with the plant."

"I'd hoped to be able to talk to you. I stopped by Cal's mom's, but—"

"I know. Frannie told me. You wrote: 'Because you were always there for me. Because I know you always will be.'"

"You were. I do."

With a sigh, she put her arms around him, laid her head on his shoulder. "All of your life, as a parent, you wonder and you worry. Did I do that right? Should I have done that, said this? Then, suddenly, in a fingersnap it seems, your children are grown. And still you wonder and you worry. Could I have done this, did I remember to say that? If you're very lucky, one day one of your children . . ." She leaned back to look into his eyes. "Because you're mine and Frannie's, too. One of your children writes you a note that arrows straight into your heart. All that worry goes away." She gave him a watery smile. "For a moment anyway. Thank you for the moment, baby."

"I wouldn't have gotten through without you and Frannie."

"I think you're wrong about that. But we damn sure helped." She laughed now, gave him a hard squeeze. "I have to go. Come and see me soon."

"I will. I'll walk you out."

"Don't be silly. I know the way." She started out, turned. "I pray for you. Being me, I cover my bases. God, the Goddess, Buddha, Allah, and so on. I pretty much tap on them all. I just want you to know that a day doesn't go by that I don't have all of you in my prayers. I'm nagging the hell out of every higher power there is. You're going to come through this, all of you. I'm not taking no for an answer."

SIX

———◦◦◦◦———

He should have known she'd be exactly on time. Not late, not early, but on the button. Cybil had that preciseness about her. She wore a shirt the color of ripe, juicy peaches with bark brown pants that cropped off a couple inches above her ankles, and sandals with a couple of thin straps that showed off those intriguing narrow feet with their toes painted to match the shirt. She'd scooped that mass of curling hair back at the temples so he could see the trio of tiny hoops on her left ear, the duet of them on her right.

She carried a brown handbag the size of a bull terrier.

"I heard you had a visitor. I'll need you to tell me about it so we're sure nothing gets lost in translation."

And right to business, he thought. "Fine." He started back toward the kitchen. If he had to run through it again, he wanted his coffee.

"Mind if I get something cold?"

"Help yourself."

She did. He watched as she pulled out the grapefruit juice and the diet ginger ale. "I'm a little put out she hasn't talked to me yet," Cybil said as she filled a glass with ice then proceeded to mix the two liquids in the glass. "But I'm trying to be big about it." She glanced over, cocked an eyebrow as she lifted the glass. "Do you want some?"

"Absolutely not."

"If I drank coffee all day the way you do, I'd be doing cartwheels off the ceiling." She glanced at the cards spread out on the counter. "I interrupted your game."

"Just passing the time."

"Hmm." She studied his card layout. "It's often called *Réussite*—or Success—in France, where some historians believe it originated. In Britain, it's Patience, which I suppose you have to have to play it. The most interesting theory I've come across is that in its early origins the outcome was a form of fortune-telling. Mind?" she asked, tapping the deck, and he shrugged his go-ahead.

She turned up the card, continued the play. "Computer play's given the game a major boost in the last couple decades. Do you play online?"

"Rarely."

"Online poker?"

"Never. I like to be in the same room as my opponents. Winning's no fun if it's anonymous."

"I tried it once. I like to try most everything once."

His mind took a side trip into the possibilities of "most everything." "How'd you do?"

"Not bad. But, like you, I found it lacked the zip of the real thing. Well, where should we do this?" She set her drink down to pull a notebook from the massive area of her purse. "We can start with you giving me the details of this morning's visitation, then—"

"I had a dream about you."

Her head angled slightly. "Oh?"

"Given the X rating, you can have the option of sharing it with the others, if you think it applies, or keeping it to yourself."

"I'd have to hear it first." Her lips curved. "In minute detail."

"You came to my bedroom upstairs. Naked."

She flipped open the notebook, began to write. "That was brazen of me."

"There was some moonlight; it gave the room a blue wash. Very sexy, very black-and-white movie. It didn't feel like the first time; there was a sense of familiarity when I touched you. The kind that said, maybe the moves would be a bit different, maybe we'd change up the rhythm, but we'd danced before."

"Did we speak?"

"Not then." There was interest in her eyes, he noted, and amusement—both on the cool side. And no pretense of embarrassment. "I knew how you'd taste, knew the sounds you'd make when I put my hands on you. I knew where you like to be touched, and how. When I was inside you, when we were . . . locked, taking each other, the room began to bleed, and burn." The interest sharpened; the amusement died. "It rolled over us, that fire, that blood. Then you spoke. Right as it took us, right as you came, you said *bestia*."

"Sex and death. It sounds more like an erotic or stress dream than foresight."

"Probably. But I thought I should pass it on." He tapped a finger on her book. "For your notes."

"It would be hard not to have sex and death on the brain, considering. But—"

"Do you have a tattoo?" He watched her eyes narrow in consideration, and knew. "About this big," he continued, holding his thumb and forefinger a couple inches apart. "At the small of your back. It looks like a three with a small wavy line coming out of the bottom curve, then a separate symbol above—a curved line with a dot in the center."

"That would be Sanskrit for the Hindu mantra of *ohm*. The four parts stand for the four stages of concentration, which are awake, asleep, dreaming, and the transcendental state."

"And here I thought it was just sexy."

"It is." Turning, Cybil lifted the back of her shirt a few inches to reveal the symbols at the small of her back. "But it also has meaning. And since you obviously saw it, we'll have to consider your dream had some meaning."

She let her shirt drop, turned back. "We both know that what we see is potential, not absolute. And that often what we see is crowded with symbolism. So, going by your dream, we have the potential to become lovers."

"Didn't need to dream to get that one."

"And as lovers we have the potential to pay a high price for the enjoyment." She kept her gaze steady on his as she spoke. "We could further speculate that while you want me on a physical level, on the emotional and mental levels, you don't. The idea of us pairing off strikes too close to following suit behind our friends, and you don't care to fall in line. Can't blame you, as I don't either. It's also irritating—an irritation I share—to consider this pairing up could be part of a larger plan put into place hundreds of years ago. How am I doing so far?"

"You're hitting the highlights."

"Then to finish up, I'd include the fact that your pessimistic nature—which I don't share—would sway your subconscious, or your gift, over to the get in, get off, get dead arena."

He let out a short laugh. "Okay."

"For me, I don't make decisions on lovers based on the possibility that orgasm might include being consumed by evil forces. It just takes all the romance out of it."

"You looking for romance, Cybil?"

"Everyone is. It's the personal definitions thereof that vary. Why don't we take this outside, on the deck? I like spring, and it doesn't last long. We might as well grab some of it while it's around."

"All right." Taking his coffee, he opened the door to the back deck. "Are you afraid?" he asked as she moved by him.

"Every day since I've come here. Aren't you?"

He left the door open behind them. "I used to be. I used to spend a lot of my life being afraid and pretending not to be. Then, along the way, I got to the fuck-it stage. Just fuck it. Now, mostly, the whole business just annoys me. It doesn't annoy you."

"Fascinates." She took sunglasses out of her purse, slid them on. "I think it's good all of us don't have the same reaction. This way we cover more ground." She sat at one of the tables on Cal's deck, facing his back gardens, and the green woods that stood along their edges. "Tell me about Ann Hawkins."

So he did, and she took her notes. "Three," she began. "Three boys, descended from her and Dent. Faith, that's Cal's area. Believing not only in himself, in you, in the town, but having the faith to accept what he can't literally see. The past, what happened before him. Hope falls to Fox, and his optimism that he can and will make a difference. His understanding and trust in what is. Which leaves the vision to you—what can be—for better or worse. A second three—Q, Layla, me—falls in with that, forming subsets. Cal and Q, Fox and Layla, and now you and me. Three into one—three men, three women, three subsets, into one unit. We've accomplished that in a very real sense. Just as we accomplished re-forming the three pieces of the bloodstone into one whole."

"Still doesn't tell us how to use it."

"But she made it clear, at least to me it's clear, that we have what we need. There's no other tangible element. That's something. Tears." Frowning, Cybil drummed her fingers on her notebook. "She wept for you, and if I'm interpreting correctly, she's saying I will. I'm happy to shed a few if it sends the Big Evil Bastard back to hell. Tears," she repeated, and closed her eyes. "They're often an ingredient used in magickal arts. I think they're usually female tears. You'll have your tears of a virgin, of a pregnant woman, of a mother, of an ancient, blah blah blah, depending. I don't know that much about it."

"There's something you don't know that much about?"

She shot him an answering smirk, tipped down her sunglasses to peer at him over them. "There are worlds I don't know much about, but almost nothing I can't find out everything about. We need to see. She appears to be saying that while the other subsets may certainly be called on to do more in their specific areas, they've done the bulk of their job there. It's time to look ahead, and that's up to you and me, partner."

"I can't whistle it up like a German shepherd."

"Of course you can. It takes practice, concentration, and attention. All of which you're capable of or you wouldn't be able to make a living playing cards. What may be more problematic is both of us being capable of calling it up together, and narrowing in on one potential future event."

She dug into her voluminous handbag again, and this time pulled out a deck of Tarot cards.

"Are you kidding me?"

"Tools," she said, and began to shuffle the oversized cards with some skill. "I also have runes, several types of crystal balls, a scrying mirror. At one point in my life I studied witchcraft very seriously, looking for answers as to why I could foretell. But like any religion or organization, there are a lot of rules. The rules began to crowd me, so after a while, I simply accepted I had this gift, and my studies spread out in wider circles."

"When did you first know?"

"That I could foretell? I'm not altogether sure. It wasn't like you, in a blinding flash. I've always had vivid dreams. I used to tell my parents about them, when I was a little girl. Or cry for them in the middle of the night if the dreams scared me. They often did. Or there would be what I'd have called déjà vu if I'd known the term as a child. My paternal grandmother, who had Romany blood, told me I had the sight. I did my best to learn how to refine it, control it. There were still dreams, some good, some bad. I often dreamed of fire. Of walking through it, of dying in it, of causing it."

She did a quick spread. The colorful illustrations on the cards drew him closer to the table. "I think I dreamed of you," she said, "long before I met you."

"Think?"

"I never saw your face. Or if I did, I couldn't keep it in my head when I woke. But in the dreams, or the visions, I knew someone was waiting for me. A lover, or so it seemed. I had my first orgasm at about fourteen during one of those dreams. I'd wake from those dreams, aroused or satisfied. Or quaking with terror. Because some-times it wasn't a lover—or not a human one—waiting for me. I never saw its face either, not even when it burned me alive." She looked up at him now. "So I learned all I could, and I learned how to keep my mind and body centered with yoga, meditation, herbs, trances—any and everything to stave off the beast in the dreams. It works most of the time. Or did."

"Harder to keep that center here in the Hollow?"

"Yes."

He sat, waved a finger at the spread. "So, what does the future hold?"

"This? Just a little personal Q and A. As to the rest . . ." She scooped the cards together, shuffled again. "Let's find out."

She set them down, said, "Cut," and when he did she fanned the deck facedown on the table. "Let's try a simple pick-a-card. You first."

Willing to play, he slid one out of the fan, and at her nod, turned it over. On the card, the couple was twined together, with her dark hair wound around their naked bodies.

"The Lovers," Cybil announced. "Shows where your mind's lodged."

"They're your cards, sugar."

"Mmm-hmm." She chose one for herself. "The Wheel of Fortune—more in your line, if we're speaking literally. Symbolizing change, chance, for good or for ill. Take another."

He turned over the Magician.

"Major Arcana, three for three." The faintest of frowns marred her brows. "It's actually one of my favorite cards, not only the art, but it stands for imagination, creativity, magic, of course. And in this case, we could say it stands for Giles Dent, your ancestor." She drew out another card, slowly turned it over. "And mine. The Devil. Greed, destruction, obsession, tyranny. Go again."

He drew the High Priestess. And without waiting, Cybil chose the Hanged Man.

"Our maternal ancestors, despite the male figure in mine. Understanding and wisdom in yours, martyrdom in mine. And still all Major Arcanas, all absolutely apt. Again."

He slid out and turned the Tower, and she Death.

"Change, potential disaster, but with the other cards you've chosen, the possibility of change for the positive, the potential to rebuild. Mine, obviously an end, and not so sunny when viewed with my other picks. Though it rarely stands for literal death, it does symbolize an absolute end."

She lifted her glass. "I need a refill."

He rose before she did, took the glass. "I'll get it. I saw how you made it."

It would give her time to settle down, Gage thought as he stepped inside. However fascinating she found the process, the results of this particular experiment had shaken her. He knew something about Tarot himself—there was no area of the occult he hadn't poked into for answers over the years. And if he'd been betting on the pulls, he wouldn't have put money on two people drawing eight Major Arcana in a row out of a deck.

He fixed her drink, switched for his next round from coffee to water. When he went outside again, she stood at the rail looking out toward the woods.

"I reshuffled, recut. And I drew eight cards at random. Only two were Major Arcana, but oddly enough they were the Devil and Death again." When she turned he noted she'd settled herself. "Interesting, isn't it? You and I together pull the most powerful and pointed cards. Because we were meant to, or because we, without direct purpose, foresaw where those cards were in the fan, and instinctively chose them."

"Why don't we try another tool? Have you got your crystal ball in that duffel bag of yours?"

"No, and it happens to be Prada. Are you willing to try to look forward, to link our ability and see what happens?"

"What did you have in mind?"

"Accepting and exploiting, hopefully, the connection. I'm better able to focus during or after meditation, but—"

"I know how to meditate."

"With all that caffeine in your system?"

He only tipped back his water bottle. "We'd better take it back inside."

"Actually, I was thinking of out here, on the grass. The gardens, the woods, the air." She took off her sunglasses, set them down on the rail, then wandered down the steps. "What do you do to relax, body and mind?"

"I play cards. I have sex. We could play strip poker, and after you lose I'll make sure we're both relaxed."

"Interesting, but I was thinking more of yoga." She slid out of her shoes, and into Prayer Position. With fluid grace she moved into a basic Sun Sign.

"I'm not doing that," Gage said as he followed her into the yard. "But I'll watch you."

"It'll just take me a minute. And on your suggestion? We made a deal. We weren't going to have sex."

"The deal was I wouldn't try to seduce you, not that we wouldn't have sex."

"Semantics."

"Specifics."

From the Down Dog position, she turned her head to look up at him. "I suppose you're right. In any case." She finished, then lowered to the grass to sit in the Lotus position.

"I'm not doing that either." But he sat across from her.

Where normally she would have rested the back of her hands on her knees, she reached out to take his. "Can you clear your mind like this?"

"I can if you can."

She smiled. "All right. Do whatever you do that works for you— other than cards and sex."

He didn't have any objections to sitting on the grass on a May afternoon with a beautiful woman. Not that he expected anything to happen. He expected her to close her eyes and float off on what-ever mantra (the *ohm* symbol at the base of her spine, that intriguing symbol on flesh the color of gold dust, right at the subtle dip from smooth back to firm ass).

Don't think about it, he warned himself. That wasn't the way to relax.

In any case, she didn't close her eyes, so he stared straight into them. A man couldn't ask for a more appealing focal point than that rich velvet brown. He timed his breathing to hers—or she to his, he wasn't sure. But in a matter of seconds they were in tune, perfectly in rhythm.

Her eyes were all he could see. Drowning pools. Her fingertips were so light on his, yet he felt weightless, as if he'd float up and away without that tenuous contact.

And he felt, for a moment, absolutely *right*, and completely connected to her.

It slammed and screamed through him, so fast, image after image ramming into the next. Fox lying by the side of the road in the rain. Cal sprawled, his shirt blood-soaked, on the floor of his office. Quinn screaming in terror, beating her hands on a locked door, and the knife that sliced down to cut her throat. Layla, bound and gagged, eyes wild with fear as flames snaked across the floor toward her.

He saw himself, by the Pagan Stone, with Cybil lying lifeless on the altar flames. And heard himself scream with rage an instant before it leaped out of the woods and took him to the dark.

Then it all jumbled together, image and sound, blurring, changing. The bloodstone fired in his hand, and voices rose with words he couldn't understand. And he was alone, alone as those flames rose from his hand toward the hot summer moon. Alone as it came out of the shadows, grinning.

He didn't know who broke contact, but the visions snapped off into a red haze of pain. He heard Cybil say his name, once, twice, and the third time with the kind of verbal slap that made him snarl.

"What?"

"Pay attention. Pay attention to the points I'm pressing. I need you to do this for me when I'm done. Are you hearing me?"

"Yeah, yeah, yeah." He could hear her, nagging at him, while his head fucking exploded. Like drilling holes in the back of his neck with her fingers was going to . . .

The pain eased from hot, stabbing knives to a dull misery. And when she took his hand, pressing, pressing on the web between his thumb and forefinger, the misery downshifted to annoying ache.

He risked opening his eyes and looked straight into hers, and saw that rich velvet was clouded. Saw her face was bone white, while she took slow, even breaths. "Okay, okay."

He pulled his hand from hers, placed his on the back of her neck. "Is this right?"

"A little to the . . . Yes. Yes. Firm, you won't hurt me."

He couldn't do worse than the visions had, so he pressed hard on the knots that pain and tension had built under her skin while she addressed the acupressure points on her own hand.

She'd tended to him first, Gage realized, and wasn't sure whether to be embarrassed or grateful. He watched those clouds of pain dissolve until she closed her eyes on a relief he understood perfectly.

"All right, that's better. That'll do. I just need to . . ." She slid back, lay down on the grass with her face to the sun, eyes closed.

"Good idea." He did exactly the same.

"We didn't control it," she said after a moment. "It just dragged us along like dogs on a leash. I couldn't stop it, or slow it down. I couldn't block the fear out."

"Proving you're a complete failure."

He heard her muffled laugh, knew her lips would be curved. "That makes two of us, tough guy. We'll do better. We have to. What did you see?"

"You first."

"All of us dead or dying. Fox, bleeding on the side of the road, in the dark and the rain. Headlights, I think the headlights from his truck." She went through them all, her voice shaking a little.

"The same for me. Then it changed."

"It was all so fast, then it got faster, more blurred, images overlapping. Ordinary things rolling into nightmares, so fast it was impossible to tell one from the other. Everything so fractured. But in the end, you had the stone."

"Yeah, everyone's dead, and I've got the stone. And the bastard killed me while it was burning in my hand."

"Did it, or was that an interpretation? What I know is that the stone was there, right through the end, that you had it, and that it held power." She rolled to her side to face him. "And I know that what we saw were possibilities. Foresight is forearmed. So we tell the others the possibilities, and we all strap it on."

"Strap what on?"

"Whatever it takes. What?" she demanded when he pressed his fingers to his eyes and shook his head.

"I just got a picture of you strapping that little pearl-handled .22 to your thigh. I must be feeling better."

"Hmm. What was I wearing?"

He dropped his hands and grinned at her. "We both must be feeling better. Why don't we . . ." This time he rolled on top of her.

"Hold on there, cowboy. A deal's a deal."

"No seduction intended."

She gave him a casual smile. "None taken."

"You're a hard case, Cybil." Testing, he took her hands, then drew her arms up over her head. Positive energy—she was big on positive energy. And Christ knew he could use some now.

She didn't resist, only continued to watch him with that half smile on her face.

"I was thinking the two of us deserve a little payoff," he told her.

"Which would be rolling around naked in Cal's backyard?"

"You read my mind."

"Not gonna happen."

"Okay. Just say when."

He took her mouth, and there was nothing testing or teasing about it. He went for the heat, and what he found spiked like a fever. Her fingers curled on his and held as her lips parted. It was more demand than invitation, more challenge than surrender. Under him, her body seemed to ripple—rising waves of energy.

Very positive.

No seduction, she thought, no persuasion, and her body responded, rejoiced, in the possession. The honesty of sheer and undisguised lust meant equal terms. Needs trapped inside her for months raced free. She'd take more, just a little more, before herding them back into the pen.

Hooking a leg around him, she arched her hips, deliberately pressing center to center before she pushed to reverse their positions. Now her mouth took command, took its fill as his hands fisted in her hair. When she heard the growl, she laughed against his lips. But when it sounded again, she felt ice slide down her spine.

Slowly, she drew her lips a breath from his. "Did you hear that?"

"Yeah."

She lifted her head another inch, and that ice floe spread. "We've got an audience."

The dog was massive, its brown fur matted and stained. Frothy drool dripped from its jowls as it lurched drunkenly out of the woods.

"That isn't Twisse," Cybil whispered.

"No."

"Meaning it's real."

"Real, and rabid. How fast can you run?"

"As fast as I need to."

"Get into the house. My gun's upstairs, on the table beside the bed. Get it, get back, and shoot the damn dog. I'll keep it off you."

Cybil ignored the rise of gorge at the thought of killing a dog. "My .22's in my bag on the deck. We can both make it."

"Go, get *inside*. Don't stop."

He dragged her up, gave her one hard shove toward the house. And the dog gathered itself, and charged.

He didn't run with her, and she didn't allow herself to think, not even when she heard the horrible sounds behind her. With her heart slamming, she flew onto the deck, shoved her hand into her bag and closed it around the butt of her revolver.

The scream she loosed when she turned was as much terror as an attempt to draw the dog's attention to her. But it only continued to roll, snap, to clamp its teeth into Gage as they fought a vicious war on Cal's pretty green grass.

She raced back, releasing the safety as she ran.

"Shoot it! Shoot the fucker!"

"I can't get a clear shot!"

His arms, his hands, were torn and bleeding. "Goddamn it, shoot!" As he shouted, he wrenched the dog's head up, looked straight into those madly snapping jaws. The dog's body jerked, once, twice, as bullets plowed into its flank, and still it tried to go for the throat. On the next shot it let out a high shriek of pain, and those mad eyes went glassy. Panting, Gage shoved the weight aside, crawled over the blood-slicked grass.

Through the haze of pain he heard weeping. Through the haze of pain he saw Cybil step up to the dying dog and fire the coup de grace into its head.

"It wasn't dead. It was suffering. Let me get you inside. God, you're torn up."

"I'll heal." But he put his arm around her shoulders, let her take his weight. He made it as far as the steps before his legs gave out. "Give me a minute. I need a minute."

She left him slumped on the steps to dash inside. Minutes later, she rushed out again with a fresh bottle of water, a basin filled with more, and several cloths. "Should I call Cal and Fox? When Fox was hurt it helped him to have you both."

"No. Not that bad."

"Let me see. I need to see." Quickly, efficiently, she drew off what was left of his shirt. Her breath might have shuddered at the tears and rips in his flesh, but she washed the wounds with a steady hand. "The shoulder's bad."

"Unnecessary information seeing as it's my shoulder." He hissed as she pressed the cool, wet cloth to the wound. "Anyway, nice shooting, Tex."

She used the bottled water to dampen a fresh cloth, then wiped it gently over his face. "I know it hurts. I know the healing hurts almost as much as the need for it."

"It's no spring picnic. Do me a favor? Get me a whiskey?"

"All right."

Inside, she braced her hands on the counter a moment. She wanted to be sick, badly wanted to be sick. But she pushed down the need, shuddered her way past it. And pulling down the bottle of Jameson, poured him a generous three fingers.

When she came back out with it, she saw that most of his surface injuries had healed, and the more serious ones had begun to close. He downed two-thirds of the whiskey she handed him in one pull, then, studying her face, held out the glass. "Down the rest, sweetheart. You look like you could use it."

She nodded, downed it. Then she did what she'd avoided doing. She turned and looked at what lay on the bloodstained grass. "I've never killed anything before. Clay pigeons, targets, shooting gallery bears. But I never put bullets into a living thing."

"If you hadn't, I might be dead. That dog weighs a good eighty pounds, mostly muscle, and it was shithouse crazy."

"It has a collar, tags." Steeling herself, she crossed the lawn, crouched. "An up-to-date rabies tag. It wasn't rabid, Gage, not in the usual sense. But I guess we both knew that."

She straightened when Gage limped over to join her. "What do we do now?" she asked him.

"We bury it."

"But . . . Gage, this was someone's dog. This wasn't a stray, he belonged to someone. They must be looking for him."

"Getting him back dead isn't going to help. Trying to explain why you put four bullets in a household pet—one who won't show rabies on any test—isn't going to help." Gage gripped her shoulders, fingers digging in for emphasis. "This is a goddamn war, do you understand? One we've been fighting a long time. More than dogs die, Cybil, so you're going to have to man up. Telling some kid that

Fido won't be home for dinner because a demon infected him isn't on the boards. We bury it, we move on."

"It must help not to have any feelings, any guilt or remorse."

"That's right, it does. Go home. We're done for the day."

"Where are you going?" she demanded when he turned away.

"To get a damn shovel."

Gritting her teeth, she marched to the garden shed ahead of him, wrenched open the door.

"I said go home."

"I say go to hell; we'll see who gets where first. I put that dog down, didn't I? So I'll help bury him." She wrenched down a shovel, all but threw it at Gage before grabbing another. "And here's something else, you son of a bitch, we're *not* done for the day. What happened here needs to be shared with the others. Whether you like it or not you're part of a team. This whole ugly business has to be reported, documented, charted. Burying it isn't enough. It's not enough. It's not."

She pressed the back of her hand to her mouth, choked back a sob as the cracks in her composure widened. When she would have pushed by him, Gage grabbed her, pulled her against him.

"Get away from me."

"Shut up. Just shut up." He held firm, ignoring her struggles, and when she gave up, gave in and clung, he held her still. "You did what you had to do," he murmured. "You did fine. You held up. Go on inside, let me finish this. You can call the others."

She leaned against him another moment. "We'll finish it. We'll bury him together. Then we'll go call the others."

SEVEN

She'd asked Quinn to bring her a change of clothes. After the horrible business of burying the dog, Cybil was filthy, sweaty, and stained. Rather than think about what stained her pants and shirt, she simply shoved them into a plastic bag, and once she'd showered, intended to shove *that* into Cal's trash.

She'd gone to pieces, she admitted as she stepped under the spray. She'd done what needed to be done, true enough, but then her shaky wall of control had broken down into emotional rubble.

So much for cool, clearheaded Cybil Kinski.

Now, if she couldn't manage cool, she could at least make a stab at the clearheaded.

Was it worse or better that she'd melted down in front of Gage? Two ways of thinking, she supposed. Worse—much—for her pride, but for the overall picture, it was best they knew what made each other tick. In order to handle their end of this successfully, knowing each other's strengths, weaknesses, and breaking points was essential.

It was a pisser she'd broken first, but she'd accept that. Eventually.

It was a tough swallow, she supposed, when she'd always perceived herself as the strong one. As the one who made the choices—the tough choices when necessary—and followed them through. Other people fell apart—her mother, her sister—but she held it together. She'd made damn sure of it.

Second swallow, she admitted, was accepting that Gage was right. A dead dog wasn't going to be the worst of it. If she couldn't handle that, she'd be useless to the others. So she'd handle it.

Bury it, as he said, and move on.

When the door opened, she felt a flash of temper along with the chilly air. "Just turn around, hotshot, and go back the way you came."

"It's Q. You okay?"

The sound of her friend's voice had tears flooding her throat again. Ruthlessly, she swallowed them down. "Better. You were quick."

"We headed right over. Cal and I. Fox and Layla will be along as soon as they can. What can I do?"

Cybil turned off the spray. "Hand me a towel." She shoved back the shower curtain and took the one Quinn held out.

"God, Cyb, you look exhausted."

"It was my first day on the job as gravedigger. I'm in damn good tune, but Jesus, Q, that's awful work. On every possible level."

As Cybil wrapped the first towel around herself, Quinn handed her a second for her hair. "Thank God you weren't hurt. You saved Gage's life."

"I'd say it was a mutual lifesaving affair." She glanced in the steamy mirror. Both emotional and physical weariness crumbled under the sheer weight of vanity. Who *was* that pale, drawn woman with the dull, bruised-looking eyes? "Oh my God. Please tell me you had the good sense to bring my makeup along with a change of clothes."

Reassured by the reaction, Quinn leaned a hip against the door. "How long have we been friends?"

"I should never have doubted you."

"Everything's on the bed. I'm going down to pour you a glass of wine while you get changed. Do you want anything else?"

"I think you've just covered the essentials."

Alone, Cybil brushed, dabbed, and blended away the signs of fatigue. She changed into the fresh clothes, did a final check, then gathered up the bag holding her soiled shirt and pants. Downstairs, she shoved the bag into the kitchen garbage, then backtracked to the front deck where Quinn sat with Cal and Gage.

Nobody, she imagined, wanted to sit on the back deck just at the moment.

She picked up her glass of wine, sat, then smiled at Cal. "So. How was your day?"

He answered her smile in kind, even as his patient gray eyes searched her face. "Not as eventful as yours. The Memorial Day committee met this morning to go over the final schedule for the day's events. Wendy Krauss, who'd had a couple of glasses of wine during today's birthday party for a league-mate, dropped a bowling ball on her foot. Broke her big toe, and a couple of teenagers got into a pushy-shovey over a dispute during a game of Foosball in the arcade."

"It's constant drama in Hawkins Hollow."

"Oh yeah."

Sipping her wine, Cybil looked out over the terraced slope, the curvy land, the winding creek. "It's a nice spot to sit after such a busy day. Your gardens are beautiful, Cal."

"They make me happy."

"Secluded spot, yet connected to the whole. You know almost everyone around here."

"Pretty much."

"You know who that dog belonged to."

He hesitated only a moment. "The Mullendores over on Fox-wood Road. Their dog went missing day before yesterday." As if he needed the contact, Cal leaned down to stroke a hand on Lump's side as his dog snored at his feet. "Their place is in town. It's a long walk for a dog from there to here, but the way Gage described him, I'd say it was the Mullendores' Roscoe."

"Roscoe." Rest in peace, she thought. "Infecting animals is a usual pattern. And I know we have a list of documented attacks by pets and wildlife in the files. Still, as you say, it's a long way from town to here, on foot—even on four feet. No reports of sightings or attacks by a rabid dog?"

"None."

"So, logically, this today was, again, target specific. The Big Evil Bastard not only infected that poor dog, but directed him here. You're often here alone during the day," she said to Gage. "Twisse couldn't know I'd be here, certainly not before he infected that dog if it's been missing for two days. So you go out, maybe take a nap in that appealing hammock Cal's got between those maple trees, or maybe Cal goes out to cut the grass. Or Quinn takes a walk through the gardens."

"Any one of us could've been alone out there," Cal agreed. "And it might not have been a dog you buried."

"A clever way to do it," Cybil mused, "or try it, with little effort or energy on its part."

"Handy, having a woman with a gun around." Gage took a slow sip of his own wine.

"And one," Cybil added, "who eventually comes around to the simple truth that she didn't kill that dog. Twisse did. Just one more thing to add to the list of payback he's earned." She glanced toward the road. "Here come Fox and Layla."

"And dinner." Quinn touched a hand to Cybil's. "I ordered up a big salad and a couple of pizzas from Gino's, figuring we'd want to stick with the simple and the staple tonight."

"Good thinking. We've got a lot of ground to cover."

———

They didn't, as they often did, talk of ordinary and easy things over the meal. The day had been too full, and the mood too urgent.

"You'll need to record this, Q," Cybil began, then turned to Gage. "Gage had a dream."

He held her gaze another few seconds, then relayed the dream of passion and death.

"Symbolism," Quinn decided quickly. "That doesn't go into the prophetic column. Obviously, no matter how good the sex might be, neither of you would just keep at it while the room burst into flame around you."

"Good point," Cybil murmured.

"Maybe it was such hot sex, they self-combusted." Fox shrugged. "Just trying to add a little levity."

"Really little." Layla poked his ribs. "We're all stressed, so violent or, ah, sexual dreams aren't surprising. And if you consider that . . . well, if you factor in that you, Gage, that you might be feeling somewhat—"

"Sexually frustrated," Quinn broke in, "and attracted to Cybil. We're all big boys and girls, and this isn't the time to be delicate. Sorry. But the fact is you and Cyb are healthy adults, not to mention really pretty, and you share an ability during a time of extreme stress. It'd be amazing if there weren't some sexual vibes buzzing about."

"Satisfy an urge, burn in hellfire?" Cal chewed on the thought as he chewed on pizza. "I don't think it's that simple, even symbolically speaking. Connect on intimate levels, there are consequences. And connect to forge another separate link in the chain the six of us have already created, increases the consequences and the power."

"I agree with that, exactly." With a nod of approval, Cybil smiled at Cal. "Too bad Q's in the way, or you and I could have hooked up."

"Staying in the way, sister."

"You're so selfish. Anyway, prophetic dreams, in my experience, are often clouded with symbolism. I think this one could go into that column, or at least be penciled into it."

"We could go upstairs now," Gage suggested. "Test the theory."

"That's a generous offer. Heroic really." Pausing, Cybil sipped her wine. "I'll pass. While I might be willing to sacrifice my body to sex for the good of the cause, I don't think it's necessary at this point."

"Just let me know when we've reached that point."

"You'll be the first. What?" she demanded as Quinn slapped a hand at the air.

"Just swatting at these damn buzzing vibes."

"Aren't you the funny one? But moving on," Cybil continued, "as the astute and handsome Caleb theorized, it's about connections, links. And there are links every bit as intimate as sex."

"Still tops my scoreboard," Fox commented. He grinned at Cybil's stony look and reached for more pizza. "But you were saying."

"Gage and I experienced one of those links when we combined our particular gifts. There was power, and there were consequences. Before that shared experience, he had another on his own. Ann Hawkins."

Cybil paused again, but this time to watch the iridescent flash of a hummingbird outside the window as it dived to the heart of a bold red blossom. "Before I left to come here, Quinn and I logged that incident, charted and mapped it. Gage went through it again for me, for my notes, in case there were any details that dropped out in the relay. There weren't, that I found."

"I thought about that off and on today," Layla put in. "She said she'd wept for him, for Gage, and that you would, Cybil. At least that's my interpretation. That it would matter."

"Tears should matter." Cybil continued to watch as the jeweled bird darted to another blossom.

"I wonder if tears are literal, like a magickal ingredient we'll need, or if they're symbolic again. Grief, joy—emotion. If it's the emotional connection that's important."

"And again, I agree exactly," Cybil added.

"We know emotions are part of it," Quinn continued. "Twisse feeds on the negative—fear, hate, anger. And it seems pretty likely the positive is one of the things that kept us all from being crisped at the Pagan Stone last trip."

"In other words, she wasn't telling us anything we don't already know."

"Positive reinforcement," Quinn said to Gage. "And she said, clearly, we have everything we need to win this. Figuring out what that everything is, and how to use it—that's the problem."

"Weaknesses versus strengths." Fox took a swig of his beer. "Twisse knows our weaknesses, and plays on them. We need to counter that, and in fact, negate that, with our strengths. Basic strategy."

"That's good." Layla nodded. "We need to make lists."

"My girl's hell on lists."

"Seriously. Our strengths and weaknesses as a group, and as individuals. It's war, isn't it? Our strengths are our weapons, and weaknesses are the gaps in our defense. Shore up the defense, or at least recognize where the gaps are, and we build up the offensive position."

"I've been teaching her chess," Fox told the group. "She catches on quick."

"It's a little late in the day for lists," Gage said.

Unoffended, Layla shook her head. "It's never too late for lists."

As Cybil picked up her wine, the hummingbird shot away like a sparkling bullet. "Next on mine is cards."

"You want to play cards?" Cal asked her. "Aren't we a little busy for a game?"

"You're never too busy for a game," Gage corrected. "But I think the lady's referring to her Tarot deck."

"I brought it with me today, and Gage and I conducted an experiment."

Though she trusted her memory, Cybil took out her notes to relate the result to the others. "All Major Arcana, all with meanings specific to both of us," she concluded. "As our resident gambler would agree, the odds of that being coincidence are in the astronomical range. The cards are open to various interpretations depending on the reader, the question, the surrounding cards, and so on. But it *feels* as though, in this case, they spoke of connection—physical, emotional, psychic connection. Then the symbol of each ancestry, and the potential for dramatic change, and consequence. I'd like to do a series of this same experiment. Cal and Quinn, Fox and Layla, all three men, all three women, and lastly, all six of us together."

"You always had a hand with Tarot," Quinn said.

"My Romany forebears. But this today was more than that."

"You did the card trick before the dog came on the scene," Fox commented. "Before the attack."

"Yeah." As the memory still unsettled her, Cybil reached for her wine. "Before."

"Maybe it was part of the trigger. That," Fox continued, "and you and Gage linking up. We still need the details on that, but if the cards weren't coincidence, and the linking generates energy and power, it doesn't seem like another coincidence that the attack came right on the heels."

"No," Cybil said slowly. "No, it really doesn't."

"You were outside," Quinn prompted. "In the backyard."

"Yeah." Cybil glanced at Gage. "Why don't you take this part?"

He didn't particularly care to give reports, but he assumed it was still difficult for her to speak of it. He ran it through, from the moment they'd sat and linked fingertips on the grass, to the moment Cybil fired the kill shot.

"Oh, honey." Her face filled with concern, Layla reached for Cybil's hand.

"Excuse me?" Gage held up a finger. "Teeth, claws, rended flesh, spilled blood. Crazy Roscoe took a chunk out of my shoulder the size of a—"

"Oh, honey." Layla rose and surprised and amused Gage by rounding the table to plant a kiss on his cheek.

"That's more like it. Anyway, that covers it."

"Gage has neglected to add that I fell apart. If we're making lists, that one has to go under weakness. I had a serious meltdown afterward. I can't guarantee it won't happen again, but I don't think it will."

"Said meltdown was intense, but brief," Gage continued. "And went into effect *after* the job was done. Personally, I don't give a rat's ass how much anybody gnashes their teeth or freaks after the job's done."

"Point well taken," Cybil decided.

"It made a mistake." Quinn spoke quietly, but her eyes were a vivid and burning blue. "It made a big goddamn mistake."

"How?" Cal asked her.

"For three of us here, a crucial element of this has all been theory before today. We've talked about what happens to people during the Seven, what they're capable of doing when infected. But only you, Fox, and Gage have ever dealt with it face-to-face. Only the three of you have ever had to defend yourselves or someone else from an attack of another living thing. An ordinary living thing that's turned into a threat. How could we know, how could we be sure, how we'd react, if we'd really be able to do what needed to be done when we were faced with it? Now we do.

"That dog today wasn't one of Twisse's nasty illusions. It was flesh and blood. Meltdown, my ass, Cyb. You didn't panic, you didn't run, you didn't freeze. You got a gun and you put it down. You saved a life. So the bastard made a big mistake with his preview of coming attractions. Because now four of us have had face-offs, and I'll be damned if Layla and I aren't just as able to stand up the way Cybil did. My vote? That's a big red check in the plus column."

"That's telling him, Blondie." Cal leaned over, kissed her.

"You're right." Fox lifted his beer in toast. "It wanted to show off, and got shot down. Literally. Psych."

Cybil continued to stare at Quinn for another moment, as the last knots of shock and grief inside her untangled. "You've always been able to cut through the bullshit, haven't you? So, okay then." She took her first truly clear breath in hours. "Let's take a moment to congratulate ourselves . . . And that's the moment. Somebody start clearing the table, and I'll get my cards."

As she left the room, Gage pushed away from the table and followed her.

"Look, you've already proved a lot today."

Reaching in her purse she hunted for her cards.

"There's no need to deal from your magic deck tonight. You're tired."

"You're right, I am tired." But it was annoying to be told so when she'd gone to the trouble to mask it. "I imagine in the days before the Seven, and during it, you and Cal and Fox function at a state well beyond tired."

"When it comes to that, choices are limited to none. It hasn't come to that yet."

"But it will. And while I'm not above needing or wanting to prove something, this isn't about that. I appreciate the concern, but—"

She broke off when he took her arm. "I don't like being concerned."

The look on his face was one of barely restrained frustration. "No, I bet you don't. I can't help you with that, Gage."

"Look. Look." The frustration rippled again, more visibly. "Let's just get something straight, right from the jump."

"By all means."

"The way the others have hooked up, that's not in the cards. Not those," he said pointing at the Tarot deck. "Not mine, not any. It's not about love songs and playing house for me."

She angled her head, kept an easy, reasonable smile on her face. "Are you under the impression I want you to sing to me, and play house?"

"Cut it out, Cybil."

"No, you cut it out, you arrogant ass. If you've got some jitters that I'm somehow going to spin you in my web until you're serenading under my window and picking out china patterns, that's your problem." She shot a finger at him and her smile was no longer easy and reasonable, but had hardened to a sneer. "If you actually have it in your tiny brain that I would want that, you're just stupid. Which is redundant due to tiny brain, and I *hate* being annoyed enough to be redundant."

"Are you going to stand there and try to tell me that when the rest of them are falling off the cliff like lemmings, you haven't given a thought to grabbing hold and dragging me off with you?"

"What a lovely image, and quite the testament to your views on our friends' feelings for each other."

"It's apt enough," he muttered. "Add in Quinn's buzzing vibes and it strikes me as pretty damn reasonable to lay it out."

"Then let me lay this out. If and when I decide I want a man for the long term, it won't be because fate crammed him down my throat. If and when," she repeated, "and contrary to what you with your sexist stupidity might believe—not every woman is looking for long-term—I won't need to grab or drag. If I did, I wouldn't want the son of a bitch. You're safe from my wiles and whims, you narcissistic jerk. If that doesn't reassure you, you can kiss my ass."

She shoved by him, marched into the dining room to slap the deck on the table. "I need to clear my head first," she said to no one in particular, then sailed out into the kitchen and through the back door.

After a quick glance at Cal, Quinn headed out after her. "She's mighty pissed," Quinn commented when Layla stepped out behind her.

"So I see."

After a rapid stride up the deck and down again, Cybil whirled to them. "Even in my current state of blind rage, I'm not going to say all men are arrogant, ignorant pigs who deserve a good kick in their precious balls."

"Just one particular man," Quinn translated.

"One particular, who just had the *nerve* to warn me that any secret, cherished dreams I might have regarding him are held in vain."

"Oh God." The hands Quinn put to her face muffled a sound caught between a groan and a snorting laugh.

"I shouldn't mistake the fact that the four of you, who've run over the cliff like lemmings, I may add, are a precursor of my future bliss with him."

"As I'm not certain his healing powers are a match for the Wrath of the Cyb, do we need to call nine-one-one?"

"If so," Layla considered, "we should let him suffer a little while longer first. Lemmings?"

"To be fair, though God knows why I should be, I'd say that remark was more due to his concern over his own situation than his opinion of any of you."

Quinn cleared her throat. "Ah, just to throw a wrench at the monkey, it's also possible he went asshat because he's projecting somewhat, due to complicated feelings for and about you."

Cybil merely shrugged at Quinn. "That would be his problem."

"Absolutely. But in your position I'd take some satisfaction from that. The possibility that he's not as worried you'll fall for him as he is he'll fall for you."

Now Cybil pursed her lips. Temper throttled back to give consideration room on the road. "Hmm. I was too mightily pissed to see that angle. I like it. I ought to give him the Treatment."

"Dear God, Cyb." With exaggerated horror on her face, Quinn gripped her friend's arm. "Not the Treatment."

"What's the Treatment?" Layla demanded. "Does it hurt?"

"The Treatment, designed and implemented by Cybil Kinski, is many faceted and multilayered," Quinn told her. "No man can hold against it."

"It's approach, attitude, response." Absently, Cybil brushed at her hair. "Knowing the quarry and adjusting that approach, attitude, and response to his specific qualifications. You can add in seduction and sex if that's acceptable to you, but it's really more about luring them to exactly where you want them. Eye contact, body language, conversation, wardrobe—all of that specifically tailored toward the man in question."

She let out a huff of breath. "But this isn't the time for that sort of thing. No matter how much he deserves it. But after this is over . . ."

"Okay, I have to know," Layla decided. "How would you tailor the Treatment for Gage?"

"It's elemental, really. He prefers sophisticated women with some style. Though he probably thinks otherwise, he's more truly attracted to—because he respects—women of strength. She shouldn't be coy about sex, but if she's sure, buddy, let's roll, he's not going to think about her twice afterward. He likes brains, leavened with humor."

"Ah, don't hit me," Layla said, "but it sounds like you're describing yourself."

That put a momentary hitch in Cybil's stride, but she continued. "Unlike Fox, we'll say, he isn't inclined to nurture. Unlike Cal, he isn't drawn to his roots, or to putting them down. He gambles, and a woman who knows how to play the game well would draw his attention. One who knows how to win, and how to lose. He can be drawn in physically—but what man can't—but only to a point. He has excellent control under most circumstances, so control would be key in drawing him."

"She'd have notes on all of this if she were going to do it." Like a proud mama, Quinn beamed at Cybil. "Then she'd do a detailed outline."

"Of course, but since this is just hypothetical . . ." Moving her shoulders, Cybil continued. "He requires challenge, so you'd have to walk the line between interest and disinterest, giving him just enough of both. No running hot and cold, which, oddly enough, some men can't resist, but finding just the right temperature—then varying it at unexpected moments to keep him just a bit off balance. And—"

She stopped, shook her head. "Doesn't matter, as I'm not going to do it. The stakes are too high to play that kind of game."

"When we were in college, she used it on this guy who cheated on me, *then* suggested we have a threesome with the girl he cheated on me with. Oink." After slinging an arm around Cybil's shoulders, Quinn gave Cybil a hard squeeze. "Cyb wound that fuckhead up like a clock, then just when he thought his alarm was going to go off, slapped him off the nightstand. It was beautiful. But yeah, probably inappropriate under our current circumstances."

"Oh well." With a shrug, Cybil shook back her hair. "It was fun thinking about it. And it calmed me down. We'd better go back in, get started."

Layla tugged Quinn back as Cybil went inside. "Am I really the only one who noticed that she just kept describing herself as the kind of woman Gage would fall for?"

"Nope. But isn't it interesting that Cyb didn't appear to get that?" Quinn draped an arm around Layla's shoulders now. "Even though, in my opinion, she was right on target. She's exactly the woman he'd fall for. Won't this be fun to watch?"

"Is it fate, Quinn, or choice? For all of us?"

"I vote choice, but you know what?" She gave Layla a pat. "I don't much care, not as long as we all live happy-ever-after."

Thinking of just that, Layla looked at Fox as she walked into the kitchen. He popped the top on a Coke, laughing at something Cal said. As his tawny eyes glanced her way, they warmed like suns.

"Ready for a little fortune-telling?" He held out a hand for hers.

"I want to ask you a question first." It was important to ask now, she realized, before those cards were turned.

"Sure, what do you need?"

"I need to know if you'll marry me."

The conversations around them stopped. For several long seconds there was no sound as he stared at her. "Okay. Now?"

"Fox."

"Because I was thinking more like February. You know what a crappy month February is? Why shouldn't there be something really great to look forward to in the mostly crappy month of February?" He took a slug of his Coke, then set it down as she stared back at him. "Plus, it was February when I saw you for the first time. But not Valentine's Day because, you know, complete cliché and way too traditional."

"You've been thinking?"

"Yeah, I've been thinking, seeing as I'm completely in love with you. But I'm glad you asked me first. Takes the pressure off." With a laugh, he lifted her off her feet. "February work for you?"

"February's perfect." She laid her hands on his cheeks, kissed him. Then lifting her head, she grinned. "Fox and I are getting married in February."

Amid the congratulations and hugs, Cybil caught Gage's eye. "Don't worry," she said quietly. "I won't propose."

She put on the kettle for tea, to keep her calm and centered when they went back to work.

EIGHT

⸺◦⸻⸻◦⸺

Gage slept poorly, and the insomnia had nothing to do with dreams or visions. He wasn't used to making serious mistakes, or worse—certainly more mortifying—clumsy missteps. Particularly with women. He made his living not just reading cards and the odds, but out of reading people, what went on behind the eyes, the words, the gestures.

It was small comfort to understand, at about three a.m., that he hadn't read Cybil incorrectly. She was just as intrigued and attracted as he, just as interested—and probably just as wary—of acting on those now-famous buzzing sexual vibes.

No, he wasn't wrong about the sexual connection between them.

His monumental mistake had been knee-jerking off a disquiet inside himself and kicking it right into her face. The second layer of the mistake being—and Christ, it was lowering—he'd been after *reassurance*. He'd wanted her to agree with him, to tell him there wasn't anything to worry about. She wasn't any more willing to get dicked around by fate than he was.

With that all tidied up, they'd work together, sleep together, fight together, hell, maybe die together, and no problem.

All that talk about emotion and emotional connection had spiced the stew he'd already had simmering inside him. Hadn't he watched both his closest friends, his brothers, fall in love? And weren't they both heading toward the altar? Any man in his right mind would take a hard look at the hand being dealt and fold before the draw.

And, with hindsight flashing like neon, he had to admit he should've kept that move, that thought, that opinion to himself. Instead, he'd fumbled it, gone on the defensive. And had, essentially, accused her of setting him up. She'd been right to kick his ass over it. No question about it. Now the question was how to put things back on a level field without having to wade through the sticky waters of an apology first. He could use the greater-good ploy, but however true it might be, it was weak.

In the end, he decided to play it by ear, and walked into the rental house. Quinn was halfway down the steps, and paused when he came in. After the briefest of hesitations, she jogged the rest of the way down. "Hi. You wouldn't be here to work, would you?"

"Actually—"

She plowed right over him with a rush of words and movement. "Because we're very shorthanded. Fox and Cal are both in meetings, and Fox's dad had a couple hours, so Layla's over at the boutique with him going over plans. It's down to me and Cyb, and actually, I need to run out to the place to get the thing. I came down to get Cyb some coffee, there's fresh in the kitchen. Get that, will you? I'll be back in twenty."

She nipped straight out the door before he could get in a word. At least half of what she'd said was bullshit manufactured on the spot. A man recognized bullshit when he was standing knee deep in it. But since it served his purposes, he just walked back to the kitchen and poured two coffees, then carried them upstairs.

That curly mass of hair tumbled this way and that out of pins Cybil had used to secure it to the top of her head. A new look for her, he thought—at least that he'd seen—and a damn sexy one. She worked with her back to him, on the big dry erase board. Another chart, he noted, and recognized the names of the cards they'd all chosen in the various rounds the night before. The music, he assumed, came from one of the laptops set up in the room. Melissa Etheridge soared.

"Wouldn't logging those into the computer be faster?"

He saw the quick jolt, and the quick recovery before she turned. The look she spared him was what he thought of as beige. Absolutely neutral. "They are logged, but this is easier on the eyes, and more accessible to the whole group. Would one of those be my coffee, or do you plan to drink both?"

He stepped over, held one out to her. "Quinn said she had to go to the place to get the thing, and would be back in twenty."

Irritation flickered over Cybil's face before she turned back to the board. "In that case, you ought to go downstairs, or outside until you have a chaperone to protect you from my wiles."

"I can handle you."

She glanced back. No beige now, Gage mused. This look was all smoke, with the faintest tinge of hot blue at the edges. "Others have thought the same. Their mistake."

Screw it, he decided as she continued to print her perfectly formed letters. When a man played his hand poorly, he had to take his losses. "I was out of line."

"Yes, we've established that much already."

"Then no problem."

"I never imagined you had one."

He drank some coffee. He watched her. He tried to figure out why her cool disinterest just pissed him off. So he set the coffee down, and took her arm to get her attention. "Look—"

"Careful." The warning dripped like molten sugar. "The last

time you started a statement that way you ended up with both feet jammed in your mouth. I imagine you'd find it as boring as I do to make the same mistake twice."

"I never said I made a mistake."

When she met this with silence, and a long, bland stare, it occurred to him she'd be a killer at the poker table. "Okay. All right. The whole day was over the top. Since I don't see you as a tease, it's pretty clear we're going to end up in bed together."

The sound she made wasn't quite a laugh, and was all insult. "I wouldn't place my bets on that just yet."

"I like the odds. But the point is, I thought we'd both want the rules laid out beforehand. The over-the-line part was making it sound as if you were looking for something more."

"That was the over-the-line part?"

"You could cut me a small break here, Cybil."

"Actually, I already have." She thought of the Treatment, and smiled. "You just don't know about it. Let me ask you something. Do you really believe you're so irresistible, so appealing, that I'll fall in love with you and start dreaming of white picket to fence you in?"

"No, I don't. That's part two of the over-the-line. Straight out?"

"Oh, yes, please."

"All the hookups, the link-ups, the subsets like you called them," he said, gesturing to her board, "started to make me uneasy. Added in the more we're in this, the more I've got an urge for you—which I know damn well is mutual—I overreacted."

And that, Cybil decided, was as close to an apology as he'd come up with, unless she beat him with a stick. All in all, it wasn't half bad. "Okay," she said, mimicking him, "all right. I'll cut you a slightly bigger break than I already have. I'll also toss in the fact that I think both of us are old enough and smart enough to resist our *urges* should we have concerns that acting on them will result in driving the other party into mad and hopeless love. Does that work for you?"

"Yeah, that works for me."

"In that case, you can either run along and do whatever it is you do, or you can stay and pitch in."

"Define 'pitch in.'"

"Lend a fresh eye with the charts, the graphs, the maps. Maybe you'll see something we're missing, or at least the potential of something. I need to finish this one, then it needs to be analyzed." She began to write again. "Then, if you're still around, it might be a good idea to try another link-up—of the psychic variety—when at least one other person's around. It occurred to me if the timing had been different yesterday, and that dog had gotten there sooner—"

"Yeah, it occurred to me, too."

"So, I think at least until we have a better handle on it, we shouldn't try that sort of thing alone, or outside."

He couldn't argue with that. "Tell me about this first, the cards."

"All right. Start with me. I've listed my cards, in the succession they were picked, and the subsets I picked with. Yours and mine here, then with Q and Layla, then with the group as a whole. There are twenty-two Major Arcana in a Tarot deck. You and I chose five cards each, all ten of them Major Arcana."

He scanned the board, nodded. "Got that."

"My female subset, five cards each, and a total of fifteen of Major Arcana. When I picked with the group as a whole, the first three were again Major Arcana, the last three—and as I elected to pull from the deck last, all twenty-two were already pulled—were the Queen of Swords, the Ten of Rods, and the Four of Cauldrons.

"Now, when you look at my three rounds, you see that in the first, and the last, I pulled both Death and the Devil. Other repeats, first and second rounds, the Hanged Man, and in all three rounds, I drew the Wheel of Fortune. Second and third, Strength."

"All of us drew repeat cards."

"That's right, so those repetitions add weight to our individual columns. And, tellingly, each woman picked a queen, each man a king. Mine, Queen of Swords, represents someone on guard. An intelligent woman who uses that intellect to gain her own way. Which I'm certainly prone to do. This queen is usually seen as a dark-haired, dark-eyed woman. Ten of Rods, a burden, a determination to succeed. Four of Cauldrons, help from a positive source, new possibilities and/or relationships."

She stepped back, frowned at the board. "My take here is, the cards from the Lesser Arcana represent not only who we are, but what we need to do individually to aid the whole. With the repeat cards representing what was set before us—individually again— what's come to be or is coming, and the eventual outcome."

"How about my king?"

"Again Swords. Represents a man of action who has an analytical mind. And though it might be seen more as Fox, as it's often someone in the legal profession, it means this man is fair, a good judge and basically, nobody's patsy. Next, you have the Six of Rods, triumph after a struggle. And last, Nine of Cauldrons. Someone who enjoys the good life, and has found material success.

"So . . ." She blew out a breath. "As Q and I are most familiar with the Tarot and its meanings, we'll work this. Shuffle it around, analyze, dig into meanings in each subset and in the order of individual picks, repeats, and so on."

"Which will tell us . . . ?"

"Strengths and weaknesses—that's a key, isn't it? For each of us, for each subset, and for the whole. And speaking of Q," Cybil continued when Quinn stepped to the doorway. "Did you get the thing from the place?" Cybil asked sweetly.

"What? Oh, that thing from that place. They were out. So, what are we up to?"

"You and I are on cards. Gage will be putting his analytical mind and his judgment into charts, maps, and graphs."

"Cool. Isn't it sweet how Cal and I picked King and Queen of

Rods?" She beamed her smile at Gage. "Both prefer country living, are loyal with strong ties to family."

"Handy." With that, Gage decided the maps needed his attention.

He wondered how many hours they'd put into all this—their pushpins and computer printouts. He understood and valued the need for research and prep work, but honestly couldn't see what help color-coded index cards were against the forces of evil.

As he studied the map of the Hollow, his mind automatically filled in houses, buildings, landmarks. How many times had he cruised those streets—on a bike, then in a car? There was the place where the dog had drowned at the dawn of the second Seven. But the summer before, he and Fox and Cal had snuck out and gone skinny-dipping in that pool one hot summer night.

The bank would be there, corner of Main and Antietam. He'd opened an account there when he'd been thirteen, to hoard money where the old man couldn't find it. And that asshole Derrick Napper had jumped Fox there one night, just for the hell of it, as Fox cut through on his way from ball practice to the Bowl-a-Rama. The Foster house had been right about there, on Parkside, and in the basement family room, he'd lost his virginity and taken that of the pretty Jenny Foster one memorable night when her parents had been out celebrating their anniversary.

Less than eighteen months later, long after he and pretty Jenny had parted ways, her mother had set the bed on fire while her father slept. There had been many fires during that Seven, and Mr. Foster one of the lucky ones. He'd awakened, put the fire out, then managed to subdue his wife before she lit up their children.

There was the bar where he and Cal and Fox had all gotten ridiculously drunk when he'd come back to celebrate their twenty-first birthday. A few years before, he recalled Lisa Hodges had stumbled out of that same bar and shot at anything that moved—and some that didn't. She'd put a bullet in his arm that Seven, Gage thought, then offered him a blow job.

Strange times.

He scanned the graphs, but as far as he could see, it didn't appear that any one area, or sector, of the Hollow experienced more episodes of violence or paranormal activity. Main Street, of course, but you had to factor in that Main got more traffic, more people used it than any of the other streets or roads in and around town. It was the primary route, with the Square the hub.

He visualized it that way, as a wheel, then as a grid, with the Square as the central point. But no particular pattern emerged. Waste of time, he thought. They could play at this for weeks, and nothing could change. All it proved was that at one time or another, nearly every place within the town limits had been hit.

The park, the ball field, the school, the old library, bowling alley, bars, shops, private homes. Documenting wasn't going to stop them from being hit again when . . .

He stepped back, used both his eyes and his memory to build Hawkins Hollow on its map. Maybe it meant nothing, but hell, the stupid pushpins were right there. Picking up the box, he began adding blue ones to the map.

"What are you doing?" Cybil demanded. "Why—"

He cut her off simply by holding up a finger as he shuffled through his memory, added more pins. There had to be more, he thought. How the hell was a man supposed to remember every applicable incident in some wild theory? And not all of them would involve him. He and Cal and Fox had been tight, but they hadn't been joined at the hip.

"Those locations were already marked," Cybil pointed out when he paused.

"Yeah, that would be the point. And these particular locations have all been hit more than once, some at each Seven. And some of those have already had an incident this time."

"Multiple hits would be logical." Quinn moved forward to study the map. "A town the size of Hawkins Hollow is limited. Other than Main Street, it's fairly spread out, but that's logical, too, as Main has more activity, more people per square foot."

"Yeah, yeah. Interesting, isn't it?"

"It might be, if we knew what the blue pins represented," Cybil said.

"Places, memories, highlights, lowlights. The bowling center. The three of us spent a hell of a lot of time there as kids. I lived on the third floor, worked there—so did Cal and Fox—for spending money. The first violent incident, at least the first we know about, happened in the center on the night of our tenth birthday. At least one act of violence happened there every Seven. Already this time, you had the mess on Valentine's Day, and Twisse shot me back to the apartment—illusion or not, it felt pretty damn real. I got the shit kicked out of me plenty of times up there."

"Violence drawing violence," Cybil murmured. "It returns to locations where you, or one of you, had a violent experience."

"Not just. See this." He tapped the map. "I had sex for the first time in the house that sits here. I was fifteen."

"Precocious," Quinn commented.

"The opportunity presented itself. Next Seven, the lady of the house tried to burn it down, with everyone in it. Didn't work out for her, fortunately. By the next Seven, my first conquest had married her college sweetheart and moved away, and the rest of the family moved to a bigger house well out of town. But the guy who bought the place broke every mirror in the place—that would be July of '01, and according to his wife, whom he attacked, started screaming about devils in the glass. The school—God knows we put in time at all three levels—we got in our share of fights there, copped our share of feels and long, wet kisses once we hit high school."

"Violent or sexual energy. Yours," Cybil added. "You, Cal, and Fox. Yes, that is interesting."

"There's bound to be more. There's also some interest in the fact that up until last month, there was never an incident of any kind at Fox's farm. It wasn't real, but it happened. Nothing ever happened at Cal's parents' place either. But it's something we should watch out for."

"I'm going to call him right now." Quinn dashed out of the room.

"Well, King of Swords, your observant and analytical mind may be on to something." Cybil tapped a finger on the map. "This is our house. No incidents here before we moved into it."

"There might have been something we didn't know about."

"No major incidents, because if there had been, you'd know. But after we move in, it starts here. Aimed at us, very likely using our own energy as part of the fuel. The first incident you're aware of happened at the bowling center when the three of you were there. This time around, the center was the scene of the first major illusionary incident, when four of the group were there. Quinn saw the demon here, when she was driving to Cal's house to meet him for the first time, which put four of the six of us in the area—for the first time."

"What are you looking for?"

"A pattern in the pattern. The second Seven, one of the first major occurrences involved a woman coming out of this bar, and firing a gun. You were hit."

"Yeah, then hit on."

"The three of you on the scene, and of course, the alcohol making the woman more susceptible. But as you were just seventeen, it's doubtful any of you spent appreciable time at that bar, or had any sort of experience there that would—"

"The old man spent plenty of time there." Understanding where she was headed, Gage checked the urge to keep that area buried. "Kicked me out, literally, when I went in looking for him. I was around seven. It was the first time he seriously laid into me. That's what you're looking for?"

"Yes."

When she offered no sympathy, no gesture of comfort, his stomach muscles relaxed again. "The last Seven we tried the ritual again, so we were at the Pagan Stone at midnight. I don't know where the first incident took place, but it was the worst of them. That year was the worst of all."

"All right, let's backtrack. You knew it was coming; you were prepared. Things happened, as they are now, before that stroke of midnight on July seventh. What do you remember happening first?"

"The dreams always come first. I came back early spring that year. We bunked in this apartment Cal had back then. I saw the little fucker crouched right on the Welcome to Hawkins Hollow sign when I first drove into town. Forgot about that. And the first night, or early morning, the three of us stayed in Cal's place, the crows hit."

"Where?"

"Main Street, that's where they like it best. But heavier on the building where we were. Yeah, that took the biggest hit. And there were a lot of fights at the high school. People put it down to end-of-year tempers and stress, but there were a lot of fights at the school."

"We can work with this, I think," Cybil responded as she swung back to her computer and began peppering the keys. "A lot of inputting, cross-referencing, and so on, but we can work this." She glanced up briefly when Quinn came back. "Is he coming?"

"As soon as he sees his parents."

"Get Fox and Layla over here, too."

"She got something?" Quinn asked Gage.

"Apparently."

"Defense is as integral to any war as offense."

"Integral," Gage repeated.

"We pinpoint the highest-risk locations, then take the necessary defensive steps."

"Which would be?"

"Evacuation, fortification." She waved the question off as she might a persistent fly. "One thing at a time."

Gage didn't put much stock in evacuation or fortification, but he followed Cybil's line of thinking. He saw the pattern within the pattern. He edged back as the others arrived, as the six of them crammed into the little office.

"We've agreed we're catalysts," Cybil began. "We know the three men released the entity we call Twisse, as that was the name it was last known by, by performing a blood ritual. We know that Quinn's first sighting was in February, the earliest we have on record—when she arrived. Layla and Quinn, both staying at the hotel, had their first shared sighting there. It's escalated since, faster and stronger. In the bowling center at the Sweetheart Dance when four of the six of us were there. The attack on Lump at Cal's when all six of us stayed there. We've logged the individual and mutual sightings this time. Again the bowling center, the Square, Fox's office and apartment, this house. So when we go back to previous Sevens, there's a locational pattern."

"Bowling center's a major site." Quinn studied the updated map. "The high school, the bar, what was the Foster house, the area around the Square. Obvious reasons for all that. But it's interesting that before this year, neither Fox's building nor this house had any incidents. We're on to something here."

"Why didn't we see this before?" Cal wondered. "How the hell did we miss it?"

"We never did charts and graphs," Fox pointed out. "We wrote stuff down, sure, but we never put it all together this way. The logical, visual way."

"And you see it every day," Cybil added. "You and Cal live here. You see the town every day, the streets, the buildings. Gage doesn't. So when he looks at the map, he sees it in a different way. And doing what he does for a living, he instinctively looks for patterns."

"What do we do with this?" Layla asked.

"We add as much data as possible from these guys' memories,"

Cybil began. "We input that, study and analyze the resulting pattern, and . . ."

"We calculate the odds on the first strike or strikes," Gage finished when she looked at him. "Bowling center year one, the bar year two. We don't know, because we were at the Pagan Stone, what took the first hit year three."

"We might." Frowning at the map, Cal pinned a finger to a spot. "My father stayed in town. He knew we were going to the clearing, to try to stop this, so he stayed in case . . . I didn't know it. He didn't tell me until after it was all over. He planted himself in the police station. A couple of guys in the bank parking lot, going at each other's cars—and each other—with tire irons."

"Did anything significant happen to any of you there?"

"Yeah." Fox hooked his thumbs in his front pockets. "Napper jumped me there once, beat half the snot out of me before I got my second wind and beat the rest of it out of him."

"Just what I'm after," Cybil told him. "Where'd you lose your virginity, Cal?"

"Well, Jesus."

"Don't be shy." Muffling laughter, Quinn bumped his shoulder.

"Backseat of my car, like any self-respecting high school senior."

"He was a late bloomer," Gage pointed out.

Cal hunched his shoulders, then deliberately straightened them again. "I've since made up for it."

"So I hear," Cybil said, and Quinn laughed again. "Where were you parked?"

"Up on Rock Mount Lane. There weren't many houses along there back then. They'd just started to develop, so . . ." He angled his head, and once again laid a finger on the map. "Here, right about here. And last Seven, two of those houses burned to the ground."

"Fox?"

"Alongside of the creek. Well outside town limits. There are a few houses tucked in there now, but they're not part of the Hollow. I don't know if that plays in this."

"We should log them in anyway. What we'll need you to do, all of you, is dig back, think back, note down anything, anywhere, that might be significant. A violent episode, a traumatic one, a sexual one. Then we'll correlate. Layla, you're a hell of a correlator."

"All right. My shop, or what will be my shop," Layla corrected. "It's been hit hard every Seven, and already took damage this time. Did anything happen there?"

"It used to be a junk shop."

The tone of Gage's voice, the quality of silence from both Cal and Fox told Cybil this wasn't only significant. It was monumental. "A kind of low-rent antique store. My mother worked there part-time off and on. We were all in there—I think maybe our mothers got together to have lunch in town, or poke around. I don't remember. But we were all in there when . . . She got sick, started to hemorrhage. She was pregnant, I can't remember how far along. But we were all in there when whatever went wrong started going wrong."

"They got an ambulance." Cal finished it so Gage wouldn't have to. "Fox's mother went with her, and mine took the three of us back to the house with her. They couldn't save her or the baby."

"The last time I saw her, she was lying on the floor of that junk shop, bleeding. I guess that's pretty fucking significant. I need more coffee."

Downstairs, he bypassed the pot and went straight out on the porch. Moments later, Cybil stepped out behind him.

"I'm sorry, so sorry this causes you pain."

"Nothing I could do then, nothing I can do now."

She moved to him, laid a hand on his arm. "I'm still sorry it causes you pain. I know what it is to lose a parent, one you loved and who loved you. I know how it can mark your life into before and after. However long ago, whatever the circumstances, there's still a place in the child that hurts."

"She told me it was going to be all right. The last thing she said to me was, 'Don't worry, baby, don't be scared. It's going to be all right.' It wasn't, but I hope she believed it."

Steadier, he turned to her. "If you're right about this, and I think you are, I'm going to find a way to kill it. I'm going to kill it for using my mother's blood, her pain, her fear to feed on. I swear a goddamn oath right here and now on that."

"Good." With her eyes on his, she held out a hand. "I'll swear it with you."

"You didn't even know her. I barely—"

She cut him off, taking his face in her hands, pulling so that his mouth met hers in a quick and fierce kiss that was more comforting than a dozen soft words. "I swear it."

Even as she drew back, her hands stayed on his face. And a single tear spilled out of her eyes to trail down her cheek. Undone, he lowered his forehead to hers.

Grateful, he took the comfort of her tears.

NINE

⸺◈⸺

nside what would be Sisters, Cybil studied the swaths of paint on the various walls. Fresh color, she thought, to cover old wounds and scars. Layla, being Layla, had created a large chart of the interior on the wall—to scale—with the projected changes and additions in place. It took little effort to visualize what could be.

And for Cybil, it took little effort to visualize what had been. The little boy, scared and confused as his mother bled on the floor of a junk shop. From that moment, Gage's life snapped, she thought. He'd glued the pieces back together, but the line of them would be forever changed by those moments in this place, the loss suffered.

She knew, as the line of her life had forever changed at the moment of her father's suicide.

Another snap in Gage's, she realized, the first time his father had raised a hand to him. Another patch, another change in the line. Then another break on his tenth birthday.

A great deal of damage and repair for one young boy. It would take a very strong and determined man not only to accept all that damage, but to build a life on it.

Because the chatter behind her had stopped, she turned to see Layla and Quinn watching her.

"It's perfect, Layla."

"You're thinking about what happened here, about Gage's mother. I've thought about it, too." Layla's eyes clouded as she looked around the shop. "I spent a lot of time thinking about it last night. There's another property a few blocks up. It might be better if I looked into renting that instead—"

"No, no, don't. This is your place." Cybil touched a hand to the chart.

"He never said a thing. Gage never said a thing, and all the times I babbled on about my plans here. Fox never . . . Or Cal. And when I asked Fox about it, he said the point was to make things what they should be, or preserve what they were meant to be. You know how he gets."

"And he's right." Fresh paint, Cybil thought again. Color and light. "If we don't keep what's ours, or take it back, we've already lost. None of us can change what happened to Gage's mother, or whatever ugliness happened since. But you can make this place live again, and to me, that's giving Twisse a major ass-kicking. As for Gage, he said his mother liked coming here. I think he'd appreciate seeing you make it somewhere she'd have enjoyed."

"I agree with that, and not just because this place is going to rock," Quinn added. "You'll put a lot of positive energy here, and that shoves it right up the ass of negative energy. That's a powerful symbol. More than that, it's damn good physics. What we're dealing with breaks down, on a lot of levels, to basic physics."

"Nature abhors a vacuum," Cybil decided, nodded. "So don't give it one. Fill it up, Layla."

Layla sighed. "As I'm about to be officially unemployed, again,

I'll have plenty of time to do that. But right now, I've got to get to the office. It's the first full day of training my replacement."

"How's she working out?" Quinn wondered.

"I think she's going to be perfect. She's smart, efficient, organized, attractive—and happily married with two teenagers. I like her; Fox is a little bit afraid of her. So, perfect." As they started out, Layla looked at Cybil. "If you talk to Gage today, would you ask him? Physics and ass-kickings aside, if it's too hard for him to have this place a part of his life—and it would be because Fox is—I can take a closer look at that other property."

"If I talk to him, I will."

After Layla locked up and turned in the opposite direction to walk to the office, Quinn hooked an arm through Cybil's. "Why don't you go do that?"

"Do what?"

"Go talk to Gage. You'll work better when you're not wondering how he's doing."

"He's a big boy, he can—"

"Cyb. We go back. First, you're involved. Even if you just thought of the guy as part of the team, you'd be involved. But it's more than that. Just you and me here," she said when Cybil stayed silent.

"All right, yes, it's more. I'm not sure how more might be defined, but it's more."

"Okay, there's the nebulous more. And you're thinking of the little boy who lost his mom, and whose father picked up the bottle instead of his son. Of the boy who took more knocks than he should have, and the man who didn't walk away when he could have. So there's the sympathy and respect elements mixed into that more."

"You're right."

"He's smart, loyal, a little bit of a hard-ass and just rough enough around some of the edges to be intriguing. And, of course, he's extremely hot."

"We do go back," Cybil agreed.

"So, go talk to him. Relieve Layla's mind, maybe get a better handle on the more, then you can concentrate on what we have to do next. Which is a lot."

"Which is why I can and should talk to him later. We've barely skimmed the surface of what we're thinking of as the hot spots. And I need a fresh look at the Tarot card draws. Most important, I'm not leaving you alone in that house. Not for anything."

"That's why laptops were invented. I'm taking mine over to the bowling center." Quinn gestured back toward the Square. "Further proof why I made the right choice in men and home base. I'll set up in Cal's office, or the vicinity, and you can swing by and get me when you're finished talking to Gage."

"Maybe that's not such a bad idea."

"Pal of mine," Quinn said as they walked into the house, "not such bad ideas are my stock and trade."

At Cal's kitchen counter, Gage dug into his memories, and with coffee at his elbow, documented them on his own laptop. Shit happened, he thought, and a lot of it had been monumentally bad shit. But in writing it down, he began to see there were a handful of locations where it happened repeatedly.

Still, it didn't all make sense. He'd experienced the worst of his life—pain, fear, grief, and fury—in that damn apartment over the bowling alley. Though incidents occurred there during every Seven, he couldn't recall a single major one. No loss of life, no burning, no looting.

And that itself was odd, wasn't it? A town institution, his child-hood home, Cal's family's center in a very true sense, Fox's favorite hangout. Yet when the infection raged, and people were burning, breaking, beating hell out of each other, the old Bowl-a-Rama stood almost untouched.

That earned a big *why* in his book, with a secondary, *how can we use it.*

There was the old library, and the three of them had certainly put in time there. Cal's great-grandmother had run the place. Ann Hawkins had lived there, and died there during the early days of the Hawkins Hollow settlement. Fox had suffered a major tragedy during the previous Seven when his fiancée took a header off the roof.

But . . . But, he mused, sipping coffee, it was the only tragedy he could remember in that location. No burning or pillaging there either. And with all those books as fuel.

The middle and high schools, hit every time, and the elementary virtually untouched. Interesting.

He shifted to study his drawing of the town map and began to speculate not only on the hot spots, but the cold ones.

The mild irritation of the knock on the front door turned into another kind of speculation when he found Cybil on the other side.

"Why don't you just come in?" he asked her. "Nobody else knocks."

"Superior breeding." She closed the door herself then tilted her head as she gave him a slow once-over. "Rough night?"

"I'd've put on a suit and tie if I'd been expecting company of superior breeding."

"A shave wouldn't hurt. I'm charged with discussing something with you. Should we discuss it standing here?"

"Is it going to take long?"

The amused glint in her eye struck a chord with him. "Aren't you the gracious host?"

"Not my house," he pointed out. "I'm working in the kitchen. You can come on back."

"Why, thank you. I believe I will." She strolled ahead of him in what he thought of as her sexy queen glide. "Mind if I make tea?"

He shrugged. "You know where everything is."

"I do." She took the kettle off the stove, walked to the sink.

He wasn't particularly annoyed that she'd come by. The fact was, it wasn't exactly a hardship to have a beautiful woman making tea in the kitchen. And that was the sticky part, he admitted. Not just any beautiful woman, but Cybil. Not just any kitchen, but for all intents and purposes right at the moment, his kitchen.

There'd been something intense between them the night before, when she'd kissed him, when she'd shed tears for him. Not sexual, or not at its core, he admitted. Sexual he could work with, he could handle. Whatever was going on between them was a hell of a lot more dangerous than sex.

She glanced over her shoulder and he felt that instant and recognizable punch of physical attraction. And there the ground held firmer under his feet.

"What are you working on?" she asked him.

"My homework assignment."

She wandered over, then gave his map an approving nod. "Nicely done."

"Do I get an A?"

Her gaze flicked up to his. "I appreciate bad moods. I have them often myself. Why don't I skip the tea, get right to the point, then I can leave you alone to enjoy yours?"

"Finish making the tea, it's no skin off mine. You can top off my coffee while you're at it. And what is the point?"

Wasn't it fascinating to watch her face while she debated between being pissed and flipping him off, or being superior and doing what she'd come to do.

She turned, got out a cup and saucer—and, he noted, ignored his request to top off his coffee. She leaned back against the opposite counter while she waited for the water to boil. "Layla's considering an alternate location for her boutique."

He waited for the rest, lifting his hands when it didn't come. "And this needs to be discussed with me because . . . ?"

"She's considering an alternative because she's concerned about your feelings."

"My feelings regarding ladies' boutiques are pretty much nonexistent. Why would she . . ."

With a nod, Cybil turned to turn off the burner under the sputtering kettle. "I see your brain's able to engage even through your bad mood. She's worried that opening her business there will hurt you. As her cards indicated, compassion and empathy are some of her strengths. You're Fox's brother in the truest sense of the word, so she loves you. She'll adjust her plans."

"There's no need for that. She doesn't have to . . . It's not . . ." He couldn't put the words together; they simply wouldn't come.

"I'll tell her."

"No, I'll talk to her." Christ. "It's just a place where something bad happened. If they boarded up all the places where something bad happened in the Hollow, there wouldn't be a town. I wouldn't give a good damn about that, but there are people I give a good damn about who do."

And loyalty, Cybil thought, was one of his strengths. "She'll make it shine. I think it's what she's meant to do. I saw her there. Two separate flashes. Two separate potentials. In one the place was burned out, the windows broken, the walls scorched. She stood alone inside the shell of the place. There was light coming through the broken front window, and that made it worse somehow. The way it beamed and burned over the ruin of her hopes."

Turning again, she poured out a cup of tea. "In the other, the light was beaming and burning in through sparkling glass, over the polished floor. She wasn't alone. There were people inside, looking at the displays, the racks. There was such movement and color. I don't know which may happen, if either. But I do know she needs to try to make that second version the truth. She'll be able to try if you tell her you're okay with it."

"Fine."

"Well, since I've completed my mission, I'll just go and leave you alone."

"Finish your damn tea."

She carried her cup over, leaned on the counter so they were face-to-face. A little sympathy shone in those big, brown eyes of hers. "Love's a weight, isn't it? And here you are loaded down with Cal and Fox, with the Hawkinses and the Barry-O'Dells. Now Layla goes and drops a big stone on the pile. There's Quinn, too, you might as well shoulder that one because she's the type who'll just keep picking it back up and dropping it on again. No wonder you're in such a sour mood."

"That's your take. To me, this just feels normal."

"In that case." She strolled around the counter to study his laptop screen over his shoulder. "My, my, you *are* doing your homework."

She smelled like the woods, he thought. Autumn woods. Nothing fragile and pastel like spring, but rich and vivid, with just a hint of distant smoke.

"A lot of locations here," she commented. "I think I get the basic idea of your groupings, but why don't you explain your—"

He didn't think about the move, he just made it. Usually a mistake, he knew, but it didn't feel like one. It didn't taste like one. He had his mouth on hers, his hands fisted in her hair before either one of them knew it was coming.

He'd jerked her off balance—he hoped in more ways than one—so her hands braced on his shoulders. She didn't shy back or pull away, but sank in. Not surrender, but like a woman who chose to enjoy.

"No seduction," he said with his mouth an inch from hers. "I don't welch on a deal, so this is straight-out. We can keep dancing around this, or we can go upstairs."

"You're right. That's definitely not seduction."

"You named the terms," he reminded her. "If you want to change them—"

"No, no. A deal's a deal." This time her mouth took his, just as hot, just as greedy. "And while I do like to dance, it's . . ." She trailed off at the knock on the door. "Why don't I see who that is? You probably need a moment or two to . . . settle down."

And so, Cybil thought as she walked out of the kitchen, did she. She had no objections to jumping into the deep end of the pool. She was, after all, a skilled and sensible swimmer. But it didn't hurt to take a couple of good, head-clearing breaths first, then decide if she wanted to jump into this particular pool at this particular time.

She took one of those breaths and opened the door. It took her a moment to recognize the man she'd seen a few times in the bowling center. She thought again that Gage favored his mother, as there was no resemblance she could see between father and son.

"Mr. Turner, I'm Cybil Kinski." He stood, Cybil thought, looking embarrassed, and a little scared. His hair had gone thin and gray. He had Gage's height, but a scrawnier build. It would be the years of drinking, she assumed, that had dug the lines in his face and webbed the broken capillaries over it. His eyes were a watered-down blue that seemed to struggle to meet hers.

"Sorry. I thought if Gage was here, I could . . ."

"Yes, he is. Come in. He's back in the kitchen. Why don't you have a seat and I'll—"

"He won't be staying." Gage's voice was brutally neutral when he stepped in. "You need to go."

"If I could have just a minute."

"I'm busy, and you're not welcome here."

"I asked Mr. Turner in." Cybil's words dropped like stones into the deep well of silence. "So I'll apologize to both of you. And I'm going to leave you alone to deal with each other. Excuse me."

Gage didn't so much as glance at her as she walked back toward the kitchen. "You need to go," he repeated.

"I just got some things to say."

"That's not my problem. I don't want to hear them. I'm living here for now, and as long as I am, you don't come around here."

Bill's jaw tightened; his mouth firmed. "I put this off since you came back to town. I can't put it off anymore. You give me five minutes, for Chrissake. Five minutes, and I won't bother you no more. I know you only come around the bowling center when I'm off. You hear me out, I'll make myself scarce anytime you want to come in, see Cal. I won't come around you, you got my word."

"Because your word always meant so much?"

Color came and went in Bill's face. "It's all I got. Five minutes, and you're rid of me."

"I've been rid of you." But Gage shrugged. "Take your five."

"Okay then." Bill cleared his throat. "I'm an alcoholic. I've been sober five years, six months, and twelve days. I let drink take over my life. I used it as an excuse to hurt you. I should've looked after you. I should've taken care of you. You didn't have nobody—anybody else, and I made it so you had nobody." His throat moved as he swallowed hard. "I used my hands and my fists and my belt on you, and I'da kept using them if you hadn't gotten big enough to stop me. I made you promises, and I broke them. Over and over again. I wasn't no kind of father to you. I wasn't no kind of man."

His voice wavered, and he looked away. While Gage said nothing, Bill took several audible breaths, then looked back into his son's face. "I can't go back and change that. I could tell you I'm sorry from now until the day I die, and it won't make up for it. I'm not going to promise you I won't drink again, but I'm not going to drink today. When I wake up tomorrow, I'm not going to drink. That's what I'm going to do, every day. And every day I'm sober, I know what I did to you, how I shamed myself as a man, and as a father. How your ma must've looked down and cried. I let her down. I let you down. I'll be sorry for that the rest of my life."

Bill took another breath. "I guess that's what I had to say. 'Cept, you made yourself into something. You did that on your own."

"Why?" If this would be the last time they faced each other,

Gage wanted the answer to the single question that had haunted him most of his life. "Why did you turn on me that way? Drinking was the excuse. That's a true thing. So why?"

"I couldn't take the belt to God." Emotion gleamed in Bill's eyes, and though his voice wavered, he continued on. "I couldn't beat God with my fists. But there you were. Had to blame someone, had to punish someone." Bill looked down at his hands. "I wasn't anything special. I could fix things, and I didn't mind hard work, but I wasn't anything special. Then she looked at me. Your ma, she made me a better man. She loved me. I'd wake up every morning, go to bed every night amazed that she was there, and she loved me. She . . . I got a couple minutes left of my five, right?"

"Finish it then."

"You oughta know . . . She was—we were—so happy when she got pregnant with you. You probably don't remember how it was . . . before. But we were happy. Cathy . . . Your ma had some problems with the pregnancy, and then it happened so fast, you coming. We didn't even get to the hospital. You come out of her heading up the pike in the ambulance."

Bill glanced away again, but this time—whether Gage wanted to see it or not—it was grief vivid in those faded blue eyes. "And there were some problems, and the doctor, he said there shouldn't be any more kids. That was okay, that was fine with me. We had you, and, Jesus, you looked just like her. I know you don't remember, but I loved you both more'n anything in the world."

"No," Gage said when Bill stopped. "I don't remember."

"I guess you wouldn't. After a while, she wanted another. She wanted another baby so bad. She'd say: Look, Bill, look at our Gage. Look what we made. Isn't he beautiful? He needs a brother or sister. And well, we started another, and she was careful. She took such good care of herself, did everything the doctor said, and no complaint. But it went wrong. They came and got me from work, and . . ."

He pulled out a bandanna, mopped at tears without any sign of shame. "I lost her, and the little girl we'd tried to make. Jim and Frannie, Jo and Brian, they helped all they could. More than most would. I started drinking, just a little here and there to get through, to get by. But it wasn't enough, so I drank more, and more yet."

His eyes dry again, he shoved the cloth back in his pocket. "I started thinking how it was my fault she died. I should've gone and gotten myself fixed, and not told her, that's all. She'd be alive if I had. Then that hurt too much, so I'd drink some more. Till I started thinking how she'd be alive if we hadn't had you. Hadn't had you, whatever messed her up inside wouldn't be, and she'd still be there when I woke in the morning. Blaming you didn't hurt so much, so I talked myself into seeing that as God's truth instead of a damned lie. Everything was your fault. Lost my job because I was drunk, but I turned that around so I lost my job because I had to look after you on my own. Anything went wrong, it was because of you, then I could drink some more, whale on you, and I wouldn't have to face the truth.

"There was nobody to blame, Gage." He let out a long sigh. "It wasn't anybody's fault. Things just went wrong, and she died. And when she died, I stopped being a man. I stopped being your daddy. What was left of me, your ma, she'd never have looked at twice. So that's the why. That's the long way around the why. I'm not asking you to forgive me. I'm not asking you to forget. I'm just asking for you to believe that I know what I did, and I'm sorry for it."

"I believe you know what you did, and you're sorry for it. You're well over your five minutes."

With a nod, Bill cast his eyes down, turned to open the door. "I won't get in your way," he said with his back to Gage. "You want to come in and see Cal, or have a beer at the grill, I won't get in your way."

When Bill closed the door behind him, Gage stood where he was. How was he supposed to feel? Was all that supposed to make a difference? All the sorry in the world didn't erase one minute of the years he'd lived in fear, of the years he'd lived in bitter anger. It did nothing to negate the shame or the sorrow.

So the old man got it off his chest, Gage thought as he strode back to the kitchen. That was fine. That was the end between them.

He saw Cybil through the window as she sat on Cal's back deck drinking her tea. He shoved open the door.

"Why the hell did you let him in? Is that your superior breeding?"

"I suppose. I've already apologized for it."

"It's the day for goddamn apologies." The anger he hadn't let him-self feel for his father—the old man wasn't entitled to it—sparked now. And flared. "You're sitting out here thinking I should forgive and forget. Poor old guy's sober now, and just trying to mend fences with his only son, the one he used to kick the shit out of regularly. But that was the booze, and the booze was the answer to grief and guilt. Be-sides, alcoholism's a disease, and he caught it like cancer. Now he's in remission, he's in his one fucking day at a time, so all's fucking for-given. I should break out the poles and see if he wants to go down to the fishing hole and drown some worms. Did your father ever punch you in the face before he blew his brains out?"

He heard her breath hitch in, release. But her voice was rock steady when she spoke. "No, he did not."

"Did he ever take a belt to your back until it bled?"

"No, he did not."

"That being the case, I'd say you lack the experience to sit out here thinking I should shrug all that off and have myself a real *Oprah* moment with the old man."

"You'd be right, absolutely. But here's another thing. You're put-ting thoughts in my head that aren't there, and words in my mouth I have no intention of saying. And I don't appreciate it. I imagine that talking with your father just now has left you feeling both raw and prickly, so I'll give you some room. In fact, I'll give you plenty of room and leave you alone to have your tantrum in private."

She made it all the way to the door before she whirled back. "No,

I will not. I'll be damned if I will. Do you want to know what I think? Are you at all interested in hearing my own opinion rather than the one you've projected on me?"

He waved a hand, a gesture so brittle with sarcasm, it all but cracked the air. "Go right ahead."

"I think you're under no obligation whatsoever to forgive anything, to forget anything. You're not required to push away the years of abuse because the abuser now chooses to be sober and in his sobriety regrets his actions. And while it may be small and unforgiving of *me*, I think people who do so at the snap of a damn finger are either liars or are in need of serious therapy. I assume you heard him out, so in my personal opinion, any debt you might owe for your existence is now paid in full. It may be fashionable to hold the opinion that terrible actions are indeed terrible, but that the person inflicting them isn't responsible due to alcohol, drugs, DNA, or goddamn PMS. He damn well *was* responsible, and if you decide to loathe him for the rest of your life, I wouldn't blame you for it. How's that?"

"Unexpected," Gage said after a moment.

"I believe the strong have an obligation to protect the weak. It's why they're the strong. I believe a parent has an obligation to protect the child. It's why they're the parent. As for my father—"

"I'm sorry." A day for apologies, he thought again. And this one might qualify as the most sincere of his lifetime. "Cybil, I'm very sorry I threw that at you."

"Regardless, he never raised a hand to me. If he were able to stand where you are right now and apologize to me for killing himself, I don't know if I'd forgive him. He ripped my life in two with that single, selfish, self-pitying act, so I think it would take more than an apology. Which would be useless since he'd still be dead. Your father's alive, and he's taken a step toward making amends. Good for him. But for my money, you can't forgive without trust, and he hasn't earned that from you. He may never, and that's not on you. His actions, his consequences. End of story."

She'd said it all, he thought. She might have said it all in the heat of temper and resentment. But everything she'd said was a comfort. "Can I start over?"

"With what?"

"I'd like to thank you for stepping out and letting me deal with that."

"You're welcome."

"And to thank you for not leaving."

"No problem."

"And last, to thank you for the kick in the ass."

She huffed out a breath, almost smiled. "That part was my pleasure."

"I bet."

He stepped to her, held out a hand. "Come upstairs."

She looked down at his hand, up into his eyes. "All right," she said, and put her hand in his.

TEN

~~~~~⬥~~~~~

Y ou surprise me."

Cybil tipped her head, gave him that long, slanted stare as
they walked through the house. "I hate to be predictable.
What's the current surprise?"

"I figured, especially after the mood-breaker, you'd say no
thanks."

"That would be shortsighted and self-defeating. I like sex. I'm
fairly sure I'm going to like sex with you." She gave a quick, careless
shrug, while that half smile stayed in place. "Why shouldn't I have
something I like?"

"I can't think of a single reason."

"Neither can I. So." At the top of the stairs she pushed him back
against the wall, crushed her mouth against his. And the easy, the
expected glide of arousal inside him banked hard, then shot straight
through him.

She bit lightly on his bottom lip once, then spoke against them—
each word a separate stroke. "Let's both have something we like."

She stepped back, gestured toward a bedroom doorway. "That one's yours, isn't it?" With one last glance over her shoulder, one that literally caused the breath to back up in his lungs, she strolled to it, and through.

This, Gage thought as he pushed off the wall, was going to be pretty damn interesting.

She was bent over the bed, straightening his disordered sheets when he came in. "I wasn't planning on using that again before tonight."

She flicked a look back at him, eyes wicked. "Isn't it nice when plans change? I'm a bed-maker myself. I like everything all . . . smooth when I slide in at night. Or . . ." She gave the sheets a last pat, turned. "Whenever."

"I don't mind a few tangles." He moved to her, gripped her hips to lift her onto her toes.

"That's good, because there's bound to be more than a few when we're finished with it, and I won't be making the bed for you." Sinuously, she hooked her arms around his neck, met his mouth in a long, slow burn of a kiss.

In one lazy glide, his hands slid up, under her shirt, over her sides with a teasing brush of thumbs over her breasts. Her shirt slithered up with the movement as he drew her arms over her head.

"Nice move," she said when her shirt dropped away.

"I've got more."

"Me, too." Smiling, she flipped open the button of his jeans, eased the zipper down barely an inch. Watching him, she grazed her nails over his belly, up to his chest. "Nice definition, for a card-player," she added as she pulled his shirt up and off.

She was a killer, he thought. "Thanks."

Both of them, he knew, understood the steps of the dance, had practiced its variations, its changing rhythms. But for this dance, their first together, he intended to take the lead.

He took her mouth again, a playful meeting of lips and tongues while he unhooked her pants. Then he lifted her off her feet in a sudden and casual show of strength that had her breath snagging even as the cotton slid down her legs to the floor. *Gotcha,* he thought, and lowered her just enough to bring her mouth to his. And when her sound of pleasure warmed his lips, when the hands on his shoulders tensed, he released her with just enough force to have her falling onto the bed.

She lay on her back, hair tumbled. Dusky skin and frothy black lace.

"You didn't get that muscle shuffling cards."

"You'd be surprised." He eased down, planted his hands on either side of her head. "Fast or slow?"

"Let's try some of both." Fisting her hands in his hair, she pulled him to her. The kiss spun out, rolls of white satin, then darkened and fired with the first hungry nips of teeth. Her hands stroked down his back, slid under his loosened jeans to ride over taut muscles. And like lightning her legs hooked around him, her body bowed up pressing them urgently center to center in a move that yanked furiously at his chain of control.

A killer, he thought again, and ravished her neck.

He had a fantastic mouth, an amazing mouth. She let her head fall back so it could sample her wherever it chose. Her skin hummed under it, and under her skin her blood began to beat. His body—long, hard, with the ripple of muscle, pressed down on hers in exactly the right way so that need gathered into tight knots that set pulses drumming.

Heat. Hunger. Hurry.

She shoved the jeans down his hips, pushing them clear as she rolled over to straddle him. He countered by levering up, fixing his mouth on hers as he flicked open the clasp of her bra.

Even as the kiss spoke of speed, of urgency, his hands skimmed, stroked, in a kind of lazy torture that kindled low fires in her belly. When his mouth lowered to taste, to possess what his hands had aroused, she bowed back to offer more.

She flowed, was all he could think, agile and eager. The beautiful lines of her, the lovely curves all in pale gold, an exotic feast for the taking. And she took, grasping her own pleasure, gliding on it. Nothing could have been more provocative to him than Cybil steeped in that inevitable rise of passion.

Had he wanted her this much? Had this clenched fist of desire been inside him all along—waiting, just waiting, to punch through caution and control? It pounded in him now, beating down all reason so he wanted to feel her tremble, to see her writhe. To hear her scream. Pinning her beneath his weight, he used his hands to plunder, to loose that slow rise into a hot, fast flood.

She came, quaking under him, her skin sheened from the heat glowing in the sunlight. Those dark eyes, those gypsy eyes seemed to hold a world of secrets when they locked on his.

"All of you," she said, and closed her hand around him. "All of you now." Wrapping her legs around him, she took him into her.

A flash, a wire sparking in the blood. She let it burn through her, crying out when it brought release, moaning as it whipped her into need again, wildly. She yielded when he shoved her legs back to go deeper, and her nails bit into his hips like spurs to urge him on. Even as the pleasure, dark and intense, battered her breathless, she rushed toward that next swamping wave.

She erupted under him, and dragged him with her into the fire.

They lay flat on their backs, side by side on the bed. He felt as if he'd been kicked off a cliff, doing the tumble down through screaming air to land in a hot river. He'd barely had the strength or the brainpower to roll off her so they could both try to get their breath back.

That hadn't been sex, he thought. Sex was anything from an enjoyable pastime to a good, sweaty bout. That had been a revelation of near-biblical proportions.

"Well, okay," he managed. "The surprises just keep coming."

"I think I saw God." Cybil's breath streamed out in something between sigh and moan. "She was pleased."

He laughed, closed his eyes. "You're like a live, female version of Gumby. Without the green."

She was silent a moment. "Since I believe that was a compliment, thanks."

"You're welcome."

"And since we're handing them out, you—" She broke off, and her hand clamped on his. "Gage."

He opened his eyes. The walls bled. Long rivers of red gushed down the walls, swam over the floor. "If that were real, Cal would be sincerely pissed off. Blood's a bitch to clean."

"It doesn't like what went on here." She took a breath, rolled to nudge him back when he started to rise. Eyes hard, face pale, she spoke in a steady voice. "Peeping Toms are so disgusting. But, we might as well give this one something to write home about. Tell me, is it true what I hear from my housemates?"

"What would that be?"

"That your healing powers include impressively fast recovery?"

He grinned at her. "Are you up for a demonstration?"

"More to the point, are you?" She tossed a leg over him, mounted him. Her head fell back, her breath shuddered out. "It's comforting to know my friends are honest. Oh God. Wait." Her hands gripped his as sensation clawed through her.

"Take your time."

"Brace yourself," she warned. "This is going to be a wild ride."

Later, though the walls and floor showed no signs of demon tantrums, he took her again in the shower. Hair damp, eyes sleepy, she dressed.

"Well, what an interesting day. Now I've got to get back to work and swing by and get Q from the bowling center."

"Maybe I'll ride in with you."

"Oh?"

"You want input, and I figure I'll cop lunch out of the deal."

"That might be arranged." When she started to walk by him, out of the room, he took her arm.

"Cybil. I'm not nearly done with you."

"Cutie." She gave his cheek a very deliberate pat. "They never are."

When she kept on going, he shook his head. He'd walked into that one, he admitted. By the time he got downstairs she'd dug a lipstick out of her cavernous bag and was sliding it, with perfect accuracy, over her lips. "How do you do that without looking?"

"Oddly, my lips remain in exactly the same place day after day, year after year. Are you going to want your laptop?"

"Yeah." He'd never considered a woman applying lipstick particularly sexy. Before. "If it gets too irritating working with you and the blonde, I'll set up somewhere."

"Gather it up then. The train's about to pull out." While he did, she took out blusher, stroked a bit over her cheeks. In seconds, she'd done something with a minute mirror and a pencil to soot up her eyes. As they walked toward the door she spritzed something from a silver tube about the size of his thumb onto her throat. And that scent, that autumn woods scent reached out and grabbed him by his.

So he grabbed her, rubbed his lips over hers. "We could blow off the day." And had the satisfaction of feeling her heart kick against his.

"Tempting. Seriously tempting, but no. I'd have to call Quinn and explain I'm not picking her up because I've decided spending the day naked in bed with you is more important than trying to find the way to destroy a demon who wants us all dead. Not that she wouldn't understand, but still."

She opened the door, stepped out on the deck.

The boy crouched on the roof of her car, a grinning gargoyle. As it flashed its teeth, Gage pushed Cybil behind him. "Get back in the house."

"Absolutely not."

With a flourish, the boy raised its hands, then chopped them down like a mad conductor. The dark fell; the wind rose.

"It's just show," Cybil shouted. "Like the walls upstairs."

"More than that this time." He could feel it in the bite of the wind. Inside in surrender, Gage thought, or out here, in challenge? If he'd been alone, it wouldn't be a question. "My car's faster."

"All right."

They started forward, pushing into the wind that shoved them back. Gage kept his eyes on the boy as it whirled in wild circles over the slope of hill, the curve of road. Debris flew, chunks of garden mulch, falling twigs, and peppering gravel. He used his body in an attempt to shield her from the worst of it. Then the boy leaped down.

"Fuck the whore while you can." The words were only uglier when shouted in that young, childish voice. "Before long, you'll watch as I make her scream in pleasure and pain. Want a taste, bitch?"

Crying out in shock, Cybil doubled over, clutching herself. Gage made the choice quickly, and letting her fall to her knees, he pulled out his knife. On a howling laugh, the boy flipped out of range in a gleeful handspring. Gage gripped Cybil's arm, wrenched her to her feet. One look at her face had her horror, her helplessness stabbing through him like his own knife.

"Get in the car. Get in the damn car." He shoved her inside, fighting off the rage as the thing in a boy's form pumped its hips obscenely. The rage pushed at him, screamed at him to go after the thing, to hack and slice. But she was curled into a ball inside the car, shaking.

Gage pulled himself in, fought to slam the door against the wind. Ruthlessly now, he shoved Cybil back, yanked the seat belt around her. Shock and pain turned her face to white marble.

"Hold on. Just hold on."

"It's in me." She gasped it out while her body jerked. "It's in me."

Gunning the engine, Gage shot into reverse, then whipped the wheel. The car bucked in the force of the wind as he sped over the bridge toward the road. Blood spat out of the sky, splatting the windshield, hissing like acid on the roof, the hood. The boy's head appeared at the top, its eyes slanted like a snake's. As it ran its tongue through the blood, Cybil moaned.

It laughed when Gage flipped the wipers on full speed, pumped the washer to spray. Laughed as though it was a fine, fine joke. Then it squealed, either with humor or with surprise, when Gage wrenched the car into a vicious three-sixty. The windshield erupted with fire.

He cut his speed rather than risk a wreck, blocked out everything but the need for a steady hand on the wheel. Slowly, the dark ebbed, the fire sputtered.

When the sun flashed on again with a gentle spring breeze, he pulled to the side of the road. She slumped back in the seat, staring up as her shoulders shook with each breath.

"Cybil."

She cringed away. "Please don't. Don't touch me."

"Okay." Nothing to say, he thought. Nothing to do but get her home. She'd been raped right in front of his eyes, and there was nothing to say, nothing to do.

When they got to the house he didn't help her inside. Don't touch me, she'd said, so he only held the door, closed it after her. "Go upstairs, lie down or . . . I'll call Quinn."

"Yes, call Quinn." But she didn't go upstairs. Instead she walked back toward the kitchen. When he went in moments later, she had a glass of brandy in her shaking hands.

"She's on her way. I don't know what you need, Cybil."

"Neither do I." She took a long drink, then a long breath. "God, neither do I, but that's a start."

"I can't leave you alone, I can't give you that. But if you want to go up and lie down, I'll stay outside the bedroom." When she shook her head, everything about her seemed to tremble. "Goddamn it, god*damn* it, scream, cry, throw something, punch me."

She shook her head again, drank the rest of the brandy. "It wasn't real, physically. But it felt real, physically, and every other way there is to feel. I'm not going to scream; I might never stop. I want Quinn, that's all. I want Quinn."

When the front door slammed open, Gage thought Quinn must have run every step. She was still running when she reached the kitchen. "Cyb."

Cybil made a sound, a mix of moan and whimper that sliced straight through Gage's belly. Even as she turned into Quinn's arms, Quinn led her away. "Come on, baby, let's go upstairs. I'll take you upstairs."

Quinn sent Gage one long, grieving look, then they were gone. Gage picked up the glass, smashed it in the sink. Changed nothing, he thought, looking down at the shards. Just a broken glass, and that changed nothing, fixed nothing, helped nothing.

Cal came in to find him standing at the sink, staring out at the sunny afternoon. "What happened? After Quinn got your call she told me to call Layla, get her here, and she ran out. Cybil, is she hurt?"

"Christ knows." His throat burned, Gage realized. Burned as if he'd swallowed flame. "It raped her. The son of a fucking bitch, and I didn't stop it."

Cal stepped up to him, laid a hand on his shoulder. "Tell me what happened."

He began coldly, almost clinically, beginning with the blood on the walls. He didn't stop or acknowledge Fox when Fox came in, but he picked up the beer Fox opened and set in front of him.

"About a mile, mile and a half from your place it stopped. It all went away. Except for Cybil. I don't know if that kind of thing ever goes away."

"You got her away," Cal pointed out. "You got her back home."

"Give me a medal and call me hero."

"I know how you feel." Fox met Gage's hot and bitter look quietly. "It's happened to Layla, so I know how you feel. Layla's upstairs now. That's going to help. And Cybil will get through it because that's the way they're made. We'll get through it because it's all we can do. We'll all get through it because we're going to make the bastard pay. That's what the fuck we're going to do."

He held out a hand. After a moment, Gage gripped it, and Cal laid his over theirs. "We'll make the bastard pay," Gage repeated. "That's what the fuck we're going to do. I swear an oath."

"We swear an oath," Cal and Fox agreed, then Cal blew out a breath and rose.

"I'll make her some tea. Tea's the thing she likes."

"Put some whiskey in it," Fox suggested.

They put it together, and after some discussion and debate, put a pony of whiskey on the side. Gage carried it up, then hesitated outside the closed bedroom door. Before he could knock, Layla opened it, jumped a little.

"Cal made this tea," Gage began.

"Perfect. I was just coming down to do exactly that. Is that whiskey?"

"Yeah. Fox's contribution."

"Good." Layla took the tray. Then studied Gage with weary eyes. "She'll be all right, Gage. Thanks for bringing this up." She closed the door and left him staring at the blank panel.

In the bathroom that linked the two bedrooms, Cybil lay in the tub. She'd had her jag, and that had left her exhausted. Oddly, the fatigue helped. Not as much as her friends, she thought, but some.

As did the hot water, and the fragrance and froth Layla had added to it. Quinn rose from the little stool beside the tub when Layla brought in the tea tray.

"That was really fast, like superpower fast."

"Gage brought it up. Cal made it, so it's probably just fine. Honey, there's whiskey here. Do you want it in the tea?"

"Oh yeah. Thanks. God." Shifting up, Cybil squeezed her burning eyes, breathed through the threatening flood of tears. "No, no, done with that."

"Maybe not." Layla doctored the tea. "I have a moment every now and again. It's okay. We're allowed."

With a nod, Cybil accepted the tea. "It wasn't the pain, though, oh Jesus, nothing's ever hurt like that. It was feeling it in me, pounding and pushing, and not being able to stop it, or fight it. It was the boy. Why is that worse? That it made me see the boy while it—" She broke off, made herself drink the spiked tea.

"It's a kind of torture, isn't it? A kind of physical and psychological torture designed to break us down." Quinn brushed a hand over Cybil's hair. "We won't be broken."

"No, we won't." She held out a hand, and in a gesture that mirrored the one made in the kitchen, Quinn took it, and Layla closed hers over theirs. "We won't break."

She dressed, and took some comfort in grooming. She wouldn't break, Cybil vowed, nor would she look like a victim. When she stepped out of the bedroom she heard the murmur of voices from the office. Not yet, she thought. Not quite ready for that. She moved quietly past, and down the stairs. Maybe after another ocean or two of tea.

In the kitchen she took the kettle to the sink and saw Gage outside, alone. Her first inclination was to back away, to slink away into some dark corner and hide. And the urge both surprised and embarrassed her. In defense, she took the opposite tact, and went outside.

He turned, stared at her. In his eyes she saw the rage and the ruin.

"Absolutely nothing I can say would sound remotely right. I thought you might want me to take off, but I didn't want to leave until I was sure you . . . What?" he said in disgust. "I don't have a clue what."

She considered for a moment. "You're not far wrong. I guess a part of me hoped you'd be gone so I didn't have to talk about this now."

"You don't have to."

"I don't like that part of me," she continued. "So let's just get this done. It came at me, the attack that's a woman's nightmare. The big fear. It made me feel that violation, and the helplessness. That horror that drove Hester Deale mad."

"I should've gone after it."

"And left me? Would you, *could* you leave me when I was completely defenseless, completely terrorized? I couldn't stop it; that's not my fault. You got me away, and getting away made it stop. You defended me when I couldn't defend myself. Thank you."

"I'm not looking for—"

"I know you're not," she interrupted. "I probably wouldn't feel as grateful if you were. Gage, if either of us feel guilty about what happened, it wins a kind of victory. So let's don't."

"Okay."

But he would, for a while yet anyway, she realized. A man would. *This* man would. Maybe she could do something to soothe them both. "Would it complicate our straightforward and mature relationship if you just held on to me for a minute?"

He put his arms around her with the wary caution of a man handling thin and priceless crystal. But when she sighed, laid her head on his shoulder, it was he who broke. His hold tightened. "Christ, Cybil. Good Christ."

"When we destroy it." She spoke clearly now, steadily now. "If it comes in a form with a dick, I will personally castrate it."

His grip tightened again, and he kissed her hair. Complicated, he realized, didn't begin to cover whatever was going on inside him. But right at that moment, he didn't give a damn.

To avoid having everyone tiptoeing around her, Cybil voted for work. The small second-floor office might've been cramped with six people inside, but she had to admit, it felt safe.

"Gage found what may be another pattern dealing with locations," she began, "that springs off the one we talked about before. We can look at them as hot spots and safe zones. The bowling center. While that was the location of the first known infection and violence and has seen other incidents, it's never sustained any damage. No fires, no vandalism. Right?"

Cal nodded. "Not really. Some fights, but most of the trouble's been outside."

"This house," Cybil continued. "Incidents since we moved in, and there may have been some during previous Sevens, but no deaths here, no fires. The old library." She paused to look at Fox. "I know you lost someone important to you there, but before Carly's death, there'd been no major incident there. And again, the building itself has never been attacked. There are several other locations, including Fox's family farm and Cal's family home that have proven to be safe zones. Fox, your office building's another. It can get in, but not physically. Only to create its illusions, so nothing it's been able to do in those places is real. Nor, more importantly, I think, have any of those locations been attacked by those infected during the Seven."

"So the questions are why, and how do we use it." Fox scanned the map. "The old library was Ann Hawkins's home, and my family farm was where she stayed and gave birth to her sons. If we go back to energy, it may be that enough of hers remains as a kind of shield."

"There you go." Quinn planted her hands on her hips. "So we dig and find out what connection the safe zones, or even those places that see less violence, have."

"I can tell you that the land the center sits on was the site of the home Ann Hawkins's sister and her husband built." Cal puffed out his cheeks. "I can check the books, and with my grandmother, but what I remember is it was originally a house, then converted to a market. It morphed and evolved over the years until my grandfather opened the original Bowl-a-Rama. But the land was always Hawkins's land."

"I think that's going to be our why," Layla commented. "But we need to remember that the old library was, well, breached, during the last Seven. It could happen to any of these locations this time."

"There wasn't a Hawkins in the library over the last Seven." Gage continued to study the map, the pattern. "Essie'd retired by then, hadn't she?"

"Yeah, she had. She still went in most every day, but . . . It wasn't hers anymore." Cal stepped up to look more closely. "They'd already started building the new library, and approved plans to make the old one a community center. It belonged to the town then. Technically, it had for years, but . . . "

"But emotionally, essentially." Cybil nodded. "It was Essie's. How long has your family owned this house, Cal?"

"I don't know. I'll find out."

"I bought my building from your dad," Fox reminded Cal. "Yeah, that's going to be the why. So how do we use it?"

"Sanctuaries," Layla said.

"Prisons," Gage corrected. "The question will be how do we hold a couple thousand infected people bent on murder and mayhem in a bowling alley, on a farm, and in a law office, to start."

"We can't. I'm not talking about the legal crap," Cal added.

"Hey, if anyone's going to talk about legal crap, it should be me." Fox took a pull from his beer. "And I'm not going to deny trampling over civil liberties isn't a big issue with me during the Seven, but the logistics won't hold."

"How many could we convince to camp out at your farm before they were infected?" Cybil met Fox's eyes as he turned to her. "And yes, I realize what an enormous risk this would be, but if a few hundred people could be talked into going there before the Seven, staying there through it—or until we kill this bastard—then others might be convinced to leave altogether for that period, or hole up in what we'll designate as safe zones, or as close to safe as we can define."

"Some leave anyway," Cal pointed out. "But the majority don't remember, don't get it, not until it's too late."

"It's different this time," Quinn added. "It's been showing itself, showing off. This is all or nothing for both sides. Even if only ten percent of the town moves out or holes up, it's a stand, isn't it?"

"Every step we take toward the positive counts," Cybil agreed.

"But doesn't kill it."

Cybil turned to Gage. "No, but it uses tactics to try to weaken us. We'll counter with those that may weaken it." She gestured toward the board with the Tarot outline. "We all have our strengths, too. Knowing who and what we are is a positive step. We have a weapon in the bloodstone, another positive. We know more, are more, and have more to work with than the three of you did before."

"If we're going to try moving anyone out who's willing, Fox needs to talk to his family. If you want to ditch the idea from the get," Cal continued, "no arguments."

"Yeah, I want to ditch it, but I'm stuck with the old free will, make your own choices song and dance I was raised on. They'll decide for themselves if they want to start a damn refugee camp. Which they will because that's how they're made. Damn."

"I'll need to talk to mine, too." Cal blew out a breath. "First, people in town tend to listen to my father, give what he says some weight. Second, we'll figure if their house or the center should be a secondary camp, or if they should stay out at the farm to help Fox's family. And we're going to need to push, and push hard on finding out how to use the stone. Having a weapon's no damn good if we don't know how to trigger it."

"We've built on the past," Quinn began, "and we have a handle on the now."

"We need to look again." Cybil nodded. "We've started on that, but—"

"We're not going there tonight." Gage's statement came cold and firm. "No point in pushing on that," he said before Cybil could argue. "It's nothing you mess with when you're already worn down. Go back to that positive energy crap you're hyping. I'd say you're running low on that tonight."

"You'd be right. Rude, which is no surprise, but accurate. In fact, I'd probably be better off hunkering down with some research, solo, for tonight. I'll do more digging on the stone because Cal's right, too."

ELEVEN

───◦◦◎◦◦───

She didn't dream, and that surprised her. Cybil had fully expected to be dogged by nightmares, portents, imagery, but instead had slept straight through the night.

Something accomplished, she supposed, as she'd gotten nowhere on the evening research. Hopefully she'd do better today, rested and focused. Rising, she walked over to take a good, hard look at herself in the mirror.

She looked the same, she thought. She was the same. What had happened to her wasn't a turning point in her life. It didn't make her less, and it hadn't broken her down. If anything, the attack had given her more incentive, made her more *involved* and more determined to win.

It may feed on humans, she realized. But it didn't understand them. And that, she supposed, could be another weapon in their arsenal.

Now she wanted a session at the gym to kick her energy level up. Sweating out the toxins, she thought, would be a kind of ritual cleansing. With any luck Quinn would be available for gym buddy. She pulled on a sports bra, bike pants, tossed what she'd need in a small tote. Stepping out, she noted Quinn's bedroom door was open, and the room empty. So, she'd grab a bottle of water out of the kitchen, and catch up with Quinn and Cal at the health club in the basement of the old library.

She strode into the kitchen, pulling up short when she saw Gage at the table with a mug of coffee and a deck of cards.

"You're out early."

"Never left." As she'd done herself, he gave her a long, hard look. "Bunked on the couch."

"Oh." It gave her a quiver in the belly. "You didn't need to do that."

"Do what?" His eyes never left her face, adding another quiver. "Stay, or bunk on the couch?"

She opened the refrigerator, got out the water. "Either. But thanks. I'm going over to the gym. I want some cardio. I assume that's where Quinn is?"

"Noises were made. Why don't you stick with the Gumby routine?"

"It's not what I'm after. Yoga relaxes me. I need to pump."

"Crap."

"What?" she demanded as he rose.

"Cal's got half his gear here. I'll find something. Wait," he ordered and strode out.

If she was going to wait, she wanted coffee, so she picked up Gage's mug and finished his off. He came back wearing a pair of gray sweats that had seen much better days, and a Baltimore Orioles T-shirt. "Let's go," he ordered.

"Am I correct in assuming you're going to the gym with me?"

"Yeah, get it moving."

She opened the fridge, took out a second bottle of water and shoved it in her tote. She doubted he could have done or said anything at that particular moment that would have meant more to her. "I'm not going to argue or tell you I can get to the gym fine by myself. First, because it would be stupid after yesterday. And second, I want to see what you've got."

"You've already seen what I've got."

She laughed, and felt better than she'd have believed possible. "Good point."

She got a solid hour in, and had the bonus of watching Gage work up a nice sweat lifting weights. It was more than the very appealing view, she realized. Watching him gave her just a little more insight into him. He didn't want to be there, particularly, but since he was, he put his time to use. Focused, thorough, patient, she thought. It might have been more the cat-at-the-mousehole kind of patience than the altruistic sort, but the results were the same. He waited.

Looser and energized, she walked back with him. "Where will you go when this is over?" she asked, then moved her shoulders at his quiet look. "That's optimism, which is positive energy. Any particular destination in mind?"

"I've kicked around a couple. Probably Europe, unless there's something happening in the States. I'll come back for the wedding—Jesus, weddings now. You?"

"I'll go back to New York, I think, at least briefly. I miss it, and that's God's truth, so I'll give myself an infusion of crowds and noise and pace. Plus, I'll need to get back to work that pays. But I expect I'll put in considerable time here. The girl part of the weddings will be more demanding than your boy part of them. If I can swing it after Quinn's, I thought a few days on a nice island—palm trees and margaritas, and balmy, tropical nights."

"That's a plan."

"A flexible one, which is my favorite kind." As they turned at the Square, she gestured to the Bowl-a-Rama. "I admire people like that. Cal and his family, who dig in and build and make a genuine mark

on a place. I'm grateful they exist, and glad of the fact that by exist-
ing and digging in and building, they allow me to make flexible
plans and visit lots of those genuine marks someone else has made."

"No burning desire to make a mark?"

"I like to think I do make them, in my own fashion. I find things
out. You need information to write a book, make a movie, rehab a
house, build a shopping center, and I can get that for you. And I can
get you information you didn't realize you needed or wanted. Maybe
all of those projects would have gotten done without me, but I can
promise you they're better with me. That's enough of a mark for me.
How about you?"

"I just like to win. I can settle for having played if the game's
solid, but winning's always better."

"Isn't it just," she agreed.

"But if I leave a mark, it gives the other players too much information, too much they might use if we faced each other over a pile
of chips again. Better to have a blank slate, as much as possible.
They don't know you, it's harder for them to read you."

"Yes." She spoke quietly. "Yes, that's exactly right. And to bring
this into our situation, I had a similar thought this morning. It
doesn't understand us. It can't really know us. It can anticipate some.
What it did to me, what it did to Fox years ago by killing Carly right
in front of him. It knows how to hurt, how to use specific weapons
to harm and to undermine. But it still doesn't get it. It doesn't seem
to comprehend that the opposite side of fear is courage. Every time
it uses our fears, it only pushes us to find more courage. It can't read
us, not accurately."

"Wouldn't flip to a bluff."

"A bluff? What bluff?"

"I don't know yet, but it's worth thinking about, because you've
got a point. I want a shower and my own clothes," he added the
minute they stepped into the house, and headed straight upstairs.

Cybil considered. She heard the voices from the kitchen. Quinn and Cal had left the gym a good twenty minutes before, and were probably finishing up breakfast and talking with Fox and Layla. She could go back, grab some coffee before going up. Or . . .

Since the shower was already running, she stripped in the bedroom before strolling in. Hair dripping, Gage narrowed his eyes when she tugged back the curtain and stepped in with him.

"Mind?"

His gaze skimmed over her, then stayed steady on hers. "There's probably enough water for both of us."

"That's what I thought." Casually, she picked up her tube of gel, squirted a generous amount into her hand. "And twofers are more efficient. Plus." Watching him, she soaped her breasts in slow circles. "I could pay you back for the night spent on the couch, and the stint at the gym."

"I don't see any money on you."

"Barter system." Slick and soapy, she pressed against him. "Unless you'd rather take an IOU."

He plunged his hand into her hair, got a good grip to jerk her face up to his. "Pay up," he demanded, then closed his mouth over hers.

There it was, she thought, outrageously grateful. There was the instant thrill, the response, the need. It had taken nothing from her. His body moved wet and hard against hers, his mouth took from hers, and there was nothing, nothing but pleasure.

"Touch me." She demanded it, using her teeth, her nails. Nothing fragile here, nothing damaged or in need of tending. Touch me, she thought, take me. Make me feel utterly, utterly human.

He'd wanted to give her time, had been prepared to give her room. And perhaps to give both to himself as well. But her need, the challenge and raw edges of it spoke to his own. So he touched, hands sliding over that sleek skin as the steam plumed and the water pounded.

And he took, pressing her back to the wet tiles, keeping his eyes on hers as he thrust into her. What he saw in hers was dark delight. He gripped her hips to anchor her, drove them both to peak.

Winded, she dropped her head to his shoulder. "Just hang on a minute."

"Same goes."

"Okay. All right. Thanks for getting into the spirit so quickly."

"Same goes."

She laughed, stayed where she was. "This might be a good time to say that I didn't like you, particularly, when we first met."

He let his eyes close, let himself steep in her scent. "I'm going to repeat myself again. Same goes."

"My first instincts are generally very accurate. Not this time. I do like you, and not just because you're very talented in bed, and in the shower."

Idly, hardly realizing he did so, he traced the tattoo at the base of her spine with a fingertip. "You're not as annoying as I initially thought."

"Here we are, all wet and naked and sentimental." Sighing now, she eased back to study him through the steam. "I trust you. That's an important issue for me. I can work with someone I don't completely trust, it just makes it a little more of a challenge. I can sleep with someone I don't completely trust, it just means it's going to be a very brief encounter. But the work's more productive, and the sex more satisfying, when I trust."

"You want to shake on that?"

She laughed again. "A superfluous gesture, under the circumstances." She lifted the gel again, turned his hand over and poured some into his palm. And turned. "But you could wash my back."

An hour later, Cybil poured her first full cup of coffee, and had to admit she felt well-buzzed without it. She went upstairs to the office where Quinn and Layla sat at laptops. On the chart, her rape was documented.

Good, Cybil thought. It was good to see it there, straight-out, and know she'd survived it intact. "I'm going to keep the setup in my room this morning," she told them. "But I asked Gage to come back later. It's time we tried another link. I'm hoping one or both of you will hang around, act as an anchor."

"We'll be here," Quinn said.

"Did you know Gage stayed, slept on the couch downstairs?"

"We talked about going back with him, to Cal's." Layla swiveled away from the keyboard. "He said he was staying. The fact is, none of us wanted to leave in case you had a bad night."

"Maybe because none of you left, I didn't have one. Thanks."

"I've got something that might perk you up, too. This house." Quinn spread her hands. "Or the land this house is on—considerably more of it at one time, but this particular plot? Ann Hawkins's grandson Patrick Hawkins, son of Fletcher, owned it. Fox is checking on his building, but I'd say we're well on the way to proving another theory."

"If this is right, and even if Gage's definition of it as prison is more accurate than mine as sanctuary," Layla continued, "it could give us a viable way to protect people. At least some people."

"The more we can protect or at least give a fighting chance to, the more we'll be able to focus on attack." Cybil nodded. "I agree. And we are going to have to attack. It's going to have to be at the Pagan Stone. I know we haven't discussed it, not in detail since the men are resistant, but whatever we do to end it is going to have to be done there. We can't be here, in town, putting out fires, trying to stop people from hurting themselves or each other. We all know when and where we'll take our stand."

"Midnight," Quinn said with a sigh. "As July seventh begins. As this Seven begins, in full. I know you're right. I think we all know it, but it feels like we're deserting the field."

"And it's going to be harder on them, the guys," Layla added. "Because they tried it before, and failed."

"We're not deserting the field. We're taking the game to ours. We won't fail this time, because we can't." Cybil looked back at the chart. "It doesn't know us. It thinks it understands, and part of its understanding is that we're weak, fragile, vulnerable. It's got reason to think that. It comes, and in a very real way, it wins. Every time. Getting stronger, every time."

"Dent took it down," Layla reminded her. "For centuries."

"Dent broke the rules, sacrificed himself. And he was a guardian." Quinn angled her head as she studied Cybil's face. "And still, it was a stopgap, still the burden and some of the power had to be passed on. Diluted, fractured. It took the six of us to reform that power and we still don't know how to use it. But . . ."

"Yes, but. We have it now, and the means to learn. We know the time and the place," Cybil said again. "We're complete with the six of us. Those images I had, of something happening to each of us. I think they were warnings. It has to try to fracture us again, to dilute what we have. We can't and we won't let that happen."

"I'll talk to Cal about ending this at the Pagan Stone. Part of him knows it has to be that way already."

"The same with Fox," Layla said. "I'll talk to him."

"Which leaves me with Gage." Cybil let out a breath.

G age paced Cal's office. "She wants to try the link again. Today."
    "Not that many todays left, son, before the big one. No point wasting any."

"You know what it's like, even pushing that on your own. It's a fucking sucker punch. She had a bad experience yesterday. The worst."

"Are you looking out for her?"

Gage stopped, baffled, annoyed. "No more than I would anybody. Plus, I'm looking out for myself. If she can't handle it—"

"Too late for that, you already put her first. Don't bother bullshitting me. You've got a thing. Why wouldn't you have a thing?"

"The thing is sex," Gage insisted. "And, sure, a mutual dependency given the circumstances. We're in this together, so we look out for each other. That's all I'm doing."

"Uh-huh."

Gage turned back with a stony look that did nothing to break Cal's grin. "Look, it's different for you."

"Sex is different for me?"

"For one thing." Frustrated, Gage jammed his hands in his pockets. "For a lot of things. You're dead-normal guy."

"Don't use the word *dead*, under the circumstances."

Jingling the change in his pocket, Gage worked it out in his head. "You're Bowl-a-Rama boy, Cal. House-in-the-country guy, with the tight family ball, the big, stupid dog—no offense," he added, glancing down at Lump, who snored away with all four feet in the air.

"None taken."

"You're a Hawkins of the Hollow, and always will be. You've got the sexy blonde who's happy to plunk her particularly fine ass down here with you and your big, stupid dog in your house in the country, and raise a brood of kids."

"Sounds about right."

"As for Fox, he's as mired here as you. Hippie kid turned town lawyer with his sprawling and interesting family who snags the pretty brunette who turns out to have a spine of steel—enough of one to open a business in this town because that works for them. Like the house with a garden and a bunch of kids will work for them. The four of you will probably be happy as lunatics."

"That's the plan."

"That's if we live, and you know, I know, we all know some of us might not make it."

"If and might." Cal nodded. "Well, life's a gamble."

"For me, gambling's life. If I get through, it's on to the next. There's no house in the country, no nine-to-five or what's for dinner, honey in me."

"And you figure that's what Cybil's looking for?"

"I don't know what she's looking for. It's not my business to know, that's the *point*." Uneasy, he raked his fingers through his dark hair. Then stopped, annoyed, knowing the gesture was one of his tells. "We're having sex," he continued. "We've got a mutual goal to kill this bastard and live to talk about it. That's it."

"Fine." Obligingly, Cal spread his hands. "Then what are you so worked up about?"

"I . . . Damned if I know," Gage admitted. "Maybe I don't want to be responsible, and linking up that way makes me responsible. They can claim equal shares all they want, but you know how it is, you know how it feels."

"Yeah, I do."

"What happened . . . What it did to her, how am I supposed to get that out of my head, Cal? How am I supposed to put that aside?"

"You can't, you don't. But that doesn't mean we can stop. We all know that, too."

"Maybe she gets to me." He let out a breath. "Okay, she gets to me, no maybe about it. Hardly a surprise, considering." His fingers itched to drag through his hair again, and he kept them firmly at his side. "This is all fucking intense."

"Caring about her doesn't equal house in the country and big, stupid dog, son."

"No." Gage let himself relax. "No, it doesn't. I could spell that out for her. Diplomatically this time."

"Sure, you do that. I'll bring the platter so your head has somewhere to sit after she knocks it off and hands it to you."

"Point," Gage muttered. "So we let it ride, that's all. But when we do the link-up, I want you and Fox there."

"Then we will be."

H e still didn't like it, but Gage was realistic enough to know a lot
of things needed doing he didn't like. He'd offset that by setting the time and place. His ground—and Cal's house was the closest to his ground as any in the Hollow—and late enough in the day
to have his brothers with him.

If anything went wrong, he'd have backup.

"Even considering Crazy Roscoe, I'd rather do this outside." Cybil glanced around the room, then zeroed in on Gage. "The fact is,
we might need to do this later on, and in the open, so we might as
well figure out how to defend ourselves if necessary."

"Fine. Hold on." Gage walked out of the room, returning moments later with his Luger.

"Don't even think about handing that to me," Fox told him.

"So grab a garden tool like last time." Gage turned to Cal.

"Okay. Shit." With considerable care, Cal took the gun.

"Safety's on."

Cybil opened her bag, took out her .22 and handed it to Quinn.
Quinn flipped open the cylinder, examined the chamber, then smoothly
locked it back in place. "Okay," she said while Cal stared at her.

"Well, the things you learn about the love of your life. Maybe
you should take the big one."

"That's okay, cutie, you can handle it."

"Quinn's an excellent shot," Cybil commented. "So, are we ready
for this?"

As they headed out the back, through the kitchen, Fox pulled
two knives from the block on Cal's counter. "Just in case," he said
when he gave one to Layla.

"Just in case."

Clouds were edging in, Gage noted, but for now there was
enough light and the breeze was easy. Like Cybil, he sat on the grass
while their friends circled around them.

"Why don't we try to focus on a specific place?" she suggested.

"Such as?"

"Right here. Cal's house. It's a good starting point. We can work our way out from there. Ease into it this time, and we might lessen the side effects."

"Okay." He took her hands. He looked into her eyes. This place, he thought. This grass, this wood, this glass, this dirt.

He saw it in his mind, the lay of the land, the slopes and rises, the lines of the house. Colors and shapes. As he let it form, the greens of spring, the blooms of it faded, withered, browned. White crept in until snow covered the ground, layered on the branches. It fell still, in fat, fast flakes. He felt them, cold and wet against his skin. In his hands, Cybil's hands chilled.

Smoke spiraled from the chimney, and a cardinal, a bright red splash, winged through the falling snow to land in the bird feeder.

Inside, he thought. Who was inside? Who'd built the fire, filled the feeder? Gripping Cybil's hand, he walked through the walls, into the kitchen. A bowl he recognized as Fox's mother's work sat on the counter holding fruit. Music drifted in, something classical that struck the first uneasy note in him. Cal wasn't the classical type, and he'd never known Quinn to go for it.

Who was listening to the music? Who'd bought the apples, the oranges in the bowl? The thought of strangers in Cal's house pushed him forward, lit a spark of anger in him. Cybil's hands tightened on his, nudged him back. He sensed, almost heard her.

No anger. No fear. Wait and see.

Locking down emotion, he moved with her.

A fire crackled in the hearth. Tulips spilled out of a clear glass vase on the mantel. And on the couch, Quinn slept under a colorful blanket. As he watched, Cal stepped to her, leaned over, and kissed her cheek. Even as the restrained tension eased out of Gage, Quinn stirred.

She smiled as her eyes opened. "Hi."

"Hi, Blondie."

"Sorry. Mozart may be good for the kid, but it puts me to sleep every time."

As she shifted, as the blanket slid down, Gage saw she was hugely pregnant. Her hands crossed over her belly, and Cal's closed over them.

It flicked off, the sounds, the images, the scents, and he was back on the grass staring into Cybil's eyes.

"It's nice to have a positive possibility for a change," she managed.

"Headache?" Quinn asked immediately. "Nausea?"

"Not really. It was easier, smoother. And the vision was a quiet one. I think that makes a difference, too. A happy one. You and Cal, in the house. It was winter, and you were sitting in front of the fire."

She squeezed Gage's hand, shot him a look. He took both as a warning, and shrugged. She didn't want to bring up the bun in the oven, fine.

"I like that better than the last one you had of us," Quinn decided. "So, how'd I look? Any disfiguring scars from demon battles?"

"Actually, you looked fabulous. Both of you did. Let's try again. Not a place this time, but people." Cybil looked up at Fox and Layla. "If that's okay with you?"

"Yeah." Layla reached for Fox's hand. "Okay."

"The same way." Cybil met Gage's eyes, settled her breathing. "Slow."

He brought them into his mind as he had Cal's house, shapes, colors, textures. He envisioned them as they were now, standing hand-in-hand behind him. Again, what was faded into what might be.

The shop, he decided. Layla's future boutique with the counters, the displays, the racks. She sat at a fancy little desk, typing something on a laptop. When the door opened, she glanced up and stood as Fox strolled in.

"Good day?" he asked.

"Good day. September's looking great, and I got more fall stock in this afternoon."

"Then congratulations and happy anniversary." He brought a bouquet of pink roses from behind his back.

"They're gorgeous! Happy anniversary."

"One month since your official grand opening."

She laughed, and as she took the flowers, the diamond on her finger caught the light and sizzled. "Then let's go home and celebrate. I'll have my one glass of wine a week."

"You're on." He put his arms around her. "We made it."

"Yes, we did."

When they came back, Cybil's hands once again squeezed his. "You take this one," she suggested.

"Your shop looks pretty slick, and so did you," he added when Layla let out a shaky breath. "That one looked pretty much like he always did. So considering these are possibilities, you've still got time to dump him."

He looked up at the sky. "We're going to get rained on before much longer."

"We've got time for another," Cybil insisted. "Let's go for the gold. The Pagan Stone."

He'd expected her to want to see herself, specifically, or the two of them. As he'd thought before, she surprised him. "We do this, that's it for tonight."

"Agreed. I've got some ideas for other avenues. Another time. Ready?"

It came too fast. He knew it the moment he opened to it, to her. Not a drift this time, but the sensation of being the pebble flying from the slingshot. The flight flung him straight into the holocaust. It rained blood and fire, each striking the scorched ground of the clearing to flash, to burn. The stone boiled with both.

He saw Cybil, her face pale as wax. Her hand bled, as did his.

His lungs strained as he fought to breathe in the smoke-thickened air. He heard the shouts around him, and braced.

For what? For what? What did he know?

It came from everywhere at once. Out of the dark, the smoke, out of the ground, the air. When he reached for his gun, his hand came up empty. When he reached for Cybil, it struck, knocking her to the ground, where she lay still as death.

He was alone with his own fear and fury. The thing that surrounded him roared in a sound of greedy triumph. Whatever sliced out at him carved a burning gash across his chest. The pain all but swallowed him whole.

Staggering, he tried to drag Cybil away. Her eyes flickered open, latched on to his. "Do it now. You have to do it now. There's no other choice."

He leaped toward the Pagan Stone, fell painfully against it. And he grasped the burning bloodstone atop it in his bare hand. With it closed in his fist, with its flames licking between his clenched fingers, he plunged with it into absolute black.

There was nothing, there was nothing, there was nothing but pain. Then he lay on the Pagan Stone as its fire consumed him.

He clawed his way back, head ringing, nausea a wretched churn in his belly. Swiping blood from his nose, he looked into Cybil's glassy eyes. "So much for slow and easy."

TWELVE

I t didn't take much of a push to convince Cybil to throttle back to research mode for a few days. They'd have to look again, she and Gage, but she couldn't claim to look forward to the experience.

Had she seen Gage's death? Had she felt her own? The question played through her mind over and over. Had it been death, or another kind of end when the black had dropped around her, leaving her blind. Had the screams she'd heard been her own?

She'd seen herself at the Pagan Stone before, and every time she did, death came for her there. Not life, not like Quinn and Layla, she mused, no celebration. Only the blood and the black.

She'd have to go back, she knew. In vision and in reality. Not only to seek answers, but to accept them. When she did, she had to go back strong. But not today. Today was a holiday with red, white, and blue bunting, with marching bands and little girls in sparkling costumes. Today's Memorial Day parade was, in her opinion, a little slice of the Hawkins Hollow pie, and sampling it helped remind her why she would go back.

And the view from the steps of Fox's office building was one of the best in the house.

"I love a parade," Quinn said beside her.

"Main Street, U.S.A. Hard to resist."

"Aw, look, there's some of the Little League guys." Quinn bounced on her toes while the pickup carting kids in the back inched by. "Those are the Blazers, proudly sponsored by the Bowl-a-Rama. Cal's dad coaches, too. They're on a three-game streak."

"You're really into all this. I mean, seriously into small-town mode."

"Who knew?" With a laugh, Quinn snaked an arm around Cybil's waist. "I'm thinking of joining a committee, and I'm going to do a discussion and signing at the bookstore. Cal's mom offered to teach me how to make pie, but I'm dodging that. There are limits."

"You're in love with this place," Cybil observed. "Not just Cal, but the town."

"I am. Writing this book changed my life, I guess. Bringing me here, realizing I was part of the lore I was researching. It brought me to Cal. But the process of writing it—beyond the hard stuff, the ugly stuff we've faced and have to face—it pulled me in, Cyb. The people, the community, the traditions, the pride. It's just exactly what I want. Not your style, I know."

"I've got nothing against it. In fact, I like it very much."

She looked out over the crowds lining the sidewalks, the fathers with kids riding their shoulders, long-legged teenage girls moving in their colorful packs, families and friends hunkered down in their folding chairs at the curbs. The air was ripe with hot dogs and candy, spicy with the heliotrope from the pots Fox had stacked on his steps. Everything was bright and clear—the blue sky, the yellow sun, the patriotic bunting flying over the streets, the red and white petunias spilling out of baskets hanging on every lamppost along Main.

Young girls in their spangles tossed batons, executed cartwheels on their way toward the Square. In the distance she heard the sound of trumpets and drums from an approaching marching band.

Most days she might prefer the pace of New York, the style of Paris, the romance of Florence, but on a sunny Saturday afternoon while May readied to give over to June, Hawkins Hollow was the perfect place to be.

She glanced over when Fox held out a glass. "Sun tea," he told her. "There's beer inside if you'd rather."

"This is great." Looking over his shoulder, she lifted an eyebrow at Gage as she sipped. "Not a parade fan?"

"I've seen my share."

"Here comes the highlight," Cal announced. "The Hawkins Hollow High School Marching Band."

Majorettes and honor guards twirled and tossed silver batons and glossy white rifles. The squad of cheerleaders danced and shook pom-poms. Crowd favorites, Cybil thought as cheers and applause erupted. And with the pair of drum majors high-stepping, the band rocked into "Twist and Shout."

"Bueller?" Cal said from behind her, and Cybil laughed.

"It's perfect, isn't it? Just absolutely."

The sweetness of it made her eyes sting. All those young faces, the bold blue and pure white of the uniforms, the tall hats, the spinning batons all moving, moving to the sheer fun of the music. People on the sidewalk began to dance, to call out the lyrics, and the sun bounced cheerfully over the bright, bright brass of instruments.

Blood gushed out of trumpets to splash over the bold blue and pure white, the fresh young faces, the high hats. It splattered from piccolos, dripped from flutes, rained up from the beat of sticks on drums.

"Oh God," Cybil breathed.

The boy swooped over the street, dropped to it to dance. She wanted to cringe back, to cower away when its awful eyes latched on to hers. But she stood, fighting off the quaking and grateful when Gage's hand dropped firmly onto her shoulder.

Overhead the bunting burst into flame. And the band played to the cheers of the crowd.

"Wait." Fox gripped Layla's hand. "Some of them see it or feel it. Look."

Cybil tore her gaze away from the demon. She saw shock and fear on some of the faces in the crowd, paleness or puzzlement on others. Here and there parents grabbed young children, pushed through the onlookers to drag them away while others only stood clapping hands to the beat.

"Bad boy! Bad boy!" A toddler screamed from her perch on her father's shoulders. And began to cry in harsh, horrible sobs. Batons flamed as they spiraled in the air. The street ran with blood. Some of the band broke ranks and ran.

Beside her, Quinn coolly, efficiently snapped pictures.

Cybil watched the boy, and as she stared, its head turned, turned, turned impossibly on its neck until its eyes met hers again. It grinned madly, baring sharp and glistening teeth.

"I'll save you for last, keep you for a pet. I'll plant my seed in you. When it ripens, when it blooms, I'll cut it from you so it can drink your blood like mother's milk."

Then it leaped, springing high into the air on a plate of fire. Riding it, it shot toward her.

She might have run, she might have stood. She'd never know. Gage yanked her back so violently she fell. Even as she shoved to her feet, he was planted in front of her. She saw the thing burst into a mass of bloody black, and vanish with the horrible echo of a boy's laughter.

Her ears rang with it, and with the brass and drums as the band continued its march up Main Street. When she pushed Gage aside to see, the buntings waved red, white, and blue. The sun bounced cheerfully off the instruments.

Cybil stepped back again. "I think I've had enough of parades for one day."

———

In Fox's office, Quinn used his computer to load and display the photographs. "What we saw doesn't come through." She tapped the screen.

"Because it wasn't real. Not all the way real," Layla said.

"Blurs and smears," Quinn noted. "And this cloudy area on each where the little bastard was. There, but not there."

"There are opposing schools of thought on paranormal photography." Calm now with something tangible to study, Cybil pushed her hair back as she leaned closer to the screen. "Some claim that digital cameras have the advantage, able to record light spectrums not visible to the human eye. Others discount them, as they can pick up refractions and reflections, dust motes and so on that cloud the issue. So a good thirty-five millimeter is recommended. But . . ."

"It's not light, but dark," Quinn finished, following the line. "An infrared lens might do better. I should've gotten my recorder out of my purse," she added, scrolling slowly through the series of photos. "It happened so fast, and I was thinking pictures not sound until . . ."

"We heard what it said," Cybil stated.

"Yeah." Quinn laid a hand over hers. "I'd like to see if and how its voice records."

"Isn't it more to the point that we weren't the only ones to see something?"

Quinn looked up at Gage. "You're right. You're right. Does it mean it's strong enough now to push through to the edges of reality, or that those who saw something, even just felt something, are more sensitive? More connected?"

"Some of both gets my vote." Fox ran a hand up and down Layla's back as they watched the photos scroll. "What Layla said about it not being completely real? That's how it felt to me. And that means it wasn't completely *not* real. I didn't see everyone who reacted, but those I noticed were part of families that've been in the Hollow for generations."

"Exactly," Cal confirmed. "I caught that, too."

"If we're able to move people out, that would be where we'd start," Fox said.

"My dad's talked to a few people, felt some of them out." Cal nodded. "We'll make it work." He glanced at his watch. "We're supposed to be heading over to my parents' pretty soon. Big backyard holiday cookout, remember? If anybody's not up for it, I'll explain."

"We should all go." Straightening, Cybil looked away from the photos. "We should all go, drink beer, eat burgers and potato salad. We've said it before. Living, doing, being normal, especially after something like this, it's saying: Up yours."

"I'm with Cybil on that. I need to run back to the house, file this memory card. Then Cal and I can head over."

"We'll lock up and ride with you." Fox looked at Gage. "Cool?"

"Yeah, we'll follow."

"Why don't you go ahead?" Cybil suggested. "We'll lock up."

"Good enough."

Gage waited until he and Cybil were alone. "What do you need to say you didn't want to say in front of them?"

"Reading people that well must come in handy, professionally. Despite the optimistic possibilities we saw, we've seen the other side of that. There are two things, actually. I realize that the last time out you tried to fight this at the Pagan Stone and it didn't work. People died. But—"

"But we have to finish this at the Pagan Stone," he interrupted. "I know it. There's no way around it. We've seen it enough times, you and I, to understand it. Cal and Fox know it, too. It's harder for them. This is their town, these are their people."

"Yours, too. At the base of it, Gage," she said before he could disagree. "It's where you come from. Whether or not it's where you end up, it's where you started. So it's yours."

"Maybe. What's the second thing?"

"I need to ask you for a favor."

He lifted his eyebrows in question. "What's the favor?"

She smiled a little. "I knew you weren't the type to just say: Name it. If things don't go the way we hope, and if you're sure we wouldn't be able to turn it around—and one more if, if I'm not able to do it myself, which would be my first choice—"

"You're going to stand there and ask me to kill you."

"You do read well. I've seen you do just that in other dreams, other visions. The other side of the coin. I'm telling you, Gage, standing here with clear mind, cool blood, that I'd rather die than live through what that thing just promised me. I need you to know that, understand that, and I'm asking you not to let it take me, what-ever has to be done."

"I won't let it take you. That's all you get, Cybil," he added when she started to speak. "I won't let it take you."

She stared into his eyes—green and direct—until she saw what she needed to see. "Okay. Let's go eat potato salad."

Because he felt he needed a distraction, Gage hunted up a poker game just outside of D.C. The stakes weren't as rich as he might have liked, but the game itself served. So, he could admit, did the temporary distance from Hawkins Hollow and from Cybil. Couldn't escape the first, he thought as he drove back on a soft June morning. But he'd let himself get much too involved with the woman.

It was stepping-back time.

When a woman looked to you to take her life to save her from worse, it was past stepping-back time. Too much responsibility, he thought as he traveled the familiar road. Too intense. Too damn real. And why the hell had he promised he'd take care of her—because that's just what he'd done. Something in the way she'd looked at him, he decided. Steady, calm as she'd asked him to end her life.

She'd meant what she'd said, flat-out meant it. More, she'd trusted him to know she meant it.

Time for a conversation, he decided. Time to make sure they both understood exactly what was on the table, and what wasn't. He didn't want anyone depending on him.

He could ask himself why he hadn't stayed over after the game, used the hotel room he'd booked. Why he hadn't moved on the signals sent by the very appealing redhead who'd given him a good run for his money at the table. All things being equal, he should be enjoying a post-sex room-service breakfast with the redhead right about now. Instead he was, again, heading for the Hollow.

So he wouldn't ask himself why. No point in asking when he didn't want the answer.

He glanced in the rearview at the sound of the sirens, then took a casual glance down at the speedometer. Only about five over the posted limit, he noted, as he wasn't in any hurry. He pulled over to the shoulder. He wasn't surprised that the view in his side mirror showed him Derrick Napper climbing out of the cruiser.

Fucking Napper, who'd hated him, Cal, and Fox since childhood. And had made it his life's work, so it seemed, to cause them trouble. Fox, particularly, Gage mused. But none of the three of them were immune.

Asshole likes to strut, Gage thought, as Napper did just that to cover the distance from the cruiser to Gage's Ferrari. How the hell did they allow such a complete bastard to strap on a weapon and pin on a badge?

Cocking a hip, Napper leaned down, gave Gage a wide, white smile. "Some people think having a fancy machine gives them the right to break the law."

"Some might."

"You were speeding, boy."

"Maybe." Without being asked, Gage offered license and registration.

"What'd this thing set you back?"

"Just write the ticket, Napper."

Napper's eyes narrowed to slits. "You were weaving."

"No," Gage said with the same dead calm, "I wasn't."

"Driving erratically, speeding. You been drinking?"

Gage tapped the to-go cup in its holder. "Coffee."

"I believe I smell alcohol on your breath. We take driving drunk serious around here, fuckhead." He smiled when he said it. "I need you to step out of the car, take a test."

"No."

Napper's hand dropped to the butt of his sidearm. "I said step out of the car, fucker."

Baiting the hook, Gage thought. It was the sort of thing that too often worked on Fox. For himself, he'd just let Deputy Asshole play it out. Slowly, Gage took the keys out of the ignition. He stepped out, clicked the locks, all the while staring into Napper's eyes. "I'm not taking a Breathalyzer, and it's within my rights to refuse."

"I say you stink of alcohol." Napper jammed a finger into Gage's chest. "I say you're a lousy drunk, just like your old man."

"Say anything you want. The opinions of dickheads don't weigh much with me."

Napper shoved Gage back against the car. Though Gage's hands curled into fists, he kept them at his sides. "I say you're drunk." To punctuate it, Napper slammed his hand on Gage's chest. "I say you resisted arrest. I say you assaulted an officer. We'll see how much that weighs when you're behind bars." He shoved Gage again, grinned. "Chicken-shit bastard." He pushed Gage around. "Spread 'em."

Coolly, Gage laid his hands on the roof of the car as Napper frisked him. "You get off on that? Is that part of the perks?" He hissed in a breath, but stayed as he was when Napper rabbit-punched him.

"You shut the fuck up." Wrenching Gage's arms behind his back, Napper cuffed him. "Maybe we'll take a little ride, you and me, before I put you in jail."

"It'll be interesting to hear you explain that, when I call in the six witnesses who drove by while you were rousting me. While you put hands on me while mine were at my sides. License numbers are in my head. I'm good with numbers." He didn't flinch when Napper pushed him violently against the car again. "And look, here comes another one."

The approaching car slowed. Gage recognized it as Joanne Barry's little hybrid. She stopped the car, rolled down the windows, and said, "Oh-oh."

"You just drive on, Ms. Barry. This is police business."

The disgusted look she sent Napper spoke volumes. "So I see. Need a lawyer, Gage?"

"Looks like. Why don't you have Fox meet me at the police station."

"I said you drive *on!*" Once again Napper's hand went to the butt of his weapon. "Or do you want me to arrest you for interfering with an officer?"

"You always were a nasty little prick. I'll call Fox, Gage." She pulled her car to the shoulder, staring at Napper as she took out her cell phone.

On an oath, Napper pushed Gage in the back of the cruiser. Gage saw his eyes latch on to the rearview as he got behind the wheel. And saw the fury in them as Joanne followed the cruiser into town, and all the way to the police station.

Gage's first twinge of fear came when both Joanne and Napper stepped out of their cars at the station, and he himself was locked inside the cruiser. No, no, he thought, witnesses here, too. Napper wouldn't lay a hand on her and if he did . . .

But he saw only a brief exchange of words before Napper unlocked the backseat and hauled him out. Joanne marched straight inside, skirted Dispatch with a "Hey, Carla," for the woman who sat there, then clipped to chief of police Wayne Hawbaker's office. "I need to file a complaint against one of your deputies, Wayne. And you need to come out here, now."

Just look at her, Gage thought. Wasn't she something?

Hawbaker came out, looked from Joanne to Gage to Napper. "What seems to be the trouble?"

"I tagged this *individual* for speeding, reckless driving. I suspected he was driving under the influence. He refused to take a Breathalyzer, resisted, and took a swing at me."

"Bullshit!"

"Joanne," Hawbaker said quietly. "Gage?"

"I'll cop to the speeding. I was about five over the limit. Joanne gave you the rest. It's bullshit."

Hawbaker's steady stare gave nothing away. "You been drinking?"

"I had a beer about ten o'clock last night. That's, what, about twelve hours ago?"

"He was driving erratically. Had an open container in the car."

"I wasn't driving erratically, and the open container was a goddamn go-coffee from Sheetz. Your boy here baited me, manhandled me, rabbit-punched me, cuffed me, and suggested we take a ride before he brought me in."

Red flags of fury rode Napper's cheeks. "He's a lying sack."

"My car's on the side of the road," Gage continued in the same even tone. "Just before Blue Mountain Lane, in front of a two-story redbrick house, white shutters, front garden. White Toyota hatchback in the driveway, Maryland vanity license plate reads Jenny4. Nice-looking brunette was out front gardening and saw it go down. You ought to check it out." He looked back at Napper now, smiled easily. "You're not very observant for a cop."

"That'd be Jenny Mullendore." Hawbaker studied Napper's face. Whatever he saw in it had his jaw tightening. Before he could speak, Fox pushed through the door.

"Quiet," he said, pointing a finger at Gage. "Why is my client in handcuffs?" he demanded.

"Derrick, uncuff him."

"I'm booking him on the aforesaid charges, and—"

"I said uncuff him. We're going to sit down and hash this out now."

Napper whirled on his chief. "You're not standing by me?"

"I want to speak to my client," Fox interrupted. "In private."

"Fox." Hawbaker dragged his hands over his bristly, graying hair. "Give me a minute here. Derrick, did you strike Gage?"

"Hell, no. I had to take him in hand when he resisted."

"Is that what Jenny Mullendore's going to tell me when I ask her?"

Napper's eyes went to furious slits. "I don't know what she's going to tell you. For all I know she's screwing him and she'll say any damn thing."

"You're quite the lover, Gage," Joanne said with a smile. "According to Deputy Napper, I'm screwing you, too."

Fox rounded on Napper, and currently cuffed, Gage could only body-bump him back. "What did you say to my mother?"

"Don't worry." Knowing her son, Joanne stepped forward, took a firm grip on his arm. "I'm filing a complaint. He told me to fuck off when I followed him in, and I followed him in because I saw him shoving Gage, who was already handcuffed. He suggested that I put out for Gage, and half the men in town."

"Jesus Christ, Derrick."

"She's lying."

"Everyone's lying but you." Gage shook his head. "That must be tough. If these cuffs aren't off in the next five seconds, I'm authorizing my attorney to file a civil suit against the deputy, and the Hawkins Hollow police department."

"Uncuff him. Now, Deputy! Carla." Chief Hawbaker turned to the wide-eyed woman at Dispatch. "Get ahold of Jennifer Mullendore."

"Um, actually, Chief, she's on the line. She just called in about, ah, an incident in front of her house."

Fox beamed a smile. "Isn't it nice when private citizens do their public duty? Are you filing charges against my client, Chief?"

This time Hawbaker scrubbed his hands over his face. "I'd appreciate it if you'd give me a few minutes on that. I'm going to take this call in my office. Deputy, come with me. If y'all would just have a seat?"

Fox sat, stretched out his legs. "Just can't stay out of trouble, can you?" he said to Gage.

"Apparently not."

"You either," he said to his mother.

"My boyfriend and I are badasses."

"He crossed the line with this," Fox said quietly. "Hawbaker's good police, he's a good chief, and he's not going to take it, not going to let it ride. If Jenny corroborates your statement, you've got grounds for those civil suits, and Hawbaker knows it. More, he knows he's got a loose cannon on his hands in Napper."

"My girlfriend hadn't come along, he would've done more. He was working himself up to it." Gage leaned over, kissed Joanne's cheek. "Thanks, honey."

"Cut that out or I'm telling my father." Fox leaned closer to Gage. "Was it just Nap the Prick, or was it more?"

"I can't say for certain, but we all know Napper doesn't need demonic help being a violent bastard. Just him, I think. He got worried when I mentioned I had plate numbers for about six cars that went by while he was shoving me around."

Gage glanced toward the closed office door when Napper's voice boomed out. "Fuck you, then. I quit." He burst out a moment later, rage burning in his eyes.

Gage noted his sidearm was missing. "There won't always be a slut around for you bastards to hide behind." He slammed out the front door of the station.

"Did he mean me or Jenny Mullendore was a slut?" Joanne wondered. "Because honestly, I don't see how she has time for slut activities with those two preschoolers of hers. Me, I've got lots of time."

"Okay, Mom." Fox patted her arm, then rose when Hawbaker stepped out of his office.

"I want to apologize to you, Joanne, for the unacceptable behavior of one of my deputies. I'd appreciate it if you'd file that complaint. I'd like to apologize to you, Gage, on behalf of my department for the harassment. Mrs. Mullendore's statement jibed with what you told me. I realize you're within your rights to file a civil action. I will tell you that due to the circumstances, I suspended Deputy Napper, with the intention of conducting a full investigation of this matter. He has elected to resign from the department."

"That works for me." Gage got to his feet.

"Unofficially, I'm going to tell you, all of you—and you can pass this to Cal, because it seems to me Derrick sees you as one. You be careful. You watch your backs. He's . . . volatile. I can have you taken back to your car, Gage, if you want."

"I've got that covered," Fox told Hawbaker. "You watch your back, too. Napper holds grudges."

Gage planned to head straight back to Cal's, grab a shower, some food, maybe some sleep. But impulse pushed him to the rental house. Cybil stood out front, in shorts and a tank that showed off long legs and long arms, and watered the pots and baskets of flowers scattered around the entrance.

She lowered the big, galvanized can, and strolled down to meet him. "I heard you had a busy morning."

"No secrets in the Hollow."

"Oh, a few. Is everything all right now?"

"I'm not in jail and Napper no longer works for the town police."

"Both good news." She angled her head. "How pissed off are you? It's difficult to tell."

"Only mildly at this point. During? I wanted to kick his ass out into the road and stomp on his face. It's hard to resist that kind of pleasure. But . . ."

"A man who controls himself has a better chance of winning."

"Something like that."

"Well, you won this one. Are you coming in, or passing by?"

Step back, go home, Gage told himself. "Any chance of getting a meal around here?"

"There might be. I guess you've earned it."

When she turned, Gage took her arm. "I wasn't going to come here today. I don't know why I did."

"For a meal?"

He pulled her to him, took her lips with a hunger that had nothing to do with food. "No. I don't know what this is, this you and me. I don't know if I like it."

"At least we're in step there, because neither do I."

"If we're alive come mid-July, I'm gone."

"So am I."

"Okay then."

"Okay. No strings on you, no strings on me." But she brushed her hands through his hair and kissed him, warmly, again. "Gage, there are a lot more important things to worry about here than what this you-and-me thing might be."

"I don't lie to women, and I don't like to misdirect them either. That's all."

"So noted. I don't like to be lied to, but I have a habit of picking my own direction. Do you want to come in and have that meal?"

"Yeah. Yeah, I do."

THIRTEEN

————◦◉◦————

He put flowers on his mother's grave, and she reached up, a slim hand spearing through earth and grass, to take them. As Gage stood in the flood of sunlight, in the quiet cemetery with its somber stones, his heart slammed into his throat. Draped in innocent white, she ascended—pretty and pale from the maw of dirt—clutching the bouquet like a bride her wedding roses.

Had they buried her in white? He didn't know.

"You used to bring me dandelions, and the wild buttercups and violets that colored the little hill near our house in the summer."

His throat ached, straining to hold his trembling heart. "I remember."

"Do you?" She sniffed the roses, red as blood against her white dress. "It's hard to know what little boys remember, what little boys forget. We used to take walks in the woods, and in the fields. Do you remember that?"

"Yes."

"There are houses in the fields now, where we used to walk. But we could walk here, for a little while."

Her skirts billowed as she turned, and with his flowers cradled in the crook of her arm, began to walk. "There's so little time left," she said. "I was afraid you wouldn't come back, not after what happened when you were here last." She looked into his eyes. "I couldn't stop it. It's very strong, and getting stronger."

"I know that, too."

"I'm proud of you for staying, for being brave. Whatever happens, I want you to know I'm proud of you. If . . . If you fail, I'll be waiting for you. I don't want you to be afraid."

"It feeds on fear."

She looked at him again. A sleek black hornet crawled out from the delicate petals of a rose, but she looked nowhere but at him. "On many things. It's had an eternity to develop its appetites. If you could stop it . . ."

"We will stop it."

"How? There are only a few weeks left, such a little bit of time. What can you do this time you didn't do before? Except be brave. What do you plan to do?"

"Whatever it takes."

"You're still looking for answers, with time running out." Her smile was soft as she nodded, soft as a second hornet, then a third squirmed, black on red. "You were always a brave and stubborn boy. All those years your father had to punish you."

"Had to?"

"What choice did he have? Don't you remember what you did?"

"What did I do?"

"You killed me, and your sister. Don't you remember? We were walking in the fields, just like this, and you ran. Even when I told you not to, you ran and ran, and fell. You cried so hard, poor little boy." Her smile was full, and somehow luminous, as the roses disgorged hornets. And the hornets began to hum.

"Your knees were all scraped and scratched. So I had to carry you, and the weight of you, the strain of it, was too much for me. You see?"

She spread her arms and the white gown blossomed with blood. Hornets swarmed in buzzing black clouds until even the roses bled. "Only a few days later, the blood and the pain. From you, Gage."

"It's a lie." It was Cybil who spoke, who was suddenly at his side. "You're a lie. Gage, it's not your mother."

"I know."

"She's not so pretty now," it said. "Want to see?"

The white dress thinned to filthy rags over rotted flesh. It laughed and laughed as fat worms writhed through the flesh, as the flesh gave way to bone.

"How about you?" it said to Cybil. "Want to see Daddy?"

The bones re-formed into a man with sightless eyes and a charming grin. "There's my princess! Come give Daddy a kiss!"

"More lies."

"Oh, I can't see! I can't see! I can't see what a worthless shit I am." It laughed uproariously. "I chose death over you." Hornets stabbed out to crawl at the corners of its grin. "Death was better than your constant *need*, your unrelenting, sickening love. Didn't have to think twice before . . ." It mimed shooting a gun with its hand. And the side of its head exploded into a ruin of blood, bone, brain.

"That's the truth, isn't it? Remember, bitch?" Its single blind eye rolled in its socket, then the image burst into flame. "I'm waiting for you, for both of you. You'll burn. They all burn."

He woke with his hand clutching Cybil's, and her eyes staring into his.

"Are you okay?"

She nodded, but stayed as she was when he sat up. Dawn spread milky light into the room as her breath shuddered in and out.

"It wasn't them," she managed. "It wasn't them, and it wasn't the truth."

"No." Because he thought they both needed it, he took her hand again. "How did you do that? Get into my dream?"

"I don't know. I could see you, hear you, but at first I was removed from it—not part of it. It was almost like watching a movie, or a play, but through a film, or a curtain. Like gauze. Then I was in it. I pushed . . ." Dissatisfied, she shook her head. "No, that's not right, not really. It was less deliberate than that, more visceral. More like a flick, the way you'd give a curtain in your way an annoyed flick. I was so angry because I thought you believed what it was saying."

"I didn't. I knew what it was from the start. Bluff me once," Gage murmured.

"You were playing it." Cybil closed her eyes a moment. "You're good."

"It's looking for our hole card, wants to know what we've got. And it told us more than we told it."

"That there's still time." Now, she sat up beside him. "However strong it's getting, however much it might be able to do, it still has to wait for the seventh for the real show."

"Give the lady a cigar. It's about time for our bluff. Time to make the bastard believe we have more than we do."

"And we'd do that by . . . ?"

Gage rose, went to the dresser, opened a drawer. "Bait."

Cybil stared at the bloodstone he held. "That's supposed to be in a safe place, not knocking around in . . . Wait. Let me see it."

Gage tossed it casually in the air, then over to her.

"This isn't our bloodstone."

"No, I picked it up at a rock shop a few days ago. But it fooled you for a minute."

"It's the same basic size, not quite the same shape. It might have power, too, Gage. The research I've done points to bloodstones as part of the Alpha Stone."

"It's not ours. Not the one it's worried about. It might be worthwhile finding out just how worried it is, and what it might do to get its hands on what it thinks is Dent's bloodstone."

"And to see how pissed off it gets when it realizes—if it does—this is a substitute."

"Can't be overstated. It's used our pain against us, our tragedies. Let's return the favor. The bloodstone helped Dent keep that thing under for three centuries. Stopped it in its tracks a good long while and set the stage for what we're doing. That's got to be one of the big losses."

"Okay. How do we con a demon?"

"I've got some ideas."

She had some of her own, but they were down avenues her research had taken her, avenues she didn't want to travel. So she kept her silence, and listened to his.

A couple hours later, Cybil stormed out of Cal's back door with sharp lashes of fury whipping from her. She spun around when Gage slammed out after her. "You've got no right, no *right* to make these plans, to make these decisions on your own."

"The hell I don't. It's my life."

"It's all our lives!" she tossed back. "We're supposed to work as a team. We're meant to work as a team."

"Meant? I'm sick to death of this destiny crap you're so high on. I make my own choices, and I deal with the results. I'm not going to let some ancient guardian make them for me."

"Oh, for God's sake." Everything about her snapped out in angry frustration, voice, hands, eyes. "We all have choices. Aren't we fighting, risking our lives, because Twisse takes away choice? But that doesn't mean any of us can just forget why we were brought together like this and go off on his own."

"I am on my own. Always have been."

"Oh, screw that! You're sick of destiny talk? Fine, *I'm* sick of your 'I'm a loner and I don't belong' refrain. It's boring. We're bound by blood, all of us."

"Is that what you think?" In contrast to her heat, his tone was brittle and cold. "You think I'm bound to you, by anything? Didn't we just cover this a little while ago? We're having sex. That's the beginning and the end of it. If you're looking for more—"

"You conceited ass. I'm talking about life and death and you're worried about me trying to get my hooks in you? Believe me, outside of the bedroom, I wouldn't have you on a bet."

Something flashed in his eyes. It might have been insult or challenge. It might have been hurt. "I'd take that bet, sister. I know your type."

"You don't know—"

"You want it all your way. You figure you're so damn smart you can run the show and everyone in it. Nobody runs me. And when this is over, you think you can keep me on the line or cut me loose, at your whim. You've got the looks, the brains, the style, what man could resist you? Well, you're looking at one."

"Is that so?" she said, her tone frigid. "Is what you were doing in bed with me last night your definition of resisting?"

"No, that's my definition of banging a willing and convenient woman."

Her angry color drained, but she inclined her head, regally. "In that case, you can consider me now unwilling and inconvenient, and do your substandard banging elsewhere."

"Part of the point. I go my way on this because this has all played out long enough for me. This fight, this town, you. All of it."

Her hands curled at her sides. "I don't care how selfish you are, how stupid you are, after this is done. But before it is, you're not going to jeopardize all the work we've done, all the progress we've made."

"Progress, my ass. Since you and your girl pals got here, we've been bogged down in charts, graphs, exploring our emotional thresholds, and other bullshit."

"Before we got here, you and your idiot brothers fumbled around on this for twenty years."

He backed her against the rail. "You haven't lived through a Seven. You think you know? What you've dealt with so far's been nothing. A few chills and spills. Wait until you see some guy disembowel himself, or try to stop some teenage girl from lighting the match after she's poured gas all over herself and her baby brother. Then you talk to me about what I can do, what I can't. You think seeing your old man put a bullet in his ear makes you some kind of expert? That was quick and clean, and you got off easy."

"You son of a bitch."

"Suck it up." His words were a slap, quick and careless. "If Twisse isn't offed before the next Seven, you're going to be dealing with a lot worse than a father who'd rather kill himself than stand up with his family."

She swung out, and there was enough behind the blow to have his head jerking back. With his ears ringing from it, he gripped her arms to ward off a second attack. "Do you want to talk about fathers, Gage? Do you really want to bring up fathers, considering your own?"

Before he could respond, Quinn rushed out. "Hold it, hold it, hold it!"

"Go back inside," Cybil ordered, "this doesn't concern you."

"The hell it doesn't. What the hell's wrong with you? Both of you?"

"Step back, Gage." Cal pushed through the door, with Fox and Layla behind him. "Just step back. Let's go inside and talk this out."

"Back off."

"Okay, okay, that's not the way to win friends and influence people." Fox moved up, put a hand on Gage's arm. "Let's take a breath here and—"

Gage shoved him off, knocked him back a step. "The back off goes for you, too, Peace and Love."

"You want to go a round with me?" Fox challenged.

"Jesus!" Layla fisted her hands in her hair. "Stop! Just because Gage is being an idiot doesn't mean you have to be one."

"Now I'm an idiot?" Fox rounded on Layla. "He shoves Cybil around, tells me to back off, and *I'm* an idiot."

"I didn't say you were an idiot, I said you didn't have to be an idiot. But apparently I'm wrong about that."

"Don't start on me. I didn't get this stupid ball rolling."

"I don't care who got it rolling." Cal held up his hands. "It stops here."

"Who gave you the gold star and put you in charge?" Gage demanded. "You don't tell me what to do. We wouldn't be in this mess in the first place without you and your ridiculous blood brothers ritual with your pussy Boy Scout knife."

It erupted then, the shouts, the accusations, each rolling over the next into an ugly mass of anger, resentment, and hurt. Words struck like fists, and none of them paid attention to the darkening sky or the oncoming rumble of thunder.

"Oh, just stop! Stop it. Shut the hell up!" Cybil pitched her voice over the chaos, silencing it to a ragged and humming silence. "Can't you see he doesn't give a damn what the rest of you think or feel? It's all about him, maybe it always has been. If he wants to go his own way, he'll go. I, for one, am done." She looked dead into Gage's eyes. "I'm done here."

Without a backward glance, she walked back into the house.

"Cyb. Shit." Quinn scalded the men with one long stare. "Nice job. Come on, Layla."

When Quinn and Layla slammed in behind Cybil, Cal swore again. "Who the hell are you to lay all this on me? Not who I thought, that's for damn sure. Maybe Cybil's right. Maybe it's time to be done with you."

"You'd better cool off," Fox managed as Cal left them. "You'd better take some time and cool the hell off unless you really do like being alone."

And alone, Gage let his mind seethe with resentment, let his thoughts travel on the stony road of blame and grievances. They turned on him, all of them, because he had the balls to take a step, because he'd decided to stop sitting around scratching his ass and studying charts. The hell with them. All of them.

He took the bloodstone out of his pocket, studied it. It meant absolutely nothing. None of it. The risks, the effort, the work, the *years*. He'd come back, time after time. He'd bled time after time. And for what?

He laid the stone on the porch rail, stared bitterly out at Cal's blooming backyard. For what? For whom? What had the Hollow ever given him? A dead mother, a drunk for a father. Pitying or suspicious looks by the *good* townspeople. And oh yeah, just recently, it got him handcuffed and shoved around by an asshole the town deemed worthy to wear a badge.

She was done? He sneered, thinking of Cybil. No, *he* was done. Hawkins Hollow and everyone in it could go straight to hell.

He turned, slammed back into the house to get his things.

It oozed out of the woods, a miasma of black. Inside the house, angry voices rang out again, and it seemed to shudder with pleasure. As it flowed over grass, pretty beds of flowers, it began to take shape. Limbs, torso, head writhing into form through the murk. Fingers, feet, eyes glowing unearthly green took shape as it crept closer to the pretty house with its generous deck and cheerful flowers raining out of glossy pots.

Ears and chin, and a grinning mouth that flashed its teeth. The thrill it felt was terrible. It smeared blood over the green of the grass, the bright petals of flowers, because it could.

Soon all would burn, all, and it would dance on the bloody ashes. The boy danced now, in greedy delight, then hopped up to crouch on the rail beside the stone. A small thing, it thought. Such a small thing to have caused so much trouble, so much time.

It cocked its head. What secrets did it hold? What power? And why were those secrets, that power blocked so that in no form could it see? Blocked from them, too, it thought. Yes, yes, the guardian had given them the key, but not the lock.

It wanted to touch the deep green and dark red of it. To steal whatever waited inside. It reached out, drew its hand back. But no, better to destroy. Always better to destroy. And it spread its hands over the stone.

"Yo," Gage said from the doorway, and shot the boy dead center of the forehead.

It screamed, and what poured from the wound was thick and black, and reeked like death. It leaped, even as Gage continued to fire, as the others rushed out of the house with him. Perched on the roof, it snarled like a mad dog.

Wind and rain erupted in a horrific gush. Taking position in the yard, Gage reloaded, prepared to fire again.

"Try not to shoot my house," Cal told him.

It leaped again, and as it slammed its fists into the air, the blood-stone exploded into dozens of fragments, into clouds of dust. The boy screamed, in triumph now, even as the blood ran from it. It spun, then it swooped, snake-fast, to latch its teeth into Gage's shoulder. As Gage dropped helplessly to his knees, it vanished.

Dimly, Gage heard voices, but they were smothered by a drowning fog of pain. He saw the sky, saw it was going blue again, but the faces that leaned over him were blurred and indistinct.

Had it killed him? If so, he wished to Christ death would get a damn move on so the agony would end. It burned, burned, boiling blood, searing bone, and inside his head he screamed. But he had no breath to make a sound, no strength even to writhe in the torment that squeezed, that clawed like flaming talons.

So he closed his eyes.

Enough, he thought. Enough now. Time to go.

So, in surrender, he began to float away from the pain.

The sharp slap to his face irritated him. The second pissed him off. Couldn't he die in relative peace?

"You come back, you son of a bitch! Do you hear me? You come back. You fight, you fucking coward. You are *not* going to die and let that bastard win."

The pain—goddamn it—the pain flooded back. When he opened his eyes in defense, Cybil's face filled his blurry vision, and her voice just kept badgering, hammering. Those dark eyes of hers were drenched with fury and tears.

He wheezed in an agonizing breath. "I wish you'd shut up."

"Cal. Fox."

"We've got him. Come on, Gage." Cal's voice came from some strange distance—miles off, it seemed, and buried in mud. "Focus. Right shoulder. It's your right shoulder. We're with you. Focus on the pain."

"How the fuck am I supposed to do anything else?"

"He's saying something." Fox's face edged into Gage's view. "Can you hear him? He's trying to tell us something."

"I am telling you something, you asshole."

"His pulse is weak. It's getting weaker."

Who was that? Gage wondered. Layla? He saw her words as pale blue lights, drifting at the corner of his eye.

"The bleeding's stopped. It's already stopped. The punctures aren't that deep now. It has to be something else. Some sort of poison."

And Quinn chimed in, Gage thought. Gang's all here. Just let me go, for God's sake. Just let me go.

"We won't. We can't." Cybil leaned closer, but this time her lips rather than her hand laid over his cheek. Blessedly cool. "Please. You have to stay. You have to come back. We can't lose you."

Tears spilled out of her eyes, dropped gently onto the wound. They washed through his blood, into the bite, and eased the burn.

"I know it hurts." She stroked his cheeks, his hair, his screaming shoulder, and wept. "I know it hurts, but you have to stay."

"He moved. His hand moved." Fox's fingers tightened on Gage's as Gage's flexed. "Cal?"

"Yeah. Yeah. Right shoulder, Gage. Start there. We've got you."

He closed his eyes again, but not in surrender this time. Bearing down, he concentrated on the source of the pain, followed it as it spread from his shoulder, down his arm, across his chest. He felt his lungs open again as if the hands that had squeezed them closed now slipped away.

"His pulse is stronger!" Layla called out.

"His color's coming back, too. He's coming back, Cyb," Quinn said.

From where she sat on the ground, cradling his head in her lap, Cybil leaned back down, watched his eyes. "It's almost over," she crooned. "Just a little more."

"Okay. Okay." He saw her clearly now, felt the grass under him, the grip of his friends' hands over his. "I've got it. Did you call me a fucking coward?"

Her breath drew in on a watery laugh. "It worked."

"Welcome back, man," Fox said to him. "The wound's closing. Let's get you inside."

"I got it," Gage repeated, but couldn't so much as lift his head. "Okay, maybe I don't."

"Give him another minute," Quinn suggested. "The wound's closed now, but . . . there's a scar."

"Let's go inside." Cybil sent looks to Quinn and Layla that said more than her words. "We'll make Gage some tea, get his bed ready."

"I don't want tea. I don't want a bed."

"You're getting both." Cybil shifted his head from her lap, patted his cheek, then rose. If she understood men at all—and Gage in particular—he'd prefer the women out of sight when his friends helped him into the house.

"I want coffee," Gage said, but the women were already headed back to the house.

"Bet you do. Quinn's right about the scar," Fox added. "Nothing's ever scarred us since the blood brothers ritual."

"None of us had a demon try to take a bite out of us either," Cal put in. "It's never been able to do anything like that before, not even during the Seven."

"Times change. Give me a hand, will you? Let's just start with sitting up." With his friends on either arm, Gage managed to make it to sitting. Where his head spun for three wicked revolutions. "Jesus." He sat, with his head braced by his updrawn knees. "I've never felt pain like that and I've had plenty of pain. Did I scream?"

"No. You went white, dropped like a stone." Cal swiped sweat off his own face.

"Inside I was screaming like a little girl. Where's my shirt?" he demanded when he lifted his head and realized he was naked to the waist.

"We had to rip it off you, get to the wound," Fox told him. "You didn't move, not a flicker, Gage. You were barely breathing. I swear to God, I thought you were gone."

"I was. Or nearly." Cautiously, Gage turned his head, pressed fingers to the scar on his shoulder. "It doesn't even ache now. I feel pretty weak, a lot shaky, but there's no pain."

"You need to sleep. You know how it goes," Cal added. "It sucks you dry, that intense a healing."

"Yeah, maybe. Get me up, will you?"

With an arm slung around each of his friends, Gage gained his rubbery legs. When half a dozen steps toward the house left him kitten-weak, he accepted he'd need that bed. But there was satisfaction in his belly as he looked at the empty porch rail.

"Bastard blew that rock to hell and back."

"Yeah, he did. Can you make the steps?"

"I can make them." In fact, he was smiling through gritted teeth when Cal and Fox all but carried him into the house.

Since he was too tired to fight off a trio of females, he drank the tea Cybil foisted on him. And he dropped onto the bed with its freshly smoothed sheets and plumped pillows.

"Why doncha lie down with me, sugar?"

"That's sweet, honey."

"Not you." Gage waved off Fox, pointed to Cybil. "Big brown eyes there. Fact, maybe all the pretty women oughta lie down here with me. Plenty of room."

"What the hell did you put in that tea?" Cal demanded.

"Secret ingredient. Go ahead." Cybil sat on the side of the bed. "I'll stay with him until he drops off."

"Come on over here and say that."

Smiling, Cybil waved off the others, then angling her head, studied Gage's face.

"Hello, gorgeous," he mumbled.

"Hello, handsome. You've had a busy morning. Go to sleep."

"Pissed you off."

"Pissed you off back. That was the plan."

"Damn good plan."

"Risky, potentially stupid plan."

He smirked. "Worked."

"You have me there."

"Didn't mean that shit about your father."

"I know. Shh." She bent down, kissed his cheek.

"Maybe meant some of the other shit—can't remember. Did you?"

"We'll talk about it later."

"She said—Ann Hawkins said—you'd cry for me. That it would matter. You did. It did. You brought me back, Cybil."

"I gave you a jumpstart. You did the rest. Gage." Shuddering once, she laid her cheek against his. "I thought you'd die. Nothing's ever scared me like that, or torn at me like that. I thought you'd die. That we'd lose you. That I would. You were dying in my arms, and until that moment, I didn't realize that I—"

She lifted her head, broke off when she saw he'd fallen asleep. "Well." She drew a long breath, then another. "Well, that's probably excellent timing for both of us. No point in humiliating myself or putting you on the spot by telling you, at a weak moment for both of us, that I've been stupid enough to fall in love with you."

Taking his hand, she sat with him a little while longer as he slept. And she wondered if she'd find the way to be smart enough to get over him.

"Do you think you must?"

Slowly, Cybil lifted her gaze from Gage's face, and looked into Ann Hawkins's. "Well, last but not least." It didn't surprise her she was so calm. She'd been waiting for this, and she'd seen much more shocking things now than a ghost by a bedside on a June morning.

"Do you think you must?" Ann repeated.

"Must what?"

"Close your heart to what you feel for him. Deny yourself the joy and the pain of it."

"I'm not a fan of pain."

"But it's life. Only the dead feel nothing."

"What about you?"

Ann's lips curved. "It is not death. My own love told me that. There is more than the dark and the light. So many shades between. I feel yet, because it is not finished. When it is, one thing ends, another begins. You are young, and may have many years in this life, in this body, in this time. Why would you live it with a closed heart?"

"Easy for you to say. Your love was returned. I know what it is to live loving someone who can't or won't love you back, or not enough."

"Your father was consumed by despair. He lost his sight, and couldn't see love."

What's the difference? Cybil thought, but shook her head. "This would be a fascinating conversation over a drink sometime, just us girls, but at the moment we're more into the life-or-death mode around here. You may have noticed."

"You are angry."

"Of course I'm angry. He nearly died today, nearly died in my arms trying to find a way to stop something that was pushed on him, on all of us. He may die yet, any or all of us might. I've seen how it might be."

"You haven't told them all you've learned, all you've seen."

Cybil looked down at Gage again. "No, I haven't."

"You will see more before it is done. Child—"

"I'm not your child."

"No, but neither are you its. Life or death, you say, and so it is. Either the light or the dark will end with the Seven. My love will either be freed, or be damned."

"And mine?" Cybil demanded.

"He will make his choice, and so will you all. I have no one but you, my hope, my faith, my courage. Only today, you used all of those. And he sleeps," Ann murmured, looking down at Gage. "Alive. More than alive, he brought back from death's shadow another answer. Another weapon."

Cybil got to her feet. "What answer? What weapon?"

"You are an educated woman with a strong and seeking mind. Find it. Use it. All is in your hands now. Yours, his, and the others'. And it fears you. His blood, its blood," she said as she began to fade, "our blood, your blood. And theirs."

Standing alone, Cybil again looked down at Gage. "His blood," she said quietly, and hurried out of the room.

FOURTEEN

When Gage woke he didn't just want coffee, he wanted it desperately. He sat up first, testing, and when the room stayed steady, stood. No weakness, no nausea, no dizziness. All good news. And no odd euphoria, he realized as his mind tracked back.

What the hell had she put in that tea?

As much as he craved coffee, he wanted a shower more, so walked into the bathroom and stripped. In the mirror, he studied his shoulder, poked at the puckered crescent marring the skin. It was odd having a scar after all these years, a tangible reminder of those keen, feral teeth tearing into him. He'd broken bones, been stabbed, shot, burned, and not a mark to show for it. But Twisse, in the form of that little bastard, manages to get a quick bite, and it appeared he'd be carrying the scar from it for the rest of his life.

However long that might be.

He showered, dressed, and headed out in search of coffee. He stopped at Cal's home office, where both Layla and Quinn were hunkered at a computer. Both looked up, both gave him the let's-have-a-look-at-you once-over.

"How are you feeling?" Layla asked him.

"I want coffee."

"Back to normal then." Quinn's look brightened into a smile. "Should be some downstairs. Cyb's down there, and you might be able to sweet-talk her into fixing you something to eat if you want it."

"Where's everybody else?"

"They ran into town. Various errands." Quinn glanced down at the computer, and the clock in the bottom corner. "They should be back any minute. Maybe I should call Cal, just have them bring food back. Cyb's burrowed, and might not be sweet-talked into cooking all that easy."

"I want coffee," he repeated, and walked away.

She didn't seem especially burrowed, Gage thought when he saw Cybil at Cal's kitchen counter. She had her laptop, her notebook, a bottle of water, but she sat right out in the open. And whatever she was doing, she stopped when he came in.

"You look better."

"Feel better. Couldn't have felt much worse." He poured the last cup of coffee, wished someone else would make a fresh pot. And so thinking, turned to study her. "How about making fresh coffee since I almost died?"

"Doing ordinary, routine things, such as making fresh coffee, would probably make you appreciate life more."

So much for sweet talk, he decided. Since there was a bag of Fritos on the counter, he dug in. "What was in the tea?"

She only smiled. "About four hours' sleep, apparently. Someone dropped by to see you while you were out."

"Who?"

"Ann Hawkins."

He considered, sipped coffee. "Is that so? Sorry I missed her."

"We had a nice chat while you sawed a few off."

"Cute. What about?"

"Life, love, the pursuit of happiness." She picked up her bottle of water. "Death, demons. You know, the usual."

"More cute. You're on a roll." And on edge, he mused. However well she masked it, he sensed nerves.

"I'm working on something that popped into my head when we talked. We'll go over it when I nail it down a bit more. She loves you."

"Sorry?"

"She loves you. I could see it in the way she looked at you while you were sleeping. And by the expression on your face now, I see that kind of talk is uncomfortable for a big he-man like you. But that's what I saw on her face, heard in her voice. For what it's worth. Now, go find something else to do and somewhere else to do it. I'm working."

Instead, he crossed over, grabbed a fistful of her hair and tugged her head back so he could crush his mouth to hers. The moment flashed, then spun, then held. He felt another hint of dizziness, another taste of euphoria before he released her.

Her eyes opened, slow and sleepy. "What was that about?"

"Just another ordinary, routine thing to help me appreciate life."

She laughed. "You're cute, too. Oh the hell with it," she said, and pulled him against her to hold on, to lay her head on his shoulder where the demon's mark rode. "Scared me. Really, really scared me."

"Me, too. I was going. It didn't seem so bad, all in all." He tipped her head back again. This face, he thought, these eyes. They'd filled his vision, his head. They'd brought him back. "Then I heard you bitching at me. You slugged me, too."

"Slapped, that time. I slugged you before, during our brilliant performance on the deck."

"Yeah. And about that. I don't remember us talking about punching."

"What can I say. I'm a genius at improv. Plus, it seriously and genuinely pissed you off and we needed plenty of anger to sucker the Big Evil Bastard in. Your plan, remember? And you said we'd all have to get rough and real to make it work."

"Yeah." He picked up her hand, studied it. "You've got a decent right jab."

"That may be, but I believe it hurt my hand more than it hurt your face."

He closed her hand into a loose fist, then brought it to his lips. Over her knuckles he saw those gorgeous eyes go wide with shock. "What? I'm not allowed to make a romantic gesture?"

"No. Yes. Yes," she said again. "It was just unexpected."

"I've got a few more, but we made a deal early on." Intrigued by her reaction, he rubbed his thumb over the knuckles he'd just kissed. "No seduction. Maybe you want to close that deal off, consider it old, finished business."

"Ah . . . maybe."

"Well then, why don't we . . ." He trailed off at the sound of the front door opening, slamming. "Continue this later?"

"Why don't we."

Fox strode in first, carting a couple of bags. "Look who's back from the dead. Got food, got stuff, got beer. Couple of twelve-packs in the car. You ought to go out, give Cal a hand bringing the rest in."

"Got coffee?" Gage demanded.

"Two pounds of beans."

"Grind and brew," Gage ordered, and walked out to help Cal.

Cybil looked at Fox, who was already pulling a Coke out of the fridge. "I don't suppose you'd take that and go away, and take the rest of your kind with you for an hour."

"Can't. Perishables." He pulled milk out of one of the grocery bags. "Plus, starving."

"Oh well." Cybil pushed away from the laptop. "I'll help you put those away. Then I guess we'll eat, and talk."

———————

She wasn't required to cook, which Cybil felt she was often cornered into doing. Apparently Cal and Fox had decided it was time for their own backyard barbecue. There were worse ways to spend a June afternoon than watching three good-looking men standing over a smoking grill.

And just look at them, she thought as she and the other women set bowls of deli potato salad, coleslaw, pickles, and condiments on the picnic table. As united over patties as they were over war. Just look at all of us. She paused a moment to do just that. They were about to have a backyard picnic, and in the same backyard hours before, one of them had bled, had suffered. Had nearly died. Now there was music pumping out of Cal's outdoor speakers, burgers sizzling on the grill, and beer frosty in the cooler.

Twisse thought he could beat them, beat *this*? No. Not in a century of Sevens. It would never beat what it could never understand, and constantly underestimated.

"You okay?" Quinn rubbed a hand over Cybil's back.

"Yes." A weight of stress and doubts dropped away. She might have to pick them up again, but for now, it was a beautiful day in June. "Yes, I am."

"Quite a view," Quinn added, nodding toward the men at the grill.

"Camera worthy."

"Excellent idea. Be right back."

"Where's she going?" Layla asked.

"I have no idea. Just as I have no idea why it apparently takes three grown men to cook some hamburgers."

"One to cook, one to kibitz, and one to insult the other two."

"Ah. Another mystery solved." Cybil lifted her brow when Quinn dashed out with her camera.

"Aren't those dogs and burgers done yet?" Quinn called out, and putting the camera on the deck rail, peered through the viewer, adjusted angles. "Hurry up. This is a photo op."

"If you were going to take pictures, you might have given us some warning so we could fix ourselves up," Cybil complained.

"You look great, Miss Fussy. Stand more over there. Cal! Come *on*."

"Just hold your pixels, Blondie."

"Fox, he doesn't need you. Stand over here between Layla and Cyb."

"I can have both?" Strolling over, Fox wrapped arms around each of their waists.

For the next five minutes, Quinn directed, ordered, adjusted until the five of them were arranged to her satisfaction. "Perfect! Set. I'll take a couple by remote." She hurried down, positioned herself between Cal and Gage.

"Food's going to get cold," Cal complained.

"Smile!" She clicked the remote. "Don't move, don't move. I want a backup."

"Starving," Fox sang out, then laughed when Layla dug her fingers into his ribs. "Mom! Layla's picking on me."

"Don't make me come over there," Quinn warned. "On three. One, two, three. Now just *stay* put while I check to make sure I got a good one."

The mutters and complaints apparently held no sway as she hurried up to the deck, bent down to call back the last two shots. "They're great. Go, Team Human!"

"Let's eat," Cal announced.

As they sat, as food was grabbed, conversation rolled, beers were uncapped, Cybil knew one true thing. They called themselves a team, and they were. But they were more than that. They were family.

It was a family who would kill the beast.

So they ate, as the June afternoon slipped into June evening, with the flowers blooming around them, and the lazy dog—sated with handouts—snoring on the soft green grass. At the edges of that soft green grass, the woods stayed silent and still. Cybil nursed a single beer through the lazy meal. When the interlude passed, she wanted her head clear for the discussion that had to follow.

"We got cake," Fox announced.

"What? Cake? What?" Quinn set down her own beer. "I can't eat cake after eating a burger and potato salad. It's against my lifestyle change. It's just not . . . Damn it, what kind of cake?"

"The kind from the bakery with the icing and the little flowers."

"You bastard." She propped her chin on her fist and looked pitifully at Fox. "Why is there cake?"

"It's for Gage."

"You got me a cake?"

"Yeah." Cal sent Gage a sober and serious nod. "We got you a Glad You Didn't Die cake. Betts at the bakery wrote that on it. She was confused, but she wrote it on. She had cherry pie, which was my first choice, but O'Dell said it had to be cake."

"We could've bought both," Fox pointed out.

"Somebody brings cake *and* pie into this house," Quinn said darkly, "somebody *will* die. By my hand."

"Anticipating that," Cal said, "we just went for the cake."

Gage considered a minute. "You guys are idiots. The appropriate Glad You Didn't Die token is a hooker and a bottle of Jack."

"We couldn't find a hooker." Fox shrugged. "Our time was limited."

"You could give him an IOU," Layla suggested.

Gage grinned at her. "All markers cheerfully accepted."

"Meanwhile, I guess we'd better clear this up, clean it up, and take a little time before we indulge in celebratory cake—of which I can have a stingy little sliver," Quinn said.

Cybil rose first. "I've been working on something, and need to explain it. After we clear the decks here, do you all want to have that explanation, and the inevitable ensuing discussion, inside or out here?"

There was another moment of silence before Gage spoke. "It's a nice night."

"Out here then. Well, as the men hunted, gathered, and cooked, I guess the cleanup's on us, ladies."

As the women cleared and carried, Gage walked over to the edge of the woods with his friends and watched Lump sniff, lift his leg, sniff, lift his leg.

"Dog's got wicked bladder control," Fox commented.

"He does that. Good instincts, too. He won't go any farther into the woods than that anymore, not without me. Wonder where the Big Evil Bastard is now," Cal asked.

"The hits it took today?" Fox's smile was fierce. "It'll need some alone time, you bet your ass. Jesus, Gage, I thought you had the bastard. Nailed it right between the eyes, ripped holes all over it. I thought: Fucking A, we're taking it out right here and now. If I hadn't gotten so goddamn smug, it might not have gotten by us and bitten you."

"I didn't die, remember? The cake says so. It's not on you," Gage continued. "Or you," he added to Cal. "Or any of us. It got under our guard and took me down. Temporarily. But it showed us something we didn't know. It's not all illusion anymore, or infection. It can take on corporeal form, or enough of one to do damage now. It's evolved. In the who-did-damage-to-who department today, I'd say we broke even. But in the strategy department? We kicked its ass."

"It was fun, too. Yelling at each other." Fox dipped his hands in his pockets. "Like therapy. I did worry that Layla was going to take a page out of Cybil's playbook and punch me. Man, she really clocked you."

"She hits like a girl."

Fox snorted. "Not from my angle. You had little X's in your eyes for a couple seconds there."

"Bullshit."

"Birdies circling over your head," Cal put in. "I was embarrassed for you and all mankind."

"You want to see some birdies?"

Cal grinned, then sobered. "Cybil was pretty quiet during dinner." He glanced over his shoulder. "I guess we'd better go find out what she's got on her mind."

Cybil switched to sun tea, and noted Gage had gone back to coffee. Though she'd been sorry to cut back on the mood, she'd turned the music off herself. It was time Team Human, as Quinn had called it, got back to business.

"I suppose it wouldn't hurt to do a quick roundup of today's events," she began. "Gage's brainstorm about using a substitute bloodstone and drawing Twisse in with our own negative and violent emotions worked."

"Points for us," Quinn commented.

"Points for us. More points for us because we have to assume that it believes it destroyed the bloodstone. It believes it's destroyed our best weapon against it. Still, our ambush had mixed results. We hurt it. Nothing screams like that unless there's pain. It hurt us. It was able to solidify its form, at least temporarily, but long enough to sink its teeth into Gage. We all saw the wound, and it looked nasty, but hardly life-threatening. And we all know he nearly died from it. We thought venom, poison. Gage, I don't know if you have a sense of what happened to you."

"It burned," he said. "I've been burned, all three of us have. But I've never felt anything like this. Felt like my goddamn bones were cooking. I could feel it spreading, closing me down. I could think, I could feel, but I couldn't move or speak. So yeah, I'd go with venom, some sort of paralytic."

Nodding absently, Cybil scribbled some notes. "There are a number of creatures both in nature and in lore that poison and paralyze their prey. Several species of marine animals and fish, arachnids, reptiles. In lore, the Din, a magical catlike beast, possesses an extra claw that holds paralytic poison. The vampire, and so on."

"We've always known it could infect the mind," Cal put in. "Now we've seen it can poison the body."

"And may have killed humans and guardians just that way," Cybil agreed. "Everything in our research, everything we've learned tells us that this demon left the last guardian for dead, but the guardian lived long enough to pass the power and the burden to a human boy. So it's very possible the guardian was poisoned, its injuries more severe and the poison more concentrated and powerful than in Gage's bite today. It's talked about devouring us, consuming us, eating us. Those may not be colorful euphemisms."

Quinn winced. "May I just say: Eewwww."

"I'll second that eewwww and add an Oh God," Layla said.

"The missing," Cybil continued. "In our documented and anecdotal evidence, there are always people missing after the demon sweeps through. We've assumed they've gone off insane, or died, killed each other—and that's very likely true for some, maybe even most. But there were likely others who it used for . . ."

"Munchies," Fox added.

"Somehow this discussion isn't making me feel more optimistic and cheerful."

"Sorry." Cybil offered Cal a smile. "I'm hoping to change that. Ann Hawkins finally decided to pay me a visit, in Gage's room while he was sleeping. I've given you the highlights of our conversation—the pep talk, we'll say. But not all the highlights, because I wanted to check some things out first. She said Gage was alive, more than alive. That he'd brought something back. Another weapon."

"I was a little out of it, but I'm pretty sure I came back empty-handed."

"Not in your hands," Cybil told him. "Its blood, our blood, their blood. And now, Gage, your blood."

"What about my blood?"

"Oh! Oh well, *shit*!" Quinn's grin spread.

"Hardly a wonder we've been friends so long." Cybil nodded at her. "You survived," she said to Gage. "Your body fought off the poison, the infection. Antibodies, immunoglobulins."

Layla raised a hand. "Sorry, science isn't my strong suit."

"Antibodies are produced by the immune system, in response to an antigen—bacteria, toxins, viruses. Basically, we've got hundreds of thousands of blood cells capable of producing a single type of antibody, and its job would be to bind with the invading antigen, and that triggers a signal for the body to manufacture more of the antibody. It neutralizes the effect of the toxin."

"Gage's blood kicked the poison's ass," Fox said. "He's got an advantage on that, like me and Cal. Our healing gifts."

"Yes. It helped him survive, and because he survived, his blood produced the antibodies that destroyed the toxin, and his blood now contains the basis for immunity. It bit you before," Cybil reminded Gage. "At the cemetery."

"I didn't have a reaction to that like I did today."

"It barely nipped you, and on the hand. Did it burn?"

"Yeah, some. Yeah, a lot, but—"

"Did you feel any nausea or dizziness?"

He started to deny it, then considered. "Maybe a little. Maybe it took longer than I expected to heal."

"You've survived two bites—one minor, and one serious—and closer to the heart. It's speculative," she hurried on, "it's not a hundred percent. But antibodies can recognize and neutralize toxins. It's a leap of faith from the science to taking what Ann said to me as what I'm suggesting now. But we don't have the time, the means, or the ability to test Gage's blood, analyze it. We don't have a sample of the poison."

"I don't think anyone's going to volunteer to get one," Fox added.

"You could be immune," Cybil said to Gage. "The way some people are to certain venoms after being bitten, or diseases after recovery from them. And your blood may be a kind of antivenom."

"You're not suggesting you send some of my blood off to the lab and have it made into a serum."

"No, first because serology is complicated and again, we don't have the means or the know-how. But this isn't just about science. It's also about parascience. It's about magicks."

Cybil laid her hands on her notebook as the moon made its slow rise through the trees. "You and Cal and Fox mixed your blood twenty-one years ago and opened the door for Twisse, as we believe Dent planned all along. The six of us mixed blood, ritualistically, and fused the three sections of the bloodstone you were given into one."

"You're banking that another blood ritual, mixing mine with all of yours, will transfer this immunity—if I have it—to the rest of you."

"Yes. Yes, I do."

"Then let's do it."

Just like that, she thought, relieved. Just like that. "I'd like to do a little more research on the ritual itself—when, how, where it should be performed."

"Don't hedge your bets, sugar. It happened here, so it should be here. It happened today, so it should be today."

Layla spoke before Cybil could. "I agree with Gage and not just because of the *eewwww, oh God*. Though that's a factor. Twisse is hurt, but it won't stay that way. We don't know how long we have before it comes back. If you think this is a defense, then let's put up the shield now."

"Cyb, you researched blood rituals inside and out before our last trip to the Pagan Stone. You know we can do this." Quinn looked around the table. "We know we can do it."

"We need words, and—"

"I'll handle it." Quinn pushed to her feet. "Writing under pressure is one of my best things. Set it up, and give me five," she added before she walked into the house.

"Well." Cybil blew out a breath. "I guess it's here and now."

She scouted through Cal's gardens for specific flowers and herbs, and continued to snip when Gage crossed the lawn to her. They stood in the wash of moonlight.

"Making a bouquet?"

"Candles, herbs, flowers, words, movements." She moved a shoulder. "Maybe they're trappings, maybe they're largely symbolic, but I believe in symbols. They're a sign of respect, if nothing else. Anytime you shed blood, anytime you ask a higher power for a favor, it should be with respect."

"You're a smart woman, Cybil."

"I am."

He took her arm, held it until she'd turned to face him. "If this works, it's because you were smart enough to put it together."

"If it doesn't?"

"It won't be because of the lack of brainpower."

"Are you seducing me by flattering my mind?"

"No." He smiled, trailed a finger over her cheek. "I'll seduce you by clouding your mind. I'm telling you this is going to work."

"Optimism? From you?"

"You're not the only one who's looked into rites and rituals. I've spent a lot of the time I'm away from here looking into those areas. Some of it's show. But some? It's faith and respect, and it's truth. It's going to work because between the six of us, we cover those bases. It's going to work because it's not just my blood, not just antibodies and science. Your tears are in me now. I felt them. So whatever I brought back, part of it's you. Get your symbols, and let's do this thing."

She stood where she was when he walked away, stood in the moonlight with flowers in her hands, and closed her eyes. Close her heart? she thought. Get over him? No, no, not if she lived a dozen lifetimes.

It was life, Ann Hawkins had told her. The joy and the pain. It was time to accept she'd have to feel both.

They lighted the candles, and sprinkled the flowers and herbs over the ground where Gage had fallen. Over them, in the center of the circle they formed, Quinn laid the photograph she'd taken of them. All six of them linked—hands or arms—with the big dog leaning adoringly against Cal's leg.

"Nice touch," Cybil commented, and Quinn smiled.

"I thought so. I kept the words simple. Pass it around," she suggested.

Cybil took the page first, and read. "You do good work." She passed it to Gage, and so the words went from hand to hand. "Everybody got it?"

Gage took Cal's Boy Scout knife, skimmed the blade across his palm. Cal took the knife, mirrored the gesture. As with the words, the knife passed from hand to hand.

And they spoke together as hands clasped, and blood mixed.

"Brother to brother, brother to sister, lover to lover. Life to life for the then, for the now, for the to be. Through faith, through hope, in truth. With blood and tears to shield light from black. Brother to brother, brother to sister, lover to lover."

Though there was no wind, the candle flames swayed and rose higher. Cal crouched. "Friend to friend," he said, and taking Lump's paw, scored a shallow cut. Lump stared, dark eyes full of trust as Cal closed his hand over the cut. "Sorry, pal." He straightened, shrugged. "I couldn't leave him out."

"He's part of the team." Quinn bent, picked up the photograph. "I don't feel any different, but I believe it worked."

"So do I." Layla crouched to gather up the flowers and herbs. "I'm going to put these in water. It just . . . seems like the right thing to do."

"It's been a good day." Fox took Layla's hand, brushed his lips over her palm. "I've got one thing to say. Who wants cake?"

FIFTEEN

—◦◦◦—

Because it was a quiet place where the three of them could meet in private, Gage and Fox joined Cal in his office in the bowling center. Time was ticking by. Gage could all but feel the days draining away. None of them had seen Twisse, in any form, since the day Gage had shot it. But there had been signs.

The increase in animal attacks, or the bloated bodies of animals on the sides of the road. Unexplained power outages and electrical fires. Tempers grew shorter, it seemed, every day. Accidents increased.

And the dreams became a nightly plague.

"My grandmother and cousin are moving into my parents' place today," Cal told them. "Somebody threw a rock through Gran's next-door-neighbor's window yesterday. I'm trying to convince them all to move out to the farm, Fox. Safety in numbers. The fact is, the way things are, we'll need to get those who're willing out there soon. I know it's earlier than we thought, I know it's a lot, but—"

"They're ready. My mom and dad, my brother and his family, my sister and her guy." Fox rubbed the back of his neck. "I had a fight with Sage over the phone last night," he added, speaking of his older sister. "She started talking about making plans to come back, to help. She's staying in Seattle—pissed at me, but she's staying. I used the fact that Paula's pregnant as leverage there."

"That's good. Enough of your family's involved in this. My two sisters are staying where they are, too. People are heading out of town every day. A couple here, a couple there."

"I stopped by the flower shop yesterday," Fox told them. "Amy told me she's closing up the end of the week, taking a couple weeks' vacation up in Maine. I've had three clients cancel appointments for next week. I'm thinking I might just close the office until after this is done."

"Find out if there's anything your family needs out at the farm. Supplies, tents. I don't know."

"I'm going to head out there later, give them a hand with some of it."

"You need help?" Gage asked.

"No, we've got it covered. I might be late heading back to Cal's if that's where we'll all bunk tonight. One of you could make sure Layla's not on her own, and gets there."

"No problem. Anybody getting any sleep?" Cal asked them, and Gage merely laughed. "Yeah. Me, too." Cal nudged the bloodstone over the desk. "I took this out of the safe when I got here this morning. I thought maybe if I just sit here, stare at the damn thing, something will come."

"We've got so much going." Fox pushed to his feet to pace. "I can feel it. Can't you feel it? We're right on the edge of it, but we just can't push over. It seems like it's all there, all the pieces of it. Except that one." He picked up the stone. "Except this one. We've got it, but we don't know how the hell to use it."

"Maybe what we need is a howitzer instead of a hunk of rock."

With a half smile, Fox turned to Gage. "I'm at the point a howitzer doesn't sound so bad. But this is what'll do the bastard. The women are spending nearly every waking hour—which is most of the time these days—trying to find the answer to this hunk of rock. But . . ."

"We can't see past that edge," Cal put in.

"Cybil and I have tried the link-up, but it's either a really crappy vision, or nothing. That interference, that static the bastard can jam things with. It's working overtime on blocking us."

"Yeah, and Quinn's working overtime to find a way around the block. This paranormal stuff's her deal," Cal said with a shrug. "Until then, we keep doing what we can do to protect ourselves, protect the town, and figure out how to use the weapons we have."

"If we can't take it down . . ." Gage began.

Fox rolled his eyes. "Here goes our Pollyanna with a penis."

"If we can't take it down," Gage repeated, "if we know it's going south, is there a way to get the women clear? To get them out? I know you've both thought the same."

Fox slumped back into a chair. "Yeah."

"I've gone around with it," Cal admitted. "Even if we could convince them, which I don't see happening, I don't see how they'd get out, not if we have to take this stand at the Pagan Stone."

"I don't like it." Fox's jaw tightened. "But that's where it has to be. The middle of Hawkins Wood, in the dark. I wish I didn't know in my gut that it has to be there, that they have to go in there with us. But I do know it. So we can't let it go south, that's all."

I t had been easier, Gage admitted, when it had just been the three of them. He loved his friends, and part of him would die if either of them did. But they'd been in it together since day one. Since minute one, he corrected, as he started downstairs.

It had been easier, too, when the women had first gotten involved. Before any of them really mattered to him. Easier before he'd seen the way Quinn meshed with Cal, or the way Fox lit up when Layla was in the room.

Easier before he'd let himself have feelings for Cybil, because, goddamn it, he had feelings. Messy, irritating, impossible feelings for Cybil. The kind of feelings that pushed him into having thoughts. Messy, irritating, impossible thoughts.

He didn't want a relationship. He sure as hell didn't want a long-term relationship. And by God, he didn't want a long-term relationship that involved plans and promises. He wanted to come and go as he pleased, and that's just what he did. Except for every seventh year. And so far, so good.

You didn't mess with a streak.

So the feelings and the thoughts would just have to find another sucker to . . . infect, he decided.

"Gage."

He stopped, saw his father at the base of the steps. Perfect, Gage thought, just one more thing to give a shine to his day.

"I know I said I wouldn't get in your way when you came in to see Cal. And I won't."

"You're standing in it now."

Bill stepped back, rubbed his hands on the thighs of his work pants. "I just wanted to ask you—I didn't want to get in the way, so I wanted to ask you . . ."

"What?"

"Jim Hawkins tells me some of the towners are going to camp out at the O'Dell farm. I thought it might be I could help them out. Haul people and supplies out and such, do runs back and forth when needs be."

In Gage's memory his father had spent every Seven skunk drunk upstairs in the apartment. "That'd be up to Brian and Joanne."

"Yeah. Okay."

"Why?" Gage demanded as Bill backed away. "Why don't you just get out?"

"It's my town, too. I never did anything to help before. I never paid much mind to it, or to what you were doing about it. But I knew. Nobody could get drunk enough not to know."

"They could use help out at the farm."

"Okay then. Gage." Bill winced, rubbed his hands over his face. "I should tell you, I've been having dreams. Last few nights, I've been having them. It's like I wake up, but I'm asleep, but it's like I wake up 'cause I hear your ma out in the kitchen. She's right there, it's so real. She's at the stove cooking dinner. Pork chops, mashed potatoes, and those little peas I always liked, the way she made them. And she . . ."

"Keep going."

"She talks to me, smiles over. She had some smile, my Cathy. She says: Hey there, Bill, supper's almost ready. I go on over, like I always did, put my arms around her while her hands are busy at the stove and kiss her neck till she laughs and wiggles away. I can smell her, in the dream, and I can taste . . ."

He yanked out his bandanna, mopped his eyes. "She tells me, like she always did, to cut that out now, unless I want my supper burned. Then, she says why don't you have a drink, Bill? Why don't you have a nice drink before supper? And there's a bottle on the counter there, and she pours the whiskey into the glass, holds it out to me. She never did that, your ma never did that in her life. And she never looked at me the way she does in the dreams. With her eyes hard and mean. I gotta sit down here a minute."

Bill lowered to the steps, wiped at the sweat that pearled on his forehead. "I wake up, covered in sweat, and I can smell the whiskey she held out to me. Not Cathy, not anymore, just the whiskey. Last night, when I woke up from it, I went on out in the kitchen to get something cold 'cause my throat was so dry. There was a bottle on the counter. It was right there. I swear to Christ, it was there. I didn't buy a bottle." His hands shook now, and fresh sweat popped out above his top lip. "I started to pick it up, to pour it down the sink. I pray to God I was going to pour it down the sink, but there was nothing there. I think I'm going crazy. I know I'll go crazy if I pick up a bottle again and do anything but pour it down the sink."

"You're not going crazy." Another kind of torture, Gage thought. The bastard didn't miss a trick. "Have you ever had dreams like this before?"

"Maybe, a few times over the years. It's hard to say because I wasn't picking up bottles to pour them down the sink back then." Bill sighed now. "But maybe a few times, around this time of year. Around the time Jim says you boys call the Seven."

"It fucks with us. It's fucking with you. Go on out to the farm, give them a hand out there."

"I can do that." Bill pushed back to his feet. "Whatever it is, it's got no right using your ma that way."

"No, it doesn't."

When Bill started to walk away, Gage cursed under his breath. "Wait. I can't forget, and I don't know if I can ever forgive. But I know you loved her. I know that's the truth, so I'm sorry you lost her."

Something came into Bill's eyes, something Gage reluctantly recognized as gratitude.

"You lost her, too. I never let myself think that, not all those years. You lost her, too, and me with her. I'll carry that the rest of my life. But I won't drink today."

Gage went straight to the rental house. He walked in, and right up the stairs. As he reached the top, Quinn stepped out of her bedroom draped in a towel.

"Oh. Well. Hi, Gage."

"Where's Cybil?"

Quinn hitched the towel a little higher. "Probably in the shower or getting dressed. We hit the gym. I was just going to . . . never mind."

He studied her face. Her cheeks seemed a little flushed, her eyes a little overbright. "Something wrong?"

"Wrong? No. Everything's good. Great. Thumbs-up. I, ah, better get dressed."

"Pack, too."

"What?"

"Pack up what you need," he told her as she stood frowning and dripping. "Seeing as you're three women, it's going to take more than one trip. Cal and Fox can come by at some point and haul more. There's no point in the three of you staying here—and by the way, do any of you ever *think* about locking the door? It's getting dangerous in town. Everyone can bunk at Cal's until this is over."

"You're making that decision for everyone involved?" Cybil asked from behind him.

He turned. She was dressed and leaning against the jamb. "Yeah."

"That's fairly presumptuous, to put it mildly. But I happen to agree with you." She looked over at Quinn. "It's just not practical to have three bases—here, Cal's, Fox's—anymore. We'd be better to consolidate. Even assuming this house is a cold spot, and safe, we're too spread out."

"Who's arguing?" Quinn adjusted her towel again. "Layla's at the boutique with Fox's dad, but Cyb and I can put some of her things together."

Cybil continued to look at Quinn. "It might be helpful if you went by there now, Gage, let her know. It's going to take a little time for us to pack up the research equipment anyway. Then you could borrow Cal's truck, and we could take the first load."

He knew when he was getting the brush-off. Cybil wanted him gone, for now. "Get it together then. And once we're at Cal's, you and I have to try the link-up again."

"Yes, we do."

"I'll be back in twenty, so get a move on."

Cybil ignored him. She stood in her doorway and Quinn in hers, watching each other until they heard the front door close behind him.

"What's up, Q?"

"I'm pregnant. Holy shit, Cyb, I'm pregnant." Tears flooded her eyes even as she moved her feet and hips into what could only be interpreted as a happy dance. "I'm knocked up, I'm on the nest, I am with child and have a bun in the oven. Holy shit."

Cybil crossed the hallway, held out her arms. They stood holding each other. "I didn't expect to be expecting. I mean, we weren't trying for it. All this going on, and planning the wedding. After, we both figured."

"How far along?"

"That's just it." Drawing back, Quinn used the towel to dry her face, then turned naked to dig out clothes. "I'm not even late, but the last few days, I've just felt sort of . . . different. And I had this feeling. I thought, *ppfftt*, no, but I couldn't shake the feeling. So I bought a—okay five—I bought five early response pregnancy tests because I went a little crazy. At the pharmacy in the next town," she said, laughing now, "because, you know—small towns."

"Yes, I know."

"I only took three—came down from crazy to obsessed. I just took them. Three of them. Pink, plus sign, and the no-frills pregnant all came up. I'm probably only a couple of weeks in, if that, but . . ." She looked down at her belly. "Wow, somebody's in there."

"You haven't told Cal."

"I didn't want to say before I knew. He'll be happy, but he'll be worried, too." She pulled on capris. "Worried because of what's coming, what we have to do, and I'm, well, in the family way."

"How do you feel, about that part of it?"

"Scared, protective. And I know nothing will ever be right for us, any of us, or for this baby if we don't end it. If we don't follow through, and I'm part of that follow-through. I guess I have to believe that this—" Quinn laid a hand on her belly. "This is a sign of hope."

"I love you, Q."

"Oh God, Cyb." Once more, Quinn went into Cybil's arms. "I'm so glad you were here. I know Cal should've been the first I told, but—"

"He'll understand. He has brothers." Gently, Cybil smoothed Quinn's damp hair back. "We're going to get through this, Q, and you and Cal? You're going to be amazing parents."

"We are. Both counts." Quinn let out a breath. "Whew. You know, maybe I'll go all hormonal on the Big Evil Bastard. That might do it."

Cybil laughed. "It just might."

When Gage returned, they loaded Cal's truck. "I'm going to need my car," Quinn said, "so I'll toss some stuff in there, and I'll pick up Layla. I need to go see Cal first." She glanced at Cybil. "So I might be a while."

"Take your time. We'll unpack this load, get things organized. Well . . . See you later." Quinn gave Cybil a hard squeeze then puzzled Gage by giving him the same. "Bye."

Gage got in the truck, started the engine. Then sat, drumming his fingers on the wheel while it ran. "What's up with Quinn?"

"Quinn's fine."

"She seems a little nervy."

"We're all a little nervy, which is why I agree with you about all of us staying at the same place now."

"Not that kind of nervy." He turned in his seat, met her eyes. "Is she pregnant?"

"Well, aren't you the insightful one? Yes, she is, and I'm only confirming that because she's going to tell Cal right now."

He sat, rubbed his hands over his face. "Christ."

"You can look at it as the glass is half empty, as you obviously are. Or that it's half full. Personally, I see the glass as overflowing. This is good, strong, positive news, Gage."

"Maybe for normal people under normal circumstances. But try to look at this from Cal's angle. Would you want the woman you love, who's carrying your child, risking her life, the life of the kid? Or would you wish her a hundred miles away from this?"

"I'd wish her a thousand miles away. Do you think I can't understand how he'll feel? I love her, enormously. But I know she can't be a thousand miles away. So I'm going to look at this, as Quinn is, as a sign of hope. We knew this was coming—or the possibility of this, Gage. We saw it. We saw her and Cal together, alive and together, with Quinn pregnant. I'm going to believe that's what will be. I have to."

"We also saw her killed."

"Please don't." Cybil closed her eyes as her belly twisted. "I know we have to prepare for the worst, but please don't. Not today."

He pulled away from the curb, let her have silence for the next several minutes. "Fox is going to close his office in a couple days anyway. If Layla wants to keep on with the rehab—"

"She will. It's another positive."

"He can go back and forth with her, work with his father some. Between them, Cal and his father, we'll have eyes and ears on the town. There's no reason for Quinn—or you for that matter—to go back into the Hollow until this is over."

"Maybe not." A reasonable compromise, she mused. Surprise.

"My old man's been having dreams," Gage said, and told her.

"Feeding on fears, pain, weaknesses." Cybil closed her hand over his a moment. "It's good that he told you. That's another positive, Gage, however you feel about him. You can feel it in town now, can't you? It's like raw nerves on the air."

"It'll get worse. People coming into the Hollow for business or whatever else will suddenly change their minds. Others who planned to drive through on their way to somewhere else will decide to take a detour. Some of the locals will pack up and go away for a couple weeks. Some of those who stay will hunker down like people do to ride out a hurricane."

He scanned the roads as he drove, braced for any sign. A black dog, a boy. "People who decide they want out after July seventh, well, they won't be able to find their way out of town. They'll drive around in circles, scared, confused. If they try to call for help, mostly the calls won't go through."

He turned onto Cal's lane. "There's a burning in the air, even before the fires start. Once they do, nobody's safe."

"They will be this time. Some will be safe out at Fox's family's farm. And when we end it, the air won't burn, Gage. And the fires will go out."

He shoved open the door of the truck, then looked back at her. "We'll get this stuff inside. Then—" He grabbed her hand, jerked her back as she opened her own door. "Stay in the truck."

"What? What is it? Oh my God."

She followed his direction and saw what slithered and writhed over Cal's front deck.

"Copperheads," Gage told her. "Maybe a dozen or so."

"Poisonous. And that many? Yes, the truck's an excellent place to be." She drew her .22 out of her purse, but shook her head. "I don't suppose we can shoot them from here, especially with this."

He reached under the seat, took out his Luger. "This would do the job, but not from here. And shit, Cal will burn my ass if I put bullet holes in his house. I've got a better idea. Stay in the truck. I get bit, it'll piss me off. You get bit, you'll be out of commission—at the least."

"Good point. What's the better idea?"

"First, trade." He handed her the Luger, took the pistol. "Any other surprises, use it."

She tested the weight and feel of the gun in her hand as he stepped out of the truck. Since she had no choice but to trust him, she watched the snakes, and tried to remember what she knew about this specific species.

Poisonous, yes, but the bite was rarely fatal. Still, a few dozen bites might prove to be. They preferred rocky hillsides, and weren't especially aggressive. Of course, they weren't usually driven mad by a demon either.

These would attack. She had no doubt of that.

On cue, several of the snakes lifted their triangular heads as Gage came around the house with a shovel.

A shovel? Cybil thought. The man had a gun but decided to use a damn shovel against a nest of crazed snakes. She started to lower the window, call out her opinion of his strategy, but he was striding up the steps, and straight into the slithering nest.

It was ugly. She'd always considered herself in possession of a strong stomach, but it rolled now as he smashed and beat and sliced. She couldn't count the number of times they struck at him, and knew despite his healing gift there was pain as fang pierced flesh.

When it was over, she swallowed hard and got out of the truck. He looked down at her, his face glistening with sweat. "That's it. I'll clean this up and bury them."

"I'll give you a hand."

"I've got it. You look a little green."

She passed a hand over her brow. "I'm embarrassed to admit I feel a little green. That was . . . Are you okay?"

"Got me a few times, but that's no big."

"Thank God we got here before Layla. I can help. I'll get another shovel."

"Cybil. I could really use some coffee."

She struggled a moment, then accepted the out he offered. "All right."

She didn't suppose there was any shame in averting her eyes from the mess of it as she went into the house. Why look if she didn't have to? In the kitchen she drank cold water, splashed a little on her face until her system re-settled. When the coffee was brewed, she carried it out to him where he dug a hole just inside the edge of the woods.

"This is turning into a kind of twisted pet cemetery," she commented. "Crazy Roscoe, and now a battalion of snakes. Take a break. I can dig. Really."

He traded her the shovel for the coffee. "More of a practical joke."

"What?"

"This. Not a big show. More of an elbow in the ribs."

"I'm still laughing. But yes, I see what you mean. You're right. Just a casual little psych-out."

"Snakes come out during the Seven. People find them in their houses, the basement, closets. Even in their cars if they're stupid enough not to close the windows when they park. Rats, too."

"Lovely. Yes, I've got the notes." The summer heat and exertion dewed her skin. "Is this deep enough?"

"Yeah, it'll do. Go on back in the house."

She glanced toward the two drywall compound buckets, and thought about what he'd had to put inside them. "I'm going to see worse than this. No pandering to the delicate female."

"Your choice."

When he dumped the contents in—and her gorge rose—she could only think she hoped she didn't see much worse. "I'll wash these out." She picked up the empty buckets. "And clean off the deck while you finish here."

"Cybil," he said as she walked away. "Delicate's not how I think of you."

Strong, he thought as he dumped the first shovelful of dirt. Steady. The kind of woman a man could trust to stick, through better or worse.

When he'd finished, he walked around the house, and stopped short when he saw her on her hands and knees, scrubbing the deck. "Okay, here's another way I haven't thought of you."

She blew hair out of her eyes, looked over. "As?"

"A woman with a scrub brush in her hand."

"While I may prefer to pay someone else to do it, I've scrubbed floors before. Though I can say this is the first time I've ever scrubbed off snake guts. It's not a pleasant, housewifely task."

He climbed up, leaned on the rail out of range of the soap and water. "What would be a pleasant, housewifely task?"

"Cooking a pretty meal when the mood strikes, arranging flowers, setting an artistic table. I'm running out, that's the short list." With sweat sliding down her back, she sat back on her heels. "Oh, and making reservations."

"For dinner?"

"For anything." Rising, she started to lift the bucket, but he put his hand over hers. "I need to dump this out, then hose this off."

"I'll take care of it."

With a smile, she tipped her head. "A not-altogether-unpleasant manly task?"

"You could say."

"Then have at it. I'll clean up and we can start unloading the truck."

They worked quickly, and in tandem. That was another thing, he thought. He couldn't remember ever working in tandem with a woman. He couldn't think of a single sane reason cleaning up with her after dealing with the mangled bodies of snakes should start up those messy thoughts and feelings.

"What do you want when this is over?" he asked as he washed up at the sink.

"What do I want when this is over?" She repeated it thoughtfully as she poured him another cup of coffee. "About twelve hours' sleep in a wonderful bed with 450 thread count sheets, followed by a pitcher of mimosas along with breakfast in bed."

"All good choices, but I meant what do you want?"

"Ah, the more philosophical and encompassing want." She poured grapefruit juice and ginger ale over ice, rattled it, then took a long drink. "A break initially. From the work, the stress, this town—not that I have anything against it. Just a celebratory break from all of it. Then I want to come back and help Quinn and Layla plan their weddings, and now help Q plan for her baby. I want to see Hawkins Hollow again. I want the satisfaction of seeing it when there's no threat hanging over it, and knowing I had a part in that. I want to go back to New York for a while, then back to work, wherever that takes me. I want to see you again. Does that surprise you?"

Everything about her surprised him, he realized. "I was thinking we might catch that twelve hours' sleep and breakfast in bed together. Somewhere that's not here."

"Is that an offer?"

"It sounds like it."

"I'll take it."

"Just like that?"

"Life's short or it's long, Gage. Who the hell knows. So, yes, just like that."

He reached out, touched her cheek. "Where do you want to go?"

"Surprise me." She lifted her hand to cover his.

"What if I said—" He broke off when they heard the front door open. "Never mind," he said. "I'll surprise you."

SIXTEEN

ayla came into the dining room, which was currently in the process of morphing into their main research area. Laptops, stacks of files, charts, maps covered the table. The dry-erase board stood wedged in a corner, and Cal crouched on the floor hooking up a printer.

"Fox says he grabbed dinner at the farm, and we should probably start without him—Gage and Cybil should start without him, that is. He might be a couple hours yet. I didn't tell him the news." She beamed at Quinn. "I had to saw my tongue off a couple times, but I thought you and Cal would want to tell him in person about the baby."

"I think I still need somebody to tell me again, a few times."

"How about if I just call you Daddy?" Quinn suggested.

He let out the breathless laugh of a man caught between the thrill and the terror. "Wow." Then shifted to where Quinn sorted the files. "Wow." When he took Quinn's hand, and the two of them just stared at each other, Layla eased out of the room.

"They're basking," she told Gage and Cybil in the kitchen.

"They're entitled." Cybil closed a cupboard door, put her hands on her hips, and did a survey of the room. "I think this'll have to do. All the perishables from our place are stowed, and we'll have to live with the spill-over in dry goods."

"I'll get what makes sense out of Fox's apartment tomorrow," Layla said. "Is there anything else I can do?"

"Flip for the guest room." Gage took a quarter out of his pocket. "Loser takes the pullout in the office."

"Oh." Layla frowned at the coin. "I want to be gracious and say you're already in there, but I've slept on that pullout. Heads. No . . . tails."

"Pick one, sweetheart."

She fisted her hands on either side of her head, wiggled her hips, squeezed her eyes tight. Gage had seen people invent stranger rituals for luck.

"Tails."

Gage flipped it, snagged it, slapped it on the back of his hand. "Should've gone with your first instinct."

She sighed over the eagle. "Oh well. Fox is going to be a while, so . . ."

"We'll try the link as soon as the dining room's set up." Cybil glanced out the window. "I guess we stick inside. It's starting to rain."

"Plus, snakes. Well, enough basking for them." Layla walked back in the dining room to help organize.

You're taking a lot on." Fox stood by his father on the back porch of the farmhouse, staring out through the steady, soaking rain.

"I was at Woodstock, kid of mine. We'll be fine."

In the distant field a handful of tents stood already pitched. He and his father, along with his brother, Ridge, and Bill Turner, had put together a wooden platform, hung a canopy over it on poles to serve as a kind of cook tent.

That wasn't so weird, Fox thought, but the line of bright blue Porta Potties along the back edge of the field? That was a strange sight.

His parents would take it in stride, Fox knew. That's what they did.

"Bill's going to hook up a few shower areas," Brian went on, adjusting the bill of his ball cap as he stood in his old work boots and ancient Levi's. "He's a handy guy."

"Yeah."

"They'll be pretty rude and crude, but it'll serve for a week or two, and supplement the schedule your mom and Sparrow are going to make up for people to use the house."

"Don't just let people have the run of the place." Fox looked into his father's calm eyes. "Come on, Dad, I *know* you guys. Not everybody's honest and trustworthy."

"You mean there are dishonest people in the world who aren't in politics?" Brian lifted his eyebrows high. "Next thing you're going to tell me there's no Easter Bunny."

"Just lock up at night for a change. Just for now."

Brian made a noncommittal sound. "Jim expects some people to start heading over within the next couple of days."

Fox surrendered. His parents would do what they would do. "Could he give you any idea how many?"

"A couple hundred. People listen to Jim. More if he can manage it."

"I'll help as much as I can."

"You don't worry about that. We'll take care of this. You do what you have to do, and goddamn it, you take care of yourself. You're the only oldest son I've got."

"That's true." He turned, gave Brian a hug. "I'll see you later."

He jogged out to his truck, through the soft summer rain. Hot shower, dry clothes, beer, he thought. In that order. Better, maybe he could talk Layla into the shower with him. He started the truck, backed around his brother's pickup to head out to the road.

He hoped Gage and Cybil had some luck, or were having some if they were into the link-up. Things had started to . . . pulse, he decided. He could feel it. The town had taken on shadows, he thought, that had nothing to do with summer rain or wet, gloomy nights. Just a couple more answers, he thought. Just a couple more pieces of the puzzle. That's all they needed.

He caught the flash of headlights, well behind him, in his rearview mirror, and made the next turn. His windshield wipers swished, and Stone Sour rocked out of the radio. Tapping his hands on the wheel, thinking of that hot shower, he drove another mile before his engine clicked and coughed.

"Oh, come on! Didn't I just give you a tune-up?" Even as he spoke, the truck shuddered, slowed. Annoyed, he eased to the side of the road, coasting when the engine simply died on him like a sick dog.

"The rain just makes it perfect, doesn't it?" He started to get out, considered. As his tawny eyes shifted to his rearview mirror, he pulled out his phone. And cursed when he saw the No Service display. "Yeah, yeah, can you hear me now?"

The road behind him was dark and fogged with rain when he closed his fingers on the handle of the door.

In the living room, Gage and Cybil sat on the floor, facing each other. And facing each other, reached out to clasp hands. "I think we should try focusing on the three of you," she said to Gage, "and the bloodstone. It came to the three of you. So we could start there. The three of you, then the stone."

"Worth a shot. Ready?"

She nodded, leveled her breathing as he did. He came first to her mind. The man, the potential. She focused on what she saw in him as much as his face, his eyes, his hands. And moved on to Cal, putting him shoulder-to-shoulder with Gage inside her head. The physical Cal, and what she considered the spiritual Cal, before pulling Fox into her head.

Brothers, she thought. Blood brothers. Men who stood for each other, believed in each other, loved each other.

The drumming of the rain increased. It all but roared in her ears. A dark road, the splatting rain. A swath of lights turning the wet pavement to black glass. Two men stood in the rain on the black glass of the pavement. For a flash, she saw Fox's face clearly, just as she saw the gun glistening as it pointed at him.

Then she was falling, cut loose so that her breath gasped in and out, so that she fumbled for a moment for the support that wrenched away. She heard Gage's voice dimly.

"It's Fox. He's in trouble. Let's go."

Dizzy, Cybil pushed to her knees as Layla rushed toward Gage, grabbed his arm. "Where? What's happening? I'm coming with you."

"No, you're not. Let's move!"

"He's right. Let them go. Let them go now." Flailing out with a hand, Cybil gripped Layla's. "I don't know how much time there is."

"I can find him. I can find him." Clutching Cybil's hand, and now Quinn's, Layla pushed everything she had toward Fox. Her eyes darkened, went glassy green. "He's close. Only a couple of miles . . . He's pushing back, pushing toward us. The first bend, the first bend on White Rock Road, heading here from the farm. Hurry. Hurry. It's Napper. He's got a gun."

Fox hunched against the rain and lifted the hood of the truck. He knew how to build things. Ask him to make a table, stud out a wall, no problem. Engines? Not so much. Basic stuff, sure—change the oil, jump the battery, go wild and replace a fan belt.

As he stood in the rain with headlights approaching, the basic stuff, and his own gift, was all he needed to assess the situation. Getting out of it in one piece? That might not be as simple.

He could run, he supposed. But it just wasn't in him. Fox shifted, angled his body, and watched Derrick Napper swagger toward him through the rain.

"Got trouble, don't you?"

"Looks like." Fox didn't see the gun Napper held in the hand he kept down at his side so much as he sensed it. "How much sugar did it take?"

"Not as stupid as you look." Now Napper raised the gun. "We're going to take a little walk back into the woods here, O'Dell. We're going to have a talk about you getting me fired."

Fox didn't look at the gun but kept his gaze level on Napper's. "I got you fired? I thought you pulled that one off all by yourself."

"You don't have your slut of a mother, or your two faggot friends around to protect you now, do you? Now you're going to find out what happens to people who fuck with me, like you've been fucking with me my whole life."

"You really see it that way?" Fox spoke almost conversationally. He changed his stance slightly, planting his feet. "I was fucking with you every time you jumped me on the playground when we were kids? When you ambushed me in the parking lot of the bank? Funny how that works. But I guess you could loosely define it as me fucking with you every time you tried to kick my ass and failed."

"You're going to wish I only beat down on you by the time I'm done."

"Put the gun down and walk away, Napper. I'd say I don't want to hurt you, but what's the point in lying? Put it down and walk away while you can."

"While *I* can?" Napper pressed the gun to Fox's chest and pushed him back a step. "You really are stupid. You're going to hurt me, is that what you think?" His voice rose to a shout. "Who's got the gun, asshole?"

Watching Napper's eyes, Fox swung up the baseball bat he'd held behind his back. He felt it crack against bone, just as he felt the vicious punch of the bullet in his arm. The gun skittered off into the wet dark. "Nobody. Asshole." Fox swung again for insurance, this time plowing the bat into Napper's belly. And holding it like a batter preparing to swing for the fences, he looked down at the man sprawled at his feet. "Pretty sure I broke your arm. I bet that hurts."

He glanced up briefly as another set of headlights cut through the rain. "I told you to walk away." Crouching, he jerked Napper's head up by the hair, stared into the pasty white face. "Was it worth it?" Fox demanded. "Jesus, was it ever worth it?"

He let Napper go, rose to wait for his friends.

They came out of Gage's car fast—like bullets, Fox thought, since bullets were on his mind. "Thanks for coming. One of you needs to call Hawbaker. I can't get cell service right here."

Cal scanned the situation, heaved out a breath. "I'll take care of it." Pulling out his cell phone, he walked a few yards down the road.

"You're bleeding," Gage commented.

"Yeah. The gun went off when I broke his arm. The bullet went right through the meat. Hurts like a mother." He stared down at Napper, who sat wheezing on the wet pavement. "His arm's going to hurt a lot longer. Don't touch that," he added as Gage bent to pick up the gun. "Let's not screw up the evidence by getting your fingerprints on his weapon."

Fox yanked out his bandanna, offered it. "Wrap it up in this, will you? And for God's sake be careful with it."

"Walk on down with Cal."

Gage's flat, frigid tone had Fox's head jerking back up, and his eyes met Gage's. He shook his head. "No. No reason for that, Gage."

"He shot you. And you know damn well he meant to kill you."

"He meant to. He wanted to. You know, I've been carrying this bat around in the truck ever since you and Cybil had that preview of me lying on the side of the road. I'm a lucky guy." He laid a hand on his arm, grimaced at the smear of red he took away. "Mostly. We're going to do this straight, according to the law."

"He doesn't give a damn about the law."

"We're not like him."

Cal walked back to them. "The chief's on his way. I called the house, too. Layla knows you're okay."

"Thanks." Fox cradled his injured arm. "So, did either of you catch any of the game? O's in New York?"

They stood in the rain, waiting for the cops, and talked baseball.

Layla streaked out of the house, launching herself at Fox as he levered himself out of the car he, Cal, and Gage had squeezed into. As Cybil and Quinn stood on the porch, Gage walked up. "He's fine."

"But what happened? What—You're all soaked." Quinn drew in a breath. "Let's get inside so you all can get into dry clothes. We'll suck it up until you are."

"All but this one thing," Cybil interrupted. "Where is he? Where is that son of a bitch?"

"In police custody." With his arm snug around Layla, Fox climbed the steps to the deck. "Getting his broken arm treated and being booked on a nice variety of charges. Christ, I want a beer."

A short time later, dry, a beer in hand, Fox filled them in. "At first I was just irritated, started to get out of the truck, pop the hood. Then I remembered what Gage and Cybil had seen, which is why I had my trusty Louisville Slugger under the seat."

"Thank God," Layla breathed, then turned her head to press her lips to his healed arm.

"I had nearly a full tank, and I'd had the truck tuned up a couple weeks ago, so I focused on the engine."

"You know zero about engines," Gage pointed out.

Fox shot up his middle finger. "Sugar in the gas tank. Engine'll run for a couple miles or so, then it coughs up and dies. Now my truck's DOA."

"That's urban myth." Cal gestured with his own beer. "It sounds like the sugar got through, clogged your fuel filter or your injectors, and that's what stopped your engine. You just need your mechanic to change the filters a few times, and drop the tank, clean it out. Cost you a couple hundred."

"Really? That's it? But I thought—"

"You're questioning MacGyver?" Gage asked him.

"Lost my head for a minute. Anyway, I got the sabotage, and it wasn't a stretch to who. I just angled myself with the bat behind me when Napper showed up."

"With a gun," Layla added.

Fox squeezed her hand. "Bullets bounce off me. Almost. And we think of it this way. Napper's going to be behind bars and out of our hair. I was prepared because of Gage and Cybil, so instead of lying by the side of the road, I'm sitting here. It's all good."

"Positive," Cybil said. "A positive outcome, and one more in the plus column for us. That's important. Over and above the fact our Fox is sitting here, he was able to turn a potentially negative outcome into a positive one. Destiny has more than one road."

"I'm real happy to be off the road for the moment. In other news . . ." Fox told them about the progress at the farm. He grinned over at Quinn when she yawned. "Boring you?"

"No. Sorry. I guess it's part of the baby thing."

"What baby thing?"

"Oh God, we didn't tell you. With all the bullets bouncing off you and Porta Potties, we forgot. I'm pregnant."

"What? Seriously? I'm busy getting shot and digging latrines, and the next thing I know we're having a baby." He pushed out of the chair to cross over and kiss her, then punched Cal in the shoulder. "Take the woman to bed. Obviously you know how."

"He does, but I can get myself there. And I think I will." Rising, Quinn laid her hands on Fox's cheeks. "Welcome home."

"I'll be right up." Cal got to his feet. "We could all use some sleep. We didn't get very far with the link, being rudely interrupted. Tomorrow?"

"Tomorrow," Gage agreed.

"I think I'll go up, too." Cybil stepped over to Fox, kissed him. "Nice work, cutie."

She heard Quinn's laugh as she passed Cal's bedroom door, and smiled. Talk about positive energy, she thought. Q had always had it in abundance. Now it would likely be pouring off her like light. And light was just what they needed.

She was a little tired herself, Cybil admitted. She supposed they all were, with the bombarding dreams and restless nights. Maybe she'd try a little yoga, or a warm bath, something to soothe her system into relaxation.

Gage came up behind her, and as she started to glance back, he took her hips, turned her. He moved her back against the door to close it, held her there.

"Well, hello."

His hands moved from her hips to her wrists, then drew her arms over her head. The system she'd thought to relax went on high alert. Braced for, anticipating the demand she saw in his eyes, she could only sigh when his mouth descended to hers. Then could only tremble when instead of demand there was tenderness.

Soft, quiet, the kiss soothed even as it aroused. While his hands held hers prisoner, adding an excited kick to her heartbeat, his mouth took its time exploring and exploiting hers. She sank into the pleasure of it, with a purr in her throat when he cuffed her wrists with one hand and stroked her body with the other.

The light, almost delicate touch stirred desire in her belly, weakened her knees. And all the while his lips slid and skimmed against hers. He flipped open the button at her waistband, danced his fingers under her skirt, closed his teeth lightly, very lightly over her jaw.

She imagined herself pouring into his hands like cream.

Then he hooked his hand in the neck of her shirt, and tore it down the center.

He saw the shock in her eyes, heard it in her quick gasp. Once again, his fingers played lightly over her skin. "Seduction shouldn't be predictable. You think you know." His mouth took hers again in a long, drugging kiss. "But you don't. You won't."

His hand tightened on her wrists, a kind of warning while the kiss shimmered like silk. He felt her melt into it, degree by degree, that lovely body yielding, those lovely limbs going limp. So he shot his hand between her legs and drove her to a fast, almost brutal peak and muffled her shocked cries with his mouth.

"I want you in ways you can't imagine."

Her breath shuddered out; her eyes stayed on his. "Yes, I can."

And he smiled. "Let's find out."

He whipped her around so she was forced to brace her hands against the door, then fist them there as he did things to her body, to her mind, things that pushed her past desperation into surrender, then ripped her back again. Then he slowed, and once again he soothed, and he lifted her into his arms. At the bed she would have turned into him, curled into him in absolute bliss, but he pinned her beneath him.

"Not quite finished."

"Oh God." She shuddered when he lowered his head to flick his tongue over her nipple. "Do we have a crash cart?"

His lips curved against her breast. "I'll bring you back." And he took her hungrily into his mouth.

She shivered under him, and she gave. She yielded under him, and she surrendered. Her body lifted, held trembling before it fell again. And always, always, he knew she was with him, bound with him, need fused to need. She was strength and beauty, beyond any he'd thought to possess, and she was with him.

When he was inside her again, hard against soft, he knew her blood pounded as his did. Knew when she said his name, they were lost. Lost together.

She floated, what else could she do but float on the warm lake of pleasure? No stress, no fatigue, no fears for tomorrow. Exhaustion was bliss, she thought. Gliding on it, she opened her eyes, and found him watching her.

She had enough energy to smile. "If you're even thinking about going again, you must've suffered brain damage the last round."

"It was a knockout." How could he explain what happened inside him when they came together? He didn't have the words. Instead, he lowered his head to touch his lips to hers. "I thought you were asleep."

"Better than asleep. In the lovely, lovely between."

He took her hand, and she saw what was in his eyes. "Oh. But—"

"When better?" he asked her. "What's more relaxing than sex? What releases more positive energy, if it's done right? And, sweetheart, we did it right. But we both have to want to try it."

She let herself breathe. He was right. Linking now when they couldn't be any closer in mind and body might break through the block that had frustrated them the last several attempts.

"All right." She shifted so they lay on the bed face-to-face, heart-to-heart. "The same way we were going to try it earlier. Focusing on you, Cal, Fox, then the stone."

Her eyes. He could see himself in them. Feel himself in them. He let himself sink, then drew himself out until he stood in the clearing with the Pagan Stone. Alone.

He thought the air smelled of her—secret, seductive. The sunlight glowed gold; the trees massed with thick green. Cal moved to his side, fully formed, his gray eyes quiet, serious. And an ax held in his hands. Fox flanked him, face fierce. He held a glistening scythe.

For a moment they stood, only the three, facing the stone atop the stone.

Then hell came.

The dark, the wind, the blood-soaked rain attacked like animals. Fire roared in bellowing walls and sheathed the stones like blazing skin. He knew, in that instant, the war they'd believed they'd fought for twenty-one years had been only skirmishes, only feints and retreats.

This was war.

Soaked with sweat and blood, the women fought with them. Blades and fists and bullets whipping through a sea of screams. The iced air choked with smoke as they fell, fought back. Something sliced across his chest like claws, ripping flesh, spilling more blood. His blood stained the ground, and sizzled.

Midnight. He heard himself think it. Nearly midnight. And smearing his hands over the wound, he reached for Cybil. With tears glistening in her eyes, she gripped his hand, reached for Cal.

In turn, one by one, they joined until their hands, their blood, their minds, their will joined as well. Until the six were one. The ground split, the fire ripped its way closer. And the mass of black took form. Once again, he looked into Cybil's eyes, and taking what he found there, he broke the chain.

Reaching into the flames, he pulled the burning stone out with his bare hand. Closing it into his fist, he leaped, alone, into the black.

Into the belly of the beast.

"Stop, stop, stop." Cybil knelt beside him on the bed, beating her hands on his chest. "Come back, come back. Oh God, Gage, come back."

Could he? Could anyone come back from that? That cold, that burn, that pain, that terror? When he opened his eyes, it rolled through him, all of it, to center like a swarm of wasps in his head.

"Your nose is bleeding," he managed.

She made a sound, something between a sob and a curse before she slid off the bed, stumbled to the bath. She came back with a cloth for each of them, pressed her own against her bone-white face. "Where . . . Where's that spot?" He fumbled for the acupressure points on her hand, her neck.

"Doesn't matter."

"It does if your head feels like mine. Might be sick." He laid still, closed his eyes. "Really hate being sick. Let's just take a minute."

Shaking, shaking, she lay beside him, wrapped close. "I thought . . . I didn't think you were breathing. What did you see?"

"That it's going to be worse than anything we've come up against, anything we imagined we would. You saw it. I felt you right there with me."

"I saw you die. Did you see that?"

The bitterness in her tone surprised him enough for him to risk sitting up. "No. I took the stone, I've seen that before. The blood, the fire, the stone. I took it, and I went right into the bastard. Then . . ." He couldn't describe what he'd seen, what he'd felt. He didn't want to. "That's it. You were punching me and telling me to come back."

"I saw you die," she repeated. "You went into it, and you were gone. Everything went mad. Everything was mad, but it got worse. And the thing, form after form after form, twisting, screaming, burning. I don't know how long. Then, the light was blinding. I couldn't see. Light and heat and sound. Then silence. It was gone, and you were lying on the ground, covered with blood. Dead."

"What do you mean it was gone?"

"Did you *hear* what I said. You were dead. Not dying, not unconscious or floating in some damn limbo. When we got to you, you were dead."

"We? All of you?"

"Yes, yes, yes." She covered her face with her hands.

"Stop it." He yanked them back down. "Did we kill it?"

Her tearful eyes met his. "We killed you."

"Bullshit. Did we destroy it, Cybil? Did taking the bloodstone into it destroy it?"

"I can't be sure—" But when he gripped her shoulders, she closed her eyes, dug for strength. "Yes. There was nothing left of it. You took it back to hell."

The light on his face burned like the fires that waited there. "Now we know how it's done."

"You can't be serious. It *killed* you."

"We saw Fox dead on the side of the road. Right now he's on the lumpy pullout sleeping like a baby or banging Layla. Potential, remember. It's one of your favorites."

"None of us are going to let you do this."

"None of you makes decisions for me."

"Why does it have to be you?"

"It's a gamble." He shrugged. "It's what I do. Relax, sugar." He gave her arm an absent stroke. "We've made it this far. We'll hash it out some yet, look at the angles, options. Let's get some sleep."

"Gage."

"We'll sleep on it, kick it around tomorrow."

But as he lay in the dark, knowing she lay wakeful beside him, Gage had already made up his mind.

SEVENTEEN

He told them in the morning, and told them straight-out. Then he drank his coffee while the arguments and the alternatives swarmed around him. If it had been any of them proposing to jump into the mouth of hell without a parachute, Gage thought, he'd be doing the same. But it wasn't any of them, and there was a good reason for that.

"We'll draw straws." Fox stood scowling, hands jammed in his pockets. "The three of us. Short straw goes."

"Excuse me." Quinn jabbed a finger at him. "There are six of us here. We'll *all* draw straws."

"Six and a fraction." Cal shook his head. "You're pregnant, and you're not playing short straw with the baby."

"If the baby's father can play, so can its mother."

"The father isn't currently gestating," Cal shot back.

"Before we start talking about stupid straws, we need to *think*." At her wit's end, Cybil whirled around from her blind stare out of the kitchen window. "We're not going to stand around here saying one of us is going to die. Gee, which one should it be? None of us is willing to sacrifice one for the whole."

"I agree with Cybil. We'll find another way." Layla rubbed a hand over Fox's arm to soothe him. "The bloodstone is a weapon, and apparently *the* weapon. It has to get inside Twisse. How do we get it inside?"

"A projectile," Cal considered. "We could rig up something."

"What, a slingshot? A catapult?" Gage demanded. "A freaking cannon? This is the way. It's not just about getting it into Twisse, it's about *taking* it there. It's about jamming it down the bastard's throat. About blood—our blood."

"If that's true, and without more we can't say it is, we're back to straws." Cal shoved his own coffee aside to lean toward Gage. "It's been the three of us since day one. You don't get to decide."

"I didn't. It's the way it is."

"Then why you? Give me a reason."

"It's my turn. Simple as that. You jammed a knife into that thing last winter, showed us we could hurt it. A couple months later, Fox showed us we could kick its ass back and live through it. We wouldn't be sitting here, this close to ending it, if the two of you hadn't done those things. If these three women hadn't come here, stayed here, risked all they've risked. So it's my turn."

"What next?" Cybil snapped at him. "Are you going to call time-out?"

He looked at her calmly. "We both know what we saw, what we felt. And if we all look back, step by step, we can see this one coming. I was given the future for a reason."

"So you wouldn't have one?"

"So, whether I do or not, you do." Gage shifted his gaze from Cybil to Cal. "The town does. So wherever the hell Twisse plans to go next when he's done here has a future. I play the cards I'm dealt. I'm not folding."

Cal rubbed the back of his neck. "I'm not saying I'm on board with this, but say I am—we are—there's time to think of a way for you to do this without dying."

"I'm all for that."

"We pull you out," Fox suggested. "Maybe there's a way to pull you out. Get a rope on you, some sort of harness rig?" He looked at Cal. "We could yank him back out."

"We could work with something like that."

"If we could get Twisse to take an actual form," Layla put in. "The boy, the dog, a man."

"And get it to hold form long enough for me to ram the stone up its ass?"

"You said down his throat."

Gage grinned at Layla over his coffee. "Metaphorically. I'm going to check with my demonologist friend, Professor Linz. Believe me, I'm not going into this unprepared. All things being equal, I'd like to come out of this alive." He shifted his gaze to Cybil. "I've got some plans for after."

"Then we'll keep thinking, keep working. I've got to get into the office," Fox said, "but I'm going to cancel or reschedule all the appointments and court dates I can for the duration."

"I'll give you a ride in."

"Why? Shit, right. Napper, truck. Which means I've got to swing by and see Hawbaker again this morning and check with the mechanic about my truck."

"I want in on the first part," Gage said. "I'll follow you in. I can run you by the mechanic if you need to go."

Cal got to his feet. "We're going to figure this out," he said to the group at large. "We're going to find the way."

With the men gone, the women sat in the kitchen.

"This is so completely stupid." Quinn rapped the heel of her hand on the counter. "Draw straws? For God's *sake*. As if we're going to say sure, one of us falls on the damn grenade while the rest of us stand back and twiddle our thumbs."

"We weren't twiddling," Cybil said quietly. "Believe me. It was horrible, Q. Horrible. The noise, the smoke, the *stink*. And the cold. It was everything, this thing. It was mammoth. No evil little boy or big, bad dog."

"But we fought it. We hurt it." Layla closed a hand around Cybil's arm. "If we hurt it enough, we'll weaken it. If we weaken it enough, it can't kill Gage."

"I don't know." She thought of what she'd seen, and of her own research. "I wish I did."

"Possibilities, Cyb. Remember that. What you see can be changed, has been changed *because* you see it."

"Some of it. We need to go upstairs. We need one of your spare pregnancy tests."

"Oh, but I took three." Distressed, Quinn pressed a hand to her belly. "And I even felt queasy this morning, and—"

"It's not for you. It's for Layla."

"Me? What? Why? I'm not pregnant. My period's not even due until—"

"I know when it's due," Cybil interrupted. "We're three women who've been living in the same house for months. Our cycles are on the same schedule."

"I'm on birth control."

"So was I," Quinn said thoughtfully. "But that doesn't explain why you think Layla's pregnant."

"So pee on a stick." Cybil rose, gave the come-ahead sign. "It's easy."

"Fine, fine, if it makes you feel better. But I'm not pregnant. I'd know. I'd sense it, wouldn't I?"

"It's harder to see ourselves." Cybil led the way upstairs, strolled into Quinn's room, sat on the bed while Quinn opened a drawer.

"Take your pick." She held out two boxes.

"It doesn't matter because it doesn't matter." Layla took one at random.

"Go pee," Cybil told her. "We'll wait."

When Layla went into the bathroom, Quinn turned to Cybil. "You want to tell me why she's in there peeing on a stick?"

"Let's just wait."

Moments later Layla came back with the test stick. "There, done. And no plus sign."

"It's been about thirty seconds since you flushed," Quinn pointed out.

"Thirty seconds, thirty minutes. I can't be pregnant. I'm getting married in February. I don't even have the ring yet. After February, and if we buy this house we're thinking about, and I decorate it, after my business is up and running smoothly, *then* I can be pregnant. Next February—our first anniversary—would be the perfect time to conceive. Everything should be in place by then."

"You really are an anal and organized soul," Cybil commented.

"Absolutely. And I know my own body, my own cycle, my own . . ." She trailed off when she glanced down at the test stick. "Oh."

"Let me see that." Quinn snatched it out of her hand. "That's a really big, really clear, really unmistakable plus for positive, Miss I Can't Be Pregnant."

"Oh. Oh. Wow."

"I said holy shit a lot." Quinn passed the stick to Cybil. "Give yourself a minute. See how you feel after the shock clears."

"That might take more than a minute. I . . . I had a sort of loose schedule worked out, for when this would happen. We want kids. We talked about it. I just thought . . . Let me see that again." Taking it from Cybil, Layla stared. "Holy shit."

"Good shit or bad shit?" Quinn asked.

"Another minute, and that one sitting down." Layla dropped onto the bed and just breathed. Then she laughed. "Good, really, really good. About a year and a half ahead of schedule, but I can adjust. Fox is going to be over the moon! I'm pregnant. How did you know?" She swiveled to Cybil. "How did you know?"

"I saw you." Moved by the radiant smile, Cybil stroked Layla's hair. "Both you and Quinn. I've been expecting this. We saw you, Quinn, Gage and I. In the winter—next winter. You were napping on the couch when he came in. And when you turned over, well, you were unmistakably pregnant."

"How'd I look?"

"Enormous. And beautiful, and wonderfully happy. You both did. And I saw Layla. You were in your boutique, which looked terrific, by the way. Fox brought you flowers. They were for your first month in business. It was sometime in September."

"We think I could open in mid-August, if . . . I'm going to open in mid-August," she corrected.

"You weren't showing yet, not really, but something you said . . . I don't think Gage caught that. A man probably wouldn't. You were all so happy." Remembering what else she'd seen, only the night before, Cybil pressed her lips together. "That's how it should be. I believe now that's how it will be."

"Honey." Quinn sat beside her, draped an arm over Cybil's shoulder. "You think Gage has to die for all this to happen for the rest of us."

"I've seen it happen. I've seen all of it happen. So has he. How much is destiny, how much is choice? I just don't know anymore." She took Layla's hand, laid her head on Quinn's shoulder. "Some of the research, it talks about the need for sacrifice, for balance— destroy the dark, the light must die, too. The stone—the power source—must be taken into the dark, by the light. I didn't tell you."

Cybil lifted her hands, held them over her face, dropped them. "I didn't tell any of you because I didn't want to believe it. Didn't want to face it. I don't know why I had to fall in love with him to lose him. Not this way."

Quinn hugged harder. "We'll find another."

"I've tried."

"We'll all be trying now," Layla reminded her. "We'll find it."

"We don't give up," Quinn insisted. "That's the one thing we don't do."

"You're right. You're right." Hope wasn't something to dismiss, Cybil reminded herself. "And this isn't the moment for gloom and doom. Let's get out of this house. Let's just get out of this house for a few hours."

"I want to tell Fox. We could drive into town, and I could tell him face-to-face. Make his day."

"Perfect."

When they learned from Fox's peppy new office manager that Fox was with a client, Layla decided to multitask.

"I'll run upstairs, get some more clothes, clean out the perishables from the kitchen. If he's not done by that time, well, I'll just wait."

"I'll let him know you're here as soon as he's free," the new office manager sang out as the three women started up the stairs.

"I'll start in the kitchen," Cybil said.

"I'll give you a hand with that. As soon as I pee." Quinn shifted from foot to foot. "It's probably psychological pee, because I know I'm pregnant. But my bladder thinks otherwise. Wow," she continued when Layla opened the door to Fox's apartment to the living room. "This place is . . ."

"The word is *habitable*." With a laugh, Layla shut the door behind them. "It's amazing what a regular cleaning woman can do."

They separated, Cybil to the kitchen, Quinn to the bathroom. Layla stepped into the bedroom, and froze with a knife point at her throat.

"Don't scream. It'll go right through you, right through, and that's not the way it has to be."

"I won't scream." Her gaze latched on to the bed—and the rope, the roll of duct tape on it. On the can of gasoline. Cybil's vision, she thought. Cybil and Gage had seen her bound and gagged, on the floor with fire crawling toward her.

"You don't want to do this. Not really. It's not you."

He eased the door shut. "It needs to burn. It all needs to burn. To purify."

She looked up at his face. She knew that face. Kaz. He delivered pizza for Gino's. He was only seventeen. But now his eyes gleamed with a kind of jittery madness she thought was ancient. And his grin was wild as he backed her toward the bed. "Take off your clothes," he said.

In the kitchen Cybil pulled milk, eggs, fruit out of the refrigerator, set them on the counter. When she turned toward a broom closet, hoping for a box or bag, she saw the broken pane in the back door. Instantly she pulled her .22 from her purse and reached for a knife in the block.

One missing, she thought, fighting panic. A knife already out of the block. Gripping hers, she spun back toward the living room just as Quinn opened the bathroom door. Cybil put her finger to her lips, pushed the knife into Quinn's hand. She gestured toward the bedroom door.

"Go get help," Cybil whispered.

"Not leaving you. Not leaving either one of you." Instead, Quinn pulled out her phone.

Inside, Layla stared at the boy who delivered the pizza, who liked to talk with Fox about sports. Keep his eyes on yours, she told herself while her heart made odd piping sounds in her chest. Talk. Keep talking to him. "Kaz, something's happened to you. It's not your fault."

"Blood and fire," he said, still grinning.

She took another backward step as he jabbed out with the knife, nicked her arm. And the hand fumbling in her purse behind her back finally clamped on its target. She did scream now, and so did he, as she spewed the pepper spray in his eyes.

At the screams, both Quinn and Cybil rushed the bedroom door.

They saw Layla scrambling for a knife on the floor, and the boy they all recognized howling with his hands over his face. Whether it was instinct, panic, or simply rage, Cybil followed through. She kicked the boy in the groin, and when he doubled over, his hands leaving his streaming eyes for his crotch, shoved him into the closet. "Quick, quick, help me push the dresser in front of the door," she ordered when she slammed the closet door.

He screamed, he wept, he battered the door.

Though her hand trembled, Quinn retrieved her phone.

Within fifteen minutes, Chief Hawbaker pulled the weeping boy out of the bedroom closet.

"What's going on?" Kaz demanded. "My eyes! I can't see. Where am I? What's going on?"

"He doesn't know," Cybil said as she stood clutching Quinn's hand. He was nothing but a hurt and confused teenage boy now. "It let him go."

After cuffing Kaz, Hawbaker nodded to the can on the floor. "That what you used on him?"

"Pepper spray." Layla sat on the side of the bed, clinging to Fox. Cybil wasn't sure if she held him to stop him from leaping at the pitiful boy, or to ground herself. "I lived in New York."

"I'm going to take him in, deal with his eyes. You need to come in, all of you, make your statements."

"We'll be in later." Fox leveled his gaze on Kaz. "I want him locked up until we get there, sort this out."

Hawbaker studied the rope, the knives, the can of gas. "He will be."

"My eyes are burning. I don't understand," Kaz wept as Hawbaker guided him out. "Fox, hey, Fox, what's *up* with this?"

"It wasn't him." Layla pressed her face to Fox's shoulder. "It wasn't really him."

"I'm going to get you some water." Cybil started out, stopped as Cal and Gage rushed through the apartment door. "We're all right. Everyone's all right."

"Don't touch anything," Fox warned. "Come on, Layla, let's get you out of here."

"It wasn't him," she repeated, and took Fox's face in her hands. "You know it wasn't his fault."

"Yeah, I know. Doesn't mean I don't want to beat him into a bloody pulp right at the moment, but I know."

"Somebody want to fill us in?" Cal demanded.

"He was going to kill Layla," Gage said tightly. "The kid. What Cybil and I saw. Strip her down, tie her up, light the place up."

"But we stopped it. The way Fox stopped Napper. It didn't happen. That's twice now." Layla let out a breath. "That's two we've changed."

"Three." Cybil gestured toward Fox's front door. "That's it, isn't it?" She turned to Gage. "That's the door we saw Quinn trying to get out of when a knife was stabbing down at her. The knife Kaz had. The one from out of the block in the kitchen. Neither of those things happened because we were prepared. We changed the potential."

"More weight on our side of the scale." Cal drew Quinn to him.

"We need to go down to the police station, deal with this. Press charges."

"Fox."

"Unless," he continued over Layla's distress, "he gets out of town. Out to the farm, or just out, until after the Seven. We'll talk to him, and his parents. He can't stay in the Hollow. We can't risk it."

Layla let out another breath. "If the rest of you could go ahead? I want a few minutes to talk to Fox."

Later, because it seemed like the thing to do, Cybil dragged Gage back to Fox's apartment to load up the food.

"What's the big fucking deal about a quart of milk and some eggs?"

"It's more than that, and besides, I don't approve of waste. And it saves Layla from even thinking about coming back up here until she's steadier. And why are you so irritable?"

"Oh, I don't know, maybe it has something to do with having a woman I like quite a lot being held at knifepoint by some infected pizza delivery boy."

"You could always tip that and be happy Layla was carrying pepper spray and between her quick reflexes and Quinn and me, we managed to handle it." As a tension headache turned her shoulders into throbbing knots of concrete, Cybil bagged the milk. "And the pizza delivery boy, who was being used, is on his way to stay with his grandparents in Virginia along with the rest of his family. That's five people out of harm's way."

"I could look at it that way."

His tone made her lips twitch. "But you'd rather be irritable."

"Maybe. And we can factor in that now we've got two pregnant women instead of one to worry about."

"Both of whom have proven themselves completely capable, particularly today. Pregnant Layla managed to keep her head, to reach into her very stylish handbag and yank out a can of pepper spray. Then to blast same in that poor kid's eyes. Saving herself, potentially saving both Quinn and me from any harm. Certainly saving that boy. I would have shot him, Gage."

She sighed as she packed up food. The tension, she realized, wasn't simply about what had happened, but what might have happened. "I would have shot that boy without an instant's hesitation. I know this. She saved me from having to live with that."

"With that toy you carry, you'd have just pissed him off."

Because her lips twitched again, she turned to him. "If that's an attempt to make me feel better, it's not bad. But Jesus, I could use some aspirin."

When he walked away, she continued bagging food. He returned with a bottle of pills, poured her a glass of water. "Medicine cabinet in the bathroom," he told her.

She downed the pills. "Back to our latest adventure, both Layla and Quinn came out of this with barely a scratch—unlike the potential outcome we saw. That's a big."

"No argument." He went behind her, put his hands on her shoulders and began to push at the knots.

"Oh God." Her eyes closed in relief. "Thanks."

"So not everything we see will happen, and things we don't see will. We didn't see pregnant Layla."

"Yes, we did." She gave his hands more credit than the aspirin for knocking back the leading edge of the headache. "You didn't recognize what you saw. We saw her and Fox in her boutique, this coming September. She was pregnant."

"How do you—never mind. Woman thing," Gage decided. "Why didn't you mention it at the time?"

"I'm not really sure. But what it tells me is that some things are meant, and some things can be changed." She turned now so they were eye-to-eye. "You don't have to die, Gage."

"I'd rather not, all in all. But I won't back off from it."

"I understand that. But the things we've seen played some part in helping our friends stay alive. I have to believe they'll help you do the same. I don't want to lose you." Afraid she might fall apart, she pushed the first of two grocery bags into his arms and spoke lightly. "You come in handy."

"As a pack mule."

She shoved the second bag at him. "Among other things." Because his arms were full, she toed up, brushed her lips over his. "We'd better get going. We'll need to stop by the bakery."

"For?"

"Another Glad You're Not Dead cake. It's a nice tradition." She opened the door, let him pass through ahead of her. "I'll tell you what, for your birthday—when you're still alive—I'll bake you one."

"You'll bake me a cake if I live."

"A spectacular cake." She closed Fox's door firmly, glanced at the plywood Gage had put up where the glass pane was broken. "Six layers, one for each of us." When her eyes stung and welled inexplicably, she pulled her sunglasses out of her bag, put them on.

"Seven," Gage corrected. "Seven's the magic number, right? It should be seven."

"July seventh, a seven-layer cake." She waited for him to put the bags in the trunk of his car. "That's a deal."

"When's your birthday?"

"November." She slid into the car. "The second of November."

"I'll tell *you* what. If I get to eat a piece of your famous seven-layer cake, I'll take you anywhere you want to go on your birthday."

Despite the ache in her belly, she sent him an easy smile. "Careful. There are a lot of places I want to go."

"Good. Same here."

That was just one of the things about her, Gage thought, that kept pushing at his mind. There were a lot of places they wanted to go. When had it stopped being he and she in his mind, and become they? He couldn't pinpoint it, but he knew that he wanted to go to all of those places with her.

He wanted to show her his favorite spots, to see hers. And he wanted to go to places neither of them had ever been, and experience them together for the first time.

He didn't want just to follow the game any longer. To simply go wherever and whenever alone. He wanted to go, to see, to do, and God knew he wanted to play, but the idea of *alone* didn't have the appeal it once had.

Irritable, she'd called him. Maybe that was part of the reason why. It was, in his opinion, a damn good reason for being irritable. It was ludicrous, he decided, and started to pace the guest room instead of checking his e-mail as he'd intended. It was absolutely insane to start thinking about long-term, about commitment, about being part of a couple instead of going solo.

But he *was* thinking about it. That was the kicker. And he could imagine it, could see how it might be—the potential of it—with Cybil. He could imagine the two of them exploring the world together without the weight of it on their shoulders. He could even imagine having a base with her somewhere. New York, Vegas, Paris—wherever.

A home with her, somewhere to come back to.

The only place he'd ever had to come back to was Hawkins Hollow. And not by choice, not really by choice.

But this could be, if he took the bet.

It might be fun talking her into it.

There was time left, he thought, enough time left for him to work out a game plan. Have to be cagey about it, he mused as he sat down at his laptop. He'd have to find just the right way to tie her up in those strings they'd both agreed they didn't want. Then once he had, he could just tie a knot here, tie a knot there. She was a smart one, but then so was he. He'd lay odds he could have her wrapped up before she realized he'd changed the game—and the rules.

Pleased with the idea, he opened an e-mail from Professor Linz. And as he read, his belly tightened; his eyes chilled.

So much, he thought, fatalistically, for planning futures. His was already set—and it had less than two weeks to run.

EIGHTEEN

Once again, Gage called for a meeting at Cal's office. Just his brothers. He'd made certain he'd been up and out of the house that morning before Cybil so much as stirred. He'd needed time to think, time alone, just as he needed time now with his two friends.

He laid out what he'd learned from Linz in calm and dispassionate terms.

"Screw that," was Fox's opinion. "Screw that, Gage."

"It's how it ends."

"Because some demon academic we don't *know*, who's never been here, never dealt with what we've dealt with says so?"

"Because it's how it ends," Gage repeated. "Everything we know, everything we've found out, everything we've dealt with leads right up to it."

"I'm going to have to go with the lawyer's technical terminology on this," Cal said after a moment. "Screw that."

Gage's eyes were green and clear; he'd made his peace with what had to be. "I appreciate the sentiment, but we all know better. None of us should have made it this far. The only reason we have is because Dent broke the rules, gave us abilities, gave us a power source. Time to pay up. Don't say 'why you.'" Gage tapped a finger in the air at Fox. "It's all over your face, and we've been over that part. It's my turn, and it's my goddamn destiny. It stops this time. This is when and how. Upside is I'm not going to have to haul my ass back here every seven years to save you guys."

"Screw that, too," Fox said, but without heat as he pushed to his feet. "There's going to be another way. You're looking at this in a straight line. You're not checking out the angles."

"Brother, angles are my business. It's either destroyed this time, or it *becomes*. Fully corporeal, fully in possession of all its former power. We've already seen that begin to happen."

Absently, Gage rubbed his shoulder where the scar rode. "I've got a souvenir. To destroy it, absolutely take it out, requires a life from our side. Blood sacrifice, to pay the price, to balance the scales. One light for the dark, and blah blah blah. I'm going to do this thing one way or the other. It'd be a hell of a lot easier if I had you behind me."

"We're not just going to sit back and watch you take one for the team," Cal told him. "We keep looking for another way."

"And if we don't find one? No bullshit, Cal," Gage added. "We've been through too much to bullshit each other."

"If we can't, can I have your car?"

Gage glanced over at Fox and felt the weight drop off his shoulders. They'd do what needed to be done. They'd stand behind him, just like always. "The way you drive? Hell no. Cybil gets it. That woman knows how to handle a car. I need you to lawyer up that kind of thing for me. I'd have that off my head."

"Okay, no problem." He shrugged off Cal's curse. "And my fee's a bet. One thousand says we not only off the Big Evil Bastard, but you walk away from the Pagan Stone with the rest of us after we do."

"I want in on that," Cal said.

"That's a bet then."

Cal shook his head, absently rubbed Lump under his desk as the dog stirred from sleep. "Only a sick son of a bitch bets a thousand he's going to die."

Gage only smiled. "Dead or alive, I like to win."

"We need to take this back to the women," Fox put in, then narrowed his eyes at Gage. "Problem?"

"Depends. If we take it back to the women—"

"There's no if," Cal interrupted. "There are six of us in this."

"*When* we take it back to the women," Gage qualified, "the three of us go in as a unified front. I'm not going to be arguing with you *and* them. The deal is, we look for another way until time runs out. When time runs out and there's no other way, it's my way. Nobody welshes."

Cal rose, preparing to come around the desk to shake on the deal. The office door burst open. Cy Hudson, one of the fixtures of the Bowl-a-Rama's leagues, rushed in, teeth bared, and madly firing a .38. One of the bullets plowed into Cal's sternum, took him down even as Gage and Fox dove at Cy.

His enormous bulk didn't topple, and his sheer madness flung them off like flies. He aimed at Cal again, shifted the gun at the last moment as Gage shouted, and Lump bunched to attack. Gage braced for the bullet, caught Fox rising up like a runner off the mark out of the corner of his eye.

Bill Turner came through the door like fury. He leaped onto Cy's back, fists pounding even as Fox went in low and the dog sprang, jaw snapping. The four of them went down in a bone-breaking tangle. The gun went off again even as Gage shoved up and grabbed a chair. He brought it down, brutally, twice on Cy's exposed head.

"Okay?" he said to Fox as Cy went limp.

"Yeah, yeah. Hey, boy, good dog." Fox hooked an arm around Lump's big neck. "Cal?"

Pushing up again, Gage dropped down beside Cal. Cal's face was bone white, his eyes glassy, and his breath came in short pants. But when Gage ripped his shirt open, he saw the spent bullet pushing up through the wound. Sidling over, Lump licked Cal's face and whined.

"It's okay, you're okay. You're pushing it out." He gripped Cal's hand, sent him all he could. "Give me something."

"Smashed a rib, I think," Cal managed. "Ripped hell out of me in there." He struggled to even his breathing as Lump nosed his shoulder. "I can't exactly tell."

"We've got it. Fox, for Christ's sake, give me a hand."

"Gage."

"What! Can't you see he's . . ." Furious, Gage whipped his head around. He saw Fox kneeling on the floor pressing the blood-soaked wad of his own shirt to Bill's chest.

"Call for an ambulance. I've got to keep the pressure on."

"Go. God." Cal pushed breath out, drew more in. He fisted his hand in Lump's fur. "I've got this. I've got this. Go."

But Gage kept Cal's hand tight in his, drew out his phone. And with his eyes locked on his father's pale face, called for help.

Cybil woke groggy, headachy. The groggy wasn't much of a surprise. Mornings weren't her finest hour, particularly after a restless night, and the dreams were a plague now. More, Gage had been closed in the night before. Barely speaking, she thought, as she grabbed a robe in case there were men in the house.

Well, his moods weren't her responsibility, she decided, and felt fairly closed in herself. She'd take her coffee out on the back deck—alone. And sulk.

The idea perked her up a little, or would have if she hadn't found both Layla and Quinn holding a whispered conference in the kitchen.

"Go away. Nobody talk to me until I've had two solid hits of caffeine."

"Sorry." Quinn blocked her path to the stove. "You'll have to put that off."

Warning flashed into her eyes. "Nobody tells me to put off my morning coffee. Move it or lose it, Q."

"No coffee until after this." She picked the pregnancy test off the counter, waved it in front of Cybil's face. "Your turn, Cyb."

"My turn for what. *Move!*"

"To pee on a stick."

Cybil's jones for coffee tripped over sheer shock. "What? Are you crazy? Just because sperm met egg for the two of you doesn't mean—"

"Isn't it funny I have this on hand just like I had one for Layla."

"Ha ha."

"And it's interesting," Layla continued, "how you pointed out yesterday the three of us are on the same cycle."

"I'm not pregnant."

Layla looked at Quinn. "Isn't that what I said?"

Nearly desperate for coffee, Cybil rolled her eyes. "I *saw* you pregnant. Both of you. I didn't see me that way."

"It's always harder to see ourselves," Quinn returned. "You've told me that a few times. Let's make it simple. You want coffee? Go pee on a stick. You won't get past both of us to the goal, Cyb."

Fuming, Cybil snatched the box. "Pregnancy's made both of you bossy and bitchy." She stalked off to the first-floor powder room.

"It has to mean something." Layla rubbed her hands over her arms, ridiculously nervous. "If we're right, or if we're wrong, it has to mean something. I just wish I could figure out what."

"I've got some ideas, but . . ." Worried, Quinn paced to the kitchen doorway. "We'll think about that later. After. And either way, we have to be with her on this."

"Well, of course. Why wouldn't . . . Oh. You mean if she is, and she doesn't want to be." With a nod, Layla stepped up so she stood beside Quinn. "No question about it. Whatever it is, whatever she needs."

They waited a few more minutes, then Quinn dragged both hands through her hair. "That's it. I can't stand it."

She marched to the door, knocked for form, then pushed the door open. "Cyb, how long does—Oh, Cybil." She knelt down immediately to gather Cybil up as her friend sat on the floor.

"What am I going to do?" Cybil managed. "What am I going to do?"

"Get off the floor to start." Briskly, Layla leaned down to help her up. "I'm going to make you some tea. We'll figure this out."

"I'm so stupid. So *stupid*." Cybil pressed her hands to her eyes as Quinn led her to the kitchen and a chair. "I should've seen it coming. All three of us. It's a perfect goddamn fit. It was right there in front of my face."

"It didn't click for me," Quinn told her. "The possibility of it didn't click in for me until the middle of the night. It's going to be all right, Cybil. Whatever you want or need, whatever you decide, Layla and I are going to be right there to make sure it's all right."

"It's not the same for me as it is for the two of you. Gage and I . . . We don't have any plans. We're not . . ." She managed a weak smile. "Linked the way you are with Cal and Fox."

"You're in love with him."

"Yes, I am." Cybil looked into Quinn's eyes. "But that doesn't mean we're together. He's not looking for—"

"Forget what he's looking for." Layla's voice was so sharp, Cybil blinked. "What are *you* looking for?"

"Well, it certainly wasn't this. I was looking to finish what we started here, and to have some time with him outside of this. If I looked further than that, and I'm not so strong and coolheaded that I didn't look further and hope that we might make something together. And not so wide-eyed and optimistic that I expect to."

"You know you don't have to decide right away." Quinn stroked Cybil's hair. "This is between the three of us, and we'll keep it that way as long as you want."

"You know we can't do that," Cybil replied. "There's a purpose in this, and that purpose might be the difference between life and death."

"Gods, demons, fate—," Layla snapped. "None of them have a right to make this choice for you."

When Layla set the tea on the table, Cybil took her hand, squeezed fiercely. "Thanks. God. Thanks. The three of us, the three of them. Ann Hawkins had three sons and they were her hope, her faith, her courage. Now there are three more—the possibilities of three more inside us. There's a symmetry there that can't be ignored. In many cultures, in much lore, the pregnant woman holds particular power. We'll use that power."

She took a deep breath, reached for the tea. "I could, when it's finished, choose to end this possibility. My choice, and yes, screw gods and demons. *My* choice. And I don't choose to end this possibility. I'm not a child, and I'm not without resources. I love the father. Whatever happens between Gage and me, I absolutely believe this was meant."

She took another breath. "I know this is the right thing for me. And I know I'm officially scared to death."

"We'll all be going through it together." Quinn took Cybil's hand, took a good, strong hold. "That's going to help."

"Yes, it is. Don't say anything yet. I need to work out the best way to tell Gage. The best time, the best method. Meanwhile, the three of us need to try to figure out how we can use this surprising bout of mutual fertility. I can contact—"

"Hold that thought," Quinn said when the phone rang. After glancing at the display, she smiled. "Hello, lover. You—" The smile dropped away, and so did her color. "We're coming. I—" She shot alarmed glances at Cybil and Layla. "All right. Yes, all right. How bad? We'll meet you there."

She hung up. "Bill Turner—Gage's father—he's been shot."

They'd taken his mother away in an ambulance, Gage thought. All the lights, the sirens, the rush. He hadn't gone with her, of course. Frannie Hawkins had bundled him away, given him milk and cookies. Kept him close.

Now it was his father—the lights, the sirens, the rush. He wasn't entirely sure how it was he was speeding behind the ambulance, wedged in between Fox and Cal in the cab of Fox's truck. He could smell the blood. Cal's, the old man's.

There had been a lot of blood.

Cal was still pale, and the healing wasn't complete. Gage felt Cal tremble—quick, light shivers—as his body continued the pain and the effort of healing itself. But Cal wasn't dead, wasn't lying in a pool of his own blood as he'd been in the vision. They'd changed that . . . potential, as Cybil would call it.

Score another for the home team.

But they hadn't seen the old man. There'd been no vision of his father—dead or alive. No foresight of the old man leaping through the door and onto crazed Cy Hudson's back. No preview of that hot, determined look in his eyes. There sure as hell hadn't been any quick peek through the window to show him the way the old man lay on the floor, bleeding through Fox's wadded-up shirt.

He'd looked broken, Gage realized. Broken and frail and old when they'd loaded him into the ambulance. It wasn't right, it wasn't the right image. It didn't match the picture of Bill Turner that Gage carried around in his head the way, he supposed, he carried the picture of his mother in his wallet.

In that, she was forever young, forever smiling.

In Gage's head, Bill Turner was a big man, hefting the sway of a beer belly. He was hard eyes, hard mouth, hard hands. That was Bill Turner. As soon backhand you as look at you Bill Turner.

Who the hell was that broken bleeding man in the ambulance up ahead? And why the hell was he following him?

It blurred on him. The road, the cars, the buildings as Fox swung toward the hospital. He couldn't quite solidify it, couldn't quite bring it into focus. His body moved—getting out of the truck, climbing out when Fox slammed to the curb of the emergency entrance, striding into the ER. Part of his brain registered odd details. The change in temperature from June warmth to the chill of air-conditioning, the different sounds, voices, the new rush as medical people descended on the broken, bleeding man. He heard phones ringing—a tinny, irritatingly demanding sound.

Answer the phone, he thought, answer the goddamn phone.

Someone spoke to him, peppering him with questions. *Mr. Turner, Mr. Turner,* and he wondered how the hell they expected the old man to answer when they'd already wheeled him off. Then he remembered *he* was Mr. Turner.

"What?"

What was his father's blood type?

Did he have any allergies?

His age?

Was he on any medications, taking any drugs?

"I don't know," was all Gage could say. "I don't know."

"I'll take it." Cal took Gage's arm, gave him a quick shake. "Sit down, get coffee. Fox."

"I'm on that."

There was coffee in his hand. How had that happened? Surprisingly good coffee. He sat with Cal and Fox in a waiting room. Gray and blue couches, chairs. A TV set on some morning show with a man and a woman laughing behind a desk.

Surgical waiting room, he remembered, as if coming out of a dream. The old man was in surgery. GSW—that's what they called it. Gunshot wound. The old man was in surgery because he had a bullet in him. Supposed to be in me, Gage remembered as his mind replayed that quick whip of the gun toward him. That .38 slug should be in me.

"I need to take a walk." As Fox started to stand with him, Gage shook his head. "No, I just need some air. I'm just . . . have to clear my head."

He rode down in the elevator with a sad-eyed woman with graying roots and a man with a seersucker blazer buttoned tight over a soccer ball belly.

He wondered if they'd left anyone broken and bleeding upstairs.

On the main level, he passed the gift shop with its forest of shiny balloons (Get Well Soon! It's a Boy!) and cold case of overpriced floral arrangements, racks of glossy magazines and paperback novels. He went straight out the front doors, turned left, and walked without any thought of destination.

Busy place, he thought idly. Cars, trucks, SUVs jammed the lots, while others circled, searching for a spot to park. Some of them would stop by the gift shop for glossy magazines and balloons. A lot of sick people around, he supposed, and wondered how many of them had a GSW. Was there an appropriate tagline on a balloon for a GSW?

He heard Cybil call his name. Though the sound of it seemed absurdly out of place, he turned. She hurried down the sidewalk toward him, at just short of a run. All that dark, curling hair was sunstruck, flying around that fabulous face.

Gage had the odd thought that if a man had to die, he could go happier knowing a woman like Cybil Kinski had once run to him.

She caught him, grabbed both his hands. "Your father?"

"In surgery. How'd you get here?"

"Cal called. Quinn and Layla went in. I saw you, so . . . Can you tell me what happened?"

"Cy brought his .38 into Cal's office, shot up the place. Cal, too."

"Cal—"

"He's okay. You know how it goes."

An ambulance roared into the lot hot, sirens, lights. Someone else in trouble, Gage thought. Another balloon on a string.

"Gage. Let's find a place to sit down."

He brought himself back to her, to Cybil with the gypsy eyes. "No, I'm . . . walking. It happened fast. Couple of fingersnaps. Let's see. Bang, bang, Cal's down. Cy aims for him again, so I yelled out. No . . ." Not quite right, he remembered.

"It doesn't matter." She hooked her arm around his waist. If she could have taken his weight, she would have. But the weight he carried wasn't physical.

"It does. It all matters."

"You're right." Gently, she guided him around so they were walking back toward the hospital. "Tell me what happened."

"We went for him first, for Cy, but the guy's built like a mountain, and you add in the infection. Shook us right off. Then I yelled. He turned the gun at me."

In his mind, it replayed in slow motion, every detail, every movement. "The dog had been asleep, as usual, under the desk. He came up like vengeance. I wouldn't have believed it if I hadn't seen it. Fox is about to charge Cy again, might've had enough time. We'll never know. The old man, he comes through the door like a freight train, jumps Cy, and the three of them go down—and the dog, too. The gun went off. Fox was okay, so I got over to Cal. Never gave the old man a thought. Fox was okay, Cal was bleeding and working on pushing the goddamn bullet out. I never gave the old man a thought."

Cybil stopped, turned to him. She said nothing, only watched his face, held his hands.

"I looked over. Fox must've pulled his shirt off. He was using it to put pressure on the wound. Chest wound. GSW. The old man, he can't push the goddamn bullet out like we can."

She released his hands to put her arms around him.

"I don't know how I'm supposed to feel."

"You don't have to decide."

"I could've taken the bullet. Odds are it wouldn't have killed me."

"Cal could've taken another, on the same scale. But you tried to stop it. That's what people do, Gage. They try to stop it."

"We didn't see this, Cybil."

"No, we didn't."

"I changed it. I called a meeting with Cal and Fox, so we were there. Instead of Cal being alone in his office when Cy came in shooting, we were there."

"Gage, listen to me." She brought their hands together between them, looked over the joining directly into his eyes. "You're asking yourself, you're wondering if being there makes you to blame for what happened. You know in your heart, in your head—you *know* after twenty-one years of fighting this what's to blame."

"Cal's alive. I know that matters to me more—"

"This isn't about more, or about less."

"He—the old man—it's the first time in my life I remember him stepping up for me. It's hard knowing it might be the last."

Standing in the June sunshine, as the scream of another ambulance hacked through the air, her heart broke for him. "We could look now, look at your father, if that would help you."

"No." He laid his cheek on the top of her head. "We'll wait."

He thought it would be hours. The waiting and the wondering and second-guessing that went with it. But Gage had barely reached the waiting room when a doctor in surgical scrubs came in. Gage knew as soon as their eyes met. He saw death in them. Inside his belly something twisted viciously, like a clenched fist jerking once, hard. Then it let go, and what was left behind was numb.

"Mr. Turner."

Gage rose, waved his friends back. He walked out to listen to the doctor tell him the old man was dead.

He'd bury the old man beside his wife and daughter. That Gage could do. He wasn't having any damn viewing, or what he thought of as the after-graveside buffet. Short, simple, done. He let Cal handle the arrangements for a graveside service as long as it was brief. God knew Cal knew Bill Turner better than he did. Certainly the Bill Turner who died on the operating table.

He retrieved his father's one good suit from the apartment and delivered it to the funeral home. He ordered the headstone, paid for it and the other expenses in cash.

At some point, he supposed, he'd need to clean out the apartment, donate everything to Goodwill or the Salvation Army. Something. Or, as the odds were Cal would be making arrangements for his own graveside service before much longer, Gage figured he could leave that little chore to Cal and Fox.

They lied to the police, which wouldn't keep Gage from sleeping at night. With Jim Hawkins's help, they'd tampered with evidence. Cy remembered nothing, and Gage figured if the old man had to die, that shouldn't be for nothing either.

He came out of the funeral home, telling himself he'd done all he could. And he saw Frannie Hawkins standing beside his car.

"Cybil said you'd be here. I didn't want to come in, to intrude."

"You've never intruded."

She put her arms around him—one good, hard hug. "I'm sorry. I know how things were between you and Bill, but I'm sorry."

"I am, too. I'm just not sure what that covers."

"However things were, however he was, in the past, in the end he did everything he could to protect you—and my boy, and Fox. And in the end, you've done exactly the right thing for them, for the Hollow, and for Bill."

"I'm laying the rap for his own death on him."

"You're saving a good man, an innocent man from a murder charge and prison." Frannie's face radiated compassion. "It wasn't Cy who shot Cal or Bill—and we know that. It isn't Cy who should spend, potentially, the rest of his life behind bars, leave his wife alone, his kids and grandkids."

"No. We talked about that. The old man's not in a position to put his two cents in, so . . ."

"Then you should understand Bill considered Cy a friend, and it was mutual. After Bill quit drinking, Cy was one of the ones who'd sit around with him, drinking coffee or Cokes. I want you to know I feel absolutely certain this is what Bill would want you to do. As far as anyone knows, Bill came in with the gun, God knows why because none of us do, and when Cy and the rest of you tried to stop him, there was an accident. Bill wouldn't want Cy punished for what was beyond his control. And nothing can hurt Bill now. You know what happened, what Bill did in the end. It doesn't matter what anyone else knows."

It helped hearing it, helped rub dull the sharper edges of guilt. "I can't feel—the grief, the anger. I can't feel it."

"If and when you need to, you will. All you need to know now is you've done what can and should be done. That's enough."

"Would you do something for me?"

"Just about anything."

"When I'm not around, will you put flowers out there now and again? For the three of them."

"Yes. I will."

He stepped over to her car, opened the door for her. "Now I'm going to ask you something."

"Ask away."

"If you knew you had a week or two to live, what would you do?"

She started to speak, stopped, and Gage understood she'd

smothered her instinctive response—for his sake. Instead, she smiled. "How am I feeling?"

"Good."

"In that case, I'd do exactly as I pleased, particularly if it was something I'd normally deny myself or hesitate over. I'd grab everything I wanted, needed. I'd make sure the people who annoyed me knew just what I thought. And more important, that everyone I loved knew how much they meant to me."

"No confessing your sins, making amends?"

"If I haven't confessed and amended by that point, screw it. It's all about me now."

Laughing, he leaned down and kissed her. "I really love you."

"I know you do."

As usual, in Gage's opinion, Frannie had her sensible finger on the heart of the matter. But first things first. He knew too well that death—anyone's death—wouldn't stop the approach of the Seven. The meeting they'd held in Cal's office now had to be open to all six.

"The deal's pretty straightforward," he began. They sat, all of them, in Cal's living room on the night before his father's burial. "Some of the books and folklore Linz accessed have fancy or fanciful language, but it boils down to this: The bloodstone—our stone— is the key. Part of the Alpha Stone, just as Cybil theorized. A power source. And oddly enough, in some of Linz's studies, this fragment is called the Pagan Stone. I don't see that as coincidence."

"What's the lock?" Quinn asked.

"Its heart. The black, festering heart of our own Big Evil Bastard. Insert key, turn, the lock opens and the Evil Bastard goes back to hell. Simple as that."

"No," Cybil said slowly, "it's not."

"Actually it is. But you've got to ante up first."

"And you're saying you're what we ante up?"

"The stakes are a little too rich for me," Layla added. "Why play its game? We'll find one of our own, and use our rules."

"It's not its game," Gage corrected. "It's the only game we've got. And one it's been trying to delay and destroy for eons. The bloodstone destroys it, which is why it came to us in threes, why we weren't able to put it together until now. Until we were old enough, until we were all a part of it. It took all six of us. The rest of it will, too. But only one of us turns the key. That's for me."

"How?" Cybil demanded. "By going inside it? By dying and going to hell with it?"

"'Into the black.' You already know this," he said, watching her face. "You've already found what Linz did."

"Some sources theorize the bloodstone—or Pagan Stone—this particular fragment of the Alpha, will destroy the dark, the black, the demon, if it pierces its heart. Can," she said quickly, "may—if it's been imbued with the blood of the chosen, if it's taken in at exactly the right time. *If, can, may.*"

"You didn't share this?"

"I'm still verifying. I'm still checking sources. No," she added after a moment of silence. "I didn't share it."

"'Into the black,'" Gage repeated. "All the lore uses that phrase or a close variation. The dark, the black. The heart of the beast, and only when it's in its true form. *Bestia.* And every living thing around it, not protected, dies when it dies. Its death requires equal sacrifice. Blood sacrifice. A light to smother the dark. And you'd found that, too," he added to Cybil.

"I found some sources that speak of sacrifice, balance." She started to qualify, to argue—*anything*—then stopped. They were all entitled to hear it. "Most of the sources I've found claim that to pierce the heart, the demon must be in his true form, and the stone must be taken into it by the guardian, by the light. And that light must go in with full knowledge that, by destroying, he will, in turn, be destroyed. The sacrifice must be made with free will."

Gage nodded. "That jibes with Linz."

"Isn't that handy? Doesn't that just tie it up in a bow?"

For a moment, as Gage and Cybil watched each other, no one spoke. Then Quinn made an *ahem* sound. "Okay, question." Quinn held up a finger. "If the bloodstone and a sacrifice does the job, why didn't Dent kill it?"

Still watching Cybil, Gage answered. "First, it came as Twisse, not in its true form."

"I think there's more," Cal said. "I've been thinking about this since Gage ran it by us. Dent had broken the rules, and intended to break more. He couldn't destroy it. It couldn't be done by his hand. So he paved the way for us. He weakened it, made certain it couldn't become, as Linz says. Not fully corporeal, not in full power. He bought time, and passed all he could down to his ancestors—to us—to finish it."

"I'll go with that. But I don't think it's the whole story." Quinn glanced at Cybil, and her eyes held sorrow and apology. "Destroying the demon was—is—Dent's mission. His reason to exist. His sacrifice—his life—wouldn't be enough. True sacrifice involves choice. We all have choices in this. Dent isn't wholly human. Despite our heritages, all of us are. This is the price, the choice to sacrifice life for the whole. Cyb—"

Cybil held up a hand. "There's always a price." She spoke steadily. "Historically, gods demand payment. Or in more pedestrian terms, nothing's free. That doesn't mean we have to accept the price is death. Not without trying to find another way to pay the freight."

"I'm all for coming up with an alternate payment plan. But," Gage added, "we all have to agree, right here and now so we get this behind us, that if we can't, I take point on this. Agree or not, that's how it's going to be. It'd be easier for me if we agreed."

No one spoke, and everyone understood Cybil had to be the first.

"We're a team," she began. "None of us would question just how completely we've become one. Within that team we've formed various units. The three men, the three women, the couples. All of those units play into the dynamics of the team. But within those units we're all individual. We're all who we are, and that's the core of what makes us what and who we are together. None of us can make a choice for another. If this is yours, I won't be responsible for making it harder, for adding to the stress, for possibly distracting you, or any of us so we make a mistake. I'll agree, believing we'll find a way where all of us walk away whole. But I'll agree, more importantly, because I believe in you. I believe in you, Gage.

"That's all I have to say. I'm tired. I'm going up."

NINETEEN

———◦◦◦———

He gave her some time. He wanted some himself. When he walked to the door of the bedroom they shared, Gage thought he knew exactly what he needed to say, and how he intended to say it.

Then he opened the door, saw her, and it all slipped away from him.

She stood at the window in a short white robe, with her hair loose, her feet bare. She'd turned the lights off, lighted candles instead. Their glow, the shifting shadows they created suited her perfectly. The look of her, what he felt for her, were twin arrows in the heart.

He closed the door quietly at his back; she didn't turn.

"I was wrong not to pass along the research I found."

"Yeah, you were."

"I can make excuses, I can tell you I felt I needed to dig deeper, gather more data, analyze it, verify, and so on. It's not a lie, but it's not altogether true."

"You know this is the way. You know it in your gut, Cybil, the

same as I do. If I don't do this thing, and do it right, it takes us all—
and the Hollow with us."

She said nothing for a moment, but only stood in the candlelight,
looking out at the distant hills. "There's still a smear of sunlight at
the very tips of the mountains," she said. "Just a hint of what's dying.
It's beautiful. I was standing here, looking out and thinking we're
like that. We still have that little bit of light, the beauty of it. A few
more days of that. So it's important to pay attention to it, to value it."

"I paid attention to what you said downstairs. I value that."

"Then you might as well hear what I didn't say. If you end up
being the hero and dying out there in those woods, it's going to take
me a long time to stop being angry with you. I will, eventually, but
it's going to take a good, long time. And after I stop being angry
with you—after that . . ." She drew a long breath. "It's going to take
me even longer to get over you."

"Would you look at me?"

She sighed. "It's gone now," she murmured as that smear of light
faded into the dark. Then she turned. Her eyes were clear, and so
deep he thought they might hold worlds inside them.

"I have things I need to say to you," he began.

"I'm sure. But there's something I need to tell you. I've been asking myself if it would be better for you if I didn't tell you, but—"

"You can decide after I say what I have to say. I got an answer on
this earlier today from someone whose opinion I respect. So . . ." He
slipped his hands into his pockets. If a man had the guts to die,
Gage thought, he ought to have the guts to tell a woman what he felt
for her.

"I'm not telling you—or not just telling you—because I may not
come through this. That's kind of the springboard for saying it now.
But I'd've landed here sooner or later. No getting around it."

"Getting around what?"

"A deal's a deal for me. But . . . the hell with that." Annoyance
ran over his face, heated his eyes to a burning green. "All bets are

off. I like my life. It works for me. What's the point of changing what works? That's one thing."

Intrigued, she angled her head. "I suppose it is."

"Don't interrupt."

Her eyebrows winged up. "Pardon me. I assumed this was a conversation, not a monologue. Should I sit down?"

"Just shut up for two damn minutes." Frustration only kicked up the annoyance factor. "I've got this push-pull thing with the whole destiny deal. No denying it pulls me in, or I'd be a few thousand miles away from here right now. But I'm damned if it pushes me where I don't want to go."

"Except you're here, and not wherever else. Sorry." She waved a hand when his eyes narrowed in warning. "Sorry."

"I make up my own mind, and I expect other people to do the same. That's what I'm saying." And all at once, he knew exactly what he was saying.

"I'm not here with you because of some grand design dictated before either of us were born. I don't feel what I feel for you because somebody, or something, decided it would be for the greater good for me to feel it. What's inside me is mine, Cybil, and it's in there because of the way you are, the way you sound, the way you smell, you look, you think. It wasn't what I was after, it's not what I was looking for, but there it is."

She stood very still while the candlelight played gold over the dark velvet of her eyes. "Are you trying to tell me you're in love with me?"

"Would you just be quiet and let me manage this on my own?"

She walked to him. "Let me put it this way. Why don't you lay your cards on the table?"

He'd had worse hands, he supposed, and walked away a winner. "I'm in love with you, and I'm almost through being annoyed about it."

Her smile bloomed, beautifully. "That's interesting. I'm in love with you, and I'm almost through being surprised by it."

"That is interesting." He took her face in his hands, said her name once. His lips brushed hers, softly at first, like a wish. Then the kiss deepened. And as her arms hooked around him, there was the warmth, and the *rightness* of her. Of them. Home, he thought, wasn't always a place. Sometimes, home was a woman.

"If things were different," he began, then tightened his grip when she shook her head. "Hear me out. If things were different, or I get really lucky, would you stick with me?"

"Stick with you?" She tipped her head back to study him. "You're having a hard time with your words tonight. Are you asking me if I'd marry you?"

Obviously thrown off, he drew back a little. "I wasn't. I was thinking of something less . . . formal. Being together. Traveling, because it's what we both do. Maybe having a base. You've got one already in New York and that could work for me. Or somewhere else. I don't think we need . . ."

He wanted to be with her, to have her not just in his life, but *of* his life. Wasn't marriage putting the chips on the line and letting them ride?

"On the other hand," he thought out loud, "what the hell, it's probably not going to be an issue. If I get really lucky, do you want to marry me?"

"Yes, I do. Which probably surprises me as much as it does you. But yes, I do. And I'd like to travel with you—and have you travel with me. I'd like to have a base together, maybe a couple of them. I think we'd be good at it. We'd be good together. Really good."

"Then that's a deal."

"Not yet." She closed her eyes. "You need to know something first. And that I won't hold you to your hypothetical proposal if it changes your mind." She stepped back until they were no longer touching. "Gage. I'm pregnant." He said nothing, nothing at all. "Sometimes destiny pushes, sometimes it pulls. Sometimes it kicks you in the ass. I've had a couple of days to think about this, and—"

Thoughts tumbled inarticulately through his head. Emotions stumbled drunkenly inside his heart. "A couple days."

"I found out the morning your father was shot. It just . . . I couldn't tell you." She took another step back from him. "Chose not to tell you when you were dealing with so much."

"Okay." He drew a breath, then walked to the window to stand as she had been. "You've had a couple days to think about it. So what do you think?"

"We'll start globally, because somehow that's easier. There's a reason the three of us conceived so closely together—very likely on the same night. You, Cal, and Fox were born at the same time. Ann Hawkins had triplets."

Her tone was brisk. In his head he saw her standing at a podium, efficiently lecturing the class. What the hell *was* this?

"Q, Layla, and I share branches on the same family tree. I believe this has happened for a purpose, an additional power that we'll need to end Twisse."

When he didn't speak, she continued. "Your blood, our blood. What's inside me, Q, Layla, combines that. Part of us, part of the three of you. I believe this is meant."

He turned then, his face unreadable. "Smart, logical, a little cold-blooded."

"As you were," she returned, "when you talked about dying."

He shrugged. "Let's shift down from global, Professor. What do you think about two weeks from now, a month from now? When this is over?"

"I don't expect—"

"Don't tell me what you expect." Sparks of anger sizzled along the edges of control. "Tell me what you want. Goddamn it, Cybil, save the lectures and tell me what the hell you want."

She didn't flinch at his words, at the tone of them—not outwardly. But he sensed her flinch, sensed her draw back, and away from him.

Let it ride, he told himself. See where the ball drops.

"All right, I'll tell you what the hell I want." Though she'd drawn back, it didn't lessen the power of her punch. "First, what I didn't want. I didn't want to find myself pregnant, to deal with something this personal, this important when the rest of *everything* is in upheaval. But that's what's happened. So."

She angled her head so their eyes were level. "I want to experience this pregnancy. I want to have this child. To give it the best life I possibly can. To be a good mother, hopefully an interesting and creative one. I want to show this child the world. I want to bring my son or daughter back here so he or she knows Quinn's and Layla's children, and sees this piece of the world we helped preserve."

Her eyes gleamed now, tears and anger. "I want you to live, you idiot, so you can have a part of that. And if you're too stupid or selfish to want a part, then I'd not only expect but demand you peel off some of your winnings every goddamn month so you help support what you helped create. Because I'm carrying part of you, and you're just as responsible as I am. I don't just want to make a family, I'm going to. With or without you."

"You're going to have the kid whether I live or die."

"That's right."

"You're going to have it if I happen to live and don't want any part of being its father, except for a check every month."

"Yes."

He nodded. "You've had a couple days to think about it. That's a lot of thinking in a short amount of time."

"I know my own mind."

"Tell me about it. Now, do you want to know mine?"

"I'm riveted."

His lips quirked. If words were fists, he'd be flat on his ass. "I'd like to send you away, tonight. This minute. Get you and what we've started in you as far away from here as possible. I've never given much thought to having kids. A lot of good reasons for that. Add on that

I'm not quite finished being annoyed to find myself in love with you, and handing out hypothetical marriage proposals, and it's a jam."

"*Tant pis.*" She shrugged at his blank stare. "Too bad."

"Okay. But I can do a lot of thinking in short amounts of time, too. It's one of my skills. Right now? Right at this moment? I don't give a flying fuck about global thinking, greater good, destiny. None of it. This is you and me, Cybil, so listen up."

"It was easier to do that when you didn't talk so damn much."

"Apparently I've got more to say to you than I used to. That kid— or whatever they call it at this stage—is as much mine as it is yours. If I happen to live past midnight on July seventh, you're both going to have to deal with that. It's not going to be you, it's going to be we. As in, we show him the world, we bring him back here. We give him the best life we can. We make a family. That's how it's going to work."

"Is that so?" Her voice trembled a little, but her eyes stayed level on his. "That being the case, you're going to have to do better than a hypothetical marriage proposal."

"We'll get to that after midnight, July seventh." He walked to her, touched her cheek, then cautiously laid his hand on her belly. "I guess we didn't see this one coming."

"Apparently we didn't look in the right place."

He pressed his hand a bit firmer against her. "I'm in love with you."

Understanding he meant both her and what they'd begun, she laid her hand over his. "I'm in love with you."

When he lifted her up, she released a watery laugh. And when he sat on the side of the bed, cradling her, she curled in, held on. They both held on.

In the morning, he stood by his father's grave. It surprised him how many people had come. Not just his own circle, but people from town—those he knew by name or face, others he couldn't place.

Many came up to speak to him, so he went through the motions, got through it on autopilot.

Then Cy Hudson reached for his hand, shook it hard while giving him a shoulder pat that was a male version of an embrace. "Don't know what to say to you." Cy stared at Gage out of his battered face. "I talked to Bill just a couple days before . . . I don't know what happened. I can't remember exactly."

"It doesn't matter, Cy."

"The doctor says it's probably getting hit in the head, and the shock and all scrambled it up in my brain or something. Maybe Bill, maybe he had a brain tumor or something like that, you know? You know how sometimes people do things they wouldn't, or—"

"I know."

"Anyway, Jim said how I should take the family on out to the O'Dell place. Seemed like a screwy thing to do, but things are screwy. I guess I will then. If you, well, you know, need anything . . ."

"Appreciate it." Standing by the grave, Gage watched his father's killer walk away.

Jim Hawkins stepped up, slid an arm around Gage's shoulders. "I know you had it rough, for a long time. Rougher and longer than you should've. All I'm going to say is you've done the right thing here. You've done right for everybody."

"You were more father to me than he was."

"Bill knew that."

They drifted away, the people from town, the ones he knew by name or face, or couldn't quite place. There were businesses to run, lives to get back to, appointments to keep. Brian and Joanne stood by him a moment longer.

"Bill was helping out at the farm the last week or two," Brian said. "I've got some of his tools, some of his things out there, if you want them."

"No. You should keep them."

"He did a lot to help us with what we're doing," Joanne told

Gage. "With what you're doing. In the end, he did what he could. That counts." She kissed Gage. "You take care."

Then it was only the six of them, and the dog who sat patiently at Cal's feet.

"I didn't know him. I knew, a little, who he was before she died. I knew, too much, who he was after. But I didn't know the man I just buried. And I don't know if I'd have wanted to, even if I'd had the chance. He died for me—for us, I guess. Seems as if that should even it all out."

He felt something. Maybe it was some shadow of grief, or maybe it was just acceptance. But it was enough. He reached out for a handful of dirt, then let it fall out of his hand onto the casket below. "So. That's that."

Cybil waited until they were back at Cal's. "I have something we need to discuss and deal with."

"You're all having triplets." Fox dropped into a chair. "That would put a cap on it."

"Not so far as I know. I've been doing a lot of research on this, but I've hesitated to bring it up. Time's too short for hesitation. We need Gage's blood."

"I'm using it right now."

"You'll have to spare some. What we did for us after the attack, we need to do for Cal's and Fox's families. In their way, they'll be on the front line. Your antibodies," she explained. "You survived the demon bite, and there's a very decent chance you're immune to its poison."

"So you're going to mix up a batch of antidemon venom in the kitchen?"

"I'm good. Not quite that good. We'd use the ritual we used before—the basic blood brothers ritual. Protection," she reminded Gage. "Your Professor Linz spoke of protection. If Twisse gets past us, or if it's able to breach the town, or worse, the farm, protection may be all we can offer."

"There are a lot of other people besides our families," Cal pointed out. "And I don't see them circling up to hold bloody hands with Gage."

"No. But there's another way. Taking it internally."

Gage sat up, leaned forward. "You want the population of Hawkins Hollow to drink my blood? Oh yeah, I bet the mayor and town council will jump right on that."

"They won't know. There was a reason I put off bringing this up, and this is it." She sat on the arm of the sofa. "Hear me out. The town has a water supply. The farm has a well. People drink water. The Bowl-a-Rama's still doing business, selling beer on tap. We wouldn't cover everyone, but this is the best shot at a broad-based immunization. I think it's worth a try."

"We're down to days left now," Fox considered. "When we go into the woods we'll be leaving the Hollow, the farm, all of it. The last time we did that, it was damn near a massacre. I'd feel easier if I knew my family had something—a chance at something. If that something's Gage's blood, let's start pumping."

"Easy for you to say." Gage rubbed the back of his neck. "The whole immune thing is a theory."

"A solid one," Cybil said, "based on science, and magicks. I've looked into both elements, studied all the angles. It could work. And if it doesn't, we're no worse off."

"Except me," Gage muttered. "How much blood?"

Cybil smiled. "Going with a magickal number, I think three pints ought to do it."

"Three? And just how are you going to get it out of me?"

"I've got that covered. I'll be right back."

"My dad gives blood to the Red Cross a few times a year," Fox commented. "He says it's no big, and after he gets OJ and a cookie."

"What kind of cookie?" Gage wanted to know, then looked

dubiously at Cybil when she came back in with a shipping carton. "What's that?"

"Everything we need. Sterile needles, tubing, container bags with anticoagulant, and so on."

"What?" The thought of what was in the box had his stomach doing a long, slow roll. "Did you go to some vampire site online?"

"I have my sources. Here." She handed Gage the bottle of water she'd set on top of the box. "It's better for you if you drink plenty of water before we draw the blood, particularly as we're going to draw about three times what's usually taken in a donation."

He took the bottle, then glanced into the box and winced. "If I'm going to have to slice some part of me open again for the ritual, why can't we just take it from there?"

"This is more efficient, and tidier." She smiled at him. "You're willing to punch a hole in a demon and die, but you're afraid of a little needle?"

"*Afraid* is a strong word. I don't suppose you ever jabbed anyone else with one of those."

"No, but I've been jabbed and I studied the procedure."

"Oh, oh! Let me do it." Fox waved a hand.

"No way in hell. She does it." Gage pointed at Layla, whose mouth dropped open in shock.

"Me? Why? Why?"

"Because of everyone here you'll worry most about hurting me." He smiled thinly at Cybil. "I know you, sweetheart. You like it rough."

"But . . . I don't want to."

"Exactly." Gage nodded at Layla. "Neither do I. That makes us the perfect team."

"I'll talk you through it," Cybil told Layla, and held up a pair of protective gloves.

"Oh, well. Shit. I'm going to go wash my hands first."

It was surprisingly simple, though Layla—whom he'd seen

literally crawl through fire—squealed breathlessly as she slid the needle into his arm. He munched on macadamia nut cookies and drank orange juice—though he'd requested a beer—while Cybil efficiently stowed the three filled bags.

"Thanks to your recuperative powers, we could do this all at once. We'll give you a little while, then go ahead and do the rituals."

"The farm should be first. We could swing by there," Fox calculated, "take care of that."

"That works. I want to take Lump out there." Cal glanced at the dog sprawled under the coffee table. "He's not going in with us this time."

"We'll take him out, then go by the Hawkinses'," Fox said, "then into town. Head out to the water supply from there." When he reached for a cookie, Gage slapped his hand aside.

"I don't see your blood in the bag, bro."

"He's good," Fox proclaimed. "Who's driving?"

It might have been a waste of their time, efforts, and Gage's blood. Cybil gnawed on that in the days—and nights—that followed. Everything that had seemed logical, everything she'd been able to document, verify, research, speculate on now seemed completely useless. What had begun for her months before as a fascinating project was now the sum total of everything that mattered. What good was intellect, she thought as she rubbed her exhausted eyes, when fate twisted what should be into the impossible?

How had time run out? How could that be? Hours now, essentially, she could count in hours the time they had left. Everything she learned, everything she saw, told her that at the end of those hours she would lose the man she loved, the father of her child. She would lose the life they might have made together.

Where were the answers she'd always been so good at finding? Why were they all the wrong ones?

She glanced up as Gage came into the dining room, then put her fingers back on the keyboard though she had no idea what she'd been typing.

"It's three in the morning," he told her.

"Yes, I know. There's a handy little clock in the bottom corner of the screen."

"You need sleep."

"I have a pretty good idea what I need." When he sat down, stretched out his legs, she shot him a single hot look. "And what I *don't* need is you sitting there staring at me while I'm trying to work."

"You've been working pretty much around the clock for days now. We've got what we've got, Cybil. There isn't any more."

"There's always more."

"One of the things I tripped over when it came to you was your brain. That's one Grade-A brain you've got. The rest of the package gets the big thumbs-up, too, but the brain's what started the fall for me. Funny, I never gave a damn, before you, if the woman I was hooked up with had the IQ of Marie Curie or an Idaho potato."

"IQ scales are considered controversial by many, and skewed toward white and middle-class."

"See." He tapped a finger in the air. "There you go. Facts and theories at the fingertips. It just kills me. Whatever the scale, you're one smart woman, Cybil, and you know we've got what we've got."

"I also know it ain't over till the fat lady sings. I'm trying to gather more information about a lost tribe in South America that may have been descended from—"

"Cybil." He reached out, laid his hand over hers. "Stop."

"How can I stop? How can you ask me to stop? It's July fourth, for God's sake. It's three hours and twelve minutes into July fourth. We only have *now*. Tonight, tomorrow, tomorrow night, before we start back to that godforsaken place, and you . . ."

"I love you." When she covered her face with her free hand and struggled with sobs, he continued to speak. Calm and clear. "That's a damn big deal for me. Never looked for it, and I sure as hell never expected it to slap me in the face like a two-by-four. But I love you. The old man told me my mother made him a better man. I get that because you make me a better man. I'm not going back to the Pagan Stone for the town. I'm not doing it just for Cal and Fox, or Quinn and Layla. I'm not doing it just for you. I'm doing it for me, too. I need you to understand that. I need you to know that."

"I do. Accepting it is the problem. I can walk into that clearing with you. I just don't know how I can walk out without you."

"I could say something corny about how I'll always be with you, but neither one of us would buy that. We've got to see how the cards fall, then we've got to play it out. That's all there is."

"I was so sure I'd find the way, find *something*." She stared blindly at the computer screen. "Save the day."

"Looks like that's going to be my job. Come on. Let's go to bed."

She rose, turned into him. "Everything's so quiet," she murmured. "The Fourth of July, but there weren't any fireworks."

"So we'll go up and make some, then get some sleep."

They slept, and they dreamed. In the dreams, the Pagan Stone burned like a furnace, and flaming blood spat from the sky. In the dreams, the writhing black mass scorched the ground, ignited the trees.

In the dreams, he died. Though she cradled him in her arms and wept over him, he did not come back to her. And even in dreams, her grief burned her heart to ashes.

She didn't weep again. Cybil shed no tears as they packed and prepared throughout the day of July fifth. She stood dry-eyed as Cal reported there were already some fires, some looting and violence in town, that his father, Chief Hawbaker, and a handful of others were doing all they could to keep order.

All that could be done had been done. All that could be said had been said.

So on the morning of July sixth, she strapped on her weapons, shouldered her pack like the others. And with the others left the pretty house on the edge of Hawkins Wood to strike out on the path to the Pagan Stone.

It was all familiar now, the sounds, the scents, the way. More shade than there had been weeks before, of course, Cybil thought. More wildflowers, and a thicker chatter from birds, but still much the same. It wouldn't have been so very different in Ann Hawkins's time. And the feelings clutched tight inside Ann as she'd left these woods, left the man she loved to his sacrifice, not so different, Cybil imagined, than what was tight in her walking into them.

But at least she would be there, with him, to the end of it.

"My knife's bigger than yours." Quinn tapped the scabbard hooked at Cybil's waist.

"Yours isn't a knife, it's a machete."

"Still, bigger. Bigger than yours, too," Quinn said to Layla.

"I'm sticking with my froe, just like last time. It's my lucky froe. How many people can say that?"

They were trying to take her mind off things, Cybil knew.

"Cybil." The word came in a conspirator's whisper, and from the left, from the deep green shadows.

When she looked, when she saw, Cybil's heart simply broke.

"Daddy."

"It's not." Gage stepped back to her, gripped her arm. "You know it's not."

When he reached for his gun, Cybil stilled his hand. "I know, I know it's not my father. But don't."

"Don't you want to come give Daddy a hug?" It spread its arms wide. "Come on, princess! Come give Daddy a great, *big* kiss!" It bared its sharklike teeth, and laughed. And laughed. Then it raked its own claws down its face, its body, to vanish in a waterfall of black blood.

"That's entertainment," Fox said under his breath.

"Poorly staged, overplayed." Shrugging it off, Cybil took Gage's hand. Nothing, she promised herself, would shake her. "We'll take point for a while," she said, and with Gage walked to the front of the group.

TWENTY

They'd planned to stop for rest at Hester's Pool, where the young, mad Hester Deale had drowned herself weeks after giving birth to the child Twisse put inside her. But the water there bubbled red. On its agitated surface, bloated bodies of birds and some small mammals bobbed and floated.

"Not exactly the right ambiance for a quick picnic," Cal decided. With his hand on Quinn's shoulder, he leaned over to brush his lips at her temple. "You okay to go another ten minutes before we break?"

"Hey, I'm the three-miles-a-day girl."

"You're the pregnant girl. One of them."

"We're good," Layla said, then dug her fingers into Fox's arm. "Fox."

Something rose out of the churning water. Head, neck, shoulders, the dirty red sludge of the pond, dripping, running. Torso, hips, legs, until it stood on the churning surface as it might a platform of stone.

Hester Deale, bearer of the demon's seed, damned by madness, dead centuries and by her own hand, stared out of wild and ravaged eyes.

"You'll birth them screaming, demons all. You are the damned, and his seed is cold. So cold. My daughters." Her arms spread. "Come, join me. Spare yourselves. I've waited for you. Take my hand."

What she held out was brittle with bone, stained with red.

"Let's go." Fox put his arm firmly around Layla's waist, drew her away. "Crazy doesn't stop with death."

"Don't leave me here! Don't leave me here alone!"

Quinn glanced back once, with pity. "Was it her, or another of Twisse's masks?"

"It's her. It's Hester." Layla didn't look back. Couldn't. "I don't think Twisse can take her form—or Ann's. They're still a presence, so it can't mimic them. Do you think when we finish this, she'll be able to rest?"

"I believe it." Cybil looked back, watched Hester—weeping now—sink back into the pool. "She's part of us. What we're doing is for her, too."

They didn't stop at all. Whether it was nerves, adrenaline, or the Nutter Butters and Little Debbies Fox passed around, they kept hiking until they'd reached the clearing. The Pagan Stone stood silent. Waiting.

"It didn't try to stop us," Cal pointed out. "Barely messed with us."

"It didn't want to waste the energy." Cybil peeled off her pack. "Storing it up. And it thinks it destroyed the one weapon we had. Bastard's feeling cocky."

"Or like the last time we came here on the eve of a Seven, it's hitting the town." Cal pulled out his cell phone, punched the key for his father's. His face, his eyes were grim when he flipped it back closed. "Nothing but static."

"Jim Hawkins will kick demon ass." Quinn put her arms around Cal. "Like father, like son."

"Fox and I could try to see," Layla began, but Cal shook his head.

"No, nothing we can do. Not there, not at the farm. And there's something to be said for saving our energies. Let's set up."

In short order Gage dumped an armload of wood near Cybil as she unpacked provisions. "Seems superfluous. If we wait a few hours, there'll be plenty of fire."

"This is our fire. An important distinction." Cybil lifted a thermos. "Want some coffee?"

"For once, no. I'm going to have a beer." He looked around as he opened one. "Funny, but I'd feel a lot better if it had come after us, like last time. Bloody rain, lashing wind, bone-snapping cold. That bit with your father—"

"Yes, I know. It was like a tip of the hat. Have a nice walk, catch you later. Arrogance is a weakness, one we'll make sure it regrets."

He took her hand. "Come here a minute."

"We need to build the fire," she began as he drew her to the edge of the clearing.

"Cal's the Boy Scout. He'll do it. There's not a lot of time left." He put his hands on her shoulders, ran them down her arms, up again. "I've got a favor to ask you."

"It's a good time to ask for one. But you'll have to live to make sure I followed through."

"I'll know. If it's a girl . . ." He saw the tears swim into her eyes, watched her will them back. "I want Catherine for her middle name—for my mother. I always felt first names should belong to the kid, but the middle one . . ."

"Catherine for your mother. That's a very easy favor."

"If it's a boy, I don't want you to name him after me. No juniors or any crap like that. Pick something, and put your father's name in the middle. That's it. And, make sure he knows—or she, whichever—not to be a sucker. You don't draw to an inside straight, don't bet what you can't afford to lose, and—"

"Should I be writing this down?"

He gave her hair a tug. "You'll remember. Give him these." Gage pulled a deck of cards out of his pocket. "The last hand I played with this deck? Four aces. So it's lucky."

"I'll hold them, until after. I have to believe—you have to let me believe—you'll be able to give them to him yourself."

"Fair enough." He put his hands on her face, skimmed his fingers up into her hair, curled them there as he brought his lips down to hers. "You're the best thing that ever came my way." He kissed her hands, then looked into her eyes. "Let's get this done."

Step by step, Cybil told herself. The fire, the stone, the candles, the words. The circle of salt. Fox had turned on a little boom box so there was music. That, too, was a step in Cybil's opinion. *We whistle while we work, you bastard.*

"Tell me what you need from me." Quinn spoke quietly as she helped Cybil arrange more candles on the table of the stone.

"Believe we'll end it—that he'll end it. And live."

"Then I will. I do. Look at me, Cybil. No one, not even Cal knows me like you. I believe."

"So do I." Layla stepped up, laid her hand over Cybil's. "I believe it."

"There, you see." Quinn closed her hand over the two of theirs. "Three pregnant women can't be . . . Whoa, what was that?"

"It . . . moved." Layla glanced up at both of them. "Didn't it?"

"Shh. Wait." Spreading her fingers over the stone under Layla's and Quinn's, Cybil fought to *feel*. "It's heating, and it's vibrating. Like it's breathing."

"The first time Cal and I touched it together, it warmed," Quinn said. "And then we were slapped back a few hundred years. If we could focus, maybe there's something we're supposed to see."

Without warning, the wind lashed out, hard, slapping hands, and knocked all three of them to the ground.

"Showtime," Fox called out as black, pulsing clouds rolled across the sky toward the setting sun.

In town, Jim Hawkins helped Chief Hawbaker drag a screaming man into the Bowl-a-Rama. Jim's face was bloody, his shirt torn, and he'd lost one of his shoes in the scuffle out on Main Street. The alleys echoed with the screams, wails, the gibbering laughter of more than a dozen they'd already pulled in and restrained.

"We're going to run out of rope." Favoring his throbbing arm where the man who'd taught his son U.S. history sank his teeth, Hawbaker secured the rope and the now-giggling teacher to a ball return. "Christ Jesus, Jim."

"A few more hours." Air wheezed in and out of Jim's lungs as he dropped down, mopped at his streaming face. They had half a dozen people locked into the old library, a scattering of others secured in what Cal told him were other safe zones. "We've just got to hold things a few more hours."

"There are hundreds of people left in town. And a handful of us still in our right mind that aren't burrowed in somewhere, hiding. Fire at the school, another in the flower shop, two more residential."

"They got them out."

"This time." Outside something crashed. Hawbaker gained his feet, drew out his service revolver.

Inside Jim's chest, his already laboring heart sprinted. Then Hawbaker turned the gun, holding it butt first toward Jim. "You need to take this."

"Shit fire, Wayne. Why?"

"My head's pounding. Like something's beating on it trying to get in." As he spoke, Hawbaker wiped at his face, shiny with sweat. "If it does, I want you holding the weapon. I want you to take care of it. Take care of me if you have to."

Jim got slowly to his feet and with considerable care, took the gun. "The way I look at it? Anybody doing what we've been doing the last couple hours is bound to have the mother of all headaches. I've got some Extra-Strength Tylenol behind the grill."

Hawbaker stared at Jim, then burst out laughing, laughed until his sides ached. "Sure, hell. Tylenol." Laughed until his eyes ran wet. Until he felt human. "That'll do her." At the next crash, he looked toward the doors and sighed. "You'd better bring the whole bottle."

I t brought the night," Cal shouted as the wind tore at them with frozen hands. Outside the circle, snakes writhed, biting, devouring each other until they burned to cinders.

"Among other things." Quinn hefted the machete, ready to slice at anything that got through.

"We can't move on it yet." Gage watched a three-headed dog pace the clearing, snapping, snarling. "It's trying to draw us out, to sucker us in."

"It's not really here." Fox shifted to try to block Layla from the worst of the wind, but it came from everywhere. "This is just . . . echoes."

"Really loud echoes." Layla clamped a hand on the handle of her froe.

"It's stronger in the dark. Always stronger in the dark." Gage watched the huge black dog pace, wondered if it was worth a bullet. "And stronger during the Seven. We're nearly there."

"Stronger now than ever. But we don't take sucker bets." Cybil bared her teeth in a grin. "And we're going to draw it in."

"If it's in town now, if it's this strong and in town . . ."

"They'll hold it." Cybil watched a rat, plump as a kitten, leap on the dog's ridged back. "And we'll reel it in."

Fox's phone beeped. "Can't read the display. It's black." Before he could flip it open, the voices poured out. Screaming, sobbing, calling his name. His mother's, his father's, dozens of others.

"It's a lie," Layla shouted. "Fox, it's a lie."

"I can't tell." He lifted desperate eyes to hers. "I can't tell."

"It's a *lie*." Before he could stop her, Layla snatched the phone, hurled it away.

With a long, appreciative whistle, Bill Turner walked out of the woods. "Sign her up! Bitch's got an arm on her. Hey, you useless little piece of shit. I got something for you." He snapped the belt held in his hands. "Come on out and take it like a man."

"Hey, asshole!" Cybil elbowed Gage aside. "He died like a man. You won't. You'll die squealing."

"Don't taunt the demon, sugar," Gage told her. "Positive human emotions, remember."

"Damn. You're right. I'll give you a positive human emotion." She spun around and in the mad wind yanked Gage to her for a deep, drowning kiss.

"I'm saving you for dessert!" The thing in Bill's form shifted, changed. She heard her father's voice boom out now. "What I plant in you will rip and claw to be born."

She closed her mind to it, poured the love she felt—so strong, so new—into Gage. "It doesn't know," she whispered against his mouth.

The wind died; the world fell silent. She thought: Eye of the storm, and took a breath. "It doesn't know," she repeated, and touched her fingers lightly to her belly. "It's one of the answers we never found. It has to be. Another way, if we can figure out how to use it."

"We've got a little over an hour left until eleven thirty—that hour of light before midnight." Cal looked up at the pure black sky. "We have to get started."

"You're right. Let's light the candles while we can." And she'd pray the answer would come in time.

Once again the candles burned. Once again the knife that had joined three boys as brothers drew blood, and those wounded hands clasped firm. But this time, Cybil thought, they weren't three, they weren't six—but the potential of nine.

On the Pagan Stone six candles burned, one to represent each other, and a seventh to symbolize their single purpose. Inside that ring of fire three small white candles flickered for the lights they'd sparked.

"It's coming." Gage looked into Cybil's eyes.

"How do you know?"

"He's right." Cal glanced at Fox, got a nod, then leaned over to kiss Quinn. "No matter what, stay inside the circle."

"I'll stay in as long as you do."

"Let's not fight, kids," Fox said before Cal could argue. "Time's a wasting."

He leaned over, kissed Layla hard. "Layla, you're my it. Quinn, Cybil, you go into the small and exclusive club of the best women I know. You guys? I wouldn't change a minute of the last thirty-one years. So when we come through the other side of this, we'll exchange manly handshakes. I'm going for big, sloppy kisses from the women, with a little something extra from my it."

"Is that your closing?" Gage demanded. The stone tucked in his pocket weighed like lead. "I'm taking big, sloppy kisses all around. One in advance." He grabbed Cybil. If his life had come down to minutes, he was taking the taste of her into the dark. He felt her hand fist on his shirt—a strong, possessive grip. Then she let him go.

"Just a down payment," she told him. With her face pale and set, she drew both her weapons. "I feel it now, too. It's close."

From somewhere in the bowels of the black woods, it roared. Trees trembled, then lashed at each other like enemies. At the edges of the clearing, fire sputtered, sparked, then spewed.

"Bang, bang, on the door, baby," Quinn murmured, and had Cal gawking at her.

"'Love Shack'?"

"I don't know why that popped in my head," she began, but Fox started laughing like a loon.

"Perfect! Knock a little louder, sugar," he sang out.

"Oh God. Bang, bang, on the door, baby," Layla repeated, and unsheathed her froe.

"Come on," Fox demanded, "put something *behind* it. I can't *hear* you."

As the fire gushed, as the stench of what came poured over the air, they sang. Foolish, maybe, Gage thought. But it was so in-your-face, so utterly and humanly defiant. Could do worse, he decided, could do a hell of a lot worse as a battle cry.

The sky hemorrhaged bloody rain that spat and sizzled on the ground, casting up a fetid haze of smoke. Through that smoke it came, while in the woods trees crashed and the wind howled like a thousand tortured voices.

The boy stood in the clearing.

It should have been ludicrous. It should, Gage thought, have been laughable. Instead it was horrible. And when the smiling child opened its mouth, the sound that ripped from it filled the world.

Still, they sang.

Gage fired, saw the bullets punch into flesh, saw the blackened blood ooze. Its scream tore gullies in the ground. Then it flew, spinning in blurry circles that spiraled smoke and dirt into a choking cloud. It changed. Boy to dog, dog to snake, snake to man, all whirling, coiling, screaming. Not its true form. The stone was useless until it took its true form.

"Bang, bang, bang," Cal shouted, and leaped out of the circle to slash, and slash, and slash with his knife.

Now it shrieked, and however inhuman the sound, there was both pain and fury in it. With a nod, Gage slipped the bloodstone out of his pocket, set it in the center of the burning candles.

As one, they rushed out of the circle, and into hell.

Blood and fire. One fell, one rose. The fierce cold bit like teeth, and the stinking smoke scored the throat. Behind them, in the center of the circle, the Pagan Stone flashed, then boiled in flame.

He saw something strike out of the smoke, rip across Cal's chest. Even as his friend staggered, Fox was rushing in, hacking at what was no longer there. Fox called out to Layla, shoved her down. This time Gage *saw* claws slice out of the smoke, and miss Layla's face by inches.

"It's playing with us," Gage shouted. Something leaped onto his back, sank its teeth into him. He tried to buck it off, to roll. Then the weight was gone and Cybil stood with her knife black with blood.

"Let it play," she said coldly. "I like it rough, remember?"

He shook his head. "Fall back. Everybody, back inside!" Shoving to his feet, he all but dragged her into the circle where the Pagan Stone ran with fire.

"We're hurting it." Layla dropped to her knees to catch her breath. "I can *feel* its pain."

"Not enough." They were all bloody, Gage thought. Every one of them splashed or stained with blood—its and their own. And time was running out. "We can't take it this way. There's only one way." He put his hand on Cybil's until she lowered her knife. "When it takes its true form."

"It'll kill you before you have a chance to kill yourself! At least when we're fighting it, we're giving it pain, we're weakening it."

"No, we're not." Fox rubbed his stinging eyes. "We're just entertaining it. Maybe distracting it a little. I'm sorry."

"But . . ." Distracting it. Cybil looked back at the Pagan Stone. That was *theirs*. She believed that. Had to believe it. It had responded when she, Quinn, and Layla had laid hands on it together.

Dropping her knife—what good was it now?—she spun to the Pagan Stone. Holding her breath, she plunged a hand through the flame to lay it on the burning altar. "Quinn! Layla!"

"What the hell are you doing?" Gage demanded.

"Distracting it. And I sincerely hope pissing it off." In the fire was heat, but no burn. This, she thought, wild with hope, was an answer. "It doesn't know." She placed her free hand on her belly as the spearing fire illuminated her face. "This is *power*. It's light. It's *us*. Q, please."

Without a moment's hesitation, Quinn shot her hand through the fire, laid it on Cybil's. "It's moving!" Quinn called out. "Layla."

But Layla was already there, and her hand closed over theirs.

It sang, Cybil thought. In her head she heard the stone sing in thousands of pure voices. The flame that shot up from the center of the stone was blinding white. Beneath them, the ground began to shake, a sudden and furious violence.

"Don't let go," Cybil called out. What had she done? she thought as her eyes blurred with tears. Oh God, what had she done.

Looking through that white shaft of flame, she met Gage's eyes. "You're one smart cookie," he said.

In the clearing, through the smoke, in the smoke, *of* the smoke, the black formed—and its hate of the light, its fury toward its radiance spewed into the air. Arms, legs, head—it was impossible to know—bulged. Eyes, eerily green, rimmed with red blinked open by the score. It grew, rolling and rising until it consumed both earth and sky. Grew until there was only the dark, the red walls of flames. And its hungry wrath.

She heard its scream of rage in her head, knew the others did, too.

I'll rip it squalling from your belly and drink it like wine.

Now, Cybil thought, *now* it knew.

"It's time. Don't let go." The stone shook under her hand, but her eyes never left Gage. "Don't let go."

"I don't plan to." He shot his hand through the fire, clutched the flaming bloodstone.

Then he turned away from her. Even then her face was in his mind. For one last moment, he stood linked with Cal and Fox. Brothers, he thought, start to finish. "Now or never," he said. "Take care of what's mine."

And with the bloodstone vised in his fist, he leaped into the black.

"No. No, no, no." Cybil's tears fell through the flame to pool on the stone.

"Hang on." Quinn clutched her hand tighter, locked an arm around her for support. On the other side, Layla did the same.

"I can't see him," Layla called out. "I can't see him. Fox!"

He came to her, and with nothing left but instinct and grief, both he and Cal laid hands on the stone. The black roared, its eyes rolled with what might have been pleasure.

"It's not going to take him, not like this." Cal shouted over the storm of sound. "I'm going after him."

"You can't." Cybil choked back a sob. "This is what he needs to finish it. This is the answer. Don't let go, of the stone, of each other. Of Gage. Don't let go."

Through the rain sliced a bolt of light. And the world quaked.

In the Hollow, Jim Hawkins collapsed on the street. Beside him, Hawbaker shielded his eyes from a sudden burst of light. "Did you hear that?" Jim demanded, but his voice was swallowed in the din. "Did you hear that?"

They knelt in the center of Main Street, washed in the brilliance, and clutched each other like drunks.

At the farm, Brian held his wife's hand as hundreds of people stood in his fields staring at the sky. "Jesus, Jo, Jesus. The woods are on fire. Hawkins Woods."

"It's not fire. Not just fire," she said as her throat throbbed. "It's . . . something else."

At the Pagan Stone, the rain turned to fire, and the fire turned to light. Those sparks of light struck the black to sizzle, to smoke. Its eyes began to wheel now, not in hunger or pleasure, but in shock, in pain, and in fury.

"He's doing it," Cybil murmured. "He's killing it." Even through her grief, she felt stunning pride. "Hold on to him. We have to hold on to him. We can bring him back."

Sensation was all he had. Pain, something so far above agony it had no name. Ferocious cold bound by intolerable heat. Thousands of claws, thousands of teeth tore and ripped at him—each wound a separate, searing misery. His own blood burned under his broken skin, and its blood coated him like oil.

Around him, the dark closed in, squeezing him in a terrible embrace so he waited to feel his own ribs snap. In his ears sounds seemed to boil—screeches, screams, laughter, pleas.

Was it eating him alive? Gage wondered.

Still he crawled and shoved through the quivering wet mass, gagging on the stench, wheezing for what little dirty air was left to him. In the heat, what was left of his shirt smoked. In the cold, his fingers numbed.

This, he thought, was hell.

And there, up there, that pulsing black mass with its burning red eye, was the heart of hell.

With his strength draining, with it simply leaking out of him like water through a sieve, he struggled for another inch, still another. Dozens of images tumbled through his brain. His mother, holding his hand as they walked across a green summer field. Cal and Fox plowing toy cars through the sand of a sandbox Brian had built at the farm. Riding bikes with them along Main Street. Pressing bloody wrists together by the campfire. Cybil, casting that sultry look over her shoulder. Moving to him. Moving under him. Weeping for him.

Nearly over, he thought. Life flashing in front of my eyes. So fucking tired. Going numb. Going out. Nearly done. And the light, he mused, dizzy now. Tunnel of light. Fucking cliché.

Cards on the table now. He felt—thought he felt—the blood-stone vibrate in his hand. As he reared back, it shot fire through his clutched fingers.

The light washed white, blinding him. In his mind, he saw a figure. The man closed his hands over his. Eyes, clear and gray, looked into his.

It is not death. My blood, her blood, our blood. Its end in the fire.

Their joined hands plunged the stone into the heart of the beast.

In the clearing, the explosion knocked Cybil off her feet. The rush of heat rolled over her, sent her tumbling like a pebble in an angry surf. The light blazed like the sun, dazzling her eyes before throwing everything into sharp relief. For a moment the woods, the stone, the sky were a single sheet of fire, and in the next stood utterly still, like the negative of a photograph.

At the edge of the clearing two figures shimmered—a man and a woman locked in a desperate embrace. In a fingersnap they were gone, and the world moved again.

A rush of wind, a last throaty call of flame, the smoke that crawled along the ground, then faded as that ground burgeoned up, swallowed it. When the wind died to a quiet breeze, the fire guttering out, she saw Gage lying motionless on that ruined earth.

She pushed up to run to him, dropping down to lay her trembling fingers at his throat. "I can't find a pulse!" So much blood. His face, his body looked as if he'd been torn to pieces.

"Come on, goddamn it." Cal knelt, gripped one of Gage's hands as Fox took the other. "Come back."

"CPR," Layla said, and Quinn was already straddling Gage, crossing her hands over his chest to pump.

Cybil started to tip his head back to begin mouth-to-mouth. And saw the Pagan Stone was still sheathed in fire, pure and white. There. She had seen him there.

"Get him on the stone. On the altar. Hurry, hurry."

Cal and Fox carried him—bloodied and lifeless—to lay him on

the simmering white flames. "Blood and fire," Cybil repeated, kissing his hand, then his lips. "I had a dream—I got it wrong, that's all. All of you on the stone, like I'd killed you, and Gage coming out of the dark to kill me. Ego, that's all. Please, Gage, please. Just my ego. Not me, not about me. All of us *around* the stone, and Gage coming out of the dark after killing *it*. Please come back. Please."

She pressed her lips to his again, willing him to breathe. Her tears fell on his face. "Death isn't the answer. Life's the answer."

She laid her lips on his again and his moved against hers.

"Gage! He's breathing. He's—"

"We've got him." Cal squeezed his hand on Gage's hand. "We've got you."

His eyes fluttered open, and met Cybil's. "I—I got lucky."

On a shudder, Cybil laid her head on his chest, listened to the beat of his heart. "We all did."

"Hey, Turner." With his grin huge, Fox leaned over so Gage could see his face. "You owe me a thousand dollars. Happy fucking birthday."

EPILOGUE

H e woke alone in bed, which he figured was a damn shame
since he felt nearly normal again. The sun blasted through
the windows. He'd probably been out for hours, Gage
thought. And small wonder. Dying took a lot out of a man.

He couldn't remember much of the trip back. The entire trip had
been one of those "one foot in front of the other" ordeals, and with
several stints of that made with his arms slung around Fox's and Cal's
shoulders. But he'd wanted to get the hell back—all of them had.

He'd been weak as a baby, that much he remembered. So weak
even after they'd gotten back to the house that Cal and Fox had had
to help him shower off the blood and dirt, and Christ only knew
what he'd brought back from hell with him.

But it no longer hurt to breathe—a good sign. And when he sat
up, nothing spun. When he got to his feet, the floor stayed steady
and nothing inside him wept with pain. Taking a moment to be sure
he remained upright, he glanced at the scar across his wrist, then
explored the one on his shoulder with his fingertips.

The light, and the dark. He'd carried both in with him.

He pulled on jeans and a shirt to go downstairs.

The front door was open, letting in more sunshine and a nice summer breeze. He spotted Cal and Fox on the front deck, with Lump laid out between their chairs. When he stepped out, both of them grinned at him—and Fox flipped the top of the cooler that sat beside him, took out a beer, offered it.

"Read my mind."

"Can do." Fox rose, as did Cal. They tapped bottles, drank.

"Kicked its ass," Fox said.

"That we did."

"Glad you're not dead," Cal added.

"So you said a couple dozen times on the way back."

"I wasn't sure you remembered. You were in and out."

"I'm in now. The Hollow?"

"My dad, Hawbaker, a few others, they held it during the worst. It got bad," Cal added, staring out at his front gardens. "Fires, looting—"

"Your usual random acts of violence," Fox continued. "There are some people in the hospital, others who'll have to decide if they want to rebuild. But Jim Hawkins. Hero time."

"He's got a broken hand, some cuts, and a lot of bruises, but he came through. The farm, too," Cal told him. "We went out to check on things, pick up Lump, and swung through town while you were getting your beauty sleep. It could've been a lot worse. Hell, it has been a lot worse. No new fatalities. Not a single one. The Hollow owes you, brother."

"Shit, it owes all of us." Gage tipped back his beer. "But yeah, especially me."

"Speaking of owing," Fox reminded him. "That'll be a grand— for each of us."

Gage lowered his beer, grinned. "It's one bet I don't mind los- ing." Then staggered back when Fox threw an arm around him, and kissed him square on the mouth.

"Changed my mind about the manly handshake."

"Jesus, O'Dell." Even as Gage lifted a hand, Cal moved in and repeated the gesture. Laughing now, Gage swiped a hand over his mouth. "Good thing nobody saw that, or I'd have to deck you both."

"Twenty-one years is a long time to say this, and mean it." Cal lifted his beer again. "Happy birthday to us."

"Fucking A." Fox lifted his.

As Gage tapped bottles, Quinn and Layla stepped out. "There he is. Pucker up, handsome."

When Quinn grabbed him, planted one on, Gage nodded. "Now that's what I'm talking about."

"My turn." Layla elbowed Quinn aside, pressed her lips to Gage's. "Are you up for a party?"

"Could be."

"We've got Fox's family and Cal's on hold. We'll give them a call if you're up for it."

A birthday party, he thought. Yeah, it had been a hell of a long time. "That'd be good."

"Meanwhile, there's someone in the kitchen who'd like to see you."

She wasn't in the kitchen, but out on the back deck, alone. When he walked out, she turned. And everything he needed bloomed on her face. Then she was in his arms, hers locked tight around him as he swung her in a circle.

"We did okay," he told her.

"We did just fine."

When he lowered her, he kissed the bruise on her temple. "How banged up are you?"

"Not very, which is another small miracle in a streak of them. I've become a fan of fate again."

"Dent. It was Dent in there with me."

She brushed back his hair, traced her fingers over his face, his shoulders. "You told us a little. You were pretty weak, a little delirious at times."

"I was going to make it—I mean finish it. I felt that. I *knew* that. But that was going to be it, that was all I had left. Then there was the light—a shaft of it, then, Jesus, an explosion of it. A nova of it."

"We saw it, too."

"I saw Dent—in my head. Or I think in my head. I had the stone in my hand. It was on fire, flames just shooting between my fingers. It started to—it sounds crazy."

"Sing," she finished. "It sang. Both stones sang."

"Yeah, it sang. A thousand voices. I felt Dent's hand close over mine. Mine over the stone, his over mine. I felt . . . linked. You know what I mean."

"Yes, exactly."

"'It is not death.' That's what he said to me, then we punched the stone right into the heart. I heard it scream, Cybil. I heard it scream, and I felt it . . . implode. From the heart out. Then that's it until I came back. Not like last time, when the bastard bit me. This was like cruising on a really good drug."

"The light tore through it," she told him. "I'd have to say vaporized it. It's the closest I can come. Gage, I saw them, for just a moment—less than a moment. I saw Giles Dent and Ann Hawkins holding each other. I saw them together, I *felt* them together. And I understood."

"What?"

"It was to be his sacrifice all along. He needed us, and he needed you to willingly offer. For you to take the stone in, knowing it would be your life. Because we did what we've done, because you were willing to give your life, he could give his instead. It is not death, he told Ann, and us, and you. He existed still, all these years. And last night, through us, through you, he was the sacrifice demanded to end it. He could finally let go. He's with Ann now, and they're—cliché time—at peace. We all are."

"It's going to take a while to get used to. But I'm all about trying." He took her hand. "I figure this. We stick around for a couple of days, until everything settles down. Then we'll take off for a couple of weeks. The way my luck's running, I figure I can win enough to buy you a ring the size of a doorknob, if you like the idea."

"I do, if that's an actual proposal rather than a hypothetical."

"How's this for actual? Let's get married in Vegas. We can talk everyone who matters into going out for it."

"In Vegas." She cocked her head, then laughed. "I don't know why, but that sounds absolutely perfect. You're on." She took his face in her hands, kissed him. "Happy birthday."

"I keep hearing that."

"Expect to hear it more. I baked you a cake."

"No joke?"

"A seven-layer cake—as promised. I love you, Gage." She slid into his arms. "I love everything about you."

"I love you, too. I've got a woman who's ready to get married in Vegas, bakes cakes, *and* has brains. I'm a lucky guy."

He laid his cheek on the top of her head, holding on while he looked out to the woods where the beaten path led to the Pagan Stone.

And at the end of the path, past Hester's Pool, where the water flowed cool and clean, the once-scorched earth of the clearing greened again. On the new ground, the Pagan Stone stood silent in the streaming sun.

Turn the page for a look at

BLOOD BROTHERS

the first book in the Sign of Seven Trilogy.

Available now from Berkley!

t crawled along the air that hung heavy as wet wool over the glade. Through the snakes of fog that slid silent over the ground, its hate crept. It came for him through the heat-smothered night.

It wanted his death.

So he waited as it pushed its way through the woods, its torch raised toward the empty sky, as it waded across the streams, around the thickets where small animals huddled in fear of the scent it bore with it.

Hellsmoke.

He had sent Ann and the lives she carried in her womb away, to safety. She had not wept, he thought now as he sprinkled the herbs he'd selected over water. Not his Ann. But he had seen the grief on her face, in the deep, dark eyes he had loved through this lifetime, and all the others before.

The three would be born from her, raised by her, and taught by her. And from them, when the time came, there would be three more.

What power he had would be theirs, these sons, who would loose their first cries long, long after this night's work was done. To leave them what tools they would need, the weapons they would wield, he risked all he had, all he was.

His legacy to them was in blood, in heart, in vision.

In this last hour, he would do all he could to provide them with what was needed to carry the burden, to remain true, to see their destiny.

His voice was strong and clear as he called to wind and water, to earth and fire. In the hearth the flames snapped. In the bowl the water trembled.

He laid the bloodstone on the cloth. Its deep green was generously spotted with red. He had treasured this stone, as had those who'd come before him. He had honored it. And now he poured power into it as one would pour water into a cup.

So his body shook and sweat and weakened as light hovered in a halo around the stone.

"For you now," he murmured, "sons of sons. Three parts of one. In faith, in hope, in truth. One light, united, to strike back dark. And here, my vow. I will not rest until destiny is met."

With the athame, he scored his palm so his blood fell onto the stone, into the water, and into the flame.

"Blood of my blood. Here I will hold until you come for me, until you loose what must be loosed again on the world. May the gods keep you."

For a moment there was grief. Even through his purpose, there was grief. Not for his life, as the sands of it were dripping down the glass. He had no fear of death. No fear of what he would soon embrace that was not death. But he grieved that he would never lay his lips on Ann's again in this life. He would not see his children born, nor the children of his children. He grieved that he would not be able to stop the suffering to come, as he had been unable to stop the suffering that had come before, in so many other life-times.

He understood that he was not the instrument, but only the vessel to be filled and emptied at the needs of the gods.

So, weary from the work, saddened by the loss, he stood outside the little hut, beside the great stone, to meet his fate.

It came in the body of a man, but that was a shell. As his own body was a shell. It called itself Lazarus Twisse, an elder of "the godly." He and those who followed had settled in the wilderness of this province when they broke with the Puritans of New England.

He studied them now in their torchlight, these men and the one who was not a man. These, he thought, who had come to the New World for religious freedom, and then persecuted and destroyed any who did not follow their single, narrow path.

"You are Giles Dent."

"I am," he said, "in this time and this place."

Lazarus Twisse stepped forward. He wore the unrelieved formal black of an elder. His high-crowned, wide-brimmed hat shadowed his face. But Giles could see his eyes, and in his eyes, he saw the demon.

"Giles Dent, you and the female known as Ann Hawkins have been accused and found guilty of witchcraft and demonic practices."

"Who accuses?"

"Bring the girl forward!" Lazarus ordered.

They pulled her, a man on each arm. She was a slight girl, barely six and ten by Giles's calculation. Her face was wax white with fear, her eyes drenched with it. Her hair had been shorn.

"Hester Deale, is this the witch who seduced you?"

"He and the one he calls wife laid hands on me." She spoke as if in a trance. "They performed ungodly acts upon my body. They came to my window as ravens, flew into my room in the night. They stilled my throat so I could not speak or call for help."

"Child," Giles said gently, "what has been done to you?"

Those fear-swamped eyes stared through him. "They called to Satan as their god, and cut the throat of a cock in sacrifice. And drank its blood. They forced its blood on me. I could not stop them."

"Hester Deale, do you renounce Satan?"

"I do renounce him."

"Hester Deale, do you renounce Giles Dent and the woman Ann Hawkins as witches and heretics?"

"I do." Tears spilled down her cheeks. "I do renounce them, and pray to God to save me. Pray to God to forgive me."

"He will," Giles whispered. "You are not to blame."

"Where is the woman Ann Hawkins?" Lazarus demanded, and Giles turned his clear gray eyes to him.

"You will not find her."

"Stand aside. I will enter this house of the devil."

"You will not find her," Giles repeated. For a moment he looked beyond Lazarus to the men and the handful of women who stood in his glade.

He saw death in their eyes, and more, the hunger for it. This was the demon's power, and his work.

Only in Hester's did Giles see fear or sorrow. So he used what he had to give, pushed his mind toward hers. *Run!*

He saw her jolt, stumble back, then he turned to Lazarus.

"We know each other, you and I. Dispatch them, release them, and it will be between us alone."

For an instant he saw the gleam of red in Lazarus's eyes. "You are done. Burn the witch!" he shouted. "Burn the devil house and all within it!"

They came with torches, and with clubs. Giles felt the blows rain on him, and the fury of the hate that was the demon's sharpest weapon.

They drove him to his knees, and the wood of the hut began to flame and smoke. Screams rang in his head, the madness of them.

With the last of his power he reached out toward the demon inside the man, with red rimming its dark eyes as it fed on the hate, the fear, the violence. He felt it gloat, he felt it *rising*, so sure of its victory, and the feast to follow.

And he ripped it to him, through the smoking air. He heard it scream in fury and pain as the flames bit into flesh. And he held it to him, close as a lover as the fire consumed them.

And with that union the fire burst, spread, destroyed every living thing in the glade.

It burned for a day and a night, like the belly of hell.